Chapter
One

Freezing rain fell throughout the morning, spattering the Highlands clearing with patches of ice and glazing the surrounding trees until the interlaced branches gleamed like fine porcelain from across the distant Cholee Sea. The raw, biting air carried the scent of half-frozen mud and wet leaves. The House of Moons, a gray two-story building, stood at one end of the winter-bare grounds, dwarfed by a huge, sprawling brown-stone complex on the other side.

Haemas Tal flung open the House of Moons' door and hesitated, her pale-gold eyes desperate. She pulled the hood of her cloak over her braided hair, then ducked her head and fought her way into the hissing downpour. The icy rain streamed off her cloak as she dashed down the crushed-gravel path that led across the grounds to Shael'donn. The chill air knifed through her lungs with each breath, but she ran faster, *faster*. Not much time, Lising had said. She had to hurry, or it would be too late. Master Ellirt would be gone forever.

The wind buffeted her, screaming like a hungry silsha prowling the lowland forest. She felt her own silshas close by, vigilant, lurking in the surrounding trees like black-furred shadows as she rounded the final turn. They picked up on her anguish and snarled in response, their voices carrying in the wet cold. Haemas's pumping legs ached and her lungs cried out for air. Ahead, the driving rain sheeted against the larger school's rough-cut brown granite. Gasping for breath, she raised her fist to beat on Shael'donn's massive door, but a startled, wide-eyed student swung it open.

She pushed inside, her hands trembling as she ripped off the

1

icy weight of her sodden cloak. The boy took it wordlessly and folded it over his arm. She turned around, the only sound her labored breathing and rain dripping on the entrance flagstones. Quiet hung in the halls like a shroud, and it seemed everything she loved about this ancient seat of learning had already died.

Healing Master Lising's long legs hurried down the main staircase toward her. He was tall and narrow, his grim face pale above the traditional healer's black tunic. Haemas pushed stray tendrils of wet white-gold hair back from her flushed cheeks and made herself meet his golden-eyed gaze. "You're sure?" She couldn't keep the disbelief out of her voice. "Master Ellirt is dying?"

Resignation flickered across his thin face. "Best you go up and say your farewells now."

She hesitated. "What about Kevisson?"

"He's been called back, Lady Haemas, but I doubt he'll get here in time."

Numb with the shock, she bowed her head and swept past him up the steps, wishing he wouldn't use her title. "Lady Haemas" was someone else entirely, someone competent and at peace with her father, who could never have been tricked into running away—someone other than Haemas Tal, Mistress of the House of Moons, the struggling mindarts academy for girls.

She hesitated outside the familiar door, then forced herself to push the latch. Inside the drapes had been drawn, although Master Ellirt had been blind from birth. A roaring fire illuminated the figure lying in the bed, swaddled in quilts up to his neck against a cold that ate at him from within, not without. The walls seemed to move inward as Haemas was overwhelmed with the muffled smell of the sickroom. She steadied herself against the mantel, fighting to speak around the knot in her throat. "Master Ellirt?"

The dimly seen figure stirred. "Come in, child."

Crossing to the narrow bed, she sank onto the wooden chair at its side, feeling as if she balanced at the edge of a black precipice. How could it have come to this? Only yesterday her

HOUSE OF MOONS

THE HOUSE OF MOONS CHRONICLES
BOOK 2

K.D. WENTWORTH

ibooks
new york
www.ibooks.net

DISTRIBUTED BY SIMON & SCHUSTER, INC.

For my wise friend David

A Publication of ibooks, inc.

Copyright © 1995 by K.D. Wentworth

An ibooks, inc. Book

Distributed by Simon & Schuster, Inc.
1230 Avenue of the Americas, New York, NY 10020

ibooks, inc.
24 West 25th Street
New York, NY 10010

The ibooks World Wide Web Site Address is:
http://www.ibooks.net

ISBN 0-7434-8002-3
First ibooks, inc. printing April 2004
10 9 8 7 6 5 4 3 2 1

Printed in the U.S.A.

old teacher had seemed hearty enough, his craggy face cheerful as he visited her classrooms and offered suggestions. She, as well as the rest of Shael'donn, had depended on him as if he would go on forever, like the towering mountains that ringed the Highlands or the clear green sky. Taking his gnarled hand, she pressed the papery skin to her cheek.

"I'm ... sorry." His voice was a hoarse whisper. "I—" He broke into a cough that wracked his lungs and brought tears to Haemas's eyes.

"Don't talk," she said as the fit subsided.

No, his mindvoice whispered, *there are ... warnings I must ... give.*

Even though speaking that way did not trouble his breathing, it took even more energy, and he had so little left. "Please—" she began.

You must listen! In her mind, Haemas heard and felt him clearly now, tasting of lemons and sunlight, sounding like his old self. *I have very little time left ... I'm not going to spend it arguing, even with someone I care as much about as you.* Master Ellirt struggled against the quilts and she loosened them so that she could prop him up on the pillows. His face was haggard in the flickering fire-shadows, the lines of strain standing out like cords. *For three years now, I have believed ... in the House of Moons, what it would stand for, what you wanted ... to do for the girls.*

If it hadn't been for her old master's persistence, the Council of Twelve would never have funded her project, and Haemas understood that better than anyone. It was against tradition to educate female children in the extended mindarts as she herself had grudgingly been allowed to train. Even though her school was smaller than she had visualized, and operated with minimal funds, it was a start and she was grateful. She tightened her fingers over his, as if by her strength alone she could hold him to this world.

If the Kashi people are to survive, we ... must use all our resources. He hesitated, moving his chilled fingers in her hand. *But the Lords will ... try ...* The white-haired head lolled back against the pillows and she thought he had passed beyond her reach. Half rising, she started to call the healer, but the gnarled fingers held on, anchoring her at his side.

I've designated . . . Kevisson as my . . . successor. His head stirred weakly. *If they . . . fight it, that will doom the House of Moons. I'm sorry . . . the House . . . so important . . . You and Kevisson . . . take care of each . . . he's a good . . . man . . .*

Dropping her mental shields, she laid herself open to him. "What can I do, Master?" Her eyes burned with scalding, unshed tears. "You showed me the way out when I had nowhere else to turn. You gave my life back to me. Tell me what I can do."

You took your own life . . . back. Remember . . . that . . .

But he had shown her the way. When her cousin, Jarid, had implanted a terrifying false memory in her mind to make her believe she had killed her father, Master Ellirt had helped her sort out the real from the false. No one else had even considered that she might not be guilty.

Watch out for . . . for . . . The old fingers suddenly spasmed in her grip, then relaxed. She reached for his mind, but found only a soft peacefulness, like the light from a shrouded lamp, slowly fading. She sat there as the fire burned down into embers, holding the familiar hand, frozen in place, feeling that until she moved he was still with her.

Outside the room, Shael'donn went on about its daily business, as yet unaware of its loss, the Kashi boys attending class, working with accomplished Andiine Masters to hone their natural mindtalents and make the best use of their innate Talent. Although Shael'donn had existed for centuries, Master Ellirt had built the school into far more than it would ever have been without him, and against custom and the displeasure of the Council of Twelve, he had made her a part of it, too, in a time when women and girls were never permitted this level of training.

Behind Haemas the door swung open. She felt the sun-gold warmth of a familiar strength enter the room as the only mind she knew as well as Master Ellirt's reached out to her. She turned. A man in green riding leathers stood in the doorway, his tan face bleak, his gold-brown eyes questioning. She answered him without words, then flew into his arms, holding Kevisson tightly against the black loss that threatened to consume them both.

Two nimble ilserin skittered around the edge of a quiet, mirror-surfaced pool in the heart of the great forest, their long green fingers exploring the trees, the brush, the drifts of dead leaves, smelling . . . listening . . . Their bright black eyes, enormous in their expressionless green faces, noted that someone had come to this sacred place and cleared the faded blue leaves away from the broad white steps leading down into the spring-fed pool. A strange, alien scent lingered, faintly acrid to sensitive ilserin noses.

Leafcurl's four limber fingers clutched convulsively at his male-brother's arm as he stared down into the pool constructed so long ago that no one, not even the venerated ilserlara—the ancient Third Ones—remembered how it had been made. He shuddered. One of the dull-green shapes that should have nestled in the sheltering mud below was gone. He turned and embraced his brother Streamleap's slim green body. Sorrow and distress echoed back and forth between them, building until it was more than either could bear. This was wrong—very, very wrong. Such pools were sacred. No one, not ilserin, ilseri, or ilserlara, would ever think of disturbing one. He trembled and buried his face in Streamleap's cool neck. Now the mothers, those ethereal, distant creatures who but rarely visited ilserin environs, must be summoned. He trembled at the thought of their mysterious, almost disturbing presence. They would be very angry, distressed beyond all measure at the terrible news he had to convey.

But, then, perhaps they would know what to do.

So the old fool was dead.

Diren Chee compressed his lips, fighting the smile that wanted to settle there. Ellirt's death eliminated the last true obstacle to his plans. Gazing around the Council Chamber, he reflected that it had certainly taken him long enough to die. The warning mentioned in the old text against vriddis berries had specifically said that, without antidote, death would occur in "one to two hours." Kniel Ellirt had somehow lasted more than a day, a wily, tough old bastard to the last.

Mind-conjured blue chispa-fire glittered from small bowls arranged along the clerestory ledge, signifying the seriousness of the occasion. Diren took his gilded seat, third from the left, at the long half-circle table of the Council of Twelve. A dozen perfumes vied as people filtered in to fill the tiered gallery. They were all dressed in their best, Lowland and Highland Houses alike, the women swathed in bright velvets and silks, the men stiff and crisp, even a few children, mostly male, wide-eyed and fidgeting. No matter what the excuse, the Kashi loved a chance to gather and gossip.

Somewhere in that blaze of a hundred different shades of golden hair sat Ellirt's replacement, the next Lord High Master of Shael'donn. Diren Chee was hoping for someone either stupid or greedy, preferably both. Stupid, greedy men seldom concerned themselves with anything beyond their personal profit.

Steepling his fingers, Diren leaned back in Chee'ayn's hereditary seat, trying not to notice that the ebari-hide covering was peeling and cracked and the silsha-fur stuffing had long since packed down to a pebbly hardness. Though he lacked the funds to remedy such humiliations at the moment, he would not have to endure them much longer. Reaching into his pocket, he fingered the cool, faceted hardness of the latteh crystal. Soon everyone would have to acknowledge the House of Chee.

At the center of the table, the Council Head, Dervlin Tal, glared at the crowd from under fierce bushy white eyebrows. He was dressed in an ornamental gold-brocaded jacket that left no doubt as to who was in charge here. Famous for his temper, Tal was another tough old bastard who might stand in Chee's way, but he would see to him soon enough. His fingers tightened around the latteh and he savored the quiescent power it contained. Everything would be taken care of in proper order.

Tal rapped on the gleaming wood of the curved table for silence. Diren stared down at his own reflection, approving the confident, golden-eyed man who gazed up at him. He straightened his collar and lounged back in his chair.

"The Council will now take up the matter of Master Ellirt's successor for the High Mastership of Shael'donn," Tal announced.

A flurry of latecomers entered the circular room. Diren recognized Haemas Tal and Kevisson Monmart as the pair passed the Council table without glancing aside. Her face was holloweyed, strain evident in the carriage of her shoulders and the set of her jaw. He had watched her at the funeral pyre for Ellirt the night before, her somber profile silhouetted against the redorange flames, always at Monmart's side. Then, as now, she had taken his breath away. He sensed both power and passion behind those reserved white-gold eyes, and meant to have them both.

Dervlin Tal scowled at their backs with undisguised animosity. The rift between the Council Head and his daughter had grown only deeper and more bitter with the passage of years, and Diren knew the fact that Haemas Tal was often seen with a person of Monmart's inadequate station did not help. Although second in Talent and training at Shael'donn only to the now-deceased Kniel Ellirt himself, Kevisson Monmart had been born of an undistinguished Lowlands House and his golden-brown hair and eyes were almost dark enough to be those of a common chierra, hardly a fitting consort for the only child of Dervlin Tal, Head of the Council of Twelve.

On Diren's right, Lord Rald bent his silver-haired head and spoke softly to Lord Killian on his other side. "You shouldn't have let that girl get away, Aaren. You could have insisted she honor the marriage contract. We would have backed your claim."

The other man's eyes glittered like amber ice. "I pride myself on knowing trouble when I see it, and that baggage is considerably more trouble than even an estate like Tal'ayn is worth."

Rald smiled back, but Diren could see the older man did not entirely agree. Neither did he. Haemas Sennay Tal represented much that even an unambitious Kashi man might want. She was a Sennay granddaughter, as denoted by her middle name, and had grown into the regal height of that ancient line. And she had inherited, from her mother's maternal line, the rare Killian coloring of white-gold hair and eyes that cropped up only once in every few generations. She was exotic, and, although too pale for popular taste, she drew him like a lightwing to the flame. This, combined with the Tal bearing and an unusually strong Talent to pass on to her children, made her desirable beyond words—not to mention the fact that the old Tal had no surviving heirs closer than maternal cousins, not even a niece or nephew. In the fullness of time, Tal'ayn would come to his daughter, whether she desired it or not.

Diren had never bothered to approach her. Chee'ayn had been impoverished before his father's father had been born. He had nothing to offer but a nit-eaten house filled with half-rotted draperies and ramshackle furniture. He didn't even dare leave the portal in operation when he was home, lest someone decide to drop in unannounced. At any rate, it was widely repeated in the Highest circles that Haemas Tal had sworn never to marry, and that mudface, Monmart, was always hanging around her in public so that it was difficult to get even the slightest moment of privacy.

He'd seen how women operated, though. As soon as the old Tal died, she'd be quick enough to move into Tal'ayn all right. No doubt Monmart was counting on being the one to live there with her.

At the center of the table, Tal cleared his throat. "As to Master Ellirt's successor, we must remember that the future of the Kashi is dependent upon the education of our young." He gazed around the circular chamber, as if daring someone to disagree. "We have always been few, while the unTalented chierra are many, but as long as we maintain our proficiency in the mindarts, we will hold our ascendancy over the chierra multitudes of this world. The day we forget that basic truth will be the beginning of the end for our way of life."

The golden heads were nodding now. Diren smiled faintly at

Tal's shameless play on their notions of superiority. It was an old topic, but one of which the Kashi'an, the People of the Light, never grew tired: their rule over the dark-haired chierra peoples of Desalaya.

"As you may know, Master Ellirt did suggest a successor." Tal's fierce golden eyes fixed Kevisson Monmart for a long moment. "Yet it was nothing more than that, a suggestion, and I am sure he never meant us to accept it without careful consideration as to what would be the best thing for Shael'donn."

Already bored, Diren shifted in his lumpy seat. Everyone knew that Monmart, who looked like a damned chierra and had no close ties to any of the great Houses, would never get the appointment. At this very second, each High House was maneuvering for influence. The High Mastership of Shael'donn was far too rich a fruit to be wasted on a nobody Lowlander.

Diren stood up, drawing the hundreds of pairs of golden eyes in the room to him. "Esteemed Head."

Tal's lined face looked down the table at him. "Yes?"

"As Talented as Lord Monmart obviously is, he is also the sole heir to Monmart'ayn, a position that I am certain will take up more of his time as the years wear on." Diren sank back into his seat, enjoying the tightening of Monmart's face.

"A valid point." Lord Rald nodded his white-haired head. "We should perhaps select someone without serious obligations to divide his attention."

Diren leaned back and laced his hands together. It was like throwing a bloody scrap before a flock of scavenging Iraels. Except for Chee'ayn and Tal'ayn, he couldn't think of a High House that didn't have its share of younger brothers, nephews, cousins, and sons to be put to some sort of gainful occupation. He could hear mental muttering as the greedy Lords squared off over the Shael'donn Mastership, none of them even remembering now that Kniel Ellirt had ever existed or left his preference.

A low clear voice rang out over the babble of voices. "Esteemed Council Head." The eyes in the circular chamber turned to Haemas Tal standing tall and straight in her ankle-

length tunic and flowing pants, the chispa-fire along the outer
rim of the chamber playing on the white-gold of her braided
hair. "I knew Master Ellirt better than many here today, and I
say we should not discard the carefully thought out decision he
left us. He had many valid reasons for naming Lord Monmart
as his successor."

"Perhaps . . ." Speaking from his seat, Diren let his voice
trail off, as if he hesitated to bring up something unpleasant.
"Perhaps it was most important to Master Ellirt that
Shael'donn is situated so closely to the House of Moons. Perhaps he couldn't bear the thought of having the two of you
parted." A muffled titter filtered through the room.

Red flushed her high cheekbones. "I will not dignify that insinuation with an answer, Lord Chee. Master Ellirt selected
Kevisson Monmart because he is the most experienced, the
most Talented, and the most qualified Master currently in residence at Shael'donn. If the Council selects anyone else today,
we will all know the appointment had little to do with any of
those qualities." Without looking at Monmart, she settled back
into her seat.

Even from across the chamber, Diren could feel the blaze of
Monmart's tight-lipped anger. He had told her not to interfere,
Diren realized. Monmart wanted to handle this on his own.

Dervlin Tal bathed his daughter with a burning look. "Your
opinion in this matter can hardly be considered unbiased." Tal
spread the sheets of parchment before him. "The chair is open
for alternate nominations."

Monmart stood, his back ramrod straight. "I wish to withdraw my name from the nominations."

"You can't." Tal held up a sheet of parchment. "Master
Ellirt nominated you and your name must be considered."

"Suit yourselves, then." His face tight with anger, Monmart
strode toward the carved doors of Old oak that stood twice as
high as a man. "I'm sure you will anyway and I have no wish
to be a part of this farce." A chierra servant darted forward to
open the door.

Diren glanced at Haemas Tal, sitting white-faced between
the empty seat on one side and that meddling old nit, Enissa

Saxbury, who fancied herself a *female* healer. He snorted. A woman healer, as if there could ever really be such a thing.

She had been Lady of Sithnal'ayn, wife to one of the High Lords and welcome in the Highest of circles—but after his death, she had abandoned her title and helped found the House of Moons, evidently content to be only a Saxbury.

A jumble of names was thrown out, mostly from the High Lords seated at the Council table. Having no idle male relatives of his own of which to dispose, Diren lounged back in his chair and monitored the list, listening for one who would suit his purposes. He hadn't gone to all this trouble to eliminate Kniel Ellirt just to watch another Lord High Master installed at Shael'donn who was clever or strongly Talented or both.

His interest was piqued when Lord Seffram Senn brought up the name of Riklin Dynd Senn, one of the younger Senn nephews, who was a Master at Shael'donn. Diren had known Riklin during his own days as a student there. They had not only been in the same form, but had roomed on the same floor. Riklin had been a stocky, slow-moving youth, quick to resent injuries and quicker yet to redress them. As far as Diren could remember, although Riklin had been competent at the mindarts, he'd never had an original thought in his entire life—the perfect picture of a man who would never notice a latteh being wielded right under his nose.

Diren studied the gallery, picking out Riklin's blunt features and curly mop of dusky-gold hair in the back. Rising, he stretched a beguiling smile across his face. "Esteemed Head," he said smoothly, "I can speak in favor of one of the candidates mentioned, a man whom I have known for many years to be honorable and Talented, a man who should serve us all exceptionally well."

Or at least as well as you deserve to be served, he thought, keeping a close watch on his shields. All around him then, he felt alliances crumbling and reforming in a swirl of new patterns as the High Houses scrambled for position.

At the end of the first ballot, Riklin Senn's name ranked third, following Leric Rald, one of the older Rald'ayn cousins who had trained at Shael'donn for many years, but was of little real account, and Alban Killian, a Killian son who had left Shael'donn several years ago. Rald was far too old, Diren thought, and Killian was a shallow womanizer with at least three bastards to his name already, a predilection at odds with the males-only environment of Shael'donn. Diren adjusted his sleeves. With a little help, even a brute like Riklin Senn might win over that pair.

Another ballot was marked, and then a third. Killian was finally eliminated, but neither Rald nor Senn could win a clear majority. The Council broke to take refreshments spread by a brace of Tal'ayn servants, and Diren worked his way through the muttering press of bodies to Seffram Senn's side.

I would like to see Riklin win this, he said in a tightly broadcast thought.

For old times' sake? Senn's lip curled disdainfully. *Don't make me laugh. Besides, Rald doesn't give a damn what you think.*

I have a few favors I can call in. Diren chewed thoughtfully on a slice of mellow cheese. *Promise me a starter flock of Old sheep, at least ten, including a good ram. And feed to last the winter.*

Senn stared stonily ahead, his eyes narrow.

They say Rald's cousin is a hard worker, although I hear that he has a quick temper, Diren continued. *I would hate to be responsible for letting him at all those young impressionable boys.* He brushed the crumbs from his hands.

All right! Senn plunged back into the milling throng from the gallery. *But he had better receive a clear majority or the deal is off!*

Drawing on his gloves, Diren drifted over to the wall, then pulled the dull-green latteh crystal out of his pocket, shielding it by turning his back. He ran a finger over the irregular facets, still amazed every time he saw it. It was, of course, illegal and forbidden, and all those other things that people always said when someone had a good idea and didn't want to share it. It was also the road back to wealth and prestige that had been stolen from Chee'ayn generations before he and his older sister, Axia, had been born. It had taken him months to locate, once he'd found descriptions of it in his father's papers, and then several more months to be able to use it. And even now, he was aware that he had barely grasped the fundamentals of the ancient art of using a latteh to control another's mind.

Opening his shields, he teased at the energy lattices within the crystal, forcing them into the pattern he had found as much through guesswork as by following directions. When it was buzzing inside his glove-protected hand, he closed his fist around it and edged toward Himret Rald, Lord of Rald'ayn, who was standing by the doors, speaking quietly with his candidate, Leric.

"Lord Rald?" Diren caught the older man's eye. "Might I have a word with you?" Diren locked his hands behind his back, caressing the latteh with his gloved thumb. "I will only need a moment and it might save us all a lot of time."

Almost imperceptibly, Rald nodded his gray-haired head, although the man's wary eyes said plainly he wanted nothing to do with him. Used to that sort of reaction, Diren smiled again. The Chee temperament had earned rather a bad reputation down through the years, but that had been his father's and grandfather's doing. It had nothing to do with him.

Rald nibbled at a chunk of pickled whiteroot. "Make it fast, Chee."

Diren brought his closed hand around. "I have something that might persuade you to change your mind."

Rald stared down at the black-gloved fist, then put his hand out as though Diren were going to offer him gold or a valuable bauble. With his free hand, Diren pressed the latteh crystal against the bare skin of the other man's palm.

Rald's face went slack, his eyes widening in shock, then rolling back. *Stand up!* Diren hissed into his mind. *In a second I will take the latteh away, after which you will announce to everyone that Leric feels unworthy of such a high honor and begs to be excused.*

He watched Rald's eyes for a moment, seeing the pupils contract to pinpoints even though he had set the latteh at only a moderate level of power. *And you will remember nothing of this. Say it!*

"I will remember nothing," Rald repeated tonelessly.

Diren pulled the crystal away, then, pocketing it with a smooth motion, reached out to Rald with the other hand. "My Lord, are you all right?"

Rald blinked, then looked about him, his lined face suddenly ashen. "I—I don't . . ."

"Come and sit down." Diren put one hand under the older man's elbow. "Perhaps something to drink—"

"No!" Rald flinched back from him and Diren felt his heart stop. "No," the other man said again, but less forcefully. "I—" He looked around. "Leric? Where's Leric?"

"Here, Himret." Leric Rald forced his way between the curious onlookers.

Rald grasped Leric's tunic with iron fingers.

"With—withdraw, Leric. It doesn't mean a damn thing anyway."

"But—!" Leric's old face sagged in surprise.

Rald's fingers tightened. "Withdraw!"

Leric turned to the Head of the Council, old Tal, and nodded stiffly, as if the motion pained him.

Tal scowled. "Let it be so, then. By default, the High Mastership of Shael'donn goes to Riklin Dynd Senn." He glared around the restless, whispering crowd for a moment. "Council is dismissed."

Rald and his cousin started slowly toward the huge outer doors, just two old men who had been beaten somehow without knowing why, then stopped as Monmart burst into the room.

"Attack!" Monmart gasped, then looked wildly around the chamber. "Lenhe'ayn has been attacked—by chierra!"

Chapter
Two

With the rest of the crowded Council chamber, Diren turned to stare at Monmart as he stood, outlined by the open doorway, his face flushed, his eyes dark and tense. Chill air from the outer passage threaded through the room.

Tal rapped on the oak table for order. "Take your seats!" The crowd of astonished Kashi, however, surged toward Monmart, buzzing with questions.

Rising, Tal banged his fist on the Council table. A fluted glass jumped and tipped over, spilling water on his notes. He cursed and hastily blotted the sheets against his shirt. "Dammit, take your seats!" The noise faded to a murmur as the onlookers drifted back to the gallery. Then Tal settled into his own thronelike chair. "Now, Monmart, you say Lenhe'ayn has been attacked?"

Monmart met the old Lord's eyes. "Yes, my Lord. On my way to the courtyard portal, I was contacted by Lady Myriel, who said chierra forces attacked earlier this afternoon, burning the unharvested fields, stealing what stock they could and slaughtering the rest, and—" He spread his hands helplessly. "—murdering her son."

A hush fell over the crowded room, deeper than the mere absence of words. Diren tapped his fingers against his chin, a study in sober reflection, while he savored their radiated shock, their inability to take it all in; the normally servile chierra had organized themselves to attack a Kashi House and had killed a Kashi heir. Such a thing had not happened within living memory. They found it unthinkable. He might have felt the same, if he hadn't been there himself.

Tal cleared his throat. "Are the attackers still there?"

Monmart shook his head. "No, my Lord."

"And what of the chierra servants—did they mutiny and join the attacking force?"

"According to Lady Lenhe," Monmart answered, "a number of the field hands actually gave their lives fighting for Lenhe'ayn."

Diren cocked his head. "How is that the Lady contacted you and no one else?" He smiled lazily, watching Haemas Tal's high-cheekboned face out of the corner of his eye. Her fingers were knotted in her lap, her skin as transparent as fine porcelain. "It had escaped me that the two of you were so—closely associated."

Monmart's golden-brown eyes jumped slightly.

He had definitely hit a nerve with that one, Diren told himself.

"We were acquainted, having met some years ago." Monmart turned away. "And so many people were sequestered here in the Council chamber, which is of course shielded. She is distraught and could locate no one else she knew."

Diren raised a questioning eyebrow and leaked just the faintest tendril of disbelief through his shields.

"Well, we must investigate at once." Tal sat back in his seat, then impatiently righted the upset glass. "This is a nasty business, chierra attacking Kashi. We can't let it go unanswered."

"Isn't Lenhe'ayn close to Monmart'ayn?" Diren asked innocently. "Perhaps Master Monmart should assess the damage, then make a report to the Council. I'm sure Lady Lenhe would appreciate his help in this difficult time." He watched Haemas Tal's face lose what little color it had.

"Yes, yes." Tal waved his hand at Monmart, dismissing him like some chierra footman. "That would most likely be best. Go down and render what aid you can. Send for more help, if you find it's needed, and bring us your report at the earliest possible moment. We must keep the closest of watches on this situation."

Monmart stood in the doorway like a pillar, his tan face distressed. It was almost too delightful, Diren thought. Here the man was actually losing the High Mastership of Shael'donn and the Tal woman in the same day, and it all fit so beautifully with Diren's own need to get her alone at some point. When that moment finally came, it would be safer if Monmart was far away in the Lowlands, too distant to be of any help.

"As you wish, my Lords," Monmart managed finally, then turned on his heel and left the room, taking Haemas Tal's pale-gold gaze with him.

The warm, lazy air currents above the edge of the sea cradled Summerstone as she drifted, spread as thinly as an oil sheen on water, soaking up the wan energies of the cold-season sun. Most of her ilseri sisters had migrated into the southern regions, seeking the more concentrated life-giving rays of the sun while the great forest lay shrouded in the shadow of winter. She alone had lingered this far north, savoring the crash of waves on the air-pocked black rocks, the frothy greenness of salt water, and the streamlined jiri that dove into the icy sea to feed, then soared back into the sky to share the clouds with her.

From far away, something teased at her consciousness, a dim sense of fear/anger/warning. Reluctantly she increased her density, gathering herself into solid form.

Come! childish voices called in the most urgent of ilserin modes. *Come now! Danger! Sorrow! Danger!*

She hesitated, her face turned up to the sun's orange disk. Ilserin were silly and prone to panic. This was probably nothing important, but she would check on the excitable young males, then spend a few days soothing their fears, perhaps teach them a new game. Soon they would be scrambling through the trees again and leaping like jiri into the wild river below the falls, dreaming of their own days to come when they would ride the sky at her side.

Fastening her barret-down cloak at her neck, Haemas hurried up the narrow stone steps leading to Tal'ayn's courtyard. It had been a disastrous meeting and the sooner she quit Tal'ayn, the better for everyone. She still found it difficult to be so close to her father's long-smoldering anger, and harder yet to visit the scene of so many painful memories.

Although twelve years had passed since her cousin Jarid's death, his ghost seemed to linger here, permeating the ancient gray stone, haunting every niche and corner, whispering that he would never leave this House for which he'd fought so savagely, that he would never forgive Haemas for winning.

She hurried to the upper door and burst outside into the frigid, snow-edged air. A short queue waited at the Tal'ayn portal up ahead as the visiting Kashi returned, mostly in ones and twos, to their own estates and lives. Joining the line, she heard the door squeak open again behind her.

"Lady Haemas!" Diren Chee's golden-haired head appeared beside her. "I would like a word with you."

She didn't turn. "I'm sorry, Lord Chee. I have pressing duties back at the House of Moons."

"Please."

She felt the heat of his presence next to her, bright as an overstoked fire. A man of average height with lean, sharply chiseled features, he had come into his inheritance after the disastrous Temporal Conclave where so many had died. He had always been courteous to her, which was more than she could say for the rest of the Council. And yet, behind his bland expression and tight shields, there was something dark and unsettling. His eyes were hungry, almost feral, and his ever-present polite smile made her uneasy.

His voice followed her across the snow-dusted cobbles as she advanced with the line. "You could help the Council pinpoint those responsible for this chierra attack."

She halted in midstep in spite of herself and turned. He wore his golden hair long and undisciplined, and his dark-flecked eyes hinted at things best not mentioned in the daylight. She shivered. Was he broadcasting at her? Strengthening her shields, she swallowed hard and looked away. "How could I possibly help?"

He reached her side again, his expression strangely hungry. "By using what the Old People taught you to travel between times."

She paled. She had been forced to go over this subject again and again with her father and various other Lords. They would never really understand what the ilseri, the natives of this world, had taught her all those years ago. In fact, most of them did not even want to understand, persisting in the mistaken belief that the temporal pathways could be put to some sort of purpose, like a hammer or an awl or any other tool—but the truth was that they could not.

"You could go back and see who attacked." Chee's angular face smiled blandly at her, but she noticed how his eyes, gone as reflective as two pools of melted gold, showed no emotion at all.

"It's not that simple." Her heart thumped inside her chest. Not now, she told herself. She couldn't handle this on top of everything else.

"Couldn't you go back?" he insisted.

"If I could find it." She saw the glittering blue temporal pathways again in her mind, the bewildering array of Whens to which one could travel if one had sufficient Talent and training—and if one were female. "The timelines exist in infinite number, but most of them are Otherwhens as far as we are concerned. The ilseri can tell the difference between Otherwhen and Truewhen, but I have always found it difficult."

"Fascinating." He moved forward beside her, his steps measured and thoughtful. "I would like to learn more."

She caught her breath; there was a strangeness about him that set her teeth on edge, and nasty rumors circulated about the House of Chee, talk of instability, madness—and murder. Coals smoldered behind this man's eyes whenever he looked at her. "Some other time, perhaps, Lord Chee."

"Yes." He smiled again without warmth. "Perhaps later would be better."

Three people ahead of her, a middle-aged man escorted his wife onto a covered platform inset above and below and at the four midpoints with pale-blue ilsera crystals. A second later, they disappeared as he mentally wrenched the energies to transport them home. Then a tall, elegant woman stepped into place—one of the Sennays, if Haemas wasn't mistaken, and a distant cousin of hers.

A young woman in front of Haemas, gowned in Rald crimson, stepped into the portal, holding a little girl dressed in lacy blue by the hand. How strange to take a child to a Council meeting, Haemas thought. Her father had never taken her anywhere, not even to a Council meeting, even though they were always held here at Tal'ayn. She had rarely left the grounds until the day she fled down into the Lowlands—when Jarid had convinced her that she'd killed her father.

"You must visit Chee'ayn," Chee said pleasantly over her shoulder. "We have the only surviving stand of pine there, right at the edge of a cliff. Chee'ayn is the one place in the Highlands where the soil is just right. When the wind blows from the north, you can smell the needles all the way up to the main house."

Haemas stepped onto the platform as soon as the woman and child disappeared, hastily throwing her mind open to the vibrations of the psi-active crystals. *North . . . south,* she recited in her mind, feeling each crystal warm in turn, *east . . . west . . . above . . . below!* She altered the vibrations to match the portal at Shael'donn. The world twisted into a chill grayness, then resolved itself into the familiar snow-covered grounds shared by the paired schools.

Kevisson stepped out of the Lenhe'ayn portal into the warmer air of the Lowlands. Smoke from the smoldering fields curled up into the clear green sky and the acrid smell of burned grain filled his lungs. After stripping off his black leather gloves, he thrust them into his belt while he surveyed the havoc wrought: the sturdy, well-kept outbuildings burned to ashes, the famous black Lenhe horses and other stock lying torn and bloodied in the dead grass, the golden fields of ripe zeli-grain now a charred ruin. An iciness ran through him; he had never known the outlying chierra people to be violent, and like all Lowlands-bred Kashi he had dealt with them his whole life.

Closing his eyes, he cast about with his mind for some hint

of the surviving Lenhes, the Kashi family that held this land. Letting his awareness drift, he passed the unhearing minds of the estate's sorrowing chierra servants, brushed against the bewildered, untrained minds of several Kashi children in the main house, then came across a tendril of broadcast pain and grief. Tracing it, he identified Myriel, the old Lord's grown daughter, in a large vaulted room somewhere nearby.

He followed her thoughts, passing several dark-haired, olive-complected chierra workers as they struggled to drag the mutilated stock to an enormous bonfire burning in one of the blackened fields. They met him with wary, strained expressions, but he stared each one down as he walked by, forcing their dark-brown eyes to lower and acknowledge him a Kashi Lord.

He didn't enjoy that, but it had been impressed upon him at an early age what his hair and eyes of golden brown meant in a society in which the lightness of a man's coloring was taken as the measure of his worth and strength. Golden eyes and hair were the genetic tag that indicated the presence of inherited mindtalents, and their absence indicated that an infant was only chierra, both head-blind and head-deaf, forever excluded from Kashi circles. Shael'donn had been the one place where none of that mattered, but Shael'donn was changing.

Stopping at a low building, he pushed open an ornately carved door and realized he had found the Lenhe family chapel. The stuffy air was thick with incense and oversweet with mounds of fall flowers. Myriel Lenhe stood at the far end, framed in a bright shaft of sunlight slanting down from a high window, her ash-gold head bent, gazing down at the still face of her murdered son—the child she had once asked of him many years ago and which, for his own reasons, he had refused to give.

"I told him to stay inside with me and the girls." Her voice had tiny cracks in it, like a crystal already shattered by the hammer and about to fall apart. "I told him to let the field hands handle the bandits when they attacked, but he just laughed and said, 'They're only chierra, Mother,' as if I didn't understand that he was a man and could do a man's work."

She stretched out trembling fingers toward the cold, alabaster-pale hand under its gossamer covering of fine Merir silk. The fluted pots of chispa-fire placed around the walls flickered as her unshielded sorrow surged through the room. "He would have been the most talented Lord in our family for generations!"

Kevisson glanced back at the additional bodies laid out on rough wooden biers at the other end of the chapel, undoubtedly all dark-haired, five-fingered chierra workers who had fallen defending the Lenhe estate beside this child.

Myriel walked slowly along the bier, studying the golden-haired boy laid out in his blue-and-gold ceremonial best. "I saw their leader, you know, when he struck Lat down." She looked at Kevisson for the first time, her reddened eyes over-large in her drawn white face. "There was something wrong with his eyes." Her hand trembled as she straightened the silken veil draped over the body. "They were the wrong color. I actually tried to kill him myself, but my mind couldn't get a grasp on him. It was like ..." She shook her head as tears welled again and trickled down her cheeks. "I can't really explain. It was like ... he was Talented."

The wrong color ... Kevisson's mouth compressed. He had once known a Lowlander with blue eyes, an oddity among a race of brown-eyed people, a freeborn chierra who had lived in the middle of the Great Forest in a nest of bandits. And that Lowlander had been protected by the ilseri. Had he been the one who attacked here today?

"Of course, I'm only rated as a Plus-One, but ..." She crossed her arms, hugging herself fiercely. "I've never had any trouble controlling our servants. It should have been enough to kill one of *them*! They have no shields, and Lat was a Plus-Four, even if he hadn't been fully trained—that should have been more than enough." Her voice dropped to a hoarse whisper. "What will I do now? Father has been dead these last three years and my other children are only girls. How long will the Council allow me to hold Lenhe'ayn without a male heir?"

Kevisson took her arm; her clammy skin was as cold as the

flagstones beneath their feet. "Why don't you come back to the house, Myriel? We'll discuss it."

"No." Suddenly she looked at him as if truly seeing him for the first time and twisted out of his grasp. "You've come from Shael'donn, haven't you? To express their sympathies." The pupils in her eyes were so dilated that he could hardly see the gold of her irises. "Well, there wouldn't have to be any so-called sympathies if you *men* had done your job. The Council is supposed to protect us. Those chierra could come back and finish us off any moment! Where are the men to keep it from happening again?"

"Myriel, you know Monmart'ayn has never held a seat on the Council." He trailed after her as she turned back to the bier. His boots echoed through the emptiness of the large room. "But I'll go back and speak to them for you."

"I asked you for help once and you refused." She gathered a double handful of the tiny white anith flowers strewn around the bier's edge and pressed them to her face. "I don't want anything from you now. Go back to Shael'donn and let your beloved books keep you warm at night. I'll take care of myself, as I've always had to."

"The Council wants me to investiga—"

"I said go!" She whirled on him, the flowers crushed between her fingers and her knuckles white. "I don't want you here! Go away!" Snowy petals drifted to the floor.

A figure dressed in gray homespun detached itself from the shadows by the wooden biers in the back and hurried toward her. "Begging your pardon, my Lord, but if you could just persuade her Ladyship to rest for a bit." Brushing past him, the old chierra servant with swollen, wet eyes slipped an arm around the staring woman and drew her gently toward the outside door. "She's not herself right now."

Myriel resisted for a moment, then turned to look at the old woman. "Dorria, what will I do?" Her voice was high-pitched and strained.

"You just let old Dorria worry about that, child." The chierra folded Myriel's head to her ample bosom and rocked her gently within her arms. "Dorria's never let you down, has she, all these years?"

Myriel began to cry, her body wracked with great convulsive sobs. The old woman glanced up at him. "If you will just go on back to the main house, your Lordship, they should be setting out supper in a bit. Her Ladyship and I will be along by and by."

Kevisson turned back to take one last look at the still, colorless face of Myriel's son, the child who might have been his had he answered her differently all those years ago. Then he walked back to the door and let himself outside into the late-afternoon sunlight.

"I never know where I stand with Kevisson." Haemas spread her palms against the chill windowpanes in her study as the flock of girl students roughhoused outside in the falling snow. The cold seeped through her hands up into her arms. "Sometimes we're so close, I feel we've a single mind between us, thinking the same thoughts. He's the other half of me. Then other times I feel as if I were sixteen again and he's come to drag me by the scruff of my neck back to my father."

"Well, wanting to help him is one thing." Enissa looked up from her thick leather-bound book of accounts. "Interfering is something else again."

The wind gusted, rattling the windowpanes and sending flurries of the dry, dustlike snow flying. Outside, the girls shrieked and ran harder, their young legs pumping, slipping, then getting up to run again. Haemas shivered. Had she ever felt as young as that, played with that kind of reckless abandon? She felt cold just watching them. "But Master Ellirt meant Kevisson to succeed him. It's not right that Shael'donn goes to someone else, especially to a man like Riklin Senn." Dropping the heavy velvet drapes, she turned away from the window's frosted panes. "What would you have done?"

"The same." Enissa's grayish-gold eyes crinkled merrily at the corners as she laid aside her pen. "I never could keep my nose where it belonged, but that's no excuse for you to be as bad." She pushed her metal spectacles back in place with her middle finger. "You should have more sense."

Haemas gazed at the older woman affectionately, thinking how difficult, even with Master Ellirt's help, it would have been to set up the House of Moons without her. She remembered the day a gray-haired stranger had shown up at Shael'donn. Brother Alidale had knocked on her door, then peeked in, his usually sober face amused. "Someone to see you," he had said, radiating a barely contained mirth through his shields.

A wave of irritation washed through her. "I don't have time." She glanced up from the raw crystal she was evaluating for a new portal set for Senn'ayn. "Tell him to come back later."

Alidale's golden eyes danced merrily. "But it isn't a 'he.' "

"Tell her to go away, then." Haemas adjusted the lathe and picked up the blue crystal again. "This set has been promised in a ten-day. I'm busy."

"Not too busy for me, I trust," said a calm, low-pitched voice from the doorway.

Haemas looked up into the plump, lined face of an older woman. "I'm afraid today is a bad time, Lady . . . ?"

"Saxbury." The round-faced woman walked into the small workroom, then dumped a large leather pouch on the floor at Haemas's feet. "But I don't intend to be Lady Saxbury anymore. I don't like her."

Alidale's mouth twitched. Haemas could see that in another second, he would be laughing in the poor woman's face. "Thank you, Brother Alidale," she said crisply. "I can handle this from here."

"As you wish." Alidale's cheeks bulged with the effort of remaining silent as he backed out the door, then closed it behind him.

"Please." Haemas rose from her seat and pulled out another one beside her work table. "Sit down."

The woman sat, folding her hands on the table and studying Haemas closely with shrewd golden eyes. She was dressed in a richly cut dark-green velvet skirt and jacket that smelled, strangely enough, of furniture polish and paint. Her mouth twisted as she glanced down and brushed at a spot of white paint on her sleeve. "Drat," she muttered. "That's what comes of always having to show servants how it's done."

"Now," Haemas said as she reseated herself, "how may I help you?"

"For a start, you can call me Enissa." The gray-haired woman nodded. "I've come to work in your House of Moons."

"I *will* be looking for staff once the house is finished next summer." Haemas turned the blue crystal over in her fingers, searching for flaws. "But I don't have a place for you until then."

"Oh, I'll just stay with you." Enissa gazed around the simple room and its overflowing bookshelves with satisfaction. "I wanted to study here when I was growing up, but, of course, Shael'donn never allowed females—until you came along." She leaned over the table and stared into Haemas's eyes. "I can't imagine how you persuaded them to train you. I'm a natural healer, myself, although no one would ever teach me."

Haemas was dumbfounded. "A healer?"

The woman reached out and pressed Haemas's right hand between her two small palms. A sense of warmth and well-being enveloped Haemas, as if sunlight were playing over her face. A faint taste of cinnamon hung in the back of her throat, and she felt a subtle, relaxing energy quite unlike anything she'd ever known.

Enissa's eyes drifted shut. "Don't get much rest, do you?" she murmured. The warmth crept up Haemas's arm, threading through her brain in slow, lazy swirls. "They keep you far too busy, and you're always afraid to say no, afraid they'll say you can't keep up, that you're not good enough." She squeezed Haemas's hand, then released it and sat back in her chair. "Being in charge will mean recognizing your own limitations as well as everyone else's. You need to remember that."

"I—" Haemas flexed her still-tingling fingers.

"Yes, yes, I know." The older woman's no-nonsense mouth frowned. "There's no such beast as a female healer, is there? At least, that's what they'd like us to think. Well, I won't put up with it anymore, not when there's finally somewhere else to go—and something that needs doing. I don't want to be a lady of a great House anymore. My children are all grown; the last of them just married a few days ago. My husband has been dead now eight years, and only the Light above knows how glad my son will be to have his wife, a proper Rald granddaughter, no less, as Lady of Sithnal'ayn instead of me. Sometimes I have to wonder at Rhydal, my departed husband. Whatever possessed him to take me, a mere Revann Saxbury with almost no dowry, to wife?"

Unable to think of a reply, Haemas stared at the older woman's unconcerned face.

"Oh, you won't get rid of me," Enissa said. "I'm here to stay."

And a good thing, too, Haemas thought now, or no telling where she and the House of Moons would be. She turned away from the window and the shrieking students, rubbing her chilled palms against her tunic. "So you think I should apologize."

Enissa winked. "Or, at the very least, lie. He's not likely to forgive you otherwise."

Haemas massaged her temples with her forefingers. She was an abominable liar, and besides, she wasn't a child anymore. Now that she was grown, the fact that Kevisson was ten years older than herself no longer mattered, and she ached for him to take her seriously. She had as much right to her opinion as he had to his. She wasn't going to give in this time.

She picked up her schedule book. "Well, I'll talk to him when he comes back from Lenhe'ayn. I'll make him understand."

Chapter Three

"Lady Myriel won't sleep, my Lord." The old chierra servant's round face was still swollen with tears. "Not for a minute, not since—" She pressed a work-worn hand over her mouth and turned away, staring at a Lenhe crest woven into the wall hanging. Her distress spread through Kevisson's mind like a dark cloud.

He laid aside the list of damages he was tallying for the Council and stood, his fingers sliding over the red spine-wood of the fine desk. The old Lord's study must have been his favorite room, he thought. From the look of the papers and ledgers still scattered about, little had been touched since Avlan Lenhe's death some three years ago. The blue-and-gold ebari-wool throws were still casually laid over the chair turned to the hearth as if the old Lord would be back in only a moment, the brocade drapes were drawn against the late-afternoon sun, the wing-backed chairs huddled close to the fire for guests who would never come. This seemed to be a house waiting for something.

"Perhaps I can be of some help—" He paused, having forgotten her name, then concentrated and plucked it lightly from the edge of her conscious thoughts. "Dorria."

"If you would be so kind. I have been that worried about her." Dorria dabbed at her reddened eyes with a worn gray shawl. "I've seen after two generations of Lenhe children now and I never failed any of them, not until—" Tears welled up in the dark-brown eyes again.

"It wasn't your fault, Dorria." He stood up and clasped her trembling shoulder. "I'm sure you've always done the very

28

best you could." *You're of no use to your Lady when you're this upset,* he murmured into her mind, using the contact of his hand on her shoulder to deepen the faint link between them. *You must calm yourself so she won't pick it up from you.*

Although the old woman's chierra mind could not hear him on a conscious level, her body began to relax. Keeping his arm lightly around her shoulder, Kevisson walked her up the winding, carpeted staircase to the family's personal wing, using his Talent to ease the terrible grief the old servant felt for Myriel, whom she had raised, and for Myriel's dead son. Although Andiine vows forbade imposing his will on others under most circumstances, blunting of grief was a widely accepted practice.

When they reached the carved expanse of Myriel's private door, Kevisson turned to the servant. "Wait out here while I speak with her. I'll call if she needs you."

Breathing somewhat more easily already, the old woman nodded and stood aside, bowing her head.

Inside, the sitting room was a shambles, as was the bedroom beyond, clothes thrown everywhere, the expensive velvets, wools, and silks ripped, then tossed aside. The fire had burned down into ashes, the air was cold, and the reek of a dozen perfumes mingled near one wall where the smashed jars lay in a heap at the baseboard. In the far corner, Myriel gazed out the window at the wild tangle of woods two fields away, her fists pressed hard against her sides.

Myriel? Kevisson closed the door softly behind him. *Why don't you lie down? It's getting dark and a lot of people will be here tomorrow.*

Myriel stiffened as he spoke directly into her mind. She was still beautiful, he thought, her tall body only slightly rounder than he remembered from all those years ago when his Search had led him into the Lowlands and he had availed himself of her father's hospitality.

"Go away!" she hissed without looking at him.

Think of your daughters. He edged closer. *They're grieving, too. You must take care of yourself for their sake.*

"My daughters!" She turned around, and he realized with a

shock that she was laughing in hard, wrenching sobs. Her face twisted. "My daughters, oh, that is just the way one of you would think!" She looked down at the green, soot-smudged gown she still wore, then brushed absently at a few blackened streaks. "I only wish I had sent my daughters out to face the chierra—then I would still have my son!"

You don't mean that. Probing beneath her shields, Kevisson blanched at the wildness seething through her mind.

"You don't understand." Her gaze turned back to the window and the charred fields beyond. "You're a man—and a son. You've never had to think about these things the way a daughter must. If I still had Lat, I would have Lenhe'ayn." A muscle twitched in her jaw. "Neither of my girls can inherit; my father entailed this estate solely upon my male heirs, of which I have none now to present to the Council."

There will be time to think about that later. Kevisson resolved to send for a healer from the House of Moons as soon as he had persuaded her to rest; she needed far more care than he could give her. *Come and lie down for a little while.* He touched her shoulder.

Unexpectedly she whirled on him like a bavval, clawing at his eyes and shoving him back against the wall. Caught off guard, he enfolded her in his arms and held her hard against his chest. *Myriel, stop this!* He poured all the strength of his Plus-Ten Talent against the inadequate defenses of her Plus-One mind. *Stop fighting me and rest!*

But grief and pain were lending her unsuspected reserves. Continuing to struggle, she worked one arm free and scratched his face. *I'll rest when I have another son!* she cried into his mind, her loss laid painfully bare before him. Her need poured over him, hot and savage. *Give me another son!* Then her lips were at his, pressing, demanding.

For a second, he almost responded. Then he drew away from her tear-ravaged face. *Perhaps you will have another son someday, but not like this.*

You refused me before.

Even as he forced her back onto the bed, he felt the aching need that she projected burning through him.

Don't say no again! Give me a son and I swear I will love him! That's why you wouldn't before, wasn't it? You thought I wouldn't love him!

It was true; he had refused her because he had caught a glimpse of himself through her mind: the disappointing reality that his eyes and hair were golden brown, not the true gold that the Kashi prized as the visible proof of their superiority to the chierra. Any child of his would likely have carried that same chierralike coloring, and he would never give his child to her or anyone else to be scorned as he had been.

It won't matter! Myriel's arms wrapped around his neck, drawing him down to her desperate need. *I swear it won't!*

For a moment, tangled in her arms, with the fire of her body pressed against his, he was tempted, almost swept beyond thinking. She was still lovely—in fact, she was all the more beautiful for the years that had transformed her from the shallow, ambitious girl he remembered into this grieving matron. But his heart had chosen long ago, for all the good it had ever done him, and it had not chosen her.

Freeing his arms, Kevisson folded her to him as if she were an ailing child and stroked the ash gold of her wild hair. His face ached where she had scratched him. *Sleep*, he whispered into her mind, knowing tomorrow would be difficult for her even if she did manage to rest. She struggled within his grip, trying to escape, but he pinned her arms, projecting an aura of calm he did not feel. *Sleep*, he commanded her again. *I won't leave you.*

Then he leaned back against the wooden headboard of her bed, using his will against hers, feeling the tension drain gradually from her body until at last his strength overpowered hers and she slept. For a long time, he watched her chest rise and fall in the evenness of a sleep that eased grief for the moment, watched until most of the lines smoothed from the curve of her still-perfect cheek.

Would he have been so firm in his refusal, he wondered, if he had never known Haemas Sennay Tal?

* * *

Even before she met Enissa in the hallway, Haemas caught Enissa's grumbling thoughts as the older woman rounded the corner. She was struggling into her heaviest wool cloak while trying to balance her medicinal pouch at the same time.

Haemas took the pouch from her. "Is there an emergency?"

A head shorter than Haemas, the older woman drew her stout body up and regarded her impatiently. "Now what else do you think could pry me out of my warm bed at this late hour? If you must know, Kevisson asked me to come down to Lenhe'ayn and see after one of the family who's in a bad way."

"Oh." Haemas's face warmed as she realized Kevisson had contacted Enissa without even leaving her a message. "Do you think you'll be back by morning? The girls seemed rather subdued at the table tonight. I'm afraid they may be upset about the attack."

A half smile quirked the edges of Enissa's mouth as she took her bulky shoulder pouch of medicines back. "There's not one among that lot who can think much beyond the cut of her next festival gown, and that's a pure fact."

Haemas started to protest, then didn't. The Kashi daughters sent from all over the Highlands as well as the Lowlands to study mindarts at the House of Moons did seem to have an overwhelming preoccupation with things other than studying, such as clothes and boys—and marriage. Softening her shields, she skimmed at the surface mindchatter of the girls housed on the upper floor and caught at the edges of a few carelessly broadcast thoughts: the latest colors in Cholee velvets . . . eligible oldest sons . . . invitations to the Dynd Naming to come in the next ten-day . . . and the undisputed goldness of young Arrich Dynd's eyes.

Haemas shook her head ruefully. "I guess you're right. Do you want me to come with you?"

"I most certainly do not." Enissa shouldered her bag. "These flighty, half-witted girls need you right here, where you can keep an eye on them." Enissa reached out with both hands and pushed her toward her own chambers. "Get some rest." She opened Haemas's door and guided her inside. "The night's half over as it is. I'll be back as soon as I can." Then she shut the door firmly in Haemas's face.

Well, good-bye to you, too, Haemas said as the older woman started down the staircase, then shook her head. The air in her sitting room was cooler than she'd expected, the fire in her blue-tiled hearth barely more than glowing red embers. Kneeling, she added more kindling, then prodded and stirred until the flames crackled again. But even though she held her hands close, the fire seemed to give off far too little warmth. Stretching her hands closer, she watched the shimmering fire, suddenly too weary to go about even the simple business of undressing for bed.

The events of the last few days swept back over her: Master Ellirt's sudden death, the appointment of Riklin Senn as the Head of Shael'donn, Kevisson's anger with her. It was all more than she could take in. Gathering her legs to her chest, she rested her chin on her knees and tried to concentrate on her schedule for the next few days.

Saatha Bramm had a Testing coming up; no doubt her father, Lord Ellric Bramm, self-important Lowlander that he was, would insist on being present to make sure the House of Moons didn't botch it. And then there was Meryet Alimn . . .

Stifling a yawn, she blinked at the yellow flames for a moment. Meryet? For some reason, she couldn't remember what had been on her mind. A chill, bone-aching weariness seeped up from the tips of her toes, spreading until she could hardly remember her own name. Reaching back, she loosened her mass of pale-gold hair from its single braid and shook it out, combing it with her fingers.

Meryet . . . Shivering, Haemas pushed herself up from the floor, then balanced there dizzily. No doubt, she should have eaten something instead of merely playing with her stew at the evening meal. Well, she scolded herself, that had been foolish. How could she expect people to trust her with their daughters when she didn't even take proper care of herself?

Something rustled behind her. Turning her head, she peered through the flickering shadows. Was someone standing there, watching her, over by the far wall? "Who's there?" she demanded, thinking that one of the girls had sneaked in.

"So, Lady," a cool voice said from the shadows, "shall we resume our discussion?"

It was Diren Chee, and she realized suddenly that her strange malaise was being projected by him. Heart pounding, she strengthened her shields and darted toward the door, but in two determined strides he caught up with her and threw his arm around her neck, jerking her almost off her feet. Before she could cry out, something hard and sharp-edged pressed against her temple and loosed a lightning bolt deep into her brain. Gasping with pain and shock, she tried to push it away.

He caught her wrist in iron fingers and twisted it behind her back. "You will come with me now," he whispered. "Say it!"

The words echoed inside her head until she thought it would burst. She threw her will against the grinding pain, trying to shield it out, but it increased twofold, then threefold. Her knees sagged as she was drawn down into a dark vortex of pain.

"Fool!" Chee shifted his arms to take her weight and keep her from falling. "Fighting only makes it worse! Do you want to kill yourself?"

Then the swirling darkness swept her beyond pain and fear.

Enissa opened her mind to the ilsera crystals set into the portal housing, concentrating on their soundless vibrations. Somewhere beyond the thicket of surrounding trees and bushes, one of the House silshas snarled and another screamed in answer, apparently enraged. A shiver ran down her spine, and, suddenly feeling something was wrong, she glanced back at the House of Moons, two stories of solemn grayness outlined in the muted glow of silvery Sedja, the largest of Desalaya's three moons.

A few late lights still shone in the girls' windows, but the sense of menace was already fading. You're getting old, she scolded herself, but that's no excuse for jumping at shadows. She sighed and turned back to the portal, focusing her mind again, then altering the wavelength to match the crystals in the

Lenhe'ayn portal, having to reproduce it from Kevisson's re-layed memory since she had never set foot on Lenhe ground.

Wouldn't her late husband, Rhydal, be scandalized if he could see her now? she mused. Here she was, setting off into the night by herself, going to a place she'd never been before, to tend a woman who wasn't even a member of one of the High Houses. It was a wonder her long-dead Sithnal husband didn't march back from the Darkness itself to haunt her.

The distance from the Highlands to the Lowlands passed in less than a flash, stealing her breath with the instantaneous bite of deep cold between. She opened her eyes to the torch-lit, white-painted portal of Lenhe'ayn.

"Enissa!" Kevisson Monmart stepped out of the shadows and reached up to take her arm. Four fiery red scratches trailed down the left side of his face. "It's good of you to come all this way, and at this hour, too."

"That's Healer Saxbury to you, young man, when you have me out in the middle of the night on a call." She smiled. She had known this boy's family all her married life—the Monmarts having been one of the few Lowland Houses, be-sides her father's, that her husband, Rhydal, would tolerate—and she had always liked young Kevisson. She had to keep reminding herself that although he was some twenty-odd years younger, he was no longer a boy at all. She peered down at him. "What in the name of Darkness happened to your face?"

Kevisson glanced back at the massive house. "Myriel is out of her mind with grief."

"She fought you?" Enissa sighed, then stepped down from the portal platform onto the crushed gravel path. "You should have called me sooner."

He turned for the main house. "We'd better get inside. I did set a guard, but I don't know how safe we are exposed out here like this. The raiders could come back, although they left little enough worth bothering. Most of the zeli fields were yet to be harvested. I don't know how Lenhe'ayn is going to make it through the winter now."

Shouldering the weight of her pouch, Enissa fell in beside

him, each of her steps equaling only half of one of his strides. "And how is your mother?"

"Complaining, as always, but I'm sure that comes as no surprise." He stopped at the side door and rapped sharply. One of the chierra servants, still dirty and smudged from the day's cleanup work, peeked out, then hastily opened the door.

A bit breathless from trying to match his pace, she followed him into the half light of the long hallway. "Naevia still wants you to come home and take over Monmart'ayn?"

"I'm afraid she speaks of nothing else." Kevisson led her to a side staircase. "Of course, if my father were still alive, it would be different. Because of my . . ." He hesitated. "My coloring, as well as my commitment to Shael'donn, he always intended my sister, Mairen, to inherit, and I really don't see why she shouldn't."

Enissa watched his strong back striding easily up the long flight of steps, then put a hand to her chest, took a deep breath, and followed him. You ought to take your own advice, she scolded herself, and lose some weight!

He waited at the top for her as she struggled up the stairs, and she stopped on the last step to ease the knot in her chest. "Was Lady Lenhe badly injured?"

His mouth straightened. "Physically, she isn't hurt. All the harm is here." His fingers brushed his temple. "Her only son was killed in the attack, and it seems the old Lord entailed this estate solely upon her male heirs. Now she won't be able to hold this land. She—" He broke off and gazed down the hall. "Perhaps I'd just better let you see her. Then you'll understand."

Enissa nodded and mounted the last step. "I'm ready."

Another few doors down, he stopped and nodded to a plump gray-haired chierra servant. "Any change, Dorria?"

"No, sir." The old woman dabbed the corner of her eye with a worn shawl. "But I didn't let no one in or out, just like you said."

He took the key from her hand. "You've done well. Now I want you to go to bed and get some sleep. We'll see after your mistress now."

"Oh, no, sir!" Dorria touched the door with trembling fingers. "I want to take care of her myself. I won't be able to sleep a single wink, knowing how she is and all."

"Dorria . . ." He reached out and put a firm hand on her shoulder. *"Go and get some sleep. I insist."*

Enissa felt him put the full force of his mind behind that statement and stared at the pair of them. Andiine Masters were well known for their restraint in such matters. Things must be very bad indeed.

Dorria's lined face looked puzzled. Then she turned to go, wrapping the shawl around her hunched shoulders and walking slowly.

Enissa frowned up at him. "I suppose that was necessary."

"She's almost as badly off as her mistress." He turned the key in the lock. She heard it click, then stepped aside as he swung the door open. Inside, the room was a terrifying mess, with clothes and other possessions ripped to shreds and thrown everywhere, vases smashed and ground into the thick carpet, furniture splintered.

"Myriel?" Kevisson stuck his head through the door, then motioned to Enissa. "She must still be asleep."

Enissa followed him in, picking her way through the wreckage of slippers and lace and cosmetics strewn across the ruined carpeting. "Grief does terrible things," she murmured.

He pointed to the blue canopied bed, then stood aside. Enissa took up the hand dangling limply off to one side and held her own fingers against the hollow of the sleeping woman's wrist, but the skin was cold, far too cold. She pressed harder, feeling for the pulse that should be there.

Appalled, she stared down at the pale form on the disordered bed, seeing the hollowed shadows under the eyes, the lines of grief so strong that they were still visible, even though Myriel Lenhe had passed beyond this world.

"I did the best I could, but I'm no healer." Kevisson leaned against the bedpost at the head of the bed and shifted uneasily. "How is she?"

Enissa laid the bloodless wrist beside the woman's body, then reached across and straightened the other arm, too. She moved back, wondering what had happened and how she was going to explain this—indeed, how Kevisson was going to explain.

"Is she worse?" He reached out and touched the white forehead, then stood there in shock.

"She's—gone." Enissa sighed and looked about the room, wondering if there were an intact length of silk left somewhere for the traditional shroud.

"She can't be!" The color drained from his face. "She was sleeping when I left her, only sleeping!"

"Perhaps she didn't want to live." Enissa took his arm and pulled him toward the door. "Wake the servants. I'm afraid there is much to be done here before morning." She stopped and thought for a moment. "Did any of the rest of the family survive, or was she the last one?"

Kevisson took a deep breath, then shook his head, his eyes dark and miserable. "She said there were two more children, both girls. I haven't seen them yet."

Enissa opened the door and guided him out. "Poor little tykes," she said. "I suppose I'll have to tell them as soon as it's light."

As she watched him walk away, his shoulders slouched in shock and weariness, she was touched by an uneasy feeling that Myriel Lenhe's death had been no accident.

Chapter Four

The pounding in Haemas's head crested, ebbed, then re-surged again until even the effort to breathe was torment. She was freezing, as if she'd been left on an exposed ledge high up on the mountains that overlooked Tal'ayn. Her body felt like an ice-riddled lump, and every inch of it ached.

She's nearly conscious!

That transmitted thought, although not aimed at her, thundered in her head and rattled around as if she were trapped inside one of the great festival drums she'd seen once in the Lowlands, bringing so much pain that she almost tumbled back into the beguiling darkness again. She groaned and her teeth chattered from the cold.

"She looks half dead," a voice said.

"That's because she fought it." The second voice paused. "We need to get some of this down her." An arm propped up her aching head and something hard was thrust against her lips. She tried to turn away. "Drink or I'll drown you in it." Although the words were hard, surprisingly the tone was not. Haemas swallowed a little of the warm tea, then choked while the rest ran down her chin.

Sometime after that, the pounding in her head receded a little, though the cold settled into a knot in her middle. Opening her eyes a crack, she gazed at a small, dingy room with only one dim, half-melted candle burning in a sconce high up on the wall. The air smelled dank and stale, as if the room hadn't been opened in years. Her fingernails dug into patched bedclothes. Something was wrong. These weren't her chambers.

Several shadowed figures stood looking down on her. "Welcome, Lady," one of them said softly, then touched his fingertips to his lips in a salute.

She felt she ought to know that mocking voice, but his identity was locked up somewhere in her head behind all the pain. The walls began to swirl. Her stomach lurched and she had to close her eyes. Who were these people? Where was Enissa? If she was ill, then Enissa should be called. She didn't want some healer employed by one of the High Houses. They were always so grim and disapproving.

Fabric rustled, then voices murmured as footsteps walked away. After a while, she found that, if she lay very still, hardly breathing, the pounding lessened even more. She opened her eyes again, staring into the unsteady half darkness, trying to understand what had happened.

Shaking, she hitched herself up on her elbows. Again, the room spun crazily. She broke into a cold sweat and thought she would lose what little was in her stomach. Clutching at the mattress, she made herself get up anyway, and staggered a few steps before sprawling facedown on the floor. The icy darkness came in waves, rolling over her until she couldn't see or hear, receding a little, then sweeping back again.

Between waves, she struggled to her knees and hung there, the pounding in her head now a blinding torment. She wanted to call Enissa or one of the girls, but the pain was a universe unto itself and there was no way out.

Slowly she pushed herself back onto her feet, then with her hands out, felt her way through the room, unable to see clearly for the agony behind her eyes. She took one step, then another, and fumbled around a corner where the light seemed to be brighter. She heard voices again, but far away, as if she were at the bottom of a deep hole.

"She's gone!" one said.

"Dammit, she can't be far! Get out there and find her."

Her legs buckled and her back slid down the wall that she had been leaning against for support.

"Lady Haemas!" a male voice suddenly cried. "You're going to hurt yourself!"

"Please . . ." Haemas tried to focus through the shimmering

waves of pain on the indistinct form before her. "You must send for Enissa!"

"Of course." A strong arm slipped around her shoulders and braced her to stand. "Just lean on me."

She wavered back onto her feet. Darkness hovered above her in a giant wave, ready to break and carry her far out into an empty black sea.

"Diren, you've found her!"

"Of course I have," the male voice said calmly. "I told you she wouldn't get far in this shape. Now lock her up the way you should have done to begin with, and see that she isn't left alone this time."

Just as the darkness crashed down on her, she finally understood she was not in the House of Moons anymore.

An icy, penetrating rain soaked the procession of mourners as the priest, Father Orcado, flung open the double doors of the Lenhe chapel and led the way through the burned fields to the towering pyre of wood that had been stacked for young Lat Lenhe and his mother, Lady Myriel.

Kevisson walked behind the two biers, watching the healer, Enissa Saxbury, steady the two remaining Lenhe daughters with a hand on each child's shoulder. Their hair, a deep shade of copper-gold, had been left undressed to flow down their backs, and quickly became soaked, as did their clothes and everything else under the freezing downpour.

He drew his sodden cloak more tightly about him, wondering again how he could have been so stupid as to leave Myriel alone last night. Whether she had somehow managed to take her own life or not, the responsibility for her death had to be laid at his feet.

One by one, the entire staff of chierra workers preceded the two biers into the ruined fields, lining up before the pyre of wood cut by field hands who had labored all night. Father Orcado pushed back the hood of his ebari-wool mantle and stood with his bald head bared to the pouring rain, his hands folded, as the chierra workers struggled to climb the pyre and position the two biers side by side at the top. The air smelled of wet wood and burnt grain.

Kevisson moved into place behind the little girls. The younger one of the two, who seemed about seven or eight, turned to stare at him with puzzled greenish-gold eyes.

"Are you our father?" she asked as the rain dripped down her young forehead.

"Be still, Adrina!" The other girl, who looked to be ten or so, reached across the healer's tunic and jerked the younger child's arm. "Mother said we would never know our father."

Adrina looked from her sister to Kevisson, then sniffled, the tears welling up in her eyes. "But—" She stopped, her chest heaving, plainly trying to control herself. "I thought that now—maybe—"

Kevisson dropped to one knee, careless of the mud mixed with charred grain underfoot, and used his thumbs to wipe the rain and tears from her face. "I wish you were mine, little one. And whoever your father is, I'm sure he would be very proud to know you."

"You mustn't say that to her." The other girl narrowed her eyes, then turned back to the pyre. Her shoulders were stiff, and she held her dripping head high. "Mother said it was wrong to want things you can never have." She studied the chierra servants picking their way back down the mountain of wood. "She said it weakens you."

Enissa pressed her lips together, then drew the younger girl to her side and held her close. *Let them be for now, Kevisson,* she said silently. *We'll have to decide what can be done for them later, after we get through this.*

Nodding, he stood up and brushed ineffectually at the chill mud soaking through his pants. Perhaps since the girls could not inherit Lenhe'ayn, he would take them back to the House of Moons, where they would at least be with other children while the Council bickered over what should become of their shattered lives. He could count on Haemas to take good care of them.

Slowly the priest circled the towering pyre, his expression solemn. Kevisson glanced through the crowd for faces he knew, but the assemblage of mourners seemed to be mostly chierra servants. One of the younger Castillans had come as a representative, since Myriel's mother had been a Castillan daughter, but there were only a few other Kashi sprinkled about, none of whom he recognized. Lenhe'ayn had been a solitary House these last few years since the old Lord's death.

Together, chierra and Kashi waited in heavy silence as the priest paced the perimeter the traditional five times, one for each appearance of the Light that had changed the people of this world, transforming them from mere humans into Kashi and chierra, rulers and ruled. His slow, measured steps through the mud were the only sound, except for the muffled sobs of the household staff and the occasional distant roll of thunder.

After the fifth and final time, he stopped before the two girls and stared down at them from under thick eyebrows. "Adrina Castillan Lenhe and Kisa Castillan Lenhe, are you the only remaining kin of this woman and this boy?"

The younger child, Adrina, only clutched at Enissa's skirts, staring back at the tall, imposing priest with tearful eyes, but the older girl dipped her chin in a faint nod.

"Then it falls to you to light their way into the next world." Father Orcado picked up a wet, unlit torch from the bottom of the pyre and thrust it toward her. "You must kindle the flame in the ancient Kashi fashion so they may be sent on."

Kevisson raised an eyebrow as young Kisa took the torch, obliged to use both hands to support its weight. Orcado couldn't mean that! He glanced around at the crowd of onlookers in surprise. Even an adult would have to use an inordinate amount of energy to light that thing in such heavy rain, and there was no way to know how much training this child had been given.

Kisa lifted her pale face to the cold rain and closed her eyes. Her fair brows furrowed and he felt her concentrating on the old ritual used to call forth the spark sacred to the Kashi'an, the People of the Light. Holding his breath, he monitored the buildup of energy in her mind, felt her tense to focus and pour it forth, and knew at the last second that it would not be enough.

The end of the torch sizzled, then smoked as the soaking rain smothered her spark. The priest shook his head, his broad face impassive. "You must try again. They can be sent on in no other way."

Kisa's mouth tightened, then she closed her eyes again. Kevisson felt the heat of Enissa's anger and found it almost matched his own. Before the priest could forbid it, he laid his hand on the back of Kisa's neck. *Concentrate*, he said into her mind. *This time you will get it.*

The young girl trembled underneath his hand, but she went through the litany again, the familiar words from *The Book of Light* taught to all Kashi children as one of the first lessons learned in the mindarts.

Fire is the first aspect of the Light. I will respect and tend it just as I would the Lord of Light himself.

Her small body tensed with the effort of her concentration. Kevisson found himself reciting the words in his mind along with her. *Feel the heat . . . see its brightness . . . hear the crackle . . . smell the smoke.*

The image of fire formed in his mind just as he, and indeed all Kashi, had been taught since time beyond knowing. He felt the warmth of flames bathing his rain-chilled face, saw the crackling yellow-orange fire in his inner vision, smelled the acridness of smoke curling through the damp air.

Take the spark— Kisa's slender young body tensed. *—and Light the Fire.*

Kevisson poised, prepared to boost her spark, but this time the child's flame was bright and true, leaping into life at the end of the sodden torch. The priest took the burning brand from her small hands and walked to the edge of the pyre. "So do we all return to the Light." Then he leaned down and fired the wet wood, holding the torch in place until it reluctantly burned with a heavy, roiling black smoke.

Slowly the priest circled the five-cornered pyre, setting the soggy timber alight every few steps, until the flames crept toward the two biers and their untimely occupants.

Exhausted by her effort, young Kisa wavered on unsteady legs as the flames slowly ate their way upward. Kevisson sensed the child had worked beyond her strength and was about to pass out where she stood. He swept her into his arms and turned back to the main house, even though traditionally family members were supposed to remain until the pyre was fully consumed.

He heard Enissa murmur to the other girl, then follow him, slogging wearily through the muddy fields. No doubt Orcado would be angry at this flaunting of tradition, but Kevisson didn't care. Tradition was going to be very cold comfort to this young pair of sisters in the foreseeable future.

Summerstone stepped out of the shimmering blue perfection of the nexus into sluggish, bitterly cold air in the deep forest. Behind her, the immense waterfall roared over the rocks, pouring down into the green river below, spilling kinetic energy into the ground and air and water with a recklessness that usually delighted her as much as the ilserin. But something was wrong. The anxious males had scattered, hiding in the surrounding trees, too upset even to play or swim.

Why have you called me? She assumed her most solid form to reassure them.

They crept down the scaly gray trunks, a host of slim young males, heads bowed, shoulders hunched, black eyes dull with misery. One finely grown son, with a long, narrow chin and round eyes, ventured nearer than any of the rest. *Gone, gone! It is gone!*

What is gone— She plucked his name from his conscious thoughts. *Leafcurl?*

He made a picture for her in his mind: a clear pool rimmed with ice, broad white steps leading down into the water, a scattering of dull-green shapes nestled in the half-frozen mud at the bottom, and one empty depression where another had rested. *Not us,* he said dejectedly. *We did not take it. Not us. Not us!*

No, not you. Summerstone examined the image, shuddering. The tendrils on her head went limp with dismay. So it had started again. After so many Interims, the ilseri had thought the pools safe, but it was as the current oldest, Frostvine, had often remarked, even back in the days when Summerstone herself had been but a callow ilserin: All Whens hinged on Now, and Now was a precarious balance that could be lost at any time.

Summerstone would have to summon the others and see what, if anything, they could do.

Although the air was warm in the room where she lay, Haemas shivered as consciousness seeped back through her. Opening her eyes slightly, she tried to remember how she had come to this unfamiliar round room, built of dark-grained stone and hung with shredding tapestries thick with webs and dust. A shaft of midmorning sunlight slanted in from a high, narrow window, and a meager fire had been built in the huge fireplace. Next to her cot, a woman with hair the color of Old wheat dozed, her hands curved around an open book.

Haemas moved her head tentatively, but there was only a dull ache in her temples instead of the pounding misery of the night before.

The woman stirred, then blinked down at her with eyes that were medium gold but flecked with odd dark specks. "Well, you certainly look like you've been to Darkness and back again. Diren's little toy was much more effective than I'd ever dreamed." Smoothing a threadbare fold of her out-of-style velvet gown, she shook her head. "The more you fight the blasted thing, the harder it hits you. My advice is to cooperate with him from now on."

"Diren?" Haemas closed her eyes again, realizing she had heard that name mentioned last night, too. "Diren—Chee?" She heard the muffled sound of boots striding down the hall.

"So, Axia," a masculine voice said, "how is our guest today?"

"See for yourself, if you really want to know," the woman replied curtly as she scraped her chair back. "You will anyway."

Haemas tried to reach out with her mind, but her brain felt as if it had been smothered in thick layers of ebari wool. She got only the haziest of impressions while her head began to throb again with a peculiar buzzing. Opening her eyes, she saw the trim frame of the Lord of Chee'ayn, dressed in unrelieved black from head to toe. "It is you!" she whispered. "But why?"

"Now, if I were lying there in your place, I would be more interested in *how*." He hefted a dull-green crystal in his hand. "Don't tell me that you've never heard of a latteh."

A latteh. Somewhere in the back of her mind it seemed she had heard of something by that name ... something ancient— and forbidden.

Chee settled in the chair beside the cot, leaning back and stretching his arms above his head as if he were a hungry silsha limbering up for the hunt. "Interesting, is it not, for you and I to be here together after all those Council Meetings when you sat in the gallery across from me, tilting that proud Tal profile into the air." The cot groaned as he put his weight on the edge. Then his finger traced a line of frozen fire down her cheekbone. She flinched from his touch and he smiled. "Well, that's behind us now. Not only are you going to grace my House, you're going to put my plans into action."

"Plans?" Haemas struggled to sit up, fighting the waves of dizziness that swept over her until the whole room seemed slanted. "What in the name of Darkness are you talking about? Whatever—possessed you to bring me here?"

"The timelines, of course." His pale face floated above his starkly black collar as if it were not connected to the rest of him at all. "Of course, you'll probably understand much better after our matrimonial."

Clouds had drifted across the two rising moons, obscuring the bright crescents as Enissa emerged from the simple Shael'donn portal, holding the younger Lenhe girl's hand. She shivered in the frost-laden air, still soaked to the skin from the Lowlands downpour. She glanced up into the dark, restless sky for a moment, then turned as Kevisson emerged from the blue mist after them, cradling the exhausted, wet form of Kisa Lenhe against his chest. Enissa shook her head, still furious. If she'd had any idea what that idiot Orcado had been up to, she would not have allowed either child to attend the service, no matter what anyone said.

The Highlands wind had a raw, bitter edge that hinted at snow before the night's end. She rubbed her arms as she peered at the wan face pillowed on Kevisson's shoulder. *How is the poor thing?*

Sleeping. He shifted her slight weight in his arms. *You have room for them at the House of Moons, don't you? I could take them over to Shael'donn, but I don't know how our new Lord High Master Senn is going to rule on the subject of females. He hardly seems the liberal type.*

Enissa sniffed. *As if I'd ever let the likes of him get his hands on this pair. They've problems enough as it is. Of course we have room, but we would keep them even if it meant we all had to sleep on the floor!*

A fleeting smile passed across Kevisson's face, only to be replaced by the brooding expression he'd worn ever since the two of them had discovered Myriel's dead body. Enissa glanced down at young Adrina's copper-gold head. "Come, child. A few more steps and then we'll get a nice room ready just for you and your sister."

Adrina glanced at the still form in Kevisson's arms. "Is she—is—" A tear welled up, then trickled down the curve of her cheek.

"Bless me, child, she's fine." Enissa placed one hand on the silken hair. "She's just worn out from lighting the torch. That was a very big job for such a small girl, you know."

Adrina pressed her lips together and looked doubtful. Enissa bent over and folded her into a damp hug. "Just you wait and see," she murmured into wet hair that smelled so much like that of her own three children, now long grown. "Now, let's go get out of these wet clothes!"

Kevisson stepped out of the portal onto the crushed gravel path and headed for the gray stone building. Taking Adrina's hand again, Enissa followed, then was startled by a low rumbling snarl.

The little girl looked around fearfully, then pressed closer to her side. "What was that?"

"That's just a silsha," Enissa said with more assurance than she really felt. Try as she might, she had never been able to work up the sort of link with the lithe, black-furred beasts for which Haemas Tal was justly famous. They never seemed anything to her except the savage killers of the forest she'd always heard about.

"A silsha?" Adrina's voice was very low. "Like the ones that go after the horses and the ebari?"

"Not exactly." Kevisson glanced back over his shoulder and winked. "These are a little larger, and they love little girls."

Enissa grimaced at him. *That's exaggerating a bit, isn't it? Well, not the size part, anyway.*

Ahead of them, the massive double doors opened and a slender figure dressed in gray dashed down the path toward them. About fifty feet away, a muscular black beast leaped to the top of the low garden wall, then threw back its tuft-eared head and roared with a full-throated rage that rattled Enissa's bones.

"Mercy!" She quickened her pace to draw even with Kevisson. "I've never known them to make such a racket before."

"I have." His lean face was grim.

"Lady Enissa!" The running figure waved at them, then slowed. "Lady Enissa, I'm so glad you're back!"

Enissa recognized young Meryet Alimn. "Goodness, Meryet, no wonder the silshas are upset. What could possibly be worth all this dashing about in the dark?"

"She's gone! We can't find her anywhere, not even a trace, and the silshas have been furious ever since last night and—" Meryet broke off to gasp a breath. "And—"

"Who, child?" Enissa shook her head. "Who's gone?"

"Oh." Meryet glanced from her face to Kevisson's, then back. "The Lady Haemas. We looked for her last night when the silshas became so loud, to calm them, but she was gone and she hasn't come back and no one has seen her! We thought maybe she went—with—" The girl faltered as she read the message written on Enissa's face.

Closing her eyes, Enissa cast her mind through the House of

Moons, then the area close by, seeking some trace of the young woman she had come to look upon as a daughter, some hint of what had become of her, but there was only a disturbing blankness.

"We're afraid—" Meryet stopped and put a hand on the bodice of her overtunic, forcing herself to take a deep breath. "I mean—she wouldn't just go off like that, not without telling someone."

Kevisson clutched the sleeping child more closely in his arms. "No, she wouldn't."

"And the silshas are so angry." Meryet glanced at the one crouching on the wall, then winced as its snarl rumbled ominously through the darkness. "It's as if they know something we don't, something terrible."

Kevisson walked toward the front doors, his long strides crunching the ice-coated gravel in the crisp stillness. "They do."

Chapter
Five

"You might as well eat it; you won't get anything else." The woman called Axia held out a chipped blue-and-white bowl of congealing meat broth in one hand, her other braced on her hip. She wore a faded, much-washed rose-colored gown and her straggling hair was pulled up into a loose knot. Her mouth was pursed, her golden eyes hard as granite. "I suppose you're used to much better fare—at Shael'donn."

Haemas stared down at the greasy soup, then rested her aching forehead on her drawn-up knees. Actually, the quality of the food at Shael'donn, where she had lived nine out of the last twelve years, varied widely since all students, herself included, were required to put in turns in the kitchens. Still, the rancid broth, along with the general air of moldering decay in this place, curdled her already unsteady stomach. She pressed her lips together, then shook her head. "No, thank you."

" 'Thank you,' is it?" The sharp-faced woman set the bowl back on the cracked lacquer tray. "That's rich—'Thank you!' Wait until Diren hears that."

"Hears what?" Diren Chee strode into the ill-lit room, his fair hair neatly combed and swept back from the harsh planes of his face.

Haemas looked up at the sound of his voice, still unable to believe he was the same man she had seen in Council year after year, never suspecting what lay behind those dark-flecked eyes. She should have paid more attention to the gossip that always seemed to be circulating about the infamous House of Chee. She straightened her shoulders.

Looping his thumbs through his wide black leather belt,

Chee scrutinized her with an assured calmness that spoke of power more eloquently than words. He cocked his head to one side, reminding her of one of her silshas stalking a rock barret. "Let's get down to business, shall we? I want the timeways."

Without answering, she tried to probe his mental shields, but her mind still felt muffled and dull. The latteh, whatever it really was, had drained her. With a shock, she realized she could not even have read someone standing across the room at that moment.

"That's not possible." She looked away. "Even among the ilseri, males can't align with the timelines. You know I can't take you, or any other man there."

"I only know you *won't*." Chee seized her upper arm and dug his fingers into her flesh until she met his eyes again. "And that's not the same thing at all, is it?" A bitter smile flitted across his face. "Besides, Jarid Ketral entered the timeways."

She jerked her arm from his grasp. "And paid for it ultimately with his life, while nearly destroying the rest of us at the same time!"

"That was his mistake." He tapped his chin with a forefinger. "I have no intention of repeating it."

Suddenly she threw open her mind and reached desperately for the ilsera crystals set into the Chee'ayn portal. Perhaps she could access the temporal nexus and leave this terrible place.

Try all you like, Lady. Chee slid into her weakened mind with a practiced oiliness. *You don't really think I'm fool enough to leave the crystals in place, do you?* His mirth was like a drenching of ice-cold water.

With an effort, she raised her shields again and shut him out of her mind, but the back of her throat tasted of burned iron and the ache in her head strengthened.

"Of course, no one understands exactly how you do it," Chee continued, "but I do know from the official notes of the last Conclave on Temporal Transference that you need a set of attuned crystals. I've separated the Chee'ayn crystals and they won't be back in place until I'm ready."

"It's pointless!" Haemas stared angrily at his triumphant

face. "You can't change anything by going back. Nothing in the past can be altered."

"Ah, Lady, you mistake me." Chee reached out one finger and tucked a lock of pale-gold hair behind her ear. "I need to learn more about how to use the latteh crystal. Although it's been forbidden for over twenty generations, I've managed to puzzle out a little of the craft. But if you give any credence to the old legends and tales, there was much, much more." Gripping his hands behind his back, he strolled over to stand before the hearth, his eyes on the meager flames. "All the old manuscripts talk of the unparalleled power wielded by the latteh in the hands of the 'true adept'—power to kill, power to heal, power to build."

Slipping one hand into his pocket, he drew the oddly cut crystal out and held it up in the palm of his hand. "But that knowledge was literally thrown away by rattle-headed thinkers who thought they could decide what was best for everyone." His fingers caressed the dull-green facets. "It would take more than a lifetime to rediscover all that by trial and error. But there is another way; you can go back and find it for me."

Her heart settled into a steadier rhythm. Although he didn't know it, he was giving her a way out; once she had entered the timelines, he couldn't follow her. No male could enter the timelines without an enormous boost of outside power, and even then it endangered the fabric of reality. She would pretend to agree, then escape him in the temporal pathways, exiting somewhere else, or even some-when else, and he would be able to do nothing to prevent it.

"Where—where do you want me to go?" she asked, concentrating fiercely on her shields.

"Not where so much as *when*." He gripped the latteh tightly in his fist. "You will have to go back into the time of the Ivram Despots or even earlier. I don't care as long as I get what I need. And if it's true I can't go with you myself—" A grim half smile twisted his mouth. "I'll send Axia in my place."

Haemas leaned her head back against the wall. "But she's not trained."

"That's your problem, isn't it?" Chee looked down and smoothed the black fabric of his long loosely fitted pants.

Again Haemas tried to think, hoping her strained shields could keep him out of her mind. How Talented could Axia be, anyway? Perhaps she could just leave her behind, too, as soon as Chee gave her access to the ilsera crystals.

He crossed his arms. "I wouldn't be so sure of that."

A sliver of ice formed between her lungs and her heart. "I have friends who will look for me." She closed her eyes. "You won't get away with this."

He laughed a brittle, hard-edged laugh. "But, Lady, I have already gotten away with it." Placing a hand on either side of her, he leaned over the cot and stared into her eyes. "And if any of these so-called friends of yours should happen to get the least bit close to the truth, or if you refuse me the timeways, I will kill every one of them, starting with the fat old meddler, Enissa Saxbury, and that tiresome dreamer, Kevisson Monmart."

The gathering ilseri clustered around the violated pool, their anguish so palpable it was as if another, darker sister had joined them to mourn. Starlight winked down through the leafless trees as Summerstone hovered above the grove, counting the new arrivals. She was more worried than she wanted the rest to know. So few had come back from the southern seas, and this was so very important! Did they not understand? What the ilseri decided now could alter the future in unforeseen ways. Every full-grown sister was needed to examine the nexus for possible courses of action before they decided which course to take.

Windsign drifted into the grouping, and Summerstone reached for her mindpresence with a profound sense of relief. They had known each other for so long that she trusted this sister's judgment more than any other ilseri of similar experience.

Windsign responded with a mental caress, then increased her density and let gravity tug her down to the forest floor as she gazed into the pool. *I thought they had forgotten.*

Summerstone joined her. *We must call Moonspeaker and learn what she knows of this matter. Perhaps she can—*

No! A young, clear mindvoice rang through their midst. *She is one of them!* The speaker coalesced into a tall, broad-shouldered sister, well grown and strong.

Seashine, we welcome your strength and vision. Summerstone regarded her gravely, remembering that this sister had not yet borne her first son. She was barely out of the trees, quite young compared to the rest of the gathering, and her judgment was still clouded occasionally with ilserin excesses.

Summerstone projected an image of the young human whom she and Windsign had once called to them, then trained in the ways of the nexus: a slender female with golden hair as pale as moonlight and eyes of the same elusive shade. *She saved this world from temporal disruption when she was hardly more than a child.* She textured the image with Moonspeaker's fierce, uncomplaining strength and her former courage in the face of fear and pain. *She has spoken well for the ilseri to her kind.*

The short green tendrils that covered Seashine's head writhed with indignation and distrust. *She is still one of them, and if they have not forgotten after so long, they never will. In the fullness of time, they will always come back.*

Let us examine the nexus for possible Whens, Windsign interrupted. *Then we will consult our sister Moonspeaker and decide what must be done.*

Kevisson hunched his shoulders against a biting Highlands wind as he trudged back across the grounds to Shael'donn. His wet clothes clung like a clammy second skin and his feet were blocks of ice, but much worse was the coldness he felt within. Why in the name of all that was holy had he turned on Haemas in front of the Council and half the members of the Highest Houses as well? No wonder she had left without telling anyone. Reaching Shael'donn, he jerked the huge door open and passed the startled student on duty without a single word.

It was his damned pride; he knew that. Born of only a Lowlands House and with his dark coloring, he had always been oversensitive to the slightest insinuation that he was not as good as his fellow Andiine Masters.

But Haemas had never seemed to see anything but simple Kevisson Monmart when she turned those pale-gold eyes on him. The image of her introspective face rose up in his mind, and he thought back to twelve years earlier, when Lord Senn had sent to the Lord High Master of Shael'donn for the best Searcher available. Kevisson had answered that summons. The charge had been to find the daughter of a High House who had attacked her father, then run away to the Lowlands. Haemas Sennay Tal had been that girl, not quite sixteen at the time. He'd found her using the ancient mind-disciplines taught by the Andiines, and in one way or another, it seemed the link he had established with her then had never been broken. He sighed. They had both come so far since those days. She was light to his dark side, a river of quiet strength and perseverance. He couldn't imagine life without her.

He ran into several more students on the steps, including one from the Eighth Form whom he had been tutoring personally. Ignoring their greetings, he swept by and felt their bewildered thoughts follow him up to his small room in the West Wing.

Finally, closing the door behind him, he leaned against the varnished wood and gave into the ache; she had left without telling him, had gone away to only-the-Light-knew-where to nurse the pain he had caused. He stared around his sparely furnished room, then squared his shoulders. Myriel and Ellirt were beyond his help, but he could still do something about Haemas. Although she probably never wanted to see him again right now, it wasn't safe for her to go off alone. She never admitted it, but the House of Moons was a sore point with the more old-fashioned Houses, especially in the Highlands where the High Lords had little interest in seeing their wives and daughters and sisters better trained and more able to decide for themselves how to live their lives. She had enemies, not the least of whom were the Killians, since she had once refused to marry a son of that House. He had to find her and make sure she was safe.

He stripped off his sodden breeches and shirt and threw them in the corner, then pulled on a loose robe. Kneeling, he started a fire in the small hearth. Once it was properly kindled, he crossed to the narrow bed that had been his ever since he had first come to Shael'donn, a frightened Lowlands boy of seven. Although he'd rated more luxurious quarters as he'd moved up through the ranks, he'd retained this room, preferring its familiarity.

He pulled a fine-linked chain over his head and fingered the gold ring threaded upon it, an ancient signet of the House of Tal: oak leaves of solid silver, chased with gold and studded with tiny green koral stones. His face warmed as he remembered the touch of her fingers as she had folded his palm around it in return for his gift—the Monmart emblem of flying caestrals, though his had not been half so fine. Try as he might to feel differently, it still rankled him that Tal'ayn was one of the Highest Houses while Monmart'ayn was little more than a Lowlands farm. Despite the fact that Haemas never seemed to care, he had always felt the distinction standing between them.

Stretching out on his back on the bed, he closed the ring into his fist for a focus and shut his eyes. Letting the sensations of his body fade from his awareness, he began to count each breath, setting his mind adrift. With each breath, he let more tension drain from his body, soaking up the faint emanations of her that still permeated the ring: her strength, her determination and stubbornness, and still, even after all this time, her sorrow. He pictured her somber expression . . . the sense of duty that ruled her even when he would have had it otherwise . . . the steady regard for him that he had come to count upon.

Finally he loosed his mind into the gray betweenness, seeking the bit of brightness that would signal his quarry. Time passed unnoticed as he spread himself over the Highlands like a sheet of water, growing thinner and thinner until his energy reserves began to fail and he knew he would have to either give up or face the consequences of overextending himself.

He wondered if she had gone to the Lowlands, perhaps to

visit the ilseri, in which case he would have to follow her over
the mountains in order to find her. Then he caught something,
the barest whisper against his mind, a faint glimmer of her familiar silvery presence, but muted or altered in some way.
Something was wrong. He concentrated on following that
slight contact through the grayness, holding on as if it were his
own life-force.

She *was* there, still in the Highlands, but off in a remote
corner, far away from the House of Moons and Shael'donn.
Holding on to the tenuous line, he gathered the shreds of his
remaining energy and emerged from the nebulousness of
Search. For a split second, he had the impression of a tall
house, crumbling gray stone, and fear mingled with mocking
laughter; then a bolt of lightning flashed, shearing the precarious link. Suddenly adrift, he cried out, then spun off helplessly into blackness.

"I won't go!" Axia rubbed her arms, then knelt to shove
another log onto the guttering fire. "If you want this information so damn badly, go yourself!"

Diren tipped the heavy mug up and drained the last of the
mead, then held the pewter up in the firelight to examine it
more closely. "Such fine work," he murmured. "What do you
suppose it cost?"

"More than we'll ever have!" Axia grimaced at her younger
brother's strange expression, remembering another golden-
haired man who had sat in that same seat and stared off in
much the same bewildering manner; sometimes Diren reminded her too much of their late father for comfort.

"Not after tomorrow." Diren nodded at the flames dancing
over the logs. The light played on his fair hair. "Not after you
go back and learn more about the latteh." His eyes left the fire
and glanced up at her. "When I have power like that, we'll
have everything we ever wanted—gold, servants, respect.
Chee'ayn will be rich again and every eligible male in the
Highlands will be clamoring for your hand. You'll have your
pick of Houses."

"Don't be stupid!" Knotting her fingers, Axia pulled up a

chair and sat down beside him, trying to make him look at her. "It didn't work on Haemas Tal. You almost killed her with it, but you never really controlled her mind." She put a tentative hand on his shoulder. "The first time you trot that little trinket out and try it on a Council member, you'll get caught and that will be the end of this House."

"Shut up!" Jerking to his feet, he dashed the pewter mug to the floor. It clattered into the wall, then spun back against her foot. "I just don't know enough about it yet to make it work right on the Tal woman. I have to learn more, and that's where you come in." His eyes burned down at her. "You'll do as you're damn well told tomorrow, or I'll use it on *you!*"

He swept up the mug, then ran his fingers over the embossed Chee crest. "Anyway, I've already tried it—on Himret Rald himself, practically in front of the entire Council." Setting the mug on the mantel over the hearth, he stepped back, then centered it. "Worked far better than prayer, I must say."

That nasty, snide edge in his voice was the same one Axia had often heard from their father, usually just before he succumbed to another violent mood swing. Although she had thought her life hardly worth living already, hearing her younger brother speak in those manic tones stole what little comfort remained.

She stared down at her folded hands, seeing how the blue veins showed through the skin. She was almost forty; no one was going to contract for her now, wealthy or not, but Diren didn't seem to understand that.

"After you come back, we'll make another trip down to Lenhe'ayn." Diren settled back into the worn chair and propped his boots up on the hearth. "There should be more crystals where we found the first one."

"What do you need more for?" She blinked in surprise. "Besides, that Lenhe woman was suspicious enough when she saw us heading for the woods last time. What if we run into her again?"

"Don't worry about her." Folding his arms behind his head, he leaned back and stretched until his bones popped. "Both she and that brat of hers are dead. One of those doddering

Rald cousins has moved in until final disposition of the property is made, but he doesn't worry me. Even the old Lord himself couldn't withstand my little toy."

The top log shifted, showering red sparks up the chimney. Axia watched them swirl into the darkness, thinking they were just like dreams she used to have. When she and Diren had been younger, it had seemed as if anything was possible. Now they were down to depending on this crystal to make their dreams come true—a thing so forbidden that death was the sole penalty for using one.

"What about the Tal woman?" she asked finally. "Since the latteh doesn't really work on her, how long do you think you can keep this up? She's supposed to be a Plus-Eleven."

"You don't believe that nonsense, do you?" A sneer twisted Diren's lips. "And it wouldn't make any difference if she were. You saw what happened when she fought the latteh. It turns your own strength back against you. The damn thing nearly killed her."

Axia went cold again, remembering the paleness of the woman's face when Diren had emerged from the Chee'ayn portal the night before. For a moment, she had thought Haemas Tal was dead. She ran her tongue over her dry lips. "What's to keep her from leaving me in the past once we're away from the latteh?"

"That's the easiest part of all." He reached into his tunic and drew out the dull-green crystal. "You just take it with you."

With a feeling of panic, Haemas saw the seneschal, Pascar, waiting for her before the dining room. He glanced pointedly at the door, his old chierra face disapproving. Late again, she thought, and then knew with an icy certainty when and where she was.

Somewhere in the back of her mind, she knew she didn't have to do this anymore, didn't have to repeat this endless pattern of guilt and shame. She started to turn away, but Pascar opened the doors for her, revealing the long table set only for four. Her stepmother, Alyssa Alimn Senn, and her cousin, Jarid Tal Ketral, looked up from their plates with amused eyes.

But Jarid was dead. He had died at Haemas's feet after trying one last time to kill her over twelve years ago.

Seeming to hear her thoughts, he ran a careless hand back over the bright-gold of his hair and laughed. "Once a skivit, always a skivit, isn't that right, Cousin?"

She flinched at the hated nickname. She didn't deserve that anymore; she was no longer the same timid, frightened girl. She watched as he poured dark-red tchallit wine into green crystal goblets. Her hand reached for the goblet even as she remembered how Jarid had drugged it on that long-ago night.

She looked up at the self-satisfied smirk on Jarid's suddenly indistinct face, blinked, and then, like wind-blown sand, his features shifted. It wasn't Jarid at all—it was Diren Chee. Her hand jerked away from the goblet as if it had burned her.

"You never learn, do you?" Chee smiled at her with predatory sharp white teeth. "I find it quite disappointing that after all this time you're still so stupid."

Laughter began then, manic laughter echoing off the walls until it deafened her. The woman sitting beside Diren Chee took her hand away from her mouth and revealed the thin-featured face of Axia Chee. The Chee woman threw back her head and laughed louder and louder until Haemas thought she would scream.

"Go ahead." Diren Chee nodded at her. "No one will hear you, of course."

Haemas bolted up, feeling as if she were drowning in the shrieking, mirthless laughter, as if she would die if she didn't get away that very second—

"Die?" Diren Chee reached into his pocket. "I suppose we can arrange that." He held his open hand out. "If you insist." A glowing green crystal lay in his palm, buzzing with deadly energy.

She backed away, knocking over a chair. It clattered on the floor and blocked her way.

"If you insist." Chee leaned across the table. "If you—"

"No!" Haemas sat bolt upright on the narrow cot in the

Chee'ayn tower and threw off the worn blanket. Breath rasped in her chest as if she had run halfway across the windswept Highlands. She glanced around in a panic, but no one was there. The only door was closed and the sparse fire had burned down to sullen red-gray coals.

Jarid was dead; she knew that, yet somehow it seemed he was with her tonight in this terrible place, laughing as she tried not to lose everything she had struggled to build since his death. She had been his victim during the hard bitter years of her childhood, the object of his envy over her place as Heir to Tal'ayn, and the instrument of his revenge against her father. But no more!

She had cast all that away when she had finally broken the false memory Jarid had inflicted upon her. Then she had renounced her inheritance, seeking instead to found a Shael'donn for Kashi daughters where they could come and freely learn the mindarts and understand that they had choices in life that went beyond marriage and childbearing. She was not going to be anyone's victim again, not now or in the future.

There had to be a way out of this. Rising from the cot, she found a chipped basin in the far corner of the room and dashed tepid water over her hot face.

Diren Chee would not get away with this. No one was ever going to use her again.

Chapter Six

Diren gazed down from the third-floor windows at the pine grove and mused that, in this one particular place, Desalaya might have passed for Old Earth itself. The green sky was hazy this morning, and when he squinted, it looked almost blue. A sense of pride suffused him; Chee'ayn might be unkept and wind-worn, but it was still the only place in the Highlands where pine could be grown freely without having to mix in Old soil. At one point in time, the gardens had flowed out to the horizon, a panorama of flower beds and hedges and pools, spectacular even in a society of similarly vast estates.

His fingers caressed the cool oblong shape of the latteh in his pocket. Soon Kashi would flock here again to see Chee'ayn's restored beauty—and then remain to kneel at his feet.

He turned the crystal and watched the sun glint on its irregular facets. "I assume you've thought about what I asked."

"You *asked* for nothing." There was a new hint of fire in Haemas's voice that made him glance around in spite of himself. "You *demanded*." Her face was freshly washed; tendrils of damp hair curled around her ears. She was as pale as newfallen snow, but composed, and her white-gold eyes were impenetrable.

"Obviously you've recovered, if you can find the energy to quibble over a few unimportant words." He almost activated the crystal to subdue her, but then changed his mind and damped it completely. He needed her will intact, along with her judgment and skills. If he used the latteh to obtain full control, he would have to override those faculties in her, and he might never get what he wanted most: her timeways craft.

Pocketing the crystal, he turned to face her. She met him with a lift of her chin.

Taken aback by the determination in her face, he sent a tendril of thought to probe at the shields enclosing her mind and was rebuffed by a distressingly solid, resistant surface. "I've been studying the notes of the last Temporal Conclave." He pulled out a rickety chair and motioned for her to sit down. "They're quite interesting."

Folding her long-fingered hands, she ignored him and walked instead to the window, putting the huge desk between them. "One-fourth of the men who attempted to broach the timeways that day died, and half of those who survived were permanently mindburned." The early sunlight fired the single plait of her hair into spun white-gold as she turned her back on him and gazed down onto the snow-dusted Chee'ayn grounds.

Noticing suddenly that Axia had dressed her in a castoff gown that barely came to her ankles, he frowned. It was typical of his older sister's sharp-edged personality to be so mean-minded. No wonder he had been unable to secure a Highlands match for her worthy of her status as a daughter of the House of Chee.

Still, the light-blue velvet flattered Haemas Tal's fair coloring in a way that the gray uniforms habitually worn at the House of Moons never had. His fingers burned suddenly to stroke the ivory curve of her cheek—and he wondered at himself. Over the years, the parade of second-rate tutors his father had provided had always blathered on at him about "having not being so satisfying a thing as wanting." In this moment, he knew finally that wasn't true. Undisputably, he had her at last, and yet he ached for her more fiercely now than at any other time since he had first seen her appear before the Council of Twelve.

On that day she had worn gray, yet she outshone every woman present, her slender figure standing straight and tall as she met the eyes of all those disapproving, stiff-necked old Lords, giving them back measure for measure what they gave her. He'd wanted her then, without even knowing who or what she was.

But then someone had explained to him that she was the old Tal's daughter, the one who had run away to the Lowlands and mysteriously reappeared, versed in the timeways craft of the almost mythical ilseri.

And it was then, after he understood the opportunity that she represented, that he had finally known how to shape his ambition: Using the latteh crystal, he would bend this woman to his will as one bent a young tree. And then, when he had the strength of her knowledge and Talent behind him, along with the very power of Time itself, they would all bow down before him—every High House and miserable Lowlands farm, and the rest of Desalaya, as well. Kashi and chierra alike, they would push their faces into the dirt and pay Chee'ayn the homage it had always deserved.

He forced a deep steadying breath into his lungs, clenching his hands into fists with the effort of not touching her. *That* would come later, once she had given him the edge he required. "Someone was Searching for you last night." He held his voice to casualness. "Did you feel it?"

Her eyes flicked toward him, then returned to the frosty view outside.

So she had. He moved close enough to gaze over her shoulder and breathe warmly on the nape of her neck. "I think I was able to break the link without killing him, but whoever it was may not be so lucky next time."

Gliding away, she pulled the single braid of hair over her shoulder, automatically smoothing the stray wisps. "Perhaps *he* will kill you instead."

Diren jogged the latteh into activity and her fingers jumped as if she'd been stung. "I doubt that very much, *Lady*." He threaded a deadly softness through his voice, then seized her arm. She flinched at his touch; her skin was covered in chill-bumps, as cold beneath his fingers as the glass in the window. "Make up your mind to it," he said. "Shortly we will meet my sister down at the courtyard portal, which you will use to take her back with you to a time when the latteh was common. I want to know everything about how they were used and what they can do."

She jerked at her arm. "And if I don't?"

"Then we will proceed with our matrimonial." He pulled her hard against his chest and pinned her arms. His breathing deepened as she struggled to free herself and the sensuous pressure of her body against his made itself known. Her cool skin burned like fire beneath his fingers. He soaked in the feel of her, the subtle fragrance of her hair and skin, his at last to do with as he pleased. Now and forever. Freeing one hand, he caressed the silken white-gold hair that hung, even braided, to her waist.

She shuddered, then her jaw stiffened and she looked away. "I have never been very far back into the past." Red circles danced in her cheeks. "I don't know if it's even possible to go that far."

Releasing her, he reached for the heavy, leather-bound book lying open on his desk. He thumbed through the fragile pages until he found what he wanted, then thrust the volume at her. "I want you to go back into the period known as the Ivram Despots, although I doubt they thought of themselves in that way."

"I don't know anything about that time." Laying the dusty volume back on the desk, she traced a finger down the page, a furrow appearing between her brows. "How could I possibly recognize that period even if I found it?"

"You had best study this book and pray that you find what I'm after, because if you cannot, I will have some use out of you, one way or another." He bent his head and nuzzled the soft hollow of her neck.

Then she did sink onto the chair that he pulled out for her, and he was pleased to see her long fingers tremble when she turned the page.

The chierra cook set the steaming bowl in front of Enissa, then returned to mixing pie dough on the pastry block at the far corner of the kitchen. The air was filled with the aroma of baking cinnamon tarts. Enissa took a bite of the zeli porridge. It slid down her throat in a warm but thoroughly unappetizing lump. She kneaded her forehead and told herself to be practical. Even if she was too worried about Haemas to have any appetite, she had to eat. She couldn't afford to behave like some high-strung, overbred Lady who got the vapors every time the cook burned the roast. With Haemas missing, a million things needed looking after here at the House of Moons, not to mention the coming wrangle with the Council over the disposition of the Lenhe children.

Since they had no close family left, she wished the girls could remain here to be trained in the mindarts, but some House, most likely Castillan'ayn, as they were Castillan grandchildren, would see their potential marriageability and demand their custody.

She spooned up another bite of porridge, then changed her mind and shoved the bowl across the scrubbed kitchen worktable. No matter that her head was telling her to be sensible, her stomach just couldn't manage. Perhaps later, if Kevisson had good news from his Search, she would be able to force something down.

"Lady Enissa?"

She jumped as a hand touched her shoulder. She twisted around to see one of the gray-uniformed older students. "Yes, what is it, Saatha?"

The short, wistful-looking girl curtseyed. "Healer Nevarr is waiting in the front room to see you about something urgent—he wouldn't say what—and Father Orcado came in just behind him."

An odd pairing, Enissa told herself as she rose from her stool. "Tell them I'll be along directly," she said, then patted her hastily pinned up hair, trying to remember if she'd worn this tunic yesterday or not.

The girl turned to go, then hesitated, indecision spilling through her half-trained shields in waves.

Enissa glanced up. "Was there something else?"

"It's—it's just that everyone's been wondering." Saatha hesitated. "About Lady Haemas—has there been any word?"

"No, Saatha. Now run along."

Clad in the long, full skirts that many of the girls preferred to tunics and pants these days, Saatha took up a double handful of material, then dashed out the door, her slippers echoing down the long hall. Enissa sighed and checked her gray tunic for stains. It never failed—every time she ran into another healer, she looked like something one of the silshas had killed and dragged through the mud. The male clique that comprised the Highlands healers had little enough regard for her without adding fuel to that particular fire.

After another moment, satisfied that she was at least presentable, she followed Saatha to the communal room often used at night for gatherings. She could feel the dark weight of disapproving impatience long before she actually laid eyes on the visitors.

Stopping in the doorway, she appraised the two men, each trouble in his own particular way. "Father Orcado." She nodded stiffly at the priest of the Light. He was a barrel-chested man in his forties, clad in traditional yellow-and-gold brocades. Clearly this was to be a formal visit. Enissa sighed inwardly and stood a little taller.

"And Healer Nevarr." She managed another nod, even more curt, at the sandy-haired Shael'donn healer. He was from a distant Lowlands House unfamiliar to her, and rather young for a full-fledged healer. She knew Master Ellirt had taken him on at Shael'donn, hoping experience might eventually season the youngster's arrogant confidence, but for now, Nevarr opposed her practice as a healer at every opportunity. She studied him. "How can I be of service?"

"I haven't got time for pleasantries, Saxbury." The healer tossed aside the leather-bound text he had been leafing through. Tension was written in the lines of his jaw and shoulders.

"Well, then, tell me what you do have time for, Nevarr." She smiled faintly as he flushed over her own pointed omission of his title.

"Master Monmart has been—injured somehow. I don't even know how it happened, but both of the other Healing Masters, Feraa and Lising, have been called out to the other side of the Highlands, and I have been able to do nothing for him." He stared at her hotly, as if it were somehow her fault. "It's—beyond my training."

Enissa felt a prickle of dread. She had never known this brash young man to admit such a thing before, no matter what the circumstances. Then she turned to the priest. "And you, Father Orcado? Is your business equally pressing?"

The priest studied her with indifferent eyes. "A request has come up before the Council concerning the Lenhe children. I am to take them before this afternoon's session."

Enissa thought of Kisa and Adrina as she had left them upstairs, listless and pale, only going through the motions of taking class with the younger students. "By the Blessed Light itself, Orcado, they're still in mourning! Surely Castillan'ayn can spare them a few more days."

"I think not." He smiled thinly as if privy to secrets at which she could only guess. "As you might imagine, Sillner Castillan is unused to waiting." He adjusted his gold-embroidered overtunic.

Abruptly she made up her mind. "Well, they cannot come today." She picked up the book that Nevarr had cast aside and carefully replaced it on the shelf. "And I speak as the one in charge of their health. Check with me tomorrow—or even better, in a few days."

"The Council will not be pleased," Orcado said.

"The Council!" Enissa forced herself to draw a deep, even breath. "The Council can check with me again at their convenience. Good day, Father Orcado."

She felt his anger threatening to boil over, but he managed to contain it. "I will be back tomorrow." Without another look, he brushed past her elbow and left.

Nevarr stared after him. "Was that wise?"

"You weren't at the Lenhe funeral pyre yesterday. Kisa Lenhe has not had time to recover from what that unfeeling—" She passed a hand over her forehead. "What *he* put her through." Enissa paused as she sent a mental call to Meryet to bring her medical pouch downstairs. "Now, what about Kevisson? Has he been able to tell you anything?"

The guarded anger in Nevarr's face was overshadowed with worry. "He's—too deep. His breathing is off and I can't get any sort of response." He grimaced, turning away. "Dammit, I don't even know what he could have been up to last night."

"I do," Enissa said grimly. "He was Searching for Haemas."

"Haemas Tal?" A hint of confusion escaped Nevarr's shields.

"She's missing, or haven't you heard?"

"Missing?" His face paled until the faint dusting of freckles stood out. "You're sure she didn't just go off by herself? You know . . ." His voice trailed away lamely.

"She did it before?" Enissa finished for him sharply. "May I remind you that she was only fifteen at the time *and* under the burden of believing she had killed her father? Or has the Highlands really forgotten what Jarid Ketral did to her? I assure you that *she* never will."

Nevarr rubbed his bloodshot eyes. "Never mind that wretched business. Nobody cares about that anymore. Several students called me around the Ninth Hour last night when they found Monmart and I've been up with him ever since."

"Never mind." Enissa turned around as Meryet ran in with her pouch. "Thank you."

The girl dropped a quick curtsey. "Will there be anything else, Lady Enissa?"

"No, thank you, unless—" She turned back to the healer and caught a stunned look on his face. "Nevarr, what is it?"

"I left a student to keep watch on Monmart." The healer's eyes widened. "He says he's stopped breathing!"

"Lord of Light!" Enissa gestured at the double doors leading outside. "Go on ahead and I'll come after you as fast as I can."

But it was a five-minute run from there to Shael'donn. She could see in his stricken eyes the knowledge that he would be too late. "Go on!" she said. "I'll be right after you."

Nevarr nodded, then dashed out the door, his strong young legs pumping. Taking a firm grip on her medical pouch, she trotted after him as fast as she could, but she was already puffing by the time she reached the first bend in the path.

I'm too old for this, she told herself as the cold air rushed in and out of her straining lungs. She stopped to catch her breath and noticed the portal set halfway between the brown stone of Shael'donn and the gray House of Moons. She thought of the ilsera crystals waiting there, singing their silent song. Kevisson would be too far gone by the time Nevarr reached Shael'donn . . . but the ilseri weren't limited by time. Wasn't there a way to use the temporal pathways to reach him before it was too late?

The back of her mind prickled as she tried to remember

what Haemas had said about walking two lines in the same
When. She shook her head and angled toward the portal.
There was some difficulty about it, some complication, but she
did know Haemas had done it once. Surely, then, she could,
too. It was at least worth a try.

Reaching the simple spine-wood portal, she threw her mind
open to the crystals' vibrations as Haemas had painstakingly
taught her, and sifted through the myriad shimmering, shifting
blue lines of power that branched out from her feet in all directions, looking for one that would lead her to Kevisson's
bedside before it was too late.

The restless words on the page seemed to crawl together,
the letters combining, then breaking apart, stubbornly refusing
to make sense. Pressing her aching temples, Haemas squeezed
her eyes shut. She couldn't even think with the latteh so close
by, much less concentrate. The pulsing vibrations were keeping time with the dull pounding misery behind her eyes and
she was so infernally cold.

"Problems, Lady?"

Opening her eyes, she looked up into Chee's mocking face.
"If you want me to be able to work, then turn that bloody
thing off!"

Chee drew the green crystal from his pocket and held it out
to her so that the vibrations were even stronger, piercing her
skull. She flinched back and he smiled lazily, like a beast
about to tear into its prey.

Taking a deep breath, she tried to shield against it, but
shields were of no use. A cold sweat broke out on her forehead and the pain continued unabated while Chee circled her.

Then it abruptly stopped. "All right." He slipped the crystal
back inside his tunic. "But don't think you can try anything."
He draped his lean frame over a patched leather chair before the
ash-clogged fire and stared moodily into the guttering flames.

Chilled to the center of her heart, Haemas passed a trembling hand over her face and sat back. Try anything? Even if
she could get away from him, there would still be the latteh
crystal. And if she fought him until it cost her life, there were

others, like Enissa, who shared knowledge of the timeways, although they were not as skilled. He would no doubt go after one of them, perhaps even one of her students. And if she went before the Council and told them what she knew, they would just laugh. They were already inclined to disregard anything she had to say, and lattehs only existed in old myths, like giants and lasers; no one believed in them anymore.

Bending back over the ancient book, she pretended to absorb herself in the stiff, twiglike script again while her mind raced. Her best chance lay in agreeing to take this Chee woman into the timelines with her, then leaving her there and transferring back to the House of Moons. It made her ashamed to even think of doing such a thing to anyone, and yet what other choice remained? Diren Chee had never seen the timeways; he knew nothing of the infinite numbers of Otherwhens coexisting alongside the Truewhens.

Haemas had not been lying; Truewhen and Otherwhen were almost indistinguishable to her, as well as to the few other women she had been able to train so far at the House of Moons. Only the ilseri seemed to be capable of easily telling the difference. Chee's demands were impossible; even if she found the period he sought, it might be in an alternative timeline where the rules for using a latteh were not the same as they had been here.

"Aren't you finished yet?"

She took a deep breath and focused again on the musty yellowed page. "Nearly."

"I would like to get started sometime this century." He unfolded himself from the chair. "Let's go."

Turning the page, she ran her eyes down the descriptions of the Ivram Period hastily, blanching even as she read. Surely this couldn't be the time that he wanted—so violent and lawless, each House obliged to hold its territory against all others, employing the mind-disciplines to kill and maim.

Seizing her arm with fingers of steel, Chee jerked her out of the chair. "Stop stalling."

Numbly she tried to match his long strides as he pulled her through the echoing halls of Chee'ayn toward his portal and the ilsera crystals that would give her entry into the timelines.

Chapter Seven

Half blinded by the dazzling array of glimmering blue temporal lines, Enissa shielded her eyes with one hand. Again she struggled to remember what Haemas had said about walking two lines in the same When, but she could only recall that it was dangerous and somehow disorienting, and the longer one attempted to do it, the harder it was to break free. She decided to seek Kevisson as close to his collapse as possible, traveling back only a few minutes at the most to limit the amount of time she would overlap herself.

As she concentrated to focus the timeways on the proper moment and place, the scenes shifted crazily around her. She formed the proper picture in her mind—Kevisson as she must find him, lying unconscious in his bed on the brink of death.

The breath wheezed in her chest and her heart raced. The ghostly blue nexus possessed a terrible beauty, but she always found it frightening, worrying each time she entered that she would never find her way out again. She turned and saw a dozen Kevissons, then a hundred, a thousand splintered images of him, each differing in some slight degree. Her heart sank; the passage of time had no meaning here, but the awesome energies of this place strained the mind and nervous system. Enissa didn't have the strength to investigate a thousand possible Whens in order to find the right one. How could she find the Truewhen, the one line that would lead her to the moment that could save his life?

She sorted through the scenes, discarding every image that showed him healthy, sitting up in bed, or, as in one large section, already dead, laid out pale and bloodless under a silken shroud. Then she centered her attention on that part of the nexus where all the lines led to his bedside and a young boy seemed to be looking up in alarm. Three of the scenes had all the necessary details. Still, they must vary from each other in some vital way. How would she ever differentiate between them?

She made herself pick one by treading firmly on the fiery blue line that led to it. Raw power crackled up through her foot, hazing her mind and throwing her off-balance. Gritting her teeth, she tried to retain her focus, but unfortunately this had never been as easy for her as it was for Haemas. She managed a second step, though it was like wading through freezing fire, and then the third and final step.

The blueness faded, leaving her safe within the solid stone walls of Shael'donn. She gasped with relief and sagged against an elegant oak chest. A snub-nosed boy stared at her from Kevisson's bedside. "Bloody Darkness! Where did you come from?"

The room looked subtly wrong, filled with expensive clothes and furniture that she was sure Kevisson had never owned. She touched the youngster's tousled bright-gold head. "Do you know me?"

Within, his young mind was as cluttered as a boy's of his age ought to be. Images burst into her mind, some familiar like the Shael'donn orchard, others not, faces, names, places . . . she probed a little deeper, then sighed. This was not the When that she sought. Here, the House of Moons had never been built and this Kevisson lay ill with a fever.

Opening her mind again to the nexus, she fought her way back through the temporal energies into the scintillating blue. The scenes danced around her, shifting even as she tried to select another. Trembling, she chose anyway and set her feet to the line, fighting the disorientation as the energies surged through her body. With the third step, the nexus faded. She drew a deep, steadying breath and noticed that the boy bent over Kevisson's bed had a touch of red in his gold hair and seemed vaguely familiar. "How is he?" she asked.

"Goodness, Healer Saxbury!" A shy grin split the youngster's face, revealing a missing front tooth. "You gave me a start, coming in so quiet." He adjusted the quilt over the motionless figure on the bed. "Master Monmart is sleeping, but his breathing's a little rough."

This Kevisson was still breathing. Either he wasn't the one she sought, or she had arrived before the situation turned desperate. She stepped closer to the narrow bed. "What does Healer Nevarr say?"

"He's been called out." The boy stood up and offered her his chair. "Healer Lising has been attending him."

Wrong again! Enissa turned away, already reaching for the nexus with her mind, but the energy drain on her was telling. Her vision swam and it was difficult to catch the vibrations.

"Have you come to see after Master Monmart?" the student asked from behind her.

Harder! She must try harder! She clenched her hands and strained to hear the vibrational signature. She caught the edges of it, like a strange, faint music, and the shimmering blue line appeared at her feet. She stumbled back into the nexus, then scanned until she found the third possible scene. Her legs were shaking and weariness dragged at her as she fought to take the first step on the proper line, then the second.

The small room she was struggling to reach had a hard, bright quality, as if it were sealed behind stained glass. She felt as if she was just a whisper from Kevisson's side, and yet infinitely far. She started to take the final step, but as her foot came closer, the line whipped crazily back and forth. Concentrating, she managed to tread down just as it writhed across her path.

"My Lady!" The small boy jumped out of the wooden chair and stared at her, his eyes wide with surprise.

Ignoring him, she crossed to the bed and placed a monitoring hand on Kevisson's chest—it was not moving. Before she could act, she had a startling flash of herself standing both here, before Kevisson's bed, and *talking to Nevarr in the House of Moons' common room, hearing the irritating, officious tone of his voice, feeling her own answering surge of annoyance* . . .

She was in both places at the same time, her consciousness divided between two separate bodies, and she found herself unable to discriminate between one set of hands and the other. Summoning more of her waning energy reserves than she could afford at this point, she strained to shut the distracting second image out. A breath later, her vision cleared, leaving only Kevisson's room. She lay her trembling hand across his clammy forehead and threw open her shields, probing down through his unconscious mind and abandoning her body with a recklessness that surprised even herself. *Breathe!* she commanded him.

His mind was filled with troubling images. He seemed to be tumbling through blackness, falling forever. *You're not falling,* she told him. *You're here in your room, your very own bed. Breathe!*

Then the other scene surged back over her—*Nevarr's shocked face, her own heart racing with the fearful knowledge that Kevisson was dying, that they would be too late.* She froze, overwhelmed by conflicting sensory information, her attention perilously divided. Drawing still more energy, she pulled herself back into only this viewpoint, the Shael'donn room where Kevisson needed her so desperately.

The House of Moons and Nevarr faded from her awareness again, but as she resumed her probe, she sensed that Kevisson was dying, his thought-processes and memories becoming fuzzier, fainter. Careless of her own safety, she plunged deeper into his mind, looking for the cause. A dysfunction so sudden and severe was no accident or disease. Someone had done this deliberately, but how could she trace the damage in time to save his life?

Then she almost passed it: a place of overload in his brain where the energies of half-completed thoughts popped and fizzed like the embers of a dying fire. It was damage from a power surge of some sort, but far more extensive than any mindburn she had ever seen. It would have taken enormous strength to inflict such an injury.

Retreating, Enissa found his breathing centers and stimulated them, making his chest rise and fall to take in life-giving air. Then, little by little, she diverted her attention to the damage, sealing off the overloaded area and rerouting the grounded energies. When the worst had been circumvented, she gradually withdrew her control until he breathed on his own. Then she concentrated fully on repairing the injury—as much as such a blow might ever be repaired. Even as she worked, she worried about what the lasting effects would be on his abilities.

When she had done what she could, she let herself ascend slowly, level by level, journeying back to the body she had left behind at his bedside. Kevisson's mind seemed quieter now as she passed through, his mental rhythms more akin to natural sleep.

"*I left a student to keep watch on Monmart.*" Nevarr's eyes widened. "*He's stopped breathing!*"

Enissa paused, confused, seeing sandy-haired Nevarr standing before her even while she was aware of being submerged in Kevisson's mind. The doubleness was overwhelming; she was lost, drawn perilously thin between two conflicting realities, and she lacked the energy to shut out the scene with Nevarr a third time.

"*Lord of Light!*" She gestured at the double doors leading outside. "*Go on ahead and I'll come after you as fast as I can.*"

Black weariness dragged at her, and she realized that, in her haste, she had neglected to delegate a portion of her mind to oversee the basic functions of her body. She had to go back immediately before her heart quit beating, but the doubled imagery of two different realities was blurring her perceptions. She couldn't feel which of her two selves was the body at Kevisson's bedside now, couldn't distinguish which way to turn.

Bewildered, Enissa seemed to be standing on her own two feet in the front room in the House of Moons and yet tumbling through the images of Kevisson's sleep, both at the same time. Dreams bubbled up, confusing her ... Haemas Tal playing with a powerful black silsha on the front steps of the House of Moons, her light-gold hair flying, laughing, batting away the huge paw that could have broken her back with one swipe . . . the fields of Lenhe'ayn, smoldering and black, with acrid gray smoke curling up into the cloudless green sky . . . Myriel Lenhe, white and still under a silken shroud . . . her fault . . .

No! she told herself. Those were his memories, not hers. Blessed Light, which was the way back to her own body?

She could see in Nevarr's stricken eyes the knowledge that he would be too late.

She had already lived through this moment, but by going back through the timelines to save Kevisson, she had entered it again and now was experiencing this particular bit of time from two vantage points. *"Go on!" she heard herself say to Nevarr. "I'll be right after you."*

If she could just hold on long enough, she would catch up to the second that she had entered the timeways and this doubleness would pass, but she was so cold and tired. Searching for the Truewhen had drained her energy, and she couldn't find the way back to her body.

Nevarr nodded, then dashed out the door, his strong young legs pumping. Taking a firm grip on her medicinal pouch, Enissa followed him as fast as she could, but she was already puffing by the time she reached the first bend in the path.

Hungry black silshas with hot yellow eyes circled her, rumbling low in their savage throats . . . the edges of Kevisson's nightmare swirled over her, closing in, blurring the distinction between herself and him . . .

I'm too old for this, she told herself as the cold air rushed in and out of her struggling lungs.

People sneering at her, despising her for the brownness of her hair and eyes, speaking in loud whispers of Shael'donn's "pet chierra" behind her back.

The back of her mind prickled as she tried to remember what Haemas had said about walking two lines in the same When. She shook her head and angled toward the portal. There was some difficulty about that, some complication, but she did know that Haemas had done it once. Surely, then, she could, too.

Falling again . . . spinning through a knowing blackness that wanted to tear her heart out, she concentrated with all her might, trying to find ... what? She could not remember.

Reaching the simple spine-wood portal, she threw her mind open to the crystals' vibrations, just as Haemas Tal had painstakingly taught her, and began to sift through the myriad shimmering, shifting blue lines of power that branched out from her feet in all directions, looking for the single line that would lead her to Kevisson's bedside before it was too late.

The double image of herself faded and she perceived her body where it had fallen against the bed, head lolling, skin temperature and breathing rate dangerously low. Wearily she stretched toward it, skirting Kevisson's dreams now, stretching back toward herself with the last of her strength.

"Healer Saxbury!"

Enissa opened blurry eyes, straining to make out the face leaning over her. "Ne—varr?"

"How—?" His mouth snapped closed, then he slid an arm around her shoulders and braced her back in the bedside chair.

An aggravating grayness ate inward at the edges of Enissa's vision. Bowing her head, she rubbed her eyes. "It doesn't matter." Then she was even more annoyed to hear how thready her voice was. "Perhaps—the lad could bring me a bit of brandy."

Nevarr mopped his sweaty face with the back of his sleeve. "Emayle, bring up a bottle from the cellar—and two glasses."

"Yes, Master!" The youngster darted to the door and wrenched at the latch with both hands; then Enissa heard his feet pelting down the hall.

Nevarr pulled off his cloak and folded the warm wool around her shoulders as the shivers came hard enough to rattle her teeth. He bent over and laid his palm on Kevisson's moving chest and some of the tension eased from his face. "There was no way for you to get here ahead of me," he said, "unless—"

"Leave it alone, Nevarr." She locked her hands together to keep them from shaking. "It doesn't matter how."

He studied her, then pressed several fingers against her temple to monitor her condition.

"Stop that!" Before she realized what she was doing, Enissa pushed his hand away. "I mean—" She broke off, not sure exactly what she did mean.

Nevarr cocked his head, a grudging respect in his eyes. "Well, I guess you'll live." He threw another log on the fire, then crossed back to the bed to peer down at Kevisson's pallid face. He bracketed the unconscious man's head with both hands for a moment, then straightened. "He's sleeping normally now, but a few minutes ago, I was afraid I would only get here in time to lay him out under his shroud."

Enissa closed her eyes, seeing again the disrupted mental energies, the disturbing images of endless falling. "That's very nearly all you did get to do."

"You were in his mind." Nevarr stirred the fire with the poker, making the sparks fly. The room smelled pleasantly of burning wood. "What happened to him? Did he have a stroke or a blood clot?"

"No." Enissa held her hands out to the crackling yellow flames, sighing as a hint of warmth crept back into her fingers. "The question is not 'what happened to him?' but 'who?' " She rubbed her hands over her arms, still half frozen. "What happened to Kevisson last night was no accident. Someone tried to kill him."

The dining hall's long tables stretched before Riklin Senn in uneven rows. The air reeked of scorched vegetables and half-cooked chops. Watching moodily as the students bickered back and forth over the noon meal, his mind kept returning to that bizarre scene before the Council. What had prompted Chee to support him like that? He remembered their time together here at Shael'donn, and there certainly had never been anything like friendship between the two of them.

Riklin realized he wasn't Ellirt's equal when it came to training Talent, but he characterized himself as a good organizer and a careful thinker. Besides, the old man had had years to perfect his techniques. Riklin was just starting his tenure, and it would take a while to sort out his own style. For the moment, he really didn't need to take a personal hand with the instruction, just keep everything running along smoothly. He was aware that the post of Lord High Master had come to him as much through his uncle's influence as for any merit he himself possessed, but that was part of the game and he meant to prove the Council had made the right choice. Already most of the teaching Masters here at Shael'donn looked at him with more respect.

Most, but not Kevisson Monmart.

He jotted down another pair of names as an undertable kicking match between several adjacent boys bloomed into a full-blown brawl. The way Monmart had withdrawn his name and stomped out of the Council instead of staying to be soundly defeated as he deserved made it look as if Riklin couldn't have won otherwise.

Damn Kniel Ellirt anyway for designating Monmart as his successor. The crazy old man should have known the Council wasn't going to stand for another Lowlander holding this crucial position. The outrage that had erupted when the High Mastership had gone to Kniel Ellirt all those years ago had never quite died down. The students at Shael'donn represented the future of the Kashi people and were far too important to leave in the hands of *another* Lowlands House, even if one overlooked Monmart's distressingly chierralike appearance—and no one was likely to do that.

At any rate, everyone was nervous about that attack down at Lenhe'ayn, especially the unexplained death of the Lenhe woman. Still, he wondered if he could make something out of that. Monmart had been alone with her, then left her there to die. Riklin's eyes narrowed. Perhaps her death could be blamed on Monmart. He felt a faint, unaccustomed smile tugging at the corners of his lips. After all, what Lord would trust someone who had been so careless with the training of his sons in the delicate mindarts? One mistake could ruin a child's Talent for life.

Yes, he told himself, perhaps the implications of this Lenhe tragedy should be presented at the next session of the Council of Twelve. It was not possible to be too careful.

Scraping his chair back from the Masters' table, Riklin eyed

the blackened chop and overcooked whiteroot on his plate.
Since all the work at Shael'donn was carried out by the students, the cuisine was abominable. Although his uncle had
promised to send him an experienced chierra cook from
Senn'ayn, so far none had appeared. It was an old pattern in
his life for people to promise him things and then forget. One
day soon, though, he was going to ensure that no one ever forgot the name of Riklin Dynd Senn again.

Diren Chee snatched a threadbare cloak from a stand in the
front entrance hall and tossed it at Haemas, then pushed her
through the door. Broaching the chill air was like walking into
a wall of ice, and the ache behind her eyes resurged. A thin,
dry layer of snow had dusted the shaggy, winter-blasted lawns
and tangled bushes, and a cutting wind gusted up over the
cliffs, carrying the sweet, pungent scent of pine.

Chee made her walk before him along the overgrown path.
The bright Highlands sun winked down, giving off light without warmth in this chill setting—as lifeless, she thought, as desire would be without love. She huddled inside the borrowed
cloak, remembering Kevisson's touch last night, the faint whisper of his mind, gone too quickly for her to even try to answer
him.

Impulsively she opened her shields and reached out across
the Highlands, seeking Kevisson's familiar golden-brown presence. *Here!* she called to him. *I'm at Chee'ayn!*

"Forget him!" Chee's fingers clamped over her arm, making
her wince breathlessly. She felt the latteh he carried phase into
a higher level of activity, turning its annoying pin-prickle hum
into a shower of needles inside her head. Her temples throbbed
as he hustled her across the unkept grounds toward the
Chee'ayn portal.

"He's probably dead," Chee said. "And even if he's not,
he's nothing, just a boorish nobody who hasn't even had the
decency to marry you!"

"I have no intention of marrying anyone!" Haemas watched
her feet navigate the rough path.

"You'll do whatever I tell you," he said grimly, then towed

her around the trailing branches of a whip-willow into sight of a wind-blistered portal.

His sister leaned over the rail, shivering, her cheeks reddened by the wind. She pushed her furred hood back on her shoulders. "What took you so long?"

Chee released Haemas and passed the palm-size latteh crystal to Axia. "Here."

His sister's mouth tightened. "Why in Darkness don't you go yourself?"

"You've read the notes of the Temporal Transference Conclave." He frowned. "You know as well as I do that men simply cannot do this. Too many of them have already died trying, and I have no wish to join the list."

He reached for Haemas's arm, but she evaded his grasp, suddenly understanding what he must intend. "She can't bring that thing into the timeways!" The knee-high dead grass crunched beneath her feet as she backed away.

Chee's feral, dark-flecked eyes narrowed, then he met Axia's gaze. She nodded and the latteh climbed another level, vibrating at a frequency high enough to shred Haemas's mind. Blinded by the pain, she turned and ran, but Chee snagged her waist within two steps.

REALLY, LADY. His mindvoice thundered inside her head. *DO YOU EXPECT TO ESCAPE ME SO EASILY? WHY DO YOU THINK THE LATTEH HAS BEEN FORBIDDEN ON THE PAIN OF DEATH FOR SO MANY HUNDREDS OF YEARS?*

The stunning volume hit Haemas like a blow. She swayed in his grasp, unable to move or speak; then, just as suddenly, the latteh subsided.

"Now," he said in a strangely reasonable voice, "perhaps we finally understand each other. You can see that Axia handles the crystal almost as well as I do." He swung Haemas up into the portal like a sack of whiteroots. She sagged against the railing, her vision beginning to clear, and fought to control her ragged breathing. Master Ellirt would not have given up, she told herself. He would have kept his head and found a way out.

After taking a leather satchel from Axia, Chee pulled out a set of pale-blue ilsera crystals and began inserting them into their slots in the portal housing. His manner was almost cheerful. "The two of you will travel back into the days when the lattehs were harvested and put to very good use by the ruling Houses. And, put plainly, unless you take Axia to that time and nowhere else, she will use the latteh to make you wish you had."

Heart pounding, Haemas gripped the weathered portal housing. "Think, Chee. The latteh is very powerful and I have no idea what effect it will have if she activates it inside the nexus. We could both die."

Pain shot up her wrist as he levered her into the center of the portal beside his sister's shorter figure. "Then you had better make sure she doesn't have to activate it, hadn't you?"

Chapter
Eight

The icy Highlands wind wailed like a lost child through the stand of pines at the edge of the cliff. Dry-mouthed, Haemas turned from Diren Chee's unrelenting eyes to Axia. The woman's bitter, angular face stared defiantly back. Her lips were pinched with cold, her mouth outlined by deep grooves that told of a lifetime of barely repressed anger and doing without.

Haemas forced her clenched hands down to her sides, then tried to focus on the task at hand. "To enter the timeways, you can either lower your shields and allow me to take you—"

Axia threw back her head and laughed. The shrill sound rang out across the deserted grounds to be swallowed by the wind.

"—or you can monitor me and try to align yourself as I do," Haemas continued. Winter-bare bushes scraped across the outside of the wooden portal. "But it's difficult. Most of the girls who come to the House of Moons cannot learn more than the simplest part of it."

Axia's lip curled. "If *you* can do it, I certainly can, too." She raised her fist and let the dull-green crystal gleam through her fingers. "Quit making excuses and show me how."

Haemas listened beyond the anger in the woman's words. Axia was strung as tight as a bow. Her eyes were white-rimmed and she shifted from foot to foot as if she'd rather be anywhere else.

"You're right to be afraid," Haemas said quietly, and glanced up at the pale-blue crystals embedded in the portal housing, trying to summon the steadiness of nerve that she needed. How long had this particular set of crystals been used without being replaced? One century? Two? Three? Lowering her shields, she listened for the single frequency hidden among all the others the ilsera emitted, the one that would give her access to the temporal pathways—the same timeways, she thought with a pang, that she had sworn to defend.

The Chee'ayn crystals sounded old and dull, almost muffled, as if something stood between her and the nexus. Closing her eyes, Haemas concentrated, pouring all of her energy into trying, but finally, out of breath and sweating, she had to desist.

"I thought you were supposed to be so bloody good at this." Axia stepped toward her. "What are you trying to—"

As she approached, the heavy dull feeling increased, and Haemas realized the latteh crystal was still broadcasting on a level almost below conscious perception. "It's that—thing. I can't focus properly when it's activated."

Standing just outside the rickety portal, his face half obscured by a weathered pillar, Diren Chee crossed his arms. "Damp it," he said to his sister.

"But—"

"I said shut the damn thing down!" The dark-flecked eyes glittered. "You can flick it on again if she tries anything."

Axia stared at him, two vivid spots of scarlet blooming in her cheeks, and the latteh faded from Haemas's awareness, draining a tension of which she had not been fully aware. She took a deep breath of the bitingly cold air.

"Now get on with it!" Axia snapped, and fear leaked through her shields. A snowflake stung Haemas's cheek and melted as she let down her shields again, and this time, though still thready, the ilsera crystals' voice rang more clearly in her mind. Concentrating, she separated out the vibrational signature she wanted and laid her mind open to Axia.

Axia gasped as she glimpsed the shimmering blue nexus with its eerie, lightning-bright lines that radiated outward in every direction. "Lord of Light!"

You have to match this frequency, Haemas said into her mind as she held onto the critical tone.

She felt the other woman struggle. It was something like using the ilsera crystals to travel from place to place, as all Kashi were taught as young children, and yet much more complicated. Perhaps Axia would not be able to do it, Haemas thought, and then she could just walk off into another When and leave all this behind.

But if she did, what would become of the latteh? And what revenge would Diren Chee take on those back at Shael'donn and the House of Moons? She had to take Axia through the timelines long enough to get that crystal away from her. After that, she would consider what to do about Chee.

With a moan, Axia wrenched herself into the nexus. Her contorted face was beaded with sweat, although Haemas could not tell if it was from pain, fear, or both. Haemas gazed around at the coruscating motes of blueness, as awed by the wild beauty of this place as the first time she had entered.

Hurry up! Axia's fingernails dug into her arm. *I don't know how long I can stand this!*

The blue timelines radiated away into a thousand fractured scenes, bright-colored, shifting. Haemas bit her lip. No matter what Chee thought, the timeways did not have a geography like the Highlands that could be mapped and navigated. Every time she entered, they were different, presenting an infinite number of Whens based mainly on what she held in her mind at that moment.

She had to at least make a show of taking Axia to Ivram'ayn, the extinct House that had long ago ruled the Highlands above all other High Houses. She had read the description of that period in Chee's book, but there had been no illustrations, so there was no way for Axia to recognize it, either. They only had to exit somewhere safe. She rotated slowly, examining the lines.

Axia's fingernails convulsed through her skin. *Hurry up!* The sticky warmth of blood dripped down Haemas's arm.

Men—Haemas saw men everywhere she looked. Men in strange clothes . . . bearded, angry, bloodied, fighting, dismembered, dying, dead. Axia's thoughts must be focusing the timelines, too, interfering with Haemas's desire to find a safe haven.

Axia's nails ripped her arm again.

If we emerge in the middle of a battle, Haemas told her, *we will die just as surely as if we were killed in our own time.*

With her free hand, Axia shoved the cold facets of the latteh against Haemas's temple. *Do it now or I swear I'll turn your brain into jelly!*

Her heart thumping wildly, Haemas looked again, but nothing was familiar. Feeling Axia activate the latteh, she chose blindly, stepping off onto a line that led into a shadowed darkness where she could see the soft blue flicker of chispa-fire and no men at all. The line thrummed beneath her foot and she felt Axia stumble after her, still pressing the latteh against her head. Where in the name of Light were they going?

She took the second step, squinting into the unknown When ahead of them. At least it didn't seem to be a battlefield. Axia's nails punished her arm again, and she knew the Chee woman was at the end of her strength. For a second, Haemas let herself wonder what would happen if she just pushed her away and abandoned her in the nexus without knowledge of how to get out. Then she thought of the latteh, and the unknown effects that such a powerful crystal might have, and took the third and final step.

The blue shimmering faded, along with the singing voice of the ilsera crystals. Haemas stared at a cavernous room with a high, vaulted ceiling and strangely fluted urns of mind-conjured chispa-fire set at irregular intervals. The mood was calm and introspective, vaguely familiar. A hint of incense lingered and long benches were lined up facing one wall—a chapel of some sort?

Axia's voice broke the silence. "Where in the name of Darkness are we?"

"In the name of Darkness?" a deep, gravelly voice asked. "Interesting. Few people come here to invoke *that*."

A frozenness came over Haemas as she heard those words spoken in a cheerful, measured tone. It was the same voice she'd heard in her dreams many times in the past few days, but nowhere else—the one voice she'd longed to consult in the midst of all Kevisson's troubles with the Council, but all the same, one that had forever passed beyond her own timeline.

Locking her hands together, she turned and stared into a craggy face topped with a thinning layer of white hair.

"Master Ellirt," she said numbly.

With each examination of the nexus, Summerstone grew more dispirited. Each emerging sister told of a multitude of Futurewhens, but always the answer was essentially the same: The possibilities were endless, but all were terrifying.

Windsign had seen one startling timeline where the orange sun shone down on a green and blue planet devoid of any sentient lifeform at all. Seashine and a number of others reported snowy scenes of great destruction where slack-jawed, staring human corpses lay scattered like fallen leaves. Summerstone herself had seen a reality where the powerful golden-haired humans occupied every arable region while a multitude of dark-haired ones toiled ceaselessly in their fields and houses, and ilseri were so long forgotten that no one even recalled they had once existed.

And, worst of all, Windsign could find no branching moment, no choice sufficient to end this ancient problem. *We must call Moonspeaker,* she said finally to the assembled sisters, and even volatile young Seashine, humbled by the inevitable tragedies that lay ahead, did not protest.

Ilseri could not go to the high places, where Moonspeaker lived with her people. The lands were too cold, the atmosphere a bit too thin. Summerstone reached instead up into the mountains with her mind, pouring her strength into the seeking. She visualized the fragile small-sister, long-limbed, solemn, quiet, for all the paleness of her hair, eyes, and skin, graceful and lovely after the fashion of her kind—

But there was nothing, no sense of the one who had fought beyond her strength when the males of her kind had almost destroyed the fabric of time with their meddling. At length, Summerstone turned to Windsign. *She is gone—and yet, if she had died, we would have felt the wrenching of her passing.*

Perhaps she walks the nexus, as we do, Windsign soothed. *She senses the danger and is already seeking the solution.*

We cannot wait for her return. Summerstone solidified enough to stand on the forest floor. *We must set the shadowfoots to watch the pools, then seek out an Oldest.*

Even though his window was closed, Kevisson heard the silshas roaring as they grew ever more agitated. Lord of Light! His aching head shifted restlessly over the pillows. They had never ventured so near Shael'donn before. If Haemas did not return soon, they would have to be tracked down and killed before they hurt someone. He had never truly appreciated the hold she had over the huge black predators before. Their seeming docility had been due only to her presence, nothing more. They were still as wild and savage as the forest that had spawned them.

He turned his head as Enissa Saxbury opened his door. "Has she—?" he asked.

"There's no word." The healer discarded her cloak and medical pouch, then crossed the room and laid her warm hand over his forehead. The tingling energy of her touch spread through his body as she assessed his condition. He'd never liked being fussed over by healers, but her mind had a warm, faintly cinnamon glow that wrapped round his weariness and soothed away the aches.

"You're exhausted." She frowned down at him, then twitched at the quilt covering his bed. "You're no good like this to Haemas or anyone else. If you don't get some sleep, I swear I'll push you under myself!"

"I was asleep." Kevisson tossed restlessly on the narrow bed, remembering the strange feeling that had woken him. "But then I thought I heard Haemas calling me."

His door swung open, revealing the black-velvet–clad frame of Riklin Senn, flanked by several other men. "Are you well enough for visitors, Monmart?"

The healer turned, planting her short, plump body firmly between Senn and the bed. "He is *not*." Her tone was crisp.

Senn's steely eyes lighted on her face. "Why don't we let him answer that?"

"I'm—fine." Kevisson struggled to sit up, then blanched as the room swam around him in great sloping circles. He broke into a sweat, hot and cold at the same time, and his vision grayed at the edges.

"He is not fine!" Enissa's mouth tightened as she pressed him back against the mound of pillows.

Senn blinked at her, then motioned his grim-faced retinue into the small room. Kevisson recognized Niels Pallin and Keehan Weald, two of his Shael'donn contemporaries who had been his most relentless tormentors during his early days as a student. Their flawlessly golden eyes met his darker ones with no hint of compassion or warmth.

Senn gave Enissa a slight nod. "We appreciate your help, Healer Saxbury, but we won't detain you any longer. Please feel free to return to your duties at the House of Moons."

"Kevisson is my patient and—"

"As you know, Shael'donn is blessed with a number of excellent healers." Senn stepped aside as a spare-framed older man with thinning dark-gold hair entered the room. "Master Lising, here, for instance."

"It's all right, Enissa." Kevisson closed his eyes to make the room stand still. "I'll be fine." He wanted to tell her that it would do no good to make a scene, but his head ached too abominably to even try a shielded thought-whisper.

"Of course he will." Lising's fingers picked up his wrist and felt for his pulse. Kevisson winced at the cool, astringent indifference in the other's touch and jerked away. The healer's face tightened and he locked his hands behind his back. The room fairly crackled with suppressed energy. Kevisson glared at Senn, daring him to get on with it.

"Well . . ." Enissa reached for her pouch. "I suppose there are a few matters that could use my urgent attention, but I'll be back in an hour to check on him."

"No need for that." Senn opened the door for her. "Have a pleasant day." He waited until she was out of earshot, then spoke to someone just outside the door. "See that she doesn't get back into the building without an escort, and that's a direct order."

Kevisson's head seemed to weigh a million pounds; he sagged back onto the pillow. "Was that necessary, Senn?"

Senn turned his heavy-lidded golden eyes toward the chair at the bedside and Keehan Weald hastened to pull it out for him. The simple frame chair creaked as Senn settled his stocky frame. "I'm afraid you'll find you have much more pressing matters on your mind in the future than an old maid's bruised ego," he said sharply.

Kevisson pressed his hands over his aching eyes. "Actually, Enissa Revann Saxbury was Lady of one of the Highest Houses before she came to the House of Moons."

"All the more scandalous that she should turn her back on her position and responsibilities." Senn sniffed. "At any rate, there's to be an inquiry into the death of the Lenhe woman."

Kevisson stared up at Senn's implacable face. "Myriel Lenhe died in her sleep."

"Yes." Senn studied the nails of his right hand. The lamplight gleamed off his carefully combed golden hair. "A sleep that you forced upon her."

"She was hysterical." Kevisson tried to swallow, but his throat was as dry as sandpaper. "I was only easing her sorrow until a healer could come, nothing more. She needed rest."

"Not a 'rest' from which she would never wake." Senn stood up again, looming over the bed. "And there are curious reports from the servants that the two of you quarreled—something about a 'child'?"

"That was only her grief!" Chill sweat broke out on Kevisson's forehead as he hitched himself up on his elbows. "Nothing more! She was worried about losing Lenhe'ayn."

Senn's lips parted in a predatory smile. "And then there is the matter of those nasty scratches on your face. They look rather like fingernail tracks." He shook his head. "At any rate, the Council will meet tomorrow to go into this further." He motioned at the door and Weald threw it open. "Rest well."

"You really should get some sleep," Master Lising added. "You don't want to make yourself worse."

Black spots wavered behind Kevisson's eyes as the healer followed Senn and the others out the door. "Rest," he muttered to himself in the empty room. Only the fire crackled in answer as his fingers strayed over the angry welts across his face.

Haemas stretched out a trembling hand to the man's lined cheek, then drew back, her heart racing. She could not give into this. He was not *her* Ellirt.

"Do we know each other, my dear?" He radiated the familiar good-natured humor that had never failed to put her at ease.

"No." And *yes*, she thought behind her shields, but he would not understand. Her chest tightened and she had to turn her eyes away; she could not look into that beloved, lost face and breathe at the same time.

Axia jerked her aside with angry fingers. "You do know this old ummit, don't you? This isn't the right time!"

"No, I—" Haemas flinched as the Chee woman keyed the latteh's annoying buzz into tooth-rattling pain. "Don't do that! We won't be able to get back!"

Master Ellirt cocked his white-haired head and stepped toward them. "Get back to where?"

"Get out of the way, old man!" Axia released Haemas to shove him.

"Axia, no!" Haemas started toward Master Ellirt as he stumbled against a long knee-high bench, then fell heavily backward. "He's blind!"

The latteh phased up another painful level. Axia seized a handful of Haemas's hair and jerked her head back. The latteh pulsed at her exposed throat. "Get us out of here, Tal, or I'll kill you!"

"There will be no killing here." Ellirt's quiet voice came from the floor. "Not today or any other day." He reached an arm toward her.

Without another sound, Axia crumpled, white-faced, into a heap on the broad flagstones, the dull-green latteh still clasped in her outstretched hand. Haemas stared down at it as the pain thundered through her head, then realized that the latteh would go on broadcasting at this level until she either died or went mad. Her only chance was to get out of its range. Turning, she began to fumble through the shadowy room.

"What is it?" Ellirt heaved himself laboriously to his feet and limped after her.

Haemas stumbled over a bench and fell to her knees with bruising force. "I—I have to—get *away* from it!"

"Wait," he said, trailing her. "Tell me what's wrong and I'll help."

Shoving the bench out of her way, she struggled on, then, her eyes full of pain-tears, tripped over something unseen in the dark room and struck her cheek. At the back of the room, a door opened, allowing outside light to silhouette two dark figures.

"Master Ellirt?" one called.

Ellirt waved. "Alidale, over here!"

The darkened room seemed to be expanding and contracting as Haemas stumbled toward the door, her streaming eyes fixed on the pale rectangle of light. Pain roared over her in great waves, shutting out everything but the need for escape.

Suddenly strong hands trapped her wrists. For a second, she fought to free herself, confused, unable to see. Then another hand, warm and callused, touched her forehead.

What is it, child? Ellirt asked her. *How can we help?*

"The latteh!" She gasped. "It—you have to let me go!"

"A latteh?" He hesitated. "Alidale, see what you can find."

An immense black abyss was yawning beneath Haemas, drawing her down into oblivion. She felt that if she let it take her, she would never return, but she was almost beyond caring.

Footsteps hurried back across the floor. "Light above us!" the other voice said. "She has one in her hand, a big one!"

The darkness had a low growly voice, rumbling like thunder from the bowels of the earth. The pain sizzled along her nerves, leaving lifeless cinders in its wake. Dimly she heard voices, but no longer understood what they were saying. She felt separated from her body, just a tiny bit of awareness tossed on a vast river of agony. Nothing could be done; she would die here in this Otherwhen and no one she loved would ever know what had happened to her.

"Alidale, help me!" Ellirt's voice was suddenly clear. "I almost have it!"

The darkness was cold and smooth, beguiling, whispering to her of an end to suffering, of perfect surcease. Her thoughts froze into shards of ice that fell behind as she slid toward it.

It's all right, someone said into her mind. *We've shut it down.*

Her freezing hands were being chafed, and something heavy and warm was wrapped around her shoulders. She became aware of flagstones, cool and hard underneath her head.

"She's in shock," someone said. "We're losing her." A mind enfolded her, tasting of sunlight and lemons, illuminating the darkness that was carrying her away. *Hold onto me,* the same voice said.

For a moment, she resisted. The vast dark was a haven from the pain and the overwhelming responsibilities that hounded her every waking moment, a respite from the strain of loving a man who had kept his distance for years, too insecure to accept what she longed to give.

But Ellirt's calm, imperturbable strength surrounded her like a well of deep, clear water that never failed; he was her teacher and friend who had never forgotten her, even at the end when he lay dying. Of all the voices in the world, his was the one she could not refuse.

That's it. Now open your eyes. Let's have a good look at you.

A pale light flickered through her eyelids, then she blinked up into a seamed face backlit by an urn of pale blue chispafire.

"That's better," he said cheerily. "For a moment, I thought we were going to lose you."

She tried to speak, but no words came.

"There," he said, his voice kindly, "give it a minute. You've had quite a turn." His golden eyes stared down at her so steadily that she finally realized he really saw her. The Master Ellirt of this When was not blind like the one she had always known.

How strange, he said. *I see in your mind that you do know me, but I swear I've never met you. Where have you and this woman come from? And where did she come by a crystal of that size?*

"Here." One of the others cradled Haemas's shoulders and brought a pewter mug of brandy to her lips.

She let the fiery liquid roll down her aching throat, wondering what she should do. She owed these men her life, but most likely in this When they knew nothing of the timeways, and it would be much better if it stayed that way. Her fingers tightened on the pewter mug.

She was so tired of trying to decide what to do. She had been weary long before Diren Chee had showed up with the latteh to destroy her life. It was too much, this trying to make decisions for people who understood nothing of the way the universe worked. She wished she could forget the timeways and live a normal life. A warm tear trailed down her cheek.

"Never mind." Ellirt brushed the tear away with a gnarled forefinger. "I'm an impatient old man, but my questions will keep a bit longer."

Only an arm's length away from him, the two women winked out of existence. Diren shook his head, suddenly much colder than the bitter wind could account for. He had glimpsed a wild, unnerving realm of blue fire in Axia's mind before she disappeared. If it had been at all possible, he would have gone himself. His older sister was Talented, but she lacked the formal training of Shael'donn and tended to panic easily.

But from the beginning she had ached for the power and prestige the latteh represented, too. He remembered their first trip down to the Great Forest where it bordered the Lenhe'ayn fields. Indeed, a few of the black Lenhe horses had watched from the shade of the ancient trees as he and Axia had followed the old map he'd found in their father's things. It had led them to a still, leaf-filled pool formed out of white stone blocks, set deep into the ground. And down in the soft mud at the bottom had rested dozens of the dull-green crystals. He had selected one of the largest and taken it back to Chee'ayn

Grasping the peeling wood of the old portal, he swung himself up onto the platform, feeling the chill wind cut through him. He wondered how long he would have to wait for the women's return. As long as the ilsera crystals had to remain in the portal, he decided he might as well pay a visit to Shael'donn. Diren smiled to himself. Even if Monmart had survived the power surge that severed his Search link, he was sure to be weak, and there were a number of interesting tricks that could be played on a powerful mind that was momentarily defenseless.

Monmart might prove useful in new and interesting ways.

Chapter
Nine

The mind-conjured chispa-fire threw flickering shadows along the curved wall of the Council's meeting room at Tal'ayn. From the threshold, Kevisson gazed out over the restless crowd filling the tiered gallery. Many of Shael'donn's Masters were in attendance, including most of those who had never accepted him. Their faces were grimly anticipatory and he caught the spillover of a brittle excitement through their shields, mingled with the sharp taste of ambition.

His stomach rolled weakly, but he had nothing in it to lose. No doubt that was a mistake; he should have forced himself to eat, but he still felt disoriented and wobbly, and the little they had offered him had turned his stomach. What had happened to him on that ill-fated Search? He retained only the vaguest memory of having found ... *something*, then an explosion of red pain, severing his link and leaving him to fall endlessly through blackness.

"Kevisson Ekran Monmart." The old Tal himself rose from his seat, radiating a sense of raw power. His hardened face floated above his gold-encrusted ceremonial jacket. "You are called before the Council of Twelve." The old man's shoulders were bent with age, his hair sparse and white, but the eyes, Kevisson thought, those golden eyes were still as fierce as a caestral swooping out of the sky to attack.

Chilled to the tips of his fingers, he walked into the circular room, past the twelve High Lords occupying the same seats in which their fathers and their fathers' fathers had sat. The hereditary makeup of the Council had not changed in over two hundred years. His own father had never set foot in this room,

Monmart'ayn being only a Lowlands House, however profitable its vast fields of zeli had proved. If not for his Shael'donn education, Kevisson would never have come here, either. Few Kashi outside the Highest Houses ever did.

He stopped before Tal's seat, locked his hands behind his back, and squared his shoulders, trying not to notice as the curved walls of the room seemed to weave. A thin sheen of perspiration broke out on his forehead.

Tal resumed his seat, then shuffled through several parchment sheets. "Lord Monmart, three days ago you were commanded to Lenhe'ayn to investigate the damage done by chierra raiders."

"Yes, my Lord." Kevisson met the old man's volcanic gaze without flinching.

Tal leaned back in his chair. "And what did you find?"

The burned fields, the slaughtered stock, the pale youth lying on a bier in the darkened chapel, all the wrenching details leaped back into his mind. "If my Lords would care to examine my memories, it might save time."

Tal shot him a look of pure loathing that took him by surprise. Kevisson's jaw tightened. He sometimes forgot whose daughter Haemas Sennay Tal actually was. It was clear, however, that her father would never forget Kevisson's involvement when Haemas had abandoned Tal'ayn to study at Shael'donn.

"I think a brief summary will prove adequate, Master Monmart." Diren Chee, youngest of the Council of Twelve, spoke blandly from his seat near the end of the table's half circle.

Kevisson took a steadying breath. "The raiders killed the only son of the family and a number of the field hands, burned the fields that bordered the Great Forest, and slaughtered half the stock."

"Yes, but what of Lady Lenhe?" Petar Alimn, an old Lord with thick silver hair and a dour expression, tapped his forefinger on the table. "She survived the raid, did she not?"

Myriel's anguished face, white as sun-bleached bone, surfaced in Kevisson's mind. "Yes, but she was so distraught at losing her son that I feared she would hurt herself. I made her sleep, then sent for a healer from the House of Moons."

"A sleep from which she never woke!" A low murmur rippled through the room and all eyes turned to the doorway where Riklin Senn stood, resplendent in a tunic of green suede trimmed with green koral stones. He swirled off his cloak and passed it to a servant. "Do you deny the two of you argued that day?" Senn's voice, heavy with accusation, rang out over the crowded room. "Do you deny that those are her marks on your face? And why did you send for an inexperienced woman when you could have had any of the finest healers at Shael'donn?"

The other man's face seemed to undulate, as if Kevisson were seeing it underwater. "She was out of her head—possibly suicidal." He tried to swallow over his parched throat. "I wanted someone to comfort her, another woman who might understand what she was feeling."

Diren Chee looked faintly amused. "Someone from the House of Moons."

A white-hot wave of anger burned through Kevisson, even as he warned himself that this was probably just what they wanted. "Yes, and why not? Over and over again, I have seen Enissa Saxbury to be a gifted healer."

"And Master Lising is not?" Senn's lip curled. "What did Lady Myriel argue with you about?" His eyes narrowed. "I can, of course, have the Lenhe servants here in a flash, if you prove unwilling to enlighten us."

A distant roaring began in Kevisson's ears, as if a great river had sprung up just out of sight. "She—wanted a child from me. To replace her dead son, so she wouldn't lose Lenhe'ayn."

"A child?" The Council Head looked incredulous. An unshielded thought rang out from him, so clear that every Kashi in the room must have heard: *The Lenhe woman would have borne your mud-colored brat?*

The watching men and women in the gallery shifted uneasily. Kevisson stiffened. "She would have been glad of a child of mine," he said slowly, "had I ever consented to give it, but I would not, twelve years ago or three days ago."

Then Riklin Senn, Lord High Master of Shael'donn in Kevisson's place, glided into the center of the room, surprisingly light on his feet for so stocky a man. "Are you sure, Monmart, that's the way it was?" A feral gleam crept into his eyes. "Or did you approach her and she fought you off, scratching your face? Isn't that how it has always been, whenever you wanted a woman? Isn't that how it was with Haemas Sennay Tal?"

Kevisson stared dumbly at Riklin's heavy face, the golden eyes glittering like two burnished rocks beneath confident, bushy eyebrows.

"Do you deny that you asked the Tal woman for her hand and she refused?"

The roaring in his ears crested, almost drowning out Senn's snide tone. His chest tightened. He had ached for Haemas so long that he couldn't remember not wanting her, but she was above him—in rank, in Talent, in appearance, in every way he could name. His hands bunched into fists. "Yes, I deny that."

"Well, then, do we at least agree that you and Haemas Tal argued just before you left for Lenhe'ayn?"

"We had a—disagreement."

Senn turned a triumphant face to the Council, then strode importantly along the curve of the table. "Fresh from a disappointment, Monmart goes to Lenhe'ayn, and, seeing an attractive woman rather more on his level, argues with Myriel Lenhe. Does anyone here truly believe *she* approached *him*?"

A titter rattled through the room.

"Enough!" Tal smacked the flat of his hand upon the gleaming oak table and glared at the gallery. "We will have order."

"Perhaps they did more than argue," Senn continued smoothly. "Perhaps he took what he wanted and, once finished, did away with the evidence."

"That's a bloody lie!" The back of Kevisson's mind prickled, then a volcanic fury exploded through him, damping every control, every bit of logic and common sense. He found his hands crushing Senn's throat before he was even aware that he'd moved. How dare this arrogant bastard speak of Myriel that way! Her pale, grief-hollowed face hovered before him, obscuring everything else. He was dimly aware of others tearing at his hands, trying to pull him off, of voices calling his name.

A sudden jolt of raw mindpower staggered him to his knees. Two servants caught his arms, holding him upright when he would have slumped to the floor. His eyes rolled back in his head, but he fought to hold onto a thin thread of consciousness.

"My Lords!" Enissa's voice rang out over the muffled din, cool and authoritative. "Please stand back."

A white-hot mist still burning behind his eyes, Kevisson clenched his now-empty hands, breathing raggedly.

"Master Monmart has been quite ill." Cradling Kevisson's temples with her hands, the older woman stared deeply into his face. Her eyes were two golden suns, drawing him toward her, easing the shock. He felt his breathing even out, the wild racing of his heart slow.

She nodded as if satisfied, then turned back to the Council. "If I had been consulted, as I should have been, I would not have approved him appearing before you today. He should be in bed this very minute."

"He seems well enough to me," Riklin Senn rasped, leaning against the Council table, his face a mottled purple, one hand pressed to his bruised neck. "Or is it that if he were feeling better, he could have killed me?"

"You're lucky he didn't." Enissa's tone was blunt. "*I* would have."

"No." Kevisson lifted his throbbing head. The room swam and he swallowed hard. "It was a mistake, stupid—"

"Shut up," she said without looking at him. "You forget, my Lords, that I was also at Lenhe'ayn that night. I can swear that Myriel Lenhe did not die at Kevisson Monmart's hand, and if you doubt my word, then examine my memories."

"And mine!" Kevisson added.

"What good would that possibly do?" Senn rubbed the red marks encircling his neck. "With the level of training you both possess, it would be almost impossible to tell a constructed memory from the real thing."

"I'll give you control," Kevisson said, then wondered at himself—give control of his mind to a creature like Riklin Senn?

A faint smile tugged at Senn's lips. "Total control?"

Enissa glared at him. "With an impartial monitor."

"Name one."

Enissa was silent. Kevisson tried to think of someone acceptable, but his mind was hazy and uncooperative. "I—don't know. I'll have to think."

"Don't take too long." Tal rose from his seat. "The Council may make a decision without considering your evidence."

"He needs at least two weeks to recover from his present injury." Enissa braced her free hand on her broad hip. "An injury that, I might add, has been much aggravated by his appearance here today."

Dervlin Tal glanced at his fellow Council members, most of whom nodded. "A ten-day is granted, then." His fierce eyes narrowed. "But we will not tolerate a repetition of this kind of behavior."

Kevisson bowed his head, glimpsing Senn's smile out of the corner of his eye.

Haemas woke suddenly on a narrow, unfamiliar cot in a night-shadowed room. Her heart pounded until she vaguely remembered Master Ellirt settling her here between fresh sheets, then sitting at her side, a wall of strength, until she drifted off. Silvery moonlight streamed through a small barred window above the bed, revealing a warm, whispering night somewhere in the depths of summer, a night that should still be half a year away.

But, of course, this was an Otherwhen, where Kniel Ellirt lived on and the forbidden craft of using latteh crystals was evidently still known and employed. How many other things had diverged? She stirred restlessly and wondered if another Haemas Tal existed somewhere out there in that balmy summer night.

Fortunately she had found that the simultaneous existence of selves born of different Whens in the same timeline was somehow different from a single self attempting to walk two lines in the same When. The latter generated a frightening and potentially lethal disorientation that interfered with the timewalker's ability to return to her own When.

She had actually seen herself once as a small child in an Otherwhen without ill effects. That other Haemas had watched her from the sheltering arms of Anyah Killian Sennay, the mother who died giving her birth in her own timeline. Anyah had been willowy and tall, with same too-pale eyes and hair, and the depth of her love for her daughter had shone from her like a beacon. The memory of that other Haemas and Anyah now warmed a corner of Haemas's mind that had stood achingly empty before.

The door opened and Master Ellirt's craggy face peered in. "Feeling better, my dear?"

"Yes, thank you." Turning her head on the pillow, Haemas drank in his familiar features, overwhelmed at how good it felt to see him again, this endlessly patient man who had been like a father to her, and a far better one than Dervlin Tal had ever bothered to be.

"Perhaps you're up to some questions now." Treading softly, he set a small lamp made of pierced tin on a low table next to the bed. The lamp was a jolting reminder that he was not the Ellirt she remembered. *Her* Master Ellirt, blind from birth, had found his way through the world by use of his psisenses and had never needed anything so ordinary as a lamp.

The spartan wooden chair next to the bed creaked as he settled onto it. "I'm very curious to find out how you know me." His straggly white hair stood out in the half darkness. "Down through the years, I have guested in a great many Houses, both in the Lowlands and up here in the Highlands, but I can't recall ever meeting you, and my memory usually serves me better than that. Perhaps you were very young at the time?"

Haemas twisted the light ebari-wool blanket in her hands. "We—" she began, and then could not finish. Somewhere in the past few days, she had forgotten how to trust. "We've never—met." She started to sit up, then flinched as her head began to pound mercilessly.

You must lie still. His mind tried to flow soothingly over hers, but, afraid that he would glimpse her secrets, she held her shields tight and shut him out.

He took her hand between both of his and tried to let his goodwill reassure her. *Relax and let me dampen the pain.*

"No!" She lay back, holding her breath until the ache dulled. "Thank you."

Ellirt sat back in the chair. "The aftereffects of a latteh of that size can be rather severe, especially set at such a high level. It's wonder you didn't die." He stared over her head out the window. "That crystal was three times the size of any latteh I've ever seen. I've fought their misuse all my life, and yet I've never seen one bigger than my little finger. At least tell me what House is responsible for it, and who that woman is."

"Axia!" She had almost forgotten. "Is she . . .?"

"No, no." He reached across and drew the light blanket over her shoulders. "She's fine. Rather more than fine, I'm afraid. Kicking and screaming is a more accurate description."

Haemas sagged back into the pillow. "What has she told you?"

"Little, except that we are to return the latteh or we'll all regret it." He hesitated. "We could *take* the information from her, of course, but the very spirit of Shael'donn is absolutely opposed to such practices."

"Shael'donn?" she whispered. "This is Shael'donn?"

"Didn't you know?" He shifted his weight. "I thought that was why you came to us."

"I think I was drawn here because I once knew someone very like you, who helped me when no one else could." She stopped, feeling lost. While she tarried here in this Otherwhen, Diren Chee was still loose back in her own timeline, no doubt with more lattehs at his disposal. If she returned without Axia, there was nothing to keep him from coming after her again, or someone else, and he would be doubly furious at the loss of his sister. She didn't know what to do.

"I would be glad to help you, too, if you would tell me what you need," Ellirt said gently. "Shael'donn is a place of peace and refuge. We offer nothing but healing here."

Her throat dry and aching, Haemas nodded. "What I need most is to learn how to fight the latteh."

"Such knowledge is dangerous in the wrong hands, my dear." He gazed down at her, so like the Ellirt forever lost to her that tears welled in her eyes. "But perhaps, later, when we have built some trust between us, there may be much that we can teach one another." A faint smile crinkled his face. "Still, it is strange. I have glimpsed myself in your mind, and you do seem familiar." He cocked his head. "You have the Killian coloring."

Killians! Haemas closed her eyes. If the House of her maternal grandfather existed here in this Otherwhen, then perhaps Tal'ayn did, too. But the thought of her father's disapproving face only gave her headache renewed vigor. She felt the old man's worn palm touch her forehead. The bright circle of his mind hovered close.

Why don't you sleep? he murmured. Soothed by his familiar presence, this time she did not resist.

Enissa stood before the low stone wall at the edge of the withered kitchen garden and watched the dark, scudding clouds overhead. The bitterly cold air was dank with leaf mold and the musty smell of decaying vegetation. She couldn't think inside with the girls nattering on about the Dynd Naming and who would have the prettiest gown or who would actually dance with Arrich Dynd. The list of their preoccupations was endless—and hopelessly banal.

She huddled against the chill gray stone as the savage wind blasted at her. First had come the shock of Myriel Lenhe's death, then Haemas's baffling disappearance, and now Kevisson's bizarre, uncharacteristic attack on Riklin Senn; the world seemed determined to turn itself inside out.

Under normal circumstances, Kevisson would never have throttled Senn, no matter what the provocation, but no one knew better than she that he was still weak and disoriented.

Just two days ago, that disastrous Search had almost killed him.

Then she realized what must have happened. It was as plain as Riklin Senn's haughty face: Someone had been at Kevisson's mind while he was weak. They had sent her away from his bedside, then planted a trigger and deliberately set it off. They wanted Kevisson to look like an out-of-control man capable of murdering Myriel Lenhe in an argument. Then he would be convicted and Shael'donn would be rid of him permanently.

But how could Enissa prove it? She had wanted to transport Myriel's body back to the Highlands for examination at Shael'donn, since she had no idea of how the poor woman had actually died, but Father Orcado had insisted she be sent on to the Light with her son, saying it was important for the Lenhe girls not to drag the tragedy out any longer than absolutely necessary.

If she could go back in the timelines to see what had happened after Kevisson left Myriel alone, that might have helped, but her recent experience in walking two lines in the same When had convinced her that it wasn't possible for her. As bad as those few moments at Kevisson's side had been, she'd had only a short wait for the bewildering doubling to end. If she returned to the night of Myriel's death, she would have to live through three days to catch up to herself. Her mind would never be able to stand the strain, and she would be of no use to Kevisson if she came out of the experience a gibbering idiot.

The back door opened and the chierra cook emerged, bending her head into the fierce wind as she carried out a pail of meat scraps for the silshas. Enissa watched the chunky servant make her way to the stone trough out at the far edge of the trees.

Over on the other side of the grounds, Shael'donn had no servants. Its advanced training in the mindarts was so sought after that each boy who came to study was expected to take his turn at the chores necessary to run the school. The House of Moons, however, had been unable to implement a similar policy. Having no particular desire to educate their daughters, the great Kashi families refused to enroll them if they were required to do the work of menials. Haemas had been forced to acquire chierra servants, thereby increasing the school's financial burden and losing the opportunity to match the cheerful, self-sufficient atmosphere of Shael'donn.

A low snarl echoed through the trees and the servant glanced about fearfully as she dumped the meat scraps, then scurried back to the house. Servants, Enissa thought as something nagged at the back of her mind. Then, as the door banged shut behind the cook, she realized what it was.

She couldn't return to the moment of Myriel's death, but someone had been there, right outside the door: the elderly servant Kevisson had left to make sure Myriel stayed in her bedchamber. If she went back to Lenhe'ayn and questioned that woman, perhaps the answer to what had happened could be uncovered after all.

Chapter
Ten

Kisa Lenhe gathered the folds of the borrowed, too-large cloak in her hands as she walked down the crushed gravel path. Night had descended, but Sedja, the largest of the three moons, had risen and she could see the moon-silvered outline of the portal up ahead, set halfway between the two schools.

Somewhere in the bordering thickets of brush, a silsha snarled. Kisa glanced around, then ran along the twisting gravel path that glittered ice-bright under the moonlight. Even if the silshas ate her, she would not go back! The girls at the House of Moons seemed to think of nothing but festivals and dresses and—her mouth straightened—*boys*. Compared to the deaths of her mother and brother, such silliness made her long to scream and push them all away. She couldn't bear it for another second. She was going home.

Leaving the path, she crunched across the dead grass. Her younger sister, Adrina, was content to sit at the older girls' feet while they prattled on about, of all things, Arrich Dynd's *eyes*. She tried to tell herself that perhaps Adrina was just too young to understand that their lives were never going to be the same, but she knew it wasn't true. Adrina took after their mother— only slightly Talented, lighthearted, content with the moment— whereas she, as her mother had told her often enough, was serious-natured and restless, more like their unnamed father.

Kisa frowned. Why had their father never come to see them, not even once? No matter what had happened between him and her mother, Kisa and Adrina were of his House. His absence was something she had never been able to understand—or forgive.

She remembered how their brother's father, a tall imposing

golden-haired man by the name of Padrik Iliim, had come once to shake Lat's hand and pronounce him a credit to the Line. But of the man who had fathered both her and Adrina, nothing had ever been explained.

Easing around a stiff, thorny bush, Kisa caught the murmur of low voices carrying across the stillness. Crouching low to the frozen ground, she crept along, shielding her thoughts as best she could so that no one would sense her.

"I'm coming with you!" The man's voice, although soft, was angry. "I have every right to know what happened down there!"

"Kevisson, you should be in bed this very minute. If you don't get some rest and let your mind heal, you'll only be a danger to yourself as well as me." The other voice was that of an older woman, calm and determined. "Look at your hands shake—you're close to collapse."

Kisa edged nearer. The inside of the portal was bathed in dim yellow light from a small lantern. Two dark figures were silhouetted against the white-painted wood, one tall and square-shouldered, the other short and round. Kisa looked closer. Wasn't that Master Monmart, the man who had helped her at the funeral pyre?

"I'm fine," he said tersely.

"And I suppose trying to choke the life out of Riklin Senn was your own idea?" The woman was Healer Saxbury, the healer who had come too late to save Kisa's mother.

"Of course not." The man's voice was low, defeated. "But I didn't kill Myriel!"

Kisa eased aside the brambles of a leafless bush. Why were they talking about her mother?

The healer laid a hand on the man's shoulder. "I know that, but we need proof, and it has to come from Lenhe'ayn."

"So go, but I'm coming, too." A note of stubbornness crept back into the man's tone.

"What if Haemas returns?" Healer Saxbury asked. "Shouldn't one of us be here to tell her what happened?"

He hesitated. "We won't be gone that long, and I have to know!"

The healer lifted the lantern up to Master Monmart's face.

He looked tired, Kisa thought, as if he hadn't slept for days and days. The healer sighed. "All right, but you'd better do as I say, or I'll pack you off to Monmart'ayn, unconscious if need be, and let your mother deal with you."

"That'll be a warm day," he muttered. The two figures stepped onto the platform together, paused, and then disappeared in a flash of blue light.

The lantern had gone with them and the portal lay in ink-black shadow again as Kisa crossed the last few yards. She could already hear the transport crystals humming in her mind, singing their preset pattern that always said, "Shael'donn" to anyone who knew how to listen. Her fingers trembled as she slid her hand over the painted wood and stepped onto the staging platform. She remembered Lenhe'ayn's signature pattern, but she had never traveled alone between portals. It wasn't that hard, she told herself; people did it all the time, dumb or smart. Her mother had traveled that way often enough, and by her own admission she had barely been Talented at all.

She lowered her shields in preparation, then was startled by a rattling snarl. She jerked around as a huge silsha padded up to the portal's lowest step, moonlight gleaming on its black velvet coat. Its hot yellow eyes studied her as she backed against the railing. Shivering, she remembered the other students saying that the silshas roaming the grounds were pets, symbolic of Haemas Tal's time in the Lowlands and her bond with the ilseri. But Haemas Tal had been missing for days now, and the silshas were strangely agitated, shadowing everyone who came and went from the House of Moons, hunting their own prey instead of eating the scraps put out for them, then tearing it to bloody bits right underneath the windows. Kisa flinched as the beast flicked a tufted ear at her, then settled on its haunches an arm's length away, a study in midnight grace.

What did it want? Kisa tried to swallow, but fear had closed her throat. It was so—big!

The silsha cocked its head at her. She felt a wave of . . . need. It wanted something . . . no, *someone*, not her, someone else, important . . . *necessary*.

"Who?" she whispered, but of course it couldn't answer. The

air eased back into her lungs as she studied the long sharp-muzzled face, the glittering yellow eyes. She felt its warm breath on her freezing face, smelled the clean musk of its coat. It was quite beautiful, really. She'd never thought about an animal that way before. They regarded one another for a dozen more breaths; then it rose and prowled unhurriedly into the surrounding thicket of trees, its black hide merging with the darkness.

With a start, Kisa remembered why she was there. The healer and Master Monmart should be far enough away from the portal by now not to notice her arriving behind them. She concentrated on the ilsera crystals above her head humming their inaudible song. As the singing tone became clear in her mind again, Kisa reached for the more familiar vibrational signature of Lenhe'ayn. An instant of chill overwhelmed her, and then she opened her eyes and looked out at the moonlit fields and buildings of her home.

Nestled as she was, in the brushy hollow of a small side valley, Frostvine almost did not hear the distraught ilseri when they found her. She had spread the fabric of her great body into the copses of trees and the meadows and the wind-washed boulders, even down into the murmuring green-voiced river in order to contemplate the slow, compelling rhythm of the bedrock below—a fascinating, somewhat irregular beat whose meaning she was only beginning to comprehend.

The highly mobile Third Ones flitted about her, solid enough to actually see, teasing at her awareness, their mindvoices faint, annoying chirps. At this density, she could not make any sense of what they wanted, and yet she was loath to be disturbed. Ilserlara and ilseri had little in common, for all that they were two forms of the same species. This precious end-time was hers, to discover and cherish what truths she could before her final moment came and she lost her atoms to the winds.

Grumbling, she increased her density to a point where she could perceive what they were trying to say.

—*pool!* Her ilseri sisters fluttered around her like so many senseless avians. *Our pool has been plundered!*

A tremor shuddered through Frostvine's vast, nebulous body.

She coalesced with unseemly haste into the densest form she could now manage, filling only half the valley. *Who has dared?*

Unknown! The agitated sister stared up at her from the ground, garbed in wispy white, her solid body as lithe and green as Frostvine had once been, many Interims ago. *What can we do?*

That same agonizing questions had been asked in her youth, but the answer had never been found. A terrible anger blossomed inside Frostvine, a raw, red flower of renewed impotence and rage. As oldest of the ilserlara, she was the last who actually remembered those bleak times, and she had thought them finished forever. She recalled the searing sense of helplessness in the face of so much loss, how they had all—ilserin, ilseri, and ilserlara alike—stood by and suffered because they could find no proper shapes in their minds that would end the threat.

It could not come to that again. She, Frostvine, could not bear this agony and do nothing, as her kind always had before. This time, she would find a way to end it.

An argument raged, the voices rising and falling like an angry tide, but Haemas could not distinguish the individual words. She eased out of bed, taking great care to be quiet. Father would be furious if he caught her eavesdropping again. She cracked open the door, overwhelmed by the sense of an old, old pattern being played out as she peered down a hall lit dimly by dripping candles in tarnished brass sconces. Everything was familiar and yet utterly strange.

The voices came more clearly now, a man and a woman, by turns strident, harsh, demanding. She slid her hand along the crumbling plaster and inched toward them, bare feet padding silently over the carpet's worn nap. Outside, wind howled through the pines, and rain hammered on the roof. At the end of the hall lay an open sitting room with a hearth fire crackling somewhere out of her line of sight. The spidery black shadows of a man and woman paced back and forth on the far wall, arms waving, voices still arguing vehemently.

"I won't stand for it!" It was Father, she realized, his voice slurred with heavy drink. Then she was puzzled. It wasn't Dervlin Tal's voice, and yet she recognized it.

"I'm taking the children to Cassidae'ayn," the woman returned angrily. "Even the Lowlands is better than this hole of Darkness!"

"You'll never leave me!" the man cried harshly. Footsteps scuffled across the floor.

"Brann, no—!" The woman broke off in a terrible shriek. Something heavy toppled.

Frozen in terror, Haemas shivered against the wall, wanting to intervene, yet knowing somehow how violent Brann Chee was when he was full of drink. Her knees ached with the strain of remaining still. She heard a muffled thump, then heavy boots crossing the floor. Without even looking, she knew what she would see: her mother, Nells Cassidae, weeping, lying where she had been thrown, her head cracked open and bleeding, while Brann Chee loomed over her hunched body, gazing into the flickering flames, and drank and drank and—

But these people were no relation to her. Haemas struggled to free herself. *Her* father was Dervlin Tal and her mother had been Anyah Sennay.

Unsteady footsteps clumped toward the hall and her hiding place that provided no cover at all. In another second he would be upon her. Then she was running down the hall, barefoot, heart bursting. She found a barred door and wrenched at the crossbar with all her strength.

My lady, you mustn't! Hands reached around and caught her wrists.

With a start, Haemas found herself standing before a heavily barred door in an unfamiliar passage, rose-tinted sunlight streaming through a row of small windows set high into the wall. She drew a deep shuddering breath, that other time and place still very strong, then strained against the anonymous arms that held her back. "He's going to kill her!"

Her captor released her wrists, then moved into view. It was Master Ellirt. He peered into her eyes, his brow furrowed. "Kill who, my dear?"

Her heart raced as the image of Brann Chee's brutal face and the woman dying at his feet flickered in—out—in, alternating with the reality of the tranquil hallway. She stretched out a trembling hand to touch the door and see if it was real. Inside her head, she still heard the storm pounding Chee'ayn. If she looked over her shoulder, she would find Chee standing over his bleeding wife.

No, you're safe here. This is Shael'donn. Master Ellirt braced his hands against her temples and a warm thought-presence cocooned her. *I see—she used your dreams to slip into your mind.* Energy surged across a light link, bolstering her shields. A wave of calm reassurance swept through her and the steadying hands lowered to her shoulders.

The nightmarish images of Chee'ayn dissolved. Haemas blinked hard and her vision cleared. "What—?" she began.

Master Ellirt drew her away from the door. "You were going to unbar the door. She must have been after you all night, knowing you were exhausted from fighting the latteh." His face tightened. "I shouldn't have left you alone, but it never occurred to me that she would try something like this." Several other white-robed masters ran up behind him, but he waved them away.

Haemas twisted around to look at the door again. "That's—Axia's room?" Axia's manic laugh bubbled up inside her head, echoing and painful until she concentrated to shut her out. The rasping laughter faded.

Shaken, she let him guide her back through the maze of hallways to what was apparently her own room. She felt sickened by Axia's mental touch, violated and used. The hallways and people they passed did not seem quite real, and a dull ache was spreading behind her eyes. She massaged her temples as he opened the door.

"We've provided some fresh clothing for you, although I'm afraid we had nothing suitable for a lady. I know it's rather early, but why don't you change and then breakfast with us? The brothers would like to discuss a few things with you."

Haemas hesitated, but then he smiled at her, the same mild, encouraging smile that she had seen a thousand times over the years, the one that always said nothing was as bad as she thought and everything would come around all right in the end. She lowered her gaze, not knowing how to respond. He was her Master Ellirt all over again, sensible, warm, and comforting, and yet he was not and never would be. She could not allow herself to be lulled into a sense of false security by his likeness to her old friend and teacher.

Seeming to sense her confusion, he backed out of the sunshine-filled room and left her alone. Still trembling, she poured water from a blue-glazed pitcher into a matching basin and stared down at her wavering reflection. Axia must have projected all her memories of that terrible night; even though she had been woken before the dream played itself out, the ending was seared into her mind. Brann Chee had dragged his wife to the edge of the cliff just below the grove of pines and cast her struggling body into the rocky abyss. Haemas blanched at the thought of a child witnessing such a thing.

After washing her face, she braided her hair, then changed into the garments that had been left on the bed for her: a hooded tunic of soft white cotton that fell all the way to her ankles, worn over long, loose, matching trousers. Opening the door, she found Ellirt waiting.

"Why, you look much better," he said before she could speak, then firmly tucked her arm over his. "Come along."

Towed down the hall at his side, she wondered what the brothers wanted to talk about.

Why, the same as I, my dear. His eyes crinkled merrily at the corners. *To know where you came by that monstrously-sized crystal and what you mean to do with it.*

Sitting before the meager spread of his breakfast in the vast kitchen that had once fed fifty chierra servants at a sitting, Diren drained a lukewarm mug of tea, then tipped his rickety chair back against the wall, thinking. For months now, he had used his seat on the Council of Twelve to block funding for the House of Moons, calling in every favor owed to his father and incurring new debts of patronage himself, all to keep the other High Houses from learning of Chee'ayn's inability to pay its share. The school was a ridiculous idea anyway. No Lord wanted a wife with more mindtraining than he possessed himself, especially one who could access the timeways. Who knew what foolishness that might engender? It was not only stupid, but impractical. Girls overeducated in that fashion would be worthless as wives and mothers, and a Kashi Lord had to make the best use of all his resources.

But somehow Haemas Tal had still convinced them, putting Chee'ayn in a bind. And now ... there was no sign of her or Axia. Diren finally admitted to himself that his grand plan might have failed. Though he didn't see how, it was possible that, once she'd entered the timeways, the Tal woman had somehow escaped Axia and the latteh. Well, he was certain she would eventually return to her precious school, the only thing besides Monmart about which she seemed to care anything at all. Sooner or later he would catch up with her there and regain control of the situation.

In the meantime, more latteh crystals lay submerged in the pool in the forest, just waiting for someone to make use of them. At the moment, there was only one Kashi living at Lenhe'ayn—one of the Rald cousins who had been sent down to look after things, if he remembered correctly. If he hurried, it was unlikely anyone would be up and about to see him come through the Lenhe portal.

He snatched his heavy traveling cloak from a peg. Sanna, one of the few remaining Chee'ayn retainers, flinched out of his way as he passed. Outside, the sky stretched overhead, a pale, washed-out green streaked with rose, heralding the rising sun. His breath steamed in the chill air as he crossed the unkept grounds to his own portal. He stepped inside and aligned his mind with the Chee'ayn pattern, then altered it to take him to Lenhe'ayn. A second later, after passing through a chill that was beyond mere ice or snow, he was breathing the warmer Lowlands air, staring out across the burned fields.

Having those chierra torch the grain had been a brilliant move, he told himself as he stepped down from the platform. Lenhe'ayn workers would now have no reason to work on this side of the estate for the remainder of the winter. It was just bad luck that both Myriel and her fool son had gotten a clear look at his face. He had considered blurring or even trying to erase their memories, but such methods were crude and untrustworthy, all too often unraveling in the hands of a truly adept Master—like Kniel Ellirt or Kevisson Monmart.

Well, he had already taken care of Ellirt—the man had been a constant threat, sensing something unusual whenever Diren carried the latteh in his presence—and Monmart couldn't expose him since he had now eliminated all the witnesses. On the other hand, Monmart did still threaten Diren's long-range plans for Haemas Tal, and she was far too attached to him. He scowled, remembering how she'd tried to call out to Monmart just before he'd forced her to take Axia into the nexus.

If Riklin Senn didn't succeed in ruining Monmart's name and reputation, he would finish Monmart himself as soon as he acquired another latteh. He'd done well enough unaided, meddling with Monmart's injured mind the other day. That little show he had put on before the Council had worked quite nicely, and it would be a long time before anyone gave any weight to Master Monmart's credibility.

No field hands were in sight yet, probably all still eating in the main kitchen. Closing his eyes, Diren skimmed for the Rald overseer's mind. If the chierra servants saw him, he could adjust their memories, but he didn't want to encounter a Kashi down here where he would be hard put to explain his presence. A faint glimmer in the main house seemed to indicate Rald, but then he detected another—and another—and then finally one more. Dumbfounded, he opened his eyes again. Four Kashi here at Lenhe'ayn when there was only supposed to be one? Did someone suspect what he had done?

He compressed his lips. The pool in the forest would have to wait an hour or two longer, until he could slip into the main house and read one of the servants to find out exactly what was going on here.

Kisa shuddered as she walked like a stranger through the vast house she had known her whole life. The tapestries, the furniture, the paintings, even the smell of baking bread down in the kitchen—everything was the same, but something vibrant and alive had fled. Even though she sensed servants in the rooms she passed, going about their duties as always, the house felt empty and hollow. The muffled pad of her boots as she climbed the carpeted steps seemed loud enough to be heard all the way back in the Highlands.

At her mother's door, she paused with her hand on the painted-china latch, trying to nerve herself to go in. Myriel had been everything to the three children—mother, playmate, tutor, friend. Knowing that she was not behind this door, and never would be again, was almost more than Kisa could bear, and yet she felt something of her mother might linger here and she might in some way derive comfort from going inside.

Then she remembered her mother speaking to her in that familiar no-nonsense tone. "Tears buy no bread, Kisa Castillan Lenhe. Never forget that. Tears bring back nothing in this world worth having."

Trembling, Kisa pressed her cheek against the dark satiny wood, then heard low voices from within. She stiffened, extending her mindsenses just enough to detect two people, one Kashi, the other chierra. What were they doing in her mother's chambers? She lifted the latch and slipped into the sitting room. The voices, both female, drifted to her from the bedchamber directly adjacent.

"Now, Dorria, there's nothing to be afraid of. I just want to glance at your memories of that night and see if something unusual occurred, something you may have forgotten."

It was the healer from the Highlands, talking to her old chierra nurse. Kisa crept behind the floor-length green drapes to listen.

"I tell you, there weren't no one come past me into that room. My poor Lady were in there, resting, and then you come back with his Lordship and she were dead! That's all I know." Kisa heard the tears in Dorria's strained voice.

"Just relax." The healer's voice was calm, soothing. "Think back on that night."

Kisa wished she could view Dorria's memories, too, but she'd never been taught how, and if she tried to eavesdrop mentally now, she was sure to give herself away. Once Healer Saxbury discovered her, she would be sent straight back to the House of Moons.

She heard the sound of their breathing, then "Yes . . . that's it . . . and after Lord Monmart left, then what?"

Silence again, endless and boring. Kisa's leg went numb and she rubbed it furiously. Just a few more minutes, she told herself, and then after the healer left, she would find Dorria and—

The hall door opened softly and snicked shut again. She pressed back against the wall, holding her shields as tightly as she could and praying that would be enough to conceal her. She and Lat had played Barret-in-the-Woodpile often enough after she'd learned to shield and he'd hardly ever found her. Thinking of her older brother brought a hard knot to her throat.

The intruder was Kashi, not one of the chierra servants; even through her shields, she could feel that much. She held her breath and squeezed her eyes shut as if that would make her harder to find.

The healer's voice continued, unaware of the intruder. "Yes, I thought so, there was someone else . . . Lord of Light, what was *he* doing here? I—"

Mental energy flared, a searing orange-red, so intense that Kisa gasped. Something thumped to the floor like a sackful of feed.

"Thought you were so clever, didn't you, Healer?" a man's voice asked. Muffled sobbing was the only answer. "Stop that sniveling!" the man ordered sharply, and the crying broke off.

A bead of perspiration trickled down Kisa's temple. Had she ever shielded for so long before?

"Now, then." The man spoke in a low murmur, obviously talking to himself. "Shall we just leave this meddlesome baggage here? After all, she is old—and fat. No one would be surprised if she died of natural causes."

Kisa shivered. Was he talking about Dorria or the healer? In the face of all she had lost, the prospect of another death was frighteningly real. A tear trailed hotly down her cheek.

"What . . . ?" Footsteps walked away, halted, then came back again, chillingly close. A hand snatched the drapes open, revealing a tall, thin-faced man with receding golden hair and eyes that burned down at her like a funeral pyre. "Well, well." She flinched as he trapped her chin between his thumb and forefinger. "What sort of tidbit do we have here?"

Chapter Eleven

The crowded dining hall was filled with the rumbling, good-natured voices of men, overlaid by the raucous higher-pitched tones of the boy students. Sunlight poured through the open windows, rich and golden, and the entire room smelled of freshly baked bread and hot porridge.

It could have been any of a thousand similar mornings in her own When, Haemas thought as Master Ellirt escorted her past a sea of white-robed Andiine Masters to several empty places at the far end of the hall. He gestured for her to sit on the long wooden bench, but then she saw the latteh crystal, dull and ugly, lying beside a bowl of fresh fruit in the middle of the table. The remembered feeling of agonized helplessness swept back over her, along with the pain and the fear. The breath caught in her throat and she backed away.

"What is it, my dear?" Ellirt turned to her with a puzzled expression.

"Nothing," she said quickly, but, unbidden, her eyes darted toward the crystal.

"That? But we deactivated it yesterday." He touched her shoulder and the sunlight-and-lemons warmth of his mindpresence was reassuring. "I thought you would remember."

"I do—remember." She detected no warning buzz, or any other indication that it was still active, but found herself unable to go nearer. The hum of conversation in the dining hall died away and a hundred pairs of golden eyes turned to stare at her.

"Even if it had been reset in the controlling mode, which

would never happen here in Shael'donn, it wouldn't affect you unless you touched it again. See?" Ellirt picked up the oblong crystal and held it out to her. "I'd almost think you'd never seen a latteh before yesterday."

Haemas tore her gaze from the proffered crystal and slid onto the bench. "A week ago, I had no idea such things really existed."

"They exist." His tone was grim as he replaced the latteh on the table, then sat beside her. "Although the crystals harvested lately grow smaller and smaller until I think that perhaps some day we will find none at all."

A sandy-headed young boy, no more than seven or eight, hurried in from the kitchen with his brow furrowed in concentration, bearing a tall mug of purple nasai juice and a steaming bowl of zeli porridge studded with a golden pat of butter. Haemas put the mug to her lips and swallowed. The sweet juice ran down her parched throat, cool and refreshing. She realized she was hungry for the first time in days.

Ellirt nodded approvingly as she took up the spoon and began to eat the grainy porridge. "That's better. You're far too pale."

The man directly across the table from her cleared his throat. "May we ask how you're called?"

Glancing up, she looked into familiar blue-flecked golden eyes.

"I'm Brother Alidale." He smiled at her, then jerked his chin at the younger man on his left. "And this is Brother Benl."

"My name is Haemas," she said slowly, trying to keep the shock out of her voice. It was strange to sit here with them: skinny, dependable Alidale, shy Benl, and over at the end of the table, burly, gruff-voiced Tillan. She had known each of them during the years she had studied at Shael'donn. But in this When, Haemas Tal had apparently never come to the Brothers at Shael'donn for refuge and training, nor founded the House of Moons.

"Lady Haemas." Alidale nodded. "Could you tell—"

"No," she broke in. "Please, just—Haemas."

Alidale hesitated, looking to Ellirt, and she caught the murmur of a shielded mental exchange between them.

"Yes, I'm sorry—Haemas. Could you tell us where this crystal was found? Legends tell of large ones like this, but none of us have ever seen one of such size."

"I don't know where it came from." She stirred the lumpy porridge without really seeing it. "But what difference does it make? I can't imagine why you don't just smash it before it hurts someone else."

Alidale blinked at her in surprise. "For the healing, of course. Why else? A crystal of that size is bound to be potent."

"Healing?" It was her turn to be surprised.

"For all that she arrived on our doorstep in the thrall of a latteh, our guest knows little of these matters." Ellirt spoke quietly at her elbow. "You must remember that very few things under the sun are good or evil in and of themselves, my dear. Although the latteh has great capacity for both, the outcome depends on the one who wields it."

"Are you from the Lowlands, then?" The Benl of this When, as freckle-faced and snub-nosed as the one she had known, glanced up shyly at her over his bowl.

"No." She thought of the timelines. "I have come from much farther away than that."

"And the woman with you?" Ellirt reached for a loaf of dark-brown bread and sawed off a thick slice.

"Axia?" She accepted a still-warm slab of bread from him. "She comes from the same place."

Ellirt gave her a measuring look. "And you can't tell us where that is?"

"It would be better for you if you don't know." She thought how much safer her own When would be if the Council had not discovered the temporal possibilities of the ilsera crystals and begun experimenting. Years ago, many lives had been lost and the disaster of disrupted time had been brought searingly close before the Council had been stopped. And, once known, such secrets were unlikely to be forgotten. The danger remained, despite anything that she might do.

"You may be right." Ellirt sighed. "Some things are better left unsaid, although I must admit to my curiosity."

Remembering his wisdom and common sense, Haemas found herself tempted to lay her problems at his feet as she had done often enough with her own Ellirt, but knowledge of the timeways would only burden these people. This When already had to cope with the latteh; that was problem enough.

Alidale pushed back his half-finished bowl of porridge. "But what are we to do, then, with this woman who nearly killed you? In Shael'donn, at least, no one is allowed to force his will upon another, and yet, if we can't send her back to her people, we can't just keep her locked up here. We don't even know who she is or why she hurt you. And what about the latteh? It has to belong to someone."

Haemas felt her face flush as she considered his unanswerable questions.

"Do you wish refuge?" Ellirt asked her. "You could stay on with us and learn the art of healing with the latteh. We can always use more help when casualties come in, and I know you are powerfully Talented, or the latteh would have overruled your will."

"I can't stay." The words burst from her without thought, but she knew they were true, even as she spoke. "But, before I go, could you teach me how to deactivate a latteh? If I could learn even that much, it might mean the difference between life and death when I return."

Ellirt nodded. "I think we can do that. But what about the woman?"

Haemas folded her hands on the plank table and met his concerned gaze. "When I leave, she must go with me."

Kevisson awoke with a start, disoriented, in a strange bedchamber with fussy floral pictures that he could have sworn he'd never seen before, his head ringing with some sound that he couldn't quite remember. Then the devastating past week swept back over him. Master Ellirt's sudden illness, Haemas's disappearance, Myriel's inexplicable death and the disastrous Search that had nearly taken his life.

Throwing off the quilts, he stood up, then seized the bedpost as his vision grayed at the edges. That damned injury! Enissa had told him that he would be more sensitive to sensory extremes of light and sound, as well as to stress and exhaustion. He eased back down on the canopied bed and held his spinning head with both hands while he tried to recall what had woken him so suddenly. He couldn't remember dreaming anything in particular. One moment he had been asleep, and then someone had seemed to shout in his ear, but he was alone and the house was still now.

Perhaps Enissa had tried to mindspeak him, not realizing he was asleep. He reached for the shirt and breeches he had draped over an armchair, then pulled aside the heavy velvet drapes. The sun was rising in a cloud-cluttered green sky, painting the clouds orange-red; it must be Eighth Hour or later. He had not meant to sleep past dawn.

They had arrived too late the night before to question the servants without frightening them, so Leric Rald, the Council-appointed caretaker for Lenhe'ayn, had agreed to put them up in guest chambers. But Eighth Hour! Why in blazes had Enissa let him sleep so late? They could have questioned half the staff of this sprawling estate and returned to the Highlands by now. Was this her way of trying to make him rest?

Pouring unheated water into a basin, he washed his face hastily and, shivering, decided to put off shaving until later. Enissa had no doubt seen scruffier-looking specimens than himself in her time. He dried his face and hands. *Enissa? Where are you? I'm up and ready to start.*

He waited a moment, but she didn't answer. He pulled his shirt over his head, then closed his eyes and concentrated, reaching for the specific pattern of the older woman's personality. He heard the faint skitterings of chierra thought-traces, some in the house, more outside, but nothing of the healer. Finally he called to Leric Rald instead.

What do you want, Monmart? An unshielded tinge of irritation permeated Rald's tone, as if he had been interrupted at something important.

Kevisson glimpsed a vague image of piles of papers and account books through Rald's eyes. *I can't seem to find Healer Saxbury. Do you know if she left the house?*

Why would she do that? I thought you wanted to question the staff.

I have no idea. Kevisson grimaced at the ungracious timbre of the other's thoughts; the old man had been noticeably more civil with Enissa last night. No doubt that had been because of her deceased husband's Highland connections rather than any real sympathy with their errand. *Would you ask the servants to keep an eye out for her? I'm going to search the grounds.*

He didn't answer, but Kevisson supposed that Rald would do as he asked. It was probably just a miscommunication anyway.

Diren Chee glanced over his shoulder. The old servant woman and the girl followed him, staring ahead with dull, half-closed eyes, riding double on a slack-jawed ummit he had filched from a Lenhe'ayn corral. For himself, he had appropriated one of the coveted black Lenhe horses that had survived the raid, a sleek gelding with a finely molded head and an arching neck. But the girl and the old chierra servant were just going deep enough into the forest to prevent their bodies from ever being found, so even a rank-smelling humped draft animal would do for them.

Since it was plausible that the Saxbury woman had died of natural causes, he had left her body behind to be discovered by the servants. Two more bodies though, especially the girl's, would have raised suspicion, and he couldn't afford more attention focused on Lenhe'ayn before he acquired another latteh.

He ducked a low-hanging branch; the forest was becoming denser, the shadows dank and cold. Damn Haemas Tal anyway. If not for her, he would still have his original crystal and know everything necessary by now to employ it fully against the Council.

Behind him, Diren felt the Kashi girl struggling against the stupor he had induced to keep her from crying out. He glanced back; her face was pale, her fingers knotted into the ummit's shaggy hair. Irritated, he increased his control another level, but maintaining it was wearing upon him. The wind gusted, drawing a chorus of clacks and clatters from the stiff tree limbs and scattering papery blue-gray leaves across his path.

Then he caught another sound, a crackling off to his right, as if something paralleled him through the dead vriddis bushes and whip-willows, something big and stealthy. The hair on the back of his neck prickled, and he skimmed the immediate area with his mind; forest predators like silshas could be large, but usually didn't range this close to civilization. He caught the primitive thought-tracings of a few tree barrets, half somnolent at this time of year, and a den of silver-furred burrowing stin-rats, but nothing bigger.

After swinging down from the saddle, he led the gelding by its headstall so he could examine the ground more closely. The pool might be hidden at this season by the dead leaves and tangled thickets. When he had last been down here, the forest had been at the height of summer, everything lush and growing, the strange stone-walled pool cool and inviting.

Then, just out of sight, something thumped. Diren listened with his mind again, but sensed nothing bigger than a fist-size bavval crawling hastily out of their path.

Suddenly the gelding tossed its head and neighed, straining at the reins. "What is it?" Diren squinted into the shadows, but could make nothing out in the miserable gray half light. Sidling, the gelding flared its nostrils and Diren picked up fear from its mind. He studied the twitching, laid-back ears. Did it smell a predator? He led the leggy horse through the trees and brambles, away from whatever had frightened it, until he broke into a stand of particularly tall imposing trees that did seem familiar. He glimpsed white stone and the shimmer of water half obscured under a drift of fallen leaves.

After looping the reins around a fallen deadwood snag, he cleared the edge of the pool until he found the broad white steps. He sat down in the dead leaves and, shivering, shed his cloak and jerked off his boots. He couldn't see the bottom of the pool beneath the water's leaf-strewn pewter surface, but the other crystal had been invisible anyway until he'd dug it out of the mud.

The first step down into the frigid water shocked his breath away, and the second crystallized his bones into ice. He fumbled down the rest of the steps on rapidly numbing feet until the water lapped at his chin, then groped with his toes along the edge for the oblong shape of a latteh. For several minutes, he found nothing but the turgid ooze of cold mud, dead leaves, and an occasional stick; then his half-numb toes encountered the irregular outlines of something hard. He tried to scrape it out with his foot, but it was stuck fast. Finally he held his breath and dived down to wrest at it with his fingers. The crystal was buried deeply, though, and he had to surface for another lungful of air. A few feet away, the two captives watched him with disinterested eyes as he gasped like a dying fish, then dived back into the searing iciness.

He clawed at the mud until he could stand it no more, then burst back to the surface again, his teeth chattering and his lips blue. One more time, he told himself, then pushed the sopping hair out of his eyes and threw himself back into the water's chill embrace. His lungs ached with the effort of holding his breath and his heart thumped sluggishly. As he pried and scraped, the icy water seemed to seep into his veins.

Then suddenly the muck gave way. Cradling the crystal against his chest, he pushed off for the surface, exuberant. It was large, perhaps even bigger than the one he'd found before. With this, he would rule the Highlands!

His head broke the surface. He gulped in the freezing air, then half walked, half floated back to the steps, his hands so numb that he could hardly feel the precious crystal between them. Shivering, he clambered out of the icy pool, then hesitated.

The bare brambles on the far side of the grove twitched as a silsha, black as a cave at midnight, emerged, prowling toward him on huge, impossibly quiet feet. Clutching the muddy crystal with hands that seemed to belong to someone else, he stumbled up the last few steps and glanced around for the gelding.

Wild-eyed at the sight of the beast, the horse's ears flattened as it reared, breaking the snagged limb and freeing the reins. He cursed himself for not tying his mount to a more solid tree, then realized he had even left his sword hung on the saddle. "Steady now." He forced his voice to remain soft and calm as his muddy hand groped for the reins trailing away from him. "It's all right. Hold on." The gelding snorted, rolling its white-edged eyes, then bolted through the gray-brown trees.

His heart thundering, Diren turned back around as the silsha snarled, never taking its baleful yellow eyes off his face.

"There, my Lord!" The frightened chierra maid pointed at the slumped body on the floor in Myriel's bedchamber.

Lying there, her hand outflung against the paneled wall, the old healer was so white and still that at first Kevisson thought she was dead. He knelt and touched her lined cheek with the back of his hand and read the faint glimmer of her mind. He glanced up at the terrified chierra. "Find Lord Rald! Tell him I said to send for a healer from Shael'donn!"

The brown eyes blinked. "Be she—be she—dead, my Lord?"

"She will be if you don't hurry!" he snapped, then tried to control his runaway pulse. "Just fetch your master. I'll do what I can for her."

The maidservant dropped a hasty curtsey and fled back through the door, her steps echoing as she pelted down the hall. Kevisson snatched a lavish rose-embroidered spread from the neatly made bed and tucked it around Enissa's crumpled body. Bending low, he touched her temple and tried to reach her mind, but there was only the activity of her autonomic functions, and even those were breaking down.

Hold on, Enissa, he told her. *You're too tough and ornery to die like this.* And you can't leave me, too, he thought. First Myriel, then Haemas, and now Enissa.

Rald's heavy steps thumped up the stairs. Feeling Enissa slipping away, Kevisson opened his shields, pouring what strength he had into her failing mind. *Fight!* he said to her.

Haemas needs you and the House of Moons needs you and even those damn silshas need you!

"Lord of Light, what happened?" Rald grasped the door jamb with perspiring fingers, red in the face and wheezing.

"I don't know." Kevisson glanced up, his head spinning from the energy drain. "Send for a Shael'donn healer. I'll try to make her hold on until then."

Dimly he heard Rald calling to Shael'donn, his mindvoice ringing out through the betweenness that separated Lenhe'ayn and the Highlands, calling for a healer to come immediately.

And all the while, Enissa's skin chilled underneath Kevisson's hand as her life dribbled away and he hovered over her, powerless to prevent it.

Chapter
Twelve

The heavy crossbar holding Axia's door scraped out of its braces and another in an apparently limitless supply of silent, well-shielded young men stepped inside her room. She glimpsed a second white-robed figure standing guard as the door swung shut. The first man carried a tray loaded with fresh bread, crumbly white cheese, and a steaming mug of keiria tea across the room, and at no point did his gaze ever quite meet hers. She eyed his sturdy shoulders and calm, unlined face angrily from her perch on the bed. They all had the same look here—serene, healthy, modest, confident, the sort of young men who would never have come to Chee'ayn to seek her hand.

But what did they know of the way the world really worked? They had never lived in Brann Chee's terrifying shadow or gone hungry and cold in the middle of a huge disintegrating house or been locked out in the snow in the dead of winter. She could still smell the musty, manure-clogged barn where she and Diren had huddled many nights. Her nails dug into her palms and she longed to slap this fool's smug, self-righteous face.

The blue-striped crockery clinked as he set the tray down on the small table by the hearth. The aromatic aroma of the tea filled the room, and she realized she was quite hungry. Still, she was in no mood to be mollified. She slid off the bed and her lip curled. "I suppose you actually expect me to eat this— slop?"

Red tinged the cheeks under his sandy beard, but like all the other denizens of this dreary place he said nothing, just thrust his hands into the pockets of his long white robe and turned back to the door.

Panic welled up in her throat like a living thing trying to escape. What were they going to do with her? No one would tell her anything. She could not stay in this claustrophobic room one second longer! She shoved him sideways into the hearthside table, then rushed the door. The loaded tray clattered to the floor as he lunged and caught her around the waist with both arms.

Let me go! She twisted, at the same time trying to compel his mind, but his shields were damnably strong and she felt the force of her will slough off him like rain from a weather-treated cloak. She clawed at his hands. *You can't keep me in this hole!*

He deposited her on the narrow bed as if she were only an errant child, then knelt silently and began to pick up the scattered slices of bread and cheese.

Axia wrapped her arms around her ribs and turned her head away. Her eyes ranged along the whitewashed wall, hot and dry. "How can you do this to me?" Her voice came out in a harsh whisper. "What did she say about me? By what right do you think you can hold the Lady of Chee'ayn?"

A faint glimmer of surprise leaked from his mind, then was hastily damped. She heard him replace the mug on the tray, then mop at the tea soaking into the rug.

"Take me before your Lord!" she said. "I demand to know why I'm being held!"

Behind her, the door creaked open, then closed. Clenching her fists, she paced a tight circle around the small room, glaring helplessly at the sunlight slanting through the tiny window set far above her head. If they didn't let her go soon, someone was going to pay!

She closed her eyes and centered down again until she was calm, then sent her mind roaming through the sprawling establishment, seeking an unshielded mind to torment. But Haemas Tal seemed to be awake now, and there were no others within reach.

As had been true her whole life, everyone was determined to thwart her.

"It will be easier if we darken the room." Ellirt drew the drapes in his small wood-paneled study against the afternoon sun.

Unaccountably cold, Haemas shifted on the edge of the wooden chair, knotting her hands in her lap. Despite his reassurances, she found it difficult to believe the latteh could do anything but hurt. She remembered too clearly being caught in its power, helpless to call out to another's mind or shield or use any of the other skills that were so ingrained by time and training that she had taken them for granted.

"Now ..." He seated himself across the small table from her, so that the crystal, as big as her palm, stared up between them in the dimness like a malevolent dull-green eye. His craggy face was thoughtful. "I want you to monitor what I'm doing without actually coming in contact with the crystal yourself."

She nodded, but as his gnarled hands reached out to cradle the odd shape, she found herself trembling.

"My dear, there is no need for you to do this." His faded-gold eyes scrutinized her face, as always, trying to look deeper than she was willing for him to see. "We can keep this crystal here at Shael'donn and use it to save lives. It will be a great boon, and no one will think any the less of you for dealing with it in that way, not after yesterday. You nearly died."

The blood pounded in her head as she considered, just for a moment, returning to her timeline and trying to take up her life where she had left off. But it was, of course, no use. If Chee had found one latteh, he most likely could get more, and as long as he had that kind of power at his disposal, she would never be able to stand against him. Her friends were in jeopardy as well as her school; her one chance to make a difference. Everything she had worked so hard for would come to nothing. Chee had made it quite clear that he would never stop until he both possessed her and controlled the Council. The feel of his hot hands on her arms came back, the burning closeness of his fevered mind . . . She shuddered. "I have no choice."

A wave of reassurance washed over her from Ellirt's mind. "Then try not to worry." He closed his eyes.

Haemas let her eyelids drift downward, too, as she softened her shields and tried to follow what he was doing. Through the buffer of his mind, she felt the latteh under his fingers, not cold and dead like an inert piece of stone, as she had expected, but vibrant, filled with flickers of green energy deep within.

This is where the power of the latteh lies. He held it up in the dim light. *When these energy pulses are organized one way, it can be used as a potent agent for healing. In another pattern altogether, it binds a person's mind and steals his will.*

The energies pulsed slowly in the quiescent crystal, random like fish darting in a pool, neither dangerous nor useful. It was like fire, Haemas thought—it could be put to either great good or great destruction, but was not inherently good or bad in itself.

Ellirt began to structure the energy pulses in a complex sequence. *Now this is the pattern used for healing, although it takes practice on the user's part.*

She watched through his mind as the energy pattern took shape, trying to memorize the complex interweaving. With each nudge into place, she became aware of a subtle harmonic building within the crystal—nothing like the buzzing dissonance that had nearly torn her mind apart before, but a throbbing harmony that made her feel better just to listen to it.

Ellirt paused. *Yes, it is beautiful, isn't it? It's a great crime against nature that something so useful can also be put to so ugly a task as mind-binding.* Concentrating, he brought the few remaining random pulses into the sequence, producing a harmonic that brought tears to her eyes. *And now . . .* His fingertips spread across her bruised cheek. *I will demonstrate, although we usually reserve such power as this for life-and-death situations.*

The bruise tingled beneath his hand, and a warmth rushed through her, like sunshine streaming through her veins, building into a golden heat that dissipated all the weariness and aches she'd accumulated since Diren Chee had abducted her from the House of Moons. Her head nodded, the relief so unexpected and welcome that, just for a second, she forgot to be afraid of anything.

You see? he murmured, then his fingers spasmed and a wave of shock washed out from him. *By the Blessed Light! It can't be!*

Belatedly she realized her shields had slipped; he must have glimpsed the last few days in her mind. She jerked away from his touch.

"Other times." He passed a hand over his ashen face. "Thousands of realities, similar, yet different from our own." He lurched to his feet, his eyes staring. "You *have* known me, in another reality, similar to this one—another Kniel Ellirt."

"He was like a father to me." She focused on her clenched hands, fighting to keep her voice even. What would happen to this When now? "Much more than my real father ever was."

His back was turned to her. "And now?"

"He's dead."

"Did this Axia kill him?"

"No, he died of a fever." She bit her lip. "But it was very sudden, and recent. I still can't believe he's gone."

"Then how did she come to attack you?"

"Her brother obtained a latteh somehow. In my time, they have been forbidden for generations and little is remembered of how they function. He used it to force me to take Axia and seek knowledge of the crystal in the timeways so he could use it—and me—more effectively." She saw the ice-blue glitter of the nexus again in her mind, felt her fear as Axia unleashed the latteh's power. "At a critical moment, without even knowing, I somehow found a When in which you still existed. I must have been drawn to you."

"And yet, in this reality, we have never met." He fell silent. "Why don't you tell who you are now? I don't see how it can hurt."

Could it? Every second she lingered in this When, every word she uttered must change things forever, and not necessarily for the better. She stared down at her hands on the table. "I was born Haemas Sennay Tal."

"Tal'ayn." She heard recognition in his voice. "One of Dervlin Tal's and Anyah Sennay's daughters?"

"Their only child." Haemas rose and crossed to the window, pulling aside the heavy brown drapes to look out on the sunlit afternoon and a pair of tow-headed boys busily trimming a curving row of whipwillows. She thrust her hands into the white tunic's spacious pockets. "Anyah died when I was born."

"Not here." His voice was soft. "If I remember right, Anyah gave him four daughters and three sons. Alidale attended the Naming of the youngest only last winter and reported him a fine strapping boy."

"And Anyah?" She had difficulty speaking around the lump in her throat.

"By all reputes, a fine mother and a good wife." Perplexed, he stared at her for a moment. "Oh, you mean does she still live?" A gentle smile tugged at his lips. "Yes."

It was as if the floor had sunk beneath her. Suddenly her legs would not hold her up. She leaned against the window and tilted her head back, letting the air cool her flushed face. Here in these Highlands, Anyah lived on with her sons and daughters—and Dervlin Tal. And perhaps he was a better man for living in her light all these years. Perhaps the other Haemas had never been driven to leave Tal'ayn, had never been unhappy at all.

Her eyes strayed to Master Ellirt's concerned face. If she had not left home, the House of Moons would not exist. She would never have met Master Ellirt, or had the opportunity to train at Shael'donn. She would be an utter stranger, someone else entirely—and she would not have Kevisson in her life.

"But how is it done, this traveling between—" He stood up from the table and gestured helplessly with his hands. "Realities?"

"The secret to that almost tore my timeline apart twelve years ago." Haemas thought again of the whirling dark-blue maelstrom of disrupted time, then sharpened the memory and laid it bare for him, the whip-crackle of disintegrating temporal patterns, the grinding dissonance of disrupted energies tearing the universe apart.

He staggered backward, his face drawn.

Haemas raised her shields. "Like the latteh, once learned, this secret is a constant danger. Would you have me loose that upon your world?"

He leaned heavily on the back of his chair and sweat glistened on his wrinkled forehead. "No, of course not."

She hesitantly reached out and took his hand. His flesh was warm against her chilled palm. "I have to go back, and no one in my world remembers how to counteract the latteh."

He nodded, then opened his mind to the crystal again, and let her feel the humming harmony of it through him. *That, at least, I can provide. Watch now and I will show you the pattern for mind-binding. You cannot understand how to undo it without first knowing how it is done.*

And even though she knew he was right, she trembled as he altered the patterning, rearranging the energy pulses in a different, more sinister structure, one that did not hum with harmony but rattled and buzzed with a raw, repressed power that set her nerves on edge. She made herself study it, memorizing the hateful sequencing. *But how is it set for just one person?* Her mouth straightened. *And more important, how do you break its hold?*

He sighed. *There is only one way to learn how to break its hold. You must see it demonstrated.* The door opened, revealing the tall thin form of Brother Alidale. Ellirt beckoned him to the table. "I called Alidale to help me demonstrate how to break it." Ellirt's lined face was grim. *Watch closely, now. I want to do this only once.*

Her mouth dry, Haemas nodded, knowing she would have found it almost impossible to do Alidale the same service that he was now rendering her.

You must set it so. Ellirt nudged the last energy pulse into alignment. *Then the next person who touches it with his bare skin will finish the job, albeit unknowingly. Until the pattern is broken, the latteh will have power over its victim, a shocking waste of something that can be put to such good in the right hands.* He hesitated. *Brother Alidale?*

Alidale's bony hand reached out and grasped the crystal. Haemas paled as his eyes glazed and his mental shields faded. A bead of sweat dripped down her neck. She remembered all too well the pain of the latteh as she had felt it before.

Alidale is in no real pain because he knows better than to fight it as you did yesterday. Ellirt took the crystal back from Alidale's unresisting hand. *And, frankly, it takes a Talent of Plus-Ten or more to resist it at all. Most people simply lack the strength. The initial shock of contact binds them too quickly to have any independent thought.* He paused, then nudged an energy pulse out of phase. *This is how you break its hold. I had difficulty freeing you because the more you struggle, the stronger its hold grows.*

Alidale straightened, his golden eyes aware again, but strained and weary. "We can go through it again, if you would like."

"No." Haemas reached out and pressed his long thin fingers between her own. "I could never forget something as important as that, Brother Alidale."

Then she glanced up to see Master Ellirt smiling at her in his old familiar way.

Poised at the edge of the icy pond, Diren swore as the terrified gelding's hoofbeats pounded through the forest. He grappled with its terrified mind, but the horse was operating on pure instinct and galloped swiftly out of range, so he turned his attention instead to trying to fend the silsha off. But, even though the beast stood there, less than an arm's length away, so close he could see the hair bristling across its muscled shoulders, the damned thing had no more mental presence than a cloud. He could find nothing to grasp.

Behind him, the ummit was shifting its hindquarters and generating vague thoughts on the merits of running away. Switching his efforts to restraining it, Diren directed his two captives to dismount, then groped through the drifted leaves with shaking hands, without taking his eyes off the silsha, for his discarded cloak. The girl slid obediently down the ummit's shaggy side, followed more stiffly by the doddering servant. The movement caught the silsha's attention and it turned its blazing gaze on them. Encouraged, Diren had the pair approach the massive beast. The old woman walked in jerks like a badly manipulated puppet, her eyes wide and white-rimmed, evidently perceiving her danger somewhere in the back of that dim-witted chierra mind. The girl, however, merely cocked her red-gold head to one side and ambled fearlessly toward the yellow-eyed creature, holding a hand out to it as if it were someone's pet tree barret. *Yes,* Diren told her, *think how soft that fur must be.*

The silsha's muzzle wrinkled in a hesitant snarl as Kisa climbed over a knobby root. Diren picked his cloak up from the ground and eased it around his shoulders, shivering so hard he could barely breathe. The silsha's ears flattened as the girl reached out. Diren waited for the rush of its attack so he could leap onto the ummit, but instead the silsha thrust its great head against the girl's palm, then butted her affectionately, almost knocking her over.

"Soft," the child murmured. She swept her arms around the huge neck and pressed her cheek against the whiskery black muzzle. Its hot yellow eyes closed in contentment and Diren drew in a shocked breath. Only one person had ever been reputed to have that kind of control over these infernal creatures—Haemas Tal.

He fumbled for the ummit's trailing reins in the dried grass, but the silsha whirled and sprang at him, snarling and spitting. Diren's hand jerked away as if he'd touched naked flame. Ears pinned back, the beast settled on its glossy haunches, submitting again to the girl's caresses. A few feet away, the old servant woman scuttled behind a tree to watch helplessly with terrified eyes.

Diren wet his parched lips. "Kisa," he said quietly, "tell the silsha to let me go."

"He doesn't like you." She bent her head over its neck so that her red-gold hair trailed over the black fur.

Closing his eyes, Diren strengthened his hold on her mind. *Tell it now!*

Kisa screwed her eyes shut, concentrating, then reopened them. "I told him not to hurt you."

Diren gathered the reins, swung up into the patched saddle, and sawed the ummit's head around. It plodded reluctantly back the way he had come. The silsha followed.

Tell the bloody thing to stay here! he ordered Kisa.

She frowned. "He says you must put back what you took."

Diren glanced at the dripping latteh in his free hand, then thrust it out of sight inside his shirt. "Don't be ridiculous."

"He says you're stealing the future." She walked beside the silsha, her hands smoothing the length of the black creature's body from the tufted ears to the end of its restless tail.

Kicking the ummit, Diren rode into the surrounding trees. As if it were his shadow, the silsha glided after him, its restless tail weaving from side to side. He heard it begin to trot and looked back to see the long white fangs gleaming in the forest's gray half light.

His heart raced. He stretched his hand out to Kisa. *Hurry!* he said to her. *Come and ride with me.*

She darted around the silsha and reached up. He grasped her wrist and swung her onto the ummit, hoping the beast wouldn't attack him as long as he held her close. Silshas rarely left the cover of the trees. He would just keep the brat with him until he was out of the forest, then get rid of her. As for the sniveling old woman, let the silsha scatter her bones and save him the bother.

Inside his shirt, the chill lump of the latteh crystal pressed into his goose-bumped skin. Tomorrow he would begin again, and if setting this crystal was no different than the previous one, he would again have what he needed to control the Council.

Ignoring the black beast prowling stealthily after him, he began to consider which member of the Council of Twelve would be most beneficial for him to go after first.

* * *

Carrying Enissa on a litter between them, Healers Lising and Nevarr stepped into the Lenhe'ayn portal and in a flash of blue light were gone. Kevisson dug his nails into the dark-finished wood. At least Enissa was still alive, although the two Shael'donn healers expressed doubt that she would live out the day.

Their diagnosis had shocked him. Lising had studied Kevisson with those classic gold Kashi eyes as if all of this were his fault. "Her mind's been blasted," he'd said, his tone sharp. "Someone obviously tried to kill her."

The idea was ridiculous, though. He and Enissa and Leric Rald, the Council-appointed caretaker for Lenhe'ayn, had been the only Kashi on the estate last night. Rald was a stiff-necked old codger, but had no reason to hurt Enissa, while Kevisson and Enissa had been working together to clear his name. He had less reason than anyone to do her harm.

"The Council will want to question you," Lising had said just before they'd picked up the litter to take Enissa back to Shael'donn.

Clearly they meant to blame this on him, along with everything else. He had to find out what had happened this morning. Enissa must have been searching Myriel's chambers, but who had been in there with her?

Back at the main house, he searched every hall and room, questioning the servants as he came upon them. Few of them had seen Enissa, but, of the ones who had, all agreed she had been looking for Dorria, the old nursemaid to the Lenhe children—and no one had seen Dorria all day.

Finally, without waiting for Leric Rald's permission, Kevisson dispatched every servant on the place to find the old chierra woman. Dorria now held the answer to not just one but two secrets: What had really happened to Myriel Lenhe, and who had attacked Enissa Saxbury?

He had to have those answers, no matter what the cost.

Chapter Thirteen

As Master Ellirt watched, Haemas's hand hovered above the latteh lying in the middle of the table, but she couldn't make herself touch the innocuous-looking crystal with her bare skin. She drew a shallow, shaky breath. Ellirt's workroom was dim and stuffy; she felt closed in, threatened. Gooseflesh crawled up her arms. She rubbed her perspiring palms on the borrowed white robes and resisted the urge to bolt from the room out into the clean afternoon sun.

"Let's try again." Ellirt placed a steadying hand on the nape of her neck and brushed her mind with his, offering strength and compassion. She leaned her head back and closed her eyes, savoring his familiar mental presence. She would have known him this way anywhere, at any time. She relaxed her shields and let his calm assurance wash through her.

When her breathing had slowed and the sick churning in her stomach faded, she steeled herself and managed this time to rest her fingertips on the latteh's surface. It felt smooth and cool, altogether unremarkable, no more frightening to touch than an ilsera crystal. She hesitantly extended her mind, sensing first the enormous reservoir of power confined within it, then the tiny individual flickers of green energy pulsing randomly through the matrix like slim green fish darting in a pond. It was these "fish" that she had to coax into the pattern for healing.

—or to bind another's will, the back of her mind whispered.

But she would not think about that. Reaching for the energy pulses, she herded them with her mind as Ellirt had demonstrated, nudging them one by one into the pattern that would generate healing energies. Even as the subtle harmonic built, though, she found the process unsettling, as if she were re-arranging the living energies of a person's mind.

She turned to the remaining stray pulses, but they were maddeningly elusive, and, in her efforts to bind them into the power lattice, she had to shut out her sensory impression of first the room and then Ellirt. Up close, the greenness had a tantalizing quality, almost a familiarity, as if she had known something very like it in some other place and time. She strained closer, then closer still, and suddenly found herself immersed in a cool electric emerald greenness that cut off all other sensation. Startled, Haemas groped for awareness of her body, but there was only cool green fire flickering all around her, like lightning in some unimaginable, silent storm, beautiful and disturbing.

Out of the seeming chaos, something seemed to notice her, something *curious*, as if the latteh were alive in some sense. She wanted to know more, but had set no controls for her breathing and heart rate and needed to regain touch with her body. She pushed hard in a random direction and felt the greenness give. She exerted more pressure and found herself able to feel her fingers and toes, the perspiration drying on her skin, Ellirt's grip on her shoulders.

You must be more careful. His relief washed over her. *You stopped breathing for a moment there.*

Leaving the half-assembled healing pattern, Haemas fully withdrew her awareness back into her body, feeling again the rasp of breath in her chest, the flutter of her eyelids. Her hands shook as she opened her eyes and gazed up at the old man's seamed face. "Where do these crystals come from?"

Ellirt pulled out a chair and sat beside her. "From the Low-lands, of course. There's no record of them ever being found anywhere else, and they have been exceedingly scarce now for generations."

A feeling nagged at the back of her mind, something she ought to remember. "Where in the Lowlands?"

"Only one kind of place, actually." He sighed and locked his hands over his paunch. "I wish it were otherwise. They can do so much good in the right hands, but they're only found in a certain sort of pool in the deep forest."

Glimpsing an image in his mind, she finally made the connection—the strange, cool beauty, the emerald greenness, the potent psionic power. She leaned over the table and examined the crystal. "Small, spring-fed pools edged with white stone?"

"Yes." His forehead furrowed. "They're not common and the locations have all been mapped for hundreds of years now."

"But—" Her throat was suddenly closed and dry. "Master Ellirt, surely you know those pools were made by the ilseri?"

"The Old People?" His eyes crinkled into a net of sun-wrinkles as he suppressed a laugh. "They're just a myth. No one has ever actually seen one. Personally, I've always thought they were a story made up by the first settlers on Desalaya to frighten children."

Haemas picked up the dull-green, irregularly faceted crystal, feeling the half-assembled harmonic within. "The Old People are real." She focused her awareness on the remaining unbound flickers of energy as they skittered here and there in much the same way that thoughts darted through a human mind. She shuddered and turned back to Master Ellirt. "The ilseri taught me the secret of the temporal pathways." She held the latteh out to him. "I'd swear this crystal is alive. I can feel it. And if they're found only in the pools, they must have some connection to the ilseri."

"Alive?" His white brows knotted as he accepted the latteh from her hands. "How can that be?"

"I don't know." She stood, a range of possibilities crowding into her mind. "But I must go back to my own timeline and ask the ilseri what they know about this. If these crystals are alive and aware, then it's wrong for you to use them."

"I agree it's wrong to use them to bind another's will." He laid the crystal on the table between them. "But what about healing? How could it be wrong to save lives?"

"I'm not sure." She felt as if she were poised on the edge

of a yawning precipice, looking straight down. "I only know that I must find out."

The answer was the same everywhere Kevisson turned: Dorria was nowhere to be found. Finally he stopped a strapping servant girl on her way to beat the rugs and made her take him to Dorria's room, a small chamber adjacent to the Lenhe children's bedrooms.

The room was sparsely furnished, with only a table, a chest, and a narrow shelf-bed covered with a faded-blue ebari-wool blanket. The unbleached muslin curtains were drawn and silence lay around him, thick as fog. He picked up the neatly arranged items from a low worktable in the corner: a worn wooden hairbrush with a few wiry gray hairs caught in the bristles, an embroidered child's nightgown in need of mending, a simple necklace made of braided leather straps. He fingered each one until he had a better sense of who this old woman was and what her mind would feel like if he met it again in the gray betweenness of Search.

It helped, of course, that he had talked to her several times about Myriel, and had even spoken directly into her mind when she was overweary. He selected the hairbrush for his focus finally, getting his strongest sense of her when he touched it.

Glancing around the small room, he decided this place would do as well as any other and stretched out on the still made up bed built into the corner. Holding the brush loosely in his hand, he conjured up the old woman's image in his mind. She was chierra, of course, dark-complected, brown-eyed, five-fingered ... simple and honest ... her shoulders bent with grief ...

He began to count his breaths, letting the rasp of the wool blanket against his skin fade away, and then the afternoon light dancing on his eyelids, centering down, focusing on an old, stooped chierra woman whose life had crumbled around her in the space of the last few days ... who had lost both the woman and the boy for whom she had cared since the hour of their births.

Sometime after he entered the gray betweenness, he sensed the muted glow of her chierra mind. She was fairly close, two to three hours away, perhaps a bit more. He saw her crouched against the twisted trunk of a winterberry, mud-spattered, her skirts torn. She was alone, terrified, dazed, and exhausted, her lined face wet with tears.

Relieved that she didn't seem to be injured, Kevisson wove a silvery thread of contact between her and himself, then reluctantly left her in the cold shade of the leafless trees and began to return through the grayness back to his body. After what could have been minutes or hours, he pried his weighted eyelids apart and gazed blearily around the cheerless room. The back of his head ached and his mouth was numb. He sat up and massaged his stiff neck. Enissa had warned him against exerting himself mentally while he was still recovering, but it couldn't be helped. The thin gray light slanting in from the tiny high-set window was failing and he cursed silently. He needed to replenish the energy that he'd just expended, but the day was almost gone.

He decided to scrounge some of the spicebread he'd smelled baking earlier and eat as he rode. He thrust the hairbrush inside his shirt and slipped through the halls toward the Lenhe kitchens, feeling a sense of urgency. Whatever turn of events had stranded the old servant out in the middle of the forest, he had sensed that she was still quite afraid.

After pursuing the stampeding gelding carrying his sword all the way to the edge of the forest, Diren finally sat back in the ummit's saddle and conceded defeat. Evidently the damned horse had headed straight back to the Lenhe barns. No doubt, in the present state of confusion there, a stable hand would unsaddle it and store the sword. The worst that could happen was that it might come into Leric Rald's possession. He would have to try to retrieve it later, when everything else had been settled.

At least the silsha had faded back into the underbrush as he'd neared civilization. Diren squinted over Kisa's head toward Lenhe'ayn, then kneed the ummit back under the cover of the forest. The crystal shifted inside his clammy shirt and, even though he was shivering, a smile tugged at his lips; swords were nothing against a latteh. A blade only commanded the body and depended on the strength and speed of a man's arm, but a latteh overwhelmed the mind, no matter what the degree of one's Talent.

When they had gone far enough, he reined in the ummit and swung his silent passenger down to the ground, mentally directing her to sit beneath a forked tree. Damn, he told himself, but it was wearying to have to control her for so long. That dive into the pool had drained his energy, and fighting the cold required even more. He had nothing left to spare. Without looking at him, Kisa sank to the leaf-covered ground and locked her arms around her skinny knees, her eyes hooded and distant.

Dismounting as well, Diren tied the weary ummit's reins around a low-hanging branch, then shivered as the winter wind shrilled through the trees. His damp shirt and leggings clung to his body. The lengthening shadows now stretched across the forest floor, chill and dark blue; it was getting late, but not late enough. He couldn't risk using the Lenhe portal until later when everyone was asleep.

Kisa curled against the tree's trunk, her compressed lips tinged with blue. At his directive, she had come into the forest without winter gear of any sort. Turning his back on her drawn face, he gathered dead wood and built a small fire, running through the old Kashi ritual to generate the initial spark. As soon as the flames caught, he cast about the immediate area and piled up more kindling until he had enough for several hours. Then he squatted on the upwind side of the fire and stretched his hands to the yellow flames, letting the crackling warmth drive away the last of chill moisture in his damp clothes.

The crystal pressed against his ribs as he shifted his weight. Which member of the Council of Twelve should he go to first? Which one would prove the key to controlling all the rest? Should he try Seffram Senn or Himret Rald or perhaps even that oh-so-proper lump of respectability, the old Tal himself? Provided he picked correctly, the first Council member to fall under his control would unravel all the rest. The Highlands would fall into his lap like a ripe fruit.

A snarl rattled the impenetrable darkness beyond the fire. Seizing a piece of wood, Diren thrust the heavy branch into the red heart of the flames until it blazed, then held it high over his head. Not more than ten feet away, the calculating yellow eyes of the silsha glittered as it sank to a crouch, its midnight coat one with the shadows.

"Tell the bloody thing to get back!" he snapped at Kisa, but the child frowned and turned her face away. After lurching to his feet, Diren rounded the fire and snagged her arm with his free hand. Her eyes came alive and he felt her mind writhe free of his mental grasp.

"Don't touch me!" She twisted and sank her teeth into his hand.

Without thinking, he hurled her to the frozen ground at his feet. She lay there, one arm thrown limply above her head like the rag dolls that Axia had played with long ago. The rumble of another snarl startled him—this one from behind, though, not in front. Whirling, he saw a second silsha weaving through the tangle of trees and underbrush, and on its left a third, and a fourth, all gliding toward him like elegant black shadows cast by something unseen. Fear shriveled his stomach. Silshas were supposed to be solitary animals. He'd never heard of them hunting in packs.

He nudged the motionless child with his foot, but Kisa's mind was silent now, blank as a wiped-off slate. He knelt and dragged her closer, seeing then the purpling knot on her forehead. The silshas growled a throaty warning and his hand flinched back. The relentless beasts paced toward him, their muscles tensed and ready, making no more sound in the dried leaves than ghosts. Diren seized a second burning brand out of the fire and held it aloft with his bitten hand, feeling the wind whip the flames high above his head.

How long? he asked himself, gazing into the savage circle of burning yellow eyes. How long did he have before his fuel was exhausted and they attacked?

* * *

Crossing the stable yard with a loaf of spicebread stuffed inside his shirt, Kevisson glimpsed a sweat-lathered black gelding standing still saddled in the open barn door, its weary head drooping to the straw-littered ground. He glanced over his shoulder and wondered why no one had put the horse up.

Well, no matter, it was a stroke of luck for him. Leric Rald was suspicious after the attack on Enissa and seemed disinclined to cooperate with him any further. Although the gelding looked tired, he would have to ride slowly in the forest anyway, and from the looks of the poor creature, it needed cooling out. He fingered a sword and scabbard lopped over the saddle's pommel, surprised at the laxness of the staff. Discipline seemed to be going to pieces under Leric Rald's administration.

He ran his hand over the gelding's lowered neck and found the skin still warm, but not dangerously so. Then he gathered up the trailing reins and swung into the saddle before anyone could protest. He closed his eyes for just a second, testing his tenuous strand of contact to Dorria, then resolutely turned the gelding's nose toward the gray-brown forest. The clip of hoofbeats sounded like thunder to his guilty ears as he rode across the cobbled stable yard, but then they passed onto the dead grass and he relaxed, letting the horse set its own pace.

About an hour later, he caught a winking glimpse of Sedja's silvery half disk as he rode under the arching trees, letting the gelding pick its way around deadfalls and the gnarled roots that twisted like giant, grasping fingers out of the frozen ground. Whatever had brought Dorria this way had followed no path or pattern that he could discern. The wind had come up fierce and bitter-edged, with a chill that numbed his unprotected fingers and face and made his eyes water.

Finally he sensed from the increasing clarity of the psionic trace that he was nearing the old servant. She hadn't moved since he had located her earlier that afternoon, which puzzled him. This wasn't that far from Lenhe'ayn. Why hadn't she at least tried to walk part of the way back?

Perhaps she was injured, he thought, but he had picked up

no hint of that earlier, just an overwhelming sense of despair and fear. All around him, the trees swayed and creaked, black against the deep-green night sky, cold and tinder-dry, ready to catch fire much more easily than he liked to think about. Dismounting, he knotted the reins around a sapling, then closed his eyes and summoned a handful of shimmering blue-white chispa-fire, not wanting to risk a real flame in so much wind.

His footsteps crunched through the stiff, frozen underbrush. "Dorria?" She didn't answer, but he could sense her weary, fear-riddled mind cowering behind a massive winterberry; she was very close now. "Dorria, it's Kevisson Monmart. I've come to take you home."

Something stirred in the darkness beyond the range of his light. The wind moaned through the trees as he strained to locate the faint rustling. "Dorria, it's all right. No one is going to hurt you."

The faint sounds of muffled weeping came to him for a second over the wind. He sighed. She wasn't going to make this easy. He reached for the subliminal line of contact between them, now quite strong. "Just stay where you are. I'll come to you." Something shifted in the interlaced branches above, and he tilted his head back and tried to make it out. Surely she was too old and tired to have climbed a tree.

As he held his cupped hands up, the chispa-fire gleamed off a moving body up there amid the tangle of dark tree limbs. The treetops were alive with lithe green bodies and large black eyes that mirrored his light. The breath caught in his throat. Were these the ilseri? Although he'd encountered the nonhumans once many years ago in the forest, he'd never actually gotten a look at one. They avoided most humans at all costs. Was this what had so terrified Dorria?

Give back what you have taken!

Kevisson's hand jerked as the angry voice shouted into his still-healing mind. White-hot pain stabbed through his head and the chispa-fire sputtered cold sparks in his palm. "What—?"

The shadowfoot saw you. The image of a roiling storm

cloud formed in his mind, full of rumbling thunder and the blaze of lightning. *It is forbidden to disturb the sacred pool!*

Sinuous bodies leaped to the ground, surrounding him with a tall living wall of bright-green flesh and bottomless black eyes that regarded him without blinking.

His heart racing, Kevisson stared back into the hard alien faces. One of them, shorter than the rest, fingered his hair; then the rest of the green creatures crowded in, probing his face and body, while dark-green tendrils danced over their round skulls as if they had a life of their own. One of the creatures bared sharp predatory rows of white teeth. *The First One is not here.*

I only came for the old woman, he said, hoping they could understand him as well he did them. *I didn't know this place was special, and I'll be more than glad to leave.*

It is only a male, like us, one said, *but that does not excuse what it has done.* It leaned over him and its breath smelled of wet earth and newly sprouted leaves. *You must put the First One back.*

I don't know what you're talking about! Kevisson tried to shoulder his way through the living wall of bodies but the creatures stood their ground, firm as young trees.

We must take him with us. Then, when the mothers come, they will know what to do. The tall green bodies pressed in on him until he couldn't breathe and his chispa-fire guttered. Stronger-than-human hands seized his arms and legs, then passed him between them hand to hand into the trees above as if he weighed nothing. Halfway up, his flailing boot connected with a smooth nonhuman torso and he wrenched free. Then the back of his head struck a branch, plunging him into a heavy green darkness that snuffed all sight and sound and thought.

Chapter
Fourteen

Riklin found the mood of the House of Moons satisfyingly somber as he passed through the wood-paneled foyer into the main house. Several downcast girls brushed past him in the hall, not meeting his eyes. Upstairs, he could hear several age groupings of students at their lessons, dutifully attempting whatever was asked by their instructors, but the spirit, the heart of the institution, was flagging. A smile tugged at his lips. According to reports, eleven families had already taken their daughters home. Events were well on their way.

He stopped before the closed sickroom door and sampled the unshielded thoughts of the student sitting with Enissa Saxbury. Such carelessness better suited the pampered daughter of some High House than a person aspiring to the complicated and delicate art of Healing. This young nit had paid precious little attention to her training, from what he could tell. Well, it was no less than he had expected. Nodding to himself, Riklin opened the door without knocking.

"Lord High Master Senn!" An ash-blond slip of a girl, no more than sixteen, jumped up and spilled an open packet of dried herbs down the front of her gray tunic and onto the floor. She spread her hands helplessly above the mess. "I'm sorry. I didn't hear you knock."

Narrowing his eyes, Riklin let the chill weight of his presence settle over the room. "Why should the Lord High Master of Shael'donn knock to gain admittance on his own grounds?"

But this is not Shael'donn, the young healer's mind blurted. Then, blushing, she turned her bluish-gold eyes away.

Poor stock, Riklin thought coldly, gauging those off-color

eyes. It was getting harder to find Kashi with the truly golden eyes and hair that had always been so prized here in the Highlands. Well, that was what came of the High Houses breeding on the whim of emotion instead of logic.

Circumventing the girl's slight form, he crossed to the bedside and studied the Saxbury woman's vacant face, noting the increased ashen quality of the skin and the ragged breathing. He found it hard to believe the old harridan wasn't already dead. "How is she?"

"No better." The girl brushed fine dark-brown powder off her gray uniform, then reached across to twitch the blanket a fraction straighter. "Master Lising attended her earlier and said he would be back tomorrow. An injury like this is beyond my training. I've—" Her voice faltered. "I've never seen anything like it."

"Of course not," Riklin said bluntly. "We haven't had an attack like this here in the Highlands for years. Well, there's no help for it. She'll have to be moved to Shael'donn."

"But my Lord!" The girl's hand froze in the middle of reaching for a basin of herb-scented water. "She's far too ill—"

"I have, of course, consulted Lising on this matter, and he concurs," Riklin continued smoothly. "Lady Saxbury will do much better at Shael'donn, where there are a number of fully trained healers to look after her, and it's out of the question for her to stay on here now that the House of Moons is being closed."

The girl stared at him blankly. "Closed?"

Riklin locked his hands behind his back and allowed a touch of pious concern to leak from his shields. "In the light of recent events, we can hardly do anything else." He pulled a chair out and sat down, turning away from the pallid face on the pillow. "First, we have the unexplained disappearance of your headmistress, then the brutal attack down at Lenhe'ayn against Lady Saxbury, and now those damn silshas are running wild, frightening the students half to death and making it dangerous to use the portal. The Council cannot allow the Kashi daughters entrusted to the care of this school to remain here in a state of dubious security and without adequate supervision."

The girl stood, her face gone white. "I assure you, Lord High Master, that all the classes are running smoothly, and although the silshas are fractious at times, they have never hurt anyone."

He frowned. "When and if Haemas Tal comes back, the Council will discuss reopening the House of Moons, although there will certainly have to be alterations in its management." Riklin swiveled his head, surveying the neatly kept sickroom with its piles of white linens and carefully labeled medications. Personally, he would rather be dead than let some female excuse for a healer touch him. "Certain aspects of this place have never been—satisfactory."

"Such as?" The girl braced her slender shoulders and met his gaze without flinching. Her cheeks were flushed, her eyes narrowed.

In spite of himself, Riklin was intrigued. He studied her oval face more carefully. He usually preferred young, downy-cheeked males, such as the students at Shael'donn, but she had a certain pliant grace. It might be amusing to feel the silk of those young arms caressing his naked skin. "What is your name, child?"

She lifted her chin. "Meryet Cassidae Alimn," she said, giving him both her maternal grandfather's and her father's surname.

Alimn'ayn, of course, was a respectable High House with a seat on the Council, but the other connection was unfortunate. She would never get a decent marriage contract. Cassidae'ayn was located so far out in the Lowlands that Riklin had never seen it marked on a map. Still, her lack of standing made an illicit liaison easier. After all, who would dare protest if he favored her with his attentions? He would have to keep an eye on this one. "Alimn'ayn," he said smoothly. "Yes, you're very like your grandfather, Staanvan."

"Great-uncle." Her body was rigid.

"Yes." He turned toward the door. "You must give him my regards."

"I've never met him."

"A pity. You really must make the effort some day." Riklin glanced back at the motionless body on the bed. "I will have Lady Saxbury moved tomorrow morning, and you must leave by then, as well. The House of Moons will be officially closed at noon tomorrow. All students will return to their homes at that time. The Castillans are coming to take the Lenhe girls." Then he crossed the room, feeling Meryet Alimn's frustration well up behind him.

And that, of course, signified what was wrong with this whole concept, he thought, lifting the latch. It gave even well-bred and carefully brought up Kashi daughters a mistaken idea of their importance in the scheme of things. There was no place in this carefully ordered society for women who would not do as they were bid.

Haemas wandered under the brick archway into the sun-filled courtyard, where the morning air still held the just-scrubbed freshness of the preceding night's rain. She breathed in the damp scent of rain-washed stone and flashed back to a similar day when she had stood on the wet cobblestones of the Shael'donn courtyard before Master Ellirt in order to be Tested. The full complement of Masters had looked on as he had plunged her into a green-black river of psionic power that had confirmed the full measure of her Talent and carried her forward into adulthood. She had made many decisions since then, both good and ill, but she had always forged her own path and sought to construct something tangible from her dreams.

A pang of homesickness stabbed through her, and she knew suddenly that she could not stay here any longer. Despite the threat Diren Chee posed, her real life was back in her own When, with the House of Moons and her students and Enissa—and Kevisson. She longed to see his face again, and feel the warmth that underlaid the restrained facade he showed most of the world, the quiet steel of his strength, the fierceness of his loyalty. Her stomach tightened as she remembered how angry he had been with her that day at the Council meeting. Strangely enough, when she had asked about his counterpart here, no one in this When recognized his name or had even heard of Monmart'ayn. He had never come to the Highlands, never trained at this Shael'donn—perhaps had never been born at all.

Master Ellirt walked up from behind and gripped her shoulder affectionately.

Haemas turned to face him. "I have to go back."

"You seemed restless, so I suspected as much." His sparse white hair ruffled in the soft breeze as he placed a black velvet bag in her hands and folded her fingers around it. "I've taken the liberty of having Alidale bring your—companion out to meet us at the portal, but you must promise to come back someday and share what you learn with us."

"Learn?" Haemas's fingers traced the shape of facets through the velvet.

"About the latteh crystals." A wistful smile flitted across his craggy face. "Whether they really are alive or not, and what, if anything, the ilseri have to do with them." His golden eyes gazed steadily at her as her own Ellirt's never had.

In the middle of the courtyard, there was a glint of blue as the portal's crystals flared. Then several haggard Andiine brothers carrying a litter with a bloodied man materialized within the simple frame structure. The two glanced around hurriedly, then stepped out of the portal and rushed toward the main doors.

Haemas's hands tightened around the crystal's velvet covering; it was so restful inside these brown stone walls that she had forgotten that this When, where House fought House, aided by the latteh, was much more troubled than her own.

Ellirt sighed, his faded-gold eyes following the pair and their urgent burden. "We have not had peace here in the Highlands now for a double handful of generations, and most of the trouble began after the discovery of the latteh. It represents power in its purest form. Few can resist that lure, no matter what their intentions, but no latteh lasts for long. Maybe the fighting will end when there are no more of them."

Before she could answer, Brother Alidale brought Axia into the courtyard. Her hair straggled around her ears, wild and uncombed. Her restless eyes were bloodshot and her hands had been bound before her with a leather thong.

Ellirt followed Haemas's glance. "Are you sure you don't want to leave this creature with us?"

"No, she has to go, too." Haemas felt her throat close, but there was no help for it. Axia did not belong here.

"Then at least take care." Ellirt squeezed her hands with his large-knuckled ones. "Good journey, my dear."

The breeze tugged at Axia's disheveled wheat-colored hair as Alidale halted her beside the portal. She examined Haemas's expression and a glimmer of hope crept into her wary face.

Haemas thrust the latteh into her pocket. "If you don't cooperate this time, I may lose you in the nexus."

Raising her rope-bound wrists, Axia tossed her hair back from her face. "Then cut me loose."

Alidale paled. "Lady, I—"

"Cut me loose or I won't go." A feral gleam crept into the Chee woman's dark-flecked eyes. "You can't force me into the nexus, and you do want me to go back, don't you? You're afraid to leave me here with these *sheep*." She smiled thinly. "Go ahead and leave me, if you dare. Now that I've been through the nexus myself, perhaps I can help them unravel its secrets."

Haemas stepped into the portal housing and stared down at Axia's calculating golden eyes. What was she planning behind that brittle smile?

Seizing Axia's arm, Alidale maneuvered her onto the portal platform next to Haemas. "Master Ellirt, if they're going to use the portal, they need to hurry. We had word from Bramm'ayn a few minutes ago. There's been another attack and they've asked to bring the worst of the wounded here."

"Of course." Ellirt looked up at Haemas. "You must go now, my dear. May the Light keep you safe until we meet again."

Meet again ... The breath caught in Haemas's chest and she had to turn away from his familiar craggy face. But it was better than the way they had parted before. Even if she never saw him again, she would always know Kniel Ellirt lived on in this timeline, the same cheerful, Talented man who had once shown her the way out of her troubles when she had nowhere to turn.

Throwing her mind open to the six pale-blue ilsera crystals set into the framework of the portal, she sifted through the crystalline voices until she found the one vibration that would key the nexus. She turned to Axia and asked, *Are you coming?* as the glittering array of the nexus sprang up to enclose her with chill blue fingers. The simple wood portal faded, supplanted by the awesome multiplicity of Whens radiating around her.

Actually, I wouldn't miss your reunion with Diren for the sun and all three moons put together. Axia lowered her shields, then slitted her eyes against the suddenly visible brilliant blueness. *Where in the name of Darkness is the way back?*

Let me think, Haemas countered, *or I might make another mistake.* She turned slowly, seeking the one line that would take them back to their own reality, their Truewhen, as the ilseri called it. Out of the corner of her eye, she saw Axia picking at the cord binding her wrists with her teeth.

The flat taste of fear rose in Haemas's mouth. Axia was going to make this difficult again, and all the scenes at the ends of the lines were so unfamiliar, filled with men and women she'd never seen before, strange landscapes and buildings, unfamiliar styles of ornate clothing. The Kashi Temporal Conclave had espoused the theory that the lines available to a temporal walker were governed by the walker's desires. Could it be that the choices appearing to her now were the ones she wanted most to see? In her deepest places, was she afraid to go back?

Axia unwound the cord from her wrists and threw it aside. *Now give me the crystal!*

The electric blueness writhed underneath their feet, whipping back and forth like a living thing, and Haemas felt Axia's mind reaching for the quiescent crystal. A shock ran through her as she realized Axia didn't have to touch the latteh in order to activate it; she needed only her mind for that, and she could quite easily set it right there in the nexus, making the next person to touch it with his or her naked skin its victim.

Axia, don't! She pulled the velvet bag out of her pocket and held it behind her. *You could disrupt the timeways if you activate that kind of power in here.* She felt the latteh begin to throb inside the velvet as Axia forced the random energies into the correct pattern. Desperately Haemas whirled, looking for some clue, anything that would signal the way home. The scenes shifted; spring bloomed at the end of a whole section of lines, seemingly the same day in endless variations, filled with blue-green vines and iridescent lightwings gliding across the clear green sky, graceful as wisps of smoke.

The latteh crystal abruptly phased into the discordant energy state for mind-binding and the temporal lines responded with a coruscating violence unmatched in any of her previous encounters. As they whipped back and forth, increasingly unstable, Axia shaded her eyes and dodged after Haemas across the shimmering pathways. Haemas retreated, then caught a fleeting glimpse of a scene at the end of one line that looked familiar: an icy clearing glittering under a pair of rising half moons, surrounded by leafless interlaced trees.

She stepped toward it, but Axia, squinting against the mounting blue fury of the nexus, leaped and knocked her sprawling. Haemas fell heavily, and her head shrilled as it made contact with the wildly gyrating electric-blue timelines.

Axia tore the velvet bag out of her numb fingers. *Yes!* She clasped it to her breast with exultant hands. Then the black velvet tore on the hard-edged facets and her sixth and smallest finger touched the naked crystal. She uttered a terrible screech, the only human sound Haemas had ever heard within the temporal nexus, then reeled backward and disappeared into the fountaining blue of the pathways.

Breathing raggedly, Haemas struggled up to follow her, but the other woman had left no trace. Black dots danced behind Haemas's eyes and her addled thoughts were like stubborn children, refusing to do as they were told. The nexus energies surged, then surged again, and the black dots coalesced into waves that threatened to sweep her away. There was too much out-of-balance power here; she had to flee before it overwhelmed her and she lost consciousness. Squinting, she tried to pick a pathway, but her vision had tunneled down into a brilliant pinprick of light that told her nothing. Her hands out before her, she took one step, and another, and then the third and final one. Her trembling knees gave way and she sank onto frozen ground.

The inhuman blueness faded into the endless green-black of a Highlands night, the stars above gazing down with indifferent alabaster eyes. The wind was a steady misery, sharp as a knife-thrust and straight out of the west, but as she gasped convulsively in the icy air, her head began to clear.

Shivering, she wrapped her arms around the loose summerweight tunic and staggered to her feet, trying to see through the darkness. Where was she? Because of the way she had just stumbled out of the nexus, this could be anywhere . . . or Anywhen. Then a snarl split the darkness behind her.

She turned around to face a yellow-eyed silsha gliding through the brush. She reached out with her mind and touched a comfortingly familiar mindpresence. "Shadowfoot!" She stretched her hand out to the whiskered black nose, and the beast padded up to nuzzle her hand. The brush rustled as another silsha approached, then a third, until three of them swirled around her and she stood waist-deep in sleek black fur.

As relieved as she was exhausted, she wrapped her arms around the twining necks and pressed her face into the clean-smelling musk of fur. Even though she couldn't see it from here, the House of Moons must be close.

It seemed she had come home after all.

The night wind whistled mournfully through the cold-stiffened trees, and occasionally Diren caught a winking glimpse of stars through the moving branches. Hunched beside the dying fire and pinned under the molten glare of silsha eyes, he stared angrily down at the unconscious child at his feet.

The little brat had to wake up! She had to! The damned fire was feeding on the remains of the last few crumbling sticks. Any minute now it would gutter out in the ashes, leaving him here in the suffocating night to face these beasts of Darkness all alone. After pulling a glove off, he turned the small face over again, searching for some sign that the fall had not fatally injured her.

Moaning faintly, Kisa flinched and he felt as if the sun had just come out. After gathering her into his arms, he edged toward the ummit, tied to a low branch a few feet away. One of the silshas leaped to its feet and trotted soundlessly after them, but Diren knew if he stopped now, he wouldn't have the courage to try again.

Kisa twisted in his arms as he tried to mount, and even though she threw him off balance and made him fall back to the ground, he was relieved. Breathing hard, he leaned against the ummit's warm, woolly side. The life of this child seemed to be the only thing standing between him and being silsha-fodder.

Clutching her against his chest, he tried again and this time swung up into the patched saddle. Then he jerked the ummit's head around, urging it back toward the edge of the forest and Lenhe'ayn. Dried leaves rustled behind him as the four huge silshas trailed after him, snarling low in their throats as they wove through the trees.

For the thousandth time that night, he reached for their minds and felt the same blankness he would have read from a tree or a stream. He shuddered. How was it, he wondered, that their minds were so effectively sealed against Kashi control? If the chierra people ever learned the secret of such a trick, the Highlands would be bathed in Kashi blood.

Settling Kisa's limp body over the ummit's hump, Diren began to rethink his plans. More of these bloody black devils roamed the shared grounds of Shael'donn and the House of Moons, and had been notably upset ever since Haemas Tal had disappeared. He couldn't avoid Shael'donn because Council business often called him there. And he had to be able to keep an eye on the House of Moons as well, in case Haemas Tal should reappear.

He decided to keep the girl with him for a few more days until the latteh secured his power. He touched the cold hard lump of the crystal inside his shirt and managed a smile. In those strangely cut, dull-green facets lay the key to such power as the Highlands had not seen for generations—and it was all his.

Chapter
Fifteen

The rumble of the great waterfall vibrated down through the frozen ground and then up into the twisted tree trunks, overriding every other sound, but since the blasted green-skinned creatures that had kidnapped him seemed to have no ears, Kevisson supposed it didn't bother them. Looping one arm around the massive gray-barked limb where they'd stranded him like a piece of wet laundry, he watched the lithe green bodies playing in the thundering icy river below. They seemed born to the white-foamed current, jumping and diving like water-skits.

The water here had a deep-green, jewellike quality to it, pouring down through the tumbled ice-coated rocks, then rushing away toward the distant Cholee coast. He shivered, wondering if these creatures had ever heard of the great western sea, then decided they probably had; Desalaya had been their world long before humans had intruded.

He rubbed the back of his hand over his grimy face, fighting the black weariness that dragged at him. It had been so long since he'd had any sleep that nothing seemed quite real, but he had to think this out. Why was everything of importance in his life disappearing before his eyes? In the space of a few days, he had lost not only Master Ellirt, but his place at Shael'donn, his reputation, and, worst of all, Haemas.

Haemas . . . his mind drifted. He braced his back against the trunk, seeing the high-cheekboned face framed in hair so pale that in strong sun it only hinted of gold, the golden eyes so light that they were either a mystery or an invitation, depending on her mood. He had steeled himself to patience during the years necessary for her to grow into the dazzling woman she'd promised to become, watching her study as avidly as any student he'd ever known and more diligently than most, but now that she was grown and mistress of her own fate, he was so unsure of himself that he often simply did not know what to say to her.

Why had she made him look like a fool that day before the Council? He tried to recall the angry things they had said to each other, the cold fury he had felt, but his mind summoned up instead the music of her low voice, the whisper of her unbound hair, the faint spice of her skin. He massaged his temples, then drew in a shuddering breath of icy air. Perhaps if he could sleep for just a few minutes, he told himself, he would be able to remember why they had quarreled. He rested his chin on the rough bark and his eyes sagged.

Male-brother!

Go away and let me sleep! He tried again to shield against the other's mindvoice, but no matter how hard he tried, he could not keep these irritating creatures out of his mind.

Sleep? Puzzlement washed over him. *What is sleep?*

The tree shook beneath him. Kevisson peeled his eyes open as the sinuous green fingers reached for his branch.

Better now. The native drew even with him. Water beaded on smooth skin that was as green as unripe apples. *You faded again.*

Kevisson glanced down to the river below as it boiled over jagged rocks coated with ice and sighed. *It's called sleep. Rest. It's natural for humans to sleep. I'm tired!*

Dark-green tendrils wandered over the smooth round skull as though in search of something. *I do not understand, male-brother.*

My name is Kevisson.

That does not mean anything. The creature probed his face with clammy, boneless fingers. *Have you no real name?*

That is my real name! Kevisson climbed out of its reach. His head swam and he had to blink hard to focus his eyes as he wedged himself into a higher fork.

Scampering above him, the native hung down by its slim

legs and gazed at him with bottomless black eyes. *Real names mean something, like Woodchip or Streamleap, or mine, Leafcurl.*

If these ilserin were related to the ilseri who had taught Haemas the secrets of the temporal pathways, Kevisson couldn't imagine how she had learned anything from such silly creatures. His fingers tightened around the branch at eye level. Well, he couldn't wait any longer. He had to try to get out of there. He shimmied backward down the tree, determined to escape this time.

Halfway down, his foot slipped. The rough bark scraped the hide off his fingers as he hung precariously by one hand while his legs dangled over the forest floor.

Gently, male-brother, Leafcurl cautioned him from above. *The trees and the rocks can still tear you. Your time is not yet.*

And that, Kevisson thought grimly, made as little sense as anything else these fey creatures had said to him. Trying to swing his legs back to the trunk, he lost his grip altogether and fell, landing on his back with an impact that drove the breath from his lungs and drowned his vision in red mist.

The ilserin surged out of the torrential river and gathered him to their icy, dripping chests, pressing close and cradling his head as if he were an injured child instead of a full-grown man. *Not yet, small-brother,* one crooned while several more stroked his hair with damp fingers. *But someday we will all float among the trees. Someday.*

The icy water soaked through Kevisson's shirt, making him shiver harder. The fact that they clutched him close was no help; these strange creatures had no warmth to their bodies like humans, and they never seemed to feel the savage bite of the winter cold. *Let me go!* he told them. *I have to get warm.*

Warm?

Warm?

The puzzled thought echoed from mind to mind. They seemed to have no better referents for "warm" than for "sleep." Pushing their chill hands away, Kevisson struggled to his feet and tried to get his bearings in the early morning light. The trip to this hidden place had been wild and confusing, and after that knock on his head, he had been at best only half conscious most of the way.

Before him, the river roared through the rocky gorge, dashing itself to silvery bits on the moss-speckled rocks below, glazing the surrounding brush with ice, then surging back up to race between deeply cut banks. Behind him, and on every side, the ancient true-tree forest loomed up the walls of the gorge, dark and forbidding, the gray-blue trunks often as big around as a house. Above the trees, the winter sun glimmered down palely through thin white clouds. The chill air frosted his breath as he looked from side to side. Just pick a direction, he told himself, any direction.

Wrapping his arms around his chest for warmth, he gritted his teeth and started toward what he hoped was the east, feeling that Lenhe'ayn might lie that way. The ilserin watched with puzzled black eyes, then swirled after him, pressing close and catching him in their sinuous arms.

You must stay until the mothers come. Until then, dance with us and sing! Their fingers played with his tunic. *Brother-sun has brought the light once more. Come and play!*

Not this time. Kevisson pushed them back determinedly, hard, then harder. *I have to go!*

Push! Their mirth saturated him like a cold rain. *Push and run! Push and run!* They shoved him backward, then suddenly scattered into the trees like insects fleeing a fire.

He gazed after them, his soaked shirt clinging to his chill-bumped skin and his teeth chattering. This had all the charm of reasoning with a two-year-old. The wind shrilled through the giant trees, an eerie, wildly lonely sound, and he was shivering so hard he could barely get his breath. Just walk, he told himself. The exercise would warm him up and maybe the strange emerald-skinned people of the forest would forget to come after him this time.

Rubbing his numb hands over his arms, he picked his way between the huge gnarled roots and trunks.

The largest of the three shadowfoots hugged Haemas's heels, a warm, reassuring presence, while she searched the

House of Moons with a handful of blue-white chispa-fire. The building stood cold and echoingly empty, from the second-floor students' dormitories to the kitchen and common rooms. Not one girl remained, nor any sign of recent habitation. In the grates, kindling had been laid, ready to be lit, but the clothes and personal items, even the food staples in the pantry, were gone as if no one had ever lived there at all.

Finally she stood in the doorway of her own chambers, gazing at the thick shadows, remembering the last time she had entered, weary from a day of frustrations, when Diren Chee had lain in wait. The shadowfoot nosed her leg and her hand dropped to stroke its satiny cheek. When she saw its white breath in the dimness and realized suddenly how cold she was, she opened her dresser and was relieved to find that her clothes, at least, were still there. She changed into a warm woolen tunic over soft flowing pants, then added a cloak.

Her hands trembled as she sat on the edge of the bed. Had she come to the wrong When after all? Or perhaps had she found the right timeline, but arrived too late? Had it been days or years since Diren Chee had stolen her from this room? She ran her fingers over her dresser. The wood was almost dust-free, so it could not have been as long as all that.

Enissa? she called. *Where are you?* There was no answer, not even a muted sense of her old friend, asleep or preoccupied. Then she reached for Kevisson, but he was not there, either. Perhaps he was still in the Lowlands, or, more sobering, perhaps he just didn't want to respond. They had, after all, parted very badly. The shadowfoot whuffed gently and she rested one hand on the warm black head. Through the window she could see the lights of Shael'donn, glittering through the early-morning grayness like beacons. If this was her own When, events had taken a mysterious turn after her abduction by Diren Chee and she would find no answers here. It seemed she would have to go to Shael'donn to even begin asking the questions.

Once they were safely through the Chee'ayn portal, Diren reached up and, one by one, disengaged the six pale-blue ilsera crystals that kept it active. He wanted no unexpected visitors. "Come on," he said over his shoulder to the Lenhe girl. Her mind still bound by his, she followed him down the portal steps without a word.

Chee'ayn loomed up before him, softened in the early light, looking almost presentable. No doubt, he thought, the immense old house had been spectacular in his grandfather's grandfather's time. Never since, though. It had been sliding downward in fortune since long before he and Axia had been born, and they were the last of their line. If they didn't bring prosperity to this estate again, some other waiting Lowlands family would get the chance after their deaths to make this land pay. Maybe Ketral or Ferah.

Or even Monmart.

Diren's lips twisted. He had seen the way Kevisson Monmart looked at Haemas Tal, heard all the rumors about the closeness of their "relationship." Well, after Diren had finished with him, that mud-face was going to be lucky to escape back to the Lowlands with his dark-haired life.

He heard Kisa gasp behind him, and then her footsteps stopped. "Bloody Darkness! Will you hurry up—" Diren whirled around and reached for her; then his mouth sagged.

A blurry, blue-shrouded apparition floated above the gravel path, one hand flung out, its face averted as though in fear. The hair crawled on the back of Diren's neck and his hands began to sweat. It was ghostly and unreal, brightening, fading, then brightening again as if something were caught half in this world and half without. He swallowed convulsively and backed away as the bizarre figure sharpened into focus. It was Axia.

Her face was terrible, contorted and yet vacant, surrounded by a blueness brighter than sunlight on glare ice, so intense that he could barely look at it. His sister turned and for a second met his eyes. Her mouth worked as if she were speaking.

"What—what—" Kisa stared almost blindly at the floating woman, her small body rigid with fear.

Diren extended his hand, but his fingers passed through the wraith with only a faint electric tingle. Axia seemed to shriek soundlessly, then the image shuddered and winked out, leaving behind only the frigid morning air. Diren brought his trembling hand down to eye level.

"Was that the—the Light?" Kisa's voice was very small, then she blinked at him as if seeing him for the first time. "Who—who are you?" Tears welled up in her eyes as she gazed fearfully around the deserted, snow-drifted grounds. "I'm cold—and I want to go home!"

Irritated, he realized the shock of the apparition had loosened his hold on her mind. Taking a deep breath, he reached for the link again, but she darted back into the bare limbs of a whip-willow, managing for the moment to shield him out. Her lip trembled. "What happened to all the trees?" Then she cocked her head, as if examining him, and the fear drained from her face, replaced by a glimmer of hope. "Are you—are you my—father?"

Diren started to deny it, then hesitated. Controlling her was draining his energy, but he still might want to return to the Lowlands in search of more lattehs and she could be useful. He made himself smile and extended his hand. "Of course I am. Why else would I have brought you here?"

Kisa blinked at him, her golden eyes standing out huge in her tear- and dirt-stained face, then finally took his hand.

The silsha pressed against Haemas's legs, comfortingly warm, as she strided across the snow-covered grounds toward Shael'donn. Its company was one of the few things holding her together while she tried to make sense of these bewildering changes.

At the front entrance, the great door swung inward before she could touch the handle. The gap-toothed boy on door-duty gaped and she caught the backwash of his half-shielded shock. She glanced at the black silsha looming at her heels. "For Light's sake, he won't hurt you."

The boy's cheeks reddened. "It's not the beast, Lady, not really. Lord High Master Senn said—everyone said—that you must be—" He probed her face with worried eyes. "—dead."

The wind gusted, rattling the rafters and driving its chill

deep into her bones. She shivered, then silently pushed past him into the warm hall and stamped the snow off her boots. The boy backed into the doorjamb as the silsha slid in behind her, sinuous as a fish. He watched it helplessly, then threw his shoulder against the massive door to shut it against the blustering wind. "Please wait here until one of the Masters can see you."

Haemas wearily pushed her hood back from her hair. "That's not necessary. I can find my way."

"No, Lady!" The boy swallowed hard. "I'm sorry, but Master Senn *said* we were not to let any more womenfolk in without an escort, especially—" He broke off in embarrassment.

Haemas recalled the calculating look in Riklin Senn's eyes that day at the Council of Twelve when she had spoken out for Kevisson's claim on the High Mastership. "He said *I* wasn't to come in, is that it?"

The boy nodded tightly.

She took a deep breath. "Never mind—I'm sorry, I've forgotten your name."

"Jallan Falt, Lady."

"Yes, Jallan." She gazed over his bright-gilt head and down the hallway. The green carpet was the same, and the dark paneling, lustrous from generations of small, trailing hands, but the familiar feel to this beloved place had fled. She might as well have been in a vastly altered Otherwhen, where fate had taken a different turn at some crucial branching and nothing was the same. She sighed. "Can you at least tell me if Master Monmart is back from Lenhe'ayn yet?"

The boy glanced up at her, his eyes wide. "No, they brought the healer back yesterday afternoon, but they said Master Monmart refused to come."

For a second, she glimpsed a pale, barely breathing face in his mind. Stricken with dread, she gripped his shoulder and made him meet her eyes. "What healer?"

"Healer Saxbury, Lady." He bit his lip. "They say she won't live. She helped my mum through her last birthing, too. Mum said no one else could have done what she did. It's not fair."

"Nothing's fair about life, Jallan," a deep voice said.

Haemas glanced up from the boy's freckled face into the heavyset countenance of Riklin Senn. Withdrawing her hand, she straightened and stared back with all the directness of Dervlin Tal's daughter. "Master Senn."

"*Lord High* Master Senn, actually, but then . . ." His narrowed eyes examined her as if she were a mare up for sale. "You've been—away, haven't you?"

She wondered suddenly if Senn had known anything of Diren Chee's plans. After all, Chee had supported this oaf's claim before the Council for no reason she had been able to understand. "Jallan tells me that Enissa has been hurt. Where has she been taken?"

"A bad business, that." Senn shook his massive head. "I can't imagine what got into Monmart, although I suppose in the end breeding will tell."

Haemas glanced at Jallan's pale face, unwilling to believe what Senn was implying. The Kevisson she knew would never have hurt anyone, much less Enissa. Jallan flushed and looked away.

"Why don't you come into my office, Lady Haemas?" With surprising smoothness for a man so large, Senn started to interpose his body between her and the boy, then drew back as the silsha bared its ivory fangs and snarled. "If you'll put the beast outside, I'll fill you in on the sad events of the last few days."

But at the word "office," Haemas had flashed back to the last time she had been in that room, hardly a month ago, when she and Ellirt had sat together discussing the curriculum for the House of Moons, a fire blazing comfortably in his fireplace, the leather chairs settled in the exact same spot as the first time she had ever come into his room, his sightless eyes, as always, fixed unerringly on her face . . .

Not there. Her fingers clenched. Anywhere but there. After meeting Ellirt's counterpart in the Otherwhen, her old friend felt both closer and more lost to her than ever. Resting her hand on the silsha's head, she ignored the arm Senn held out to her. "Just tell me where Enissa is."

"You can't see her now." Senn edged closer, his eyes resting uneasily on the silsha. "Lising and Nevarr are attending her."

"She's *here*?"

Jallan nodded soberly. "South Wing, Lady," he said before Senn could silence him with a scowl.

South Wing. The Healer's Wing, where Enissa had once trained under the disapproving eyes of the other healers, honing her natural talents, while Haemas planned for the House of Moons. Dimly she was aware that Senn was still talking to her, but she brushed past his velvet-clad chest and took the stairs two at a time, opening her shields enough to listen for Enissa's mind, trusting the shadowfoot at her heels to prevent any interference.

All around her, she felt the school stirring, boys stumbling sleepily down the halls toward steaming bowls of zeli porridge in the dining hall, Masters emerging from their chambers in North Wing, students on cooking duty grumbling—everything as it ought to be, except that everyone she cared for most was dead or in grave danger or missing.

The halls had never seemed so endless when she'd lived and studied here. She stopped and tried to remember which healers were attending Enissa—Lising and . . . Nevarr? Closing her eyes, she reached for Havil Nevarr's mental pattern, never having known Lising well enough to recognize him that way.

She caught a glimmer of the healer, one floor up and half a wing away. Catching her intentions, the silsha bounded up the narrow stairs before her, growling deep in its throat. She followed it, then hurried down the long hall until she reached Nevarr's location.

After wrenching the door open, she saw the two healers standing over the bedside, gazing down at a still form buried in thick quilts. Nevarr's sandy head turned to look at her in dismay. "Lady Haemas! But—"

Bidding the shadowfoot stay in the hall, Haemas slipped between the two men to Enissa's side. Touching her friend's cheek, she was shocked to find her skin so cold. "What—happened?"

"Mindburn." Lising's voice was short. "One of the worst cases I've ever seen."

And Lising had been at Senn'ayn with her on that terrible day twelve years ago, Haemas thought numbly, attending the survivors of the Temporal Conclave where so many had died. Laying her hand on Enissa's chilled forehead, she closed her eyes, reaching deep into the still mind for some indication that her friend might know her. *Enissa?* she said softly, then louder. *Enissa?*

Nevarr took her arm. "She can't hear you, Lady Haemas. I'm afraid it's just a matter of time now."

"No!" Wrenching away from him, she gazed down at Enissa's still white face, her eyes hot and tearless. "How—" She stopped, forcing herself to control her voice. "How did this happen?"

"We're not sure." Lising's gaze was bleak. "She and Monmart returned to Lenhe'ayn, supposedly to find some evidence that would clear him of Myriel Lenhe's death. The next day, Leric Rald called up here for help, and we brought her back like this." He folded his arms.

"Myriel Lenhe's death?" she echoed numbly.

Nevarr crossed to a porcelain basin on the nightstand and poured out a measure of water. "She died the night that Monmart went down to Lenhe'ayn. And when an inquiry was conducted into her death, Monmart attacked Riklin Senn in front of everyone—tried to choke the life out of him and might have succeeded, too, if they'd been alone."

Haemas's throat felt dry and achingly tight. "He couldn't have done that."

"Only two days ago, I saw him attack Senn with my own eyes." Nevarr soaped his hands, rinsed, then reached for a towel. "He was completely out of control."

She clenched her hands by her sides to keep them from shaking. One thing at a time, she told herself. First take care of Enissa—then she could find out what had happened to Kevisson. "All right, what can we do for her?"

"I'm afraid there's nothing that can be done." Lising's

weary eyes met hers. "I only wish there were, but the damage is too great. All we can do is make her comfortable."

She glanced in shock from Lising's stony face to Nevarr's. "You can't just give up."

"We can't do anything else, unless . . ." Lising scowled and turned away.

"Unless what?" she demanded.

"Unless you know some trick of healing that we don't." Nevarr threw the towel down in disgust.

Some trick . . . Haemas turned back to Enissa and fumbled for the limp, cold hand under the layered covers. The latteh could heal, but it was lost in the nexus with Axia.

"How long?" she heard her voice ask calmly from far away. "How long does she have?"

"A day, perhaps two."

Gently she replaced Enissa's hand beneath the quilts. "Look after her," she said. "I'll be back as soon as I can."

"Lady Haemas, don't be foolish!" Nevarr called after her as she ran out the door. "There's nothing anyone can do!"

But there might be, she thought, if only doing it didn't make her as unscrupulous as Diren Chee.

Chapter
Sixteen

Kisa disliked the vast, drafty kitchen full of unswept crumbs and dust mites that would have sent her chierra nurse, Dorria, into an angry cleaning frenzy. She craned her neck, taking in the grimy windows, the crooked cabinet doors—many hanging from a single rusty hinge—and the feeling of abandonment that hung over the entire house. She swung her feet back and forth above the worn stone, studying this stranger clad in black who was her father. "When can we fetch Adrina?"

"Who?" He looked up from the meager breakfast of cold roast savok and coarse brown bread. His hollow-cheeked face made his fierce golden eyes stand out. His hair was as bright-gold as the new coin her mother had given her when last they had gone to a fair, much brighter than her mother's or grandfather's.

"My sister, Adrina." Kisa poked the meat with a finger. It was nasty stringy stuff, she decided, and pushed her chipped plate away.

"Not now." Her father chewed, his expression distant. "I have too much to do." He speared another bite of roast.

Kisa picked up the chunk of hard bread and turned it over in her fingers. "Where's the butter and jam?"

He glanced at her, his gold eyebrows knotting together over the sharp nose. His eyes glittered like an iced-over field after a winter storm. "There isn't any."

At home, she'd always had steaming porridge for breakfast, topped with yellow pats of butter made fresh from milk that came from one of the finest herds of Old dairy cattle to be found anywhere in the Lowlands, her grandfather had always said. And there had been tall mugfuls of chilled milk and all the honey and yellow callyt jam she wanted. Her chin trembled as she remembered the sweetness of callyt on her tongue and her mother's ready smile across the bountiful breakfast table. "I want to go home."

His eyes drilled her. "Stop that sniveling and eat."

Laying her hands in her lap, she pressed her lips together. She would not cry! she told herself severely. For years she had longed for a father, and now she had one—so what if he was not as she had expected? Mother had always insisted nothing in life was ever perfect. Why, hadn't Mother wanted sons who could inherit Lenhe'ayn, when she'd borne Kisa and Adrina? If Kisa had been a boy, surely her father would have been proud of her and would have come for her long ago, instead of waiting until now.

Suddenly she felt his mind hammering at her, pushing at her shields, insisting. Shocked, she watched her hand reach for the stale bread without her willing it. She broke away from him and stared back with frightened eyes. Mother had never used her Talent to force her or her sister and brother to do anything. It was wrong! Mother had always insisted upon that. The three of them were never to do that to anyone, not even the chierra servants, with whom it would have been ever so easy.

"Eat your breakfast or I'll make you." His voice was threaded with quiet menace.

Her heart racing, Kisa picked up the bread and managed a cold, tasteless nibble. In her short life, she had sometimes been lonely or sad, but she suddenly realized that she had seldom been truly frightened—until now.

Haemas crunched through the ankle-deep crust of snow. The silsha prowled at her heels, and she was comforted by its daunting presence. Three of the forest predators resided with her up here in the Highlands, but this particular silsha was the one that the ilseri had sent to her so long ago in the Great Forest, and the bond between them was especially strong. It was twelve years older now, a length of time that would have aged a horse or a dog, yet it was as lithe and vigorous as the first time she'd seen it.

The grounds between Shael'donn and the House of Moons lay eerily quiet, with the odd hush of a lull between violent storms, and the air was so cold that Haemas felt she could have reached out and snapped a portion of it in two between her hands. Ice glittered on the spiny branches of the surrounding trees and patchy gray clouds scudded overhead. She pulled her cloak closer as she trudged toward the two schools' shared portal. Questions chased each other round and round through her head like barrets playing in a tree. What were the latteh crystals, really? Were they alive in some way, as she had seemed to sense, or some sort of ilseri artifact? If they were alive, why were they found only in ilseri pools? But perhaps the most sobering thought of all was what Riklin Senn and the other Masters at Shael'donn would be lawfully bound to do if they caught her at Enissa's bedside with something so blatantly forbidden as a latteh.

She shivered in the icy stillness, her head spinning like a child's top. Well, before she could do anything else, she had to go to Windsign and Summerstone, the ilseri who had first befriended and taught her all those years ago, and learn what they could tell her on this matter.

Grasping the portal's outside rail, she stepped onto the staging platform, then watched in surprise as the persistent shadowfoot flowed up the steps. She laid her hand on the black-furred head and stared down into the inscrutable yellow eyes. The silshas, although fond of her, were usually wary of other humans, but this one had followed her in and out of buildings all morning with hardly the flick of an ear. It seemed to radiate an uneasy vigilance. Did it somehow sense that she was in danger?

She slid an arm around the sleek powerful neck, maintaining contact in order to transport it with her. Opening her shields, she aligned her mind with the voice of the crystals, activating them in the pattern learned long ago: *north . . . south*—she felt each crystal warm in turn—*east . . . west . . . above . . . below*. At the sequence's completion, the world around her dissolved and she flashed through the silent gray betweenness, reaching not for the pattern of another portal but the remembered voices of ilsera crystals set into the rim of a certain secluded ilseri pool.

The silsha snarled softly as they emerged in a wintery stillness only slightly less cold than the one they had just left behind in the Highlands. Ice crystals pinged as the trees shifted in the wind. Haemas glimpsed patches of leaden sky overhead, somber and brooding, through the interwoven true-tree branches. When last she had been there, the grove had been alive with blue-leaved branches and rich with the scent of water and warm moist soil. She knelt at the edge of the white-walled pool and peered down through the thin rime of ice.

Moonspeaker, why have you come? The ilseri voice rang with the strength of stone struck by a hammer.

Summerstone? Haemas turned her head, hoping to see the familiar green-skinned form, although the natives often dissipated their mass too thinly to be visible.

A gust of wind rattled the frozen tree branches. *It has begun again.*

What? Haemas asked, but only the wind moaning through the trees answered. She shivered, feeling suddenly alone in this place as she never had before. The shadowfoot stood motionless on the other side of the half-frozen pool, gazing at her as if, within the space of a single breath, she had become someone else—and unwelcome. Doubt burned in its yellow eyes, along with distrust. *What's wrong?* she asked Summerstone. *What have I done to displease you?*

Your kind, not you. Another mindvoice, less harsh, more sorrowful. *Still, it will not matter in the end.*

It was Windsign. Haemas hesitated, then asked, *Does it have anything to do with the latteh?* She brought forth the image of the irregular dull-green crystal in her mind, remembering the feel of it in her hand. *What do you know about such crystals? Are they really found in your pools?*

A vague green haze settled downward through the branches. *What you speak of are not crystals.*

Then what are they? Haemas stepped back as a second greenness formed in the air above the pool.

The future. The green mist contracted, coalescing into the roughly humanoid shape of an adult female ilseri garbed in flowing white. *We thought your kind had finally forgotten.*

The future? she echoed, realizing what Windsign's words must mean, and understanding at the same time that if she was right, the ilseri would never allow her to take a latteh back to the Highlands.

Our children. Summerstone's body solidified and her bottomless black eyes stared at Haemas. *What you think of as latteh crystals are First Ones, the beginning form of our kind, and now two have been stolen from their birthing pool. If they are not returned, they will die.*

The clouds had thickened, further obscuring the sun. Kevisson stared hopelessly at the closely set trees that surrounded him on all sides; each one looked identical to the next. Scratched and aching, light-headed from lack of sleep and hunger, he could not delude himself any longer. He had no idea which direction he was traveling.

He pushed his way through another thicket, and without warning the forest grew abruptly colder. The bark snapped and popped. His breath froze in his lungs and his heart lurched sluggishly. He doubled over, teeth chattering, a vague impression skirting the edges of his mind that something was approaching. "Who's there?" he called through clenched teeth. "What do you want?"

A vast, chill presence settled over him, threading through brain and blood and bone, leaving him huddled in a knot on the forest floor with his shivering muscles locked, so numb that he could not feel any part of his body. The cold presence wanted, no, *demanded* something, perhaps some*one*, but he could not make out what. Blackness ate at his vision; he watched as the ice crystals in his breath plumed out white before him, slow, then more slowly, finally ceasing altogether.

As abruptly as it had come, the coldness withdrew. Kevisson's diaphragm convulsed and he drew in lungfuls of icy air. His fingers began to tingle painfully, followed by his face and toes. He forced himself to pile a handful of twigs and run through the ritual to start a fire. A tiny spark flared, fierce and golden. He bent to blow on it, then fed it with dry leaves and larger twigs until it was burning strongly. He drew in the welcome scent of woodsmoke and held his palms out to the blessed heat, feeling as if now he might survive.

Danger, male-brother! Run! Suddenly the branches around him were alive with agile green bodies that swirled down and scattered his fire.

Where in the name of Darkness had they come from? Kevisson could have sworn he had left them behind hours ago. "Go away!" He struggled to regain his feet, but an army of green arms wrestled him facefirst to the frozen ground.

We cannot play this game anymore. Four-fingered hands gently plucked dead leaves out of his hair. *The Oldest says you must go back to the river.*

They hauled Kevisson to his feet and he tried to push them away. "I have to go home. Can you understand that? This isn't a goddamned game!"

A wave of sorrow from the alien minds washed unexpectedly over him, deep as the grief he'd felt standing before his father's funeral pyre. Startled, he stared into the shiny black eyes of the single ilserin that imprisoned him in its arms.

You must give them back, male-brother. Absently the native patted his cheek with limber, too-long fingers. *The mothers are angry, and even the Oldests know what you have done.*

Kevisson concentrated, struggling to shield the aching sorrow out of his mind, but as before, his defenses seemed worthless with these creatures. Their projected sadness overwhelmed him, tearing at him until he would have thrown himself off a cliff to end it if they had permitted it.

The ilserin pulled him back toward the fierce green river with its immense, thundering falls. Dizzy with cold and hunger and sorrow, he let them take him, not even watching where his feet fell.

* * *

Haemas huddled against the leeward side of a giant sturdy tree, avoiding the worst of the stinging sleet that came in spurts with the north wind. The grove was empty now. Windsign and Summerstone had withdrawn, and even the faithful shadowfoot had stalked off into the brush. She scuffed her heel in a drift of dead leaves, thinking that she should probably return to Shael'donn to sit with Enissa. If she could not help her friend, at least she should not leave her to die alone.

The pattern begins now again and will continue until broken by one side or the other. The mindvoice startled her; it was huge and unfamiliar, laced with an icy, dark rage that she had not even known an ilseri was capable of feeling.

What pattern? She craned her head, looking for a hint of movement among the stiff, gray-barked branches.

They have called me because alone of all the ilserlara, the Last Ones, I remember.

A feeling of immensity crept over Haemas, as if she had walked under the boughs of an incredibly ancient tree or beneath the sheer face of an overhanging cliff. *Who are you?*

Frostvine, last of the hunted ones.

Cold gripped her, a heavy, biting chill that seemed to halt the blood flowing in her veins. She huddled into her cloak, shivering violently. *Hunted by the Kashi?*

The coldness intensified, settling down through the trees like an impenetrable fog of ice. *Long ago, in a time even before mine, your kind discovered the birthing pools and our First Ones who must lie there until the Change.* The throbbing mindvoice was vast, seeming to come from everywhere at once. *When the First Ones are taken from the pool, they no longer grow and, depending on how near they are to the Change, eventually die.*

Beloved children, crumbling into dust . . . never to grow into nimble ilserin and play among the trees of the Great Forest . . . never to join their sister ilseri . . . never to know the freedom of the Oldests. Haemas shuddered as Frostvine drove the agonizing images deep into her mind: countless generations of ilseri children never born because humans, Kashi, had removed them from their nurturing birthwaters and used them as tools, as if they were no more than unknowing rocks or sticks.

Enough! A faint glimmer of Summerstone's warmth seeped through the mantle of ice. *This small sister has always done her best to speak between our two kinds.*

Which has availed us naught. Frostvine's tone was caustic. *The destruction begins again and even she can see where it must end. How many of our First Ones will be left by the next Interim?*

The air stung like ice crystals in Haemas's lungs as she clung to the twisted trunk. She thought suddenly of the Otherwhen where she had found Ellirt again. What was it the old master had said to her about the ilseri? *They're just a myth. No one has ever actually seen one.* In his timeline, the latteh was still used for both good and evil as it had been for countless generations, but very few were found, and no one had seen an ilseri for so long that the brothers of Shael'donn didn't believe they had ever existed.

Her fingers tightened on the rough bark. If the pools were once again robbed, the ilseri would die out here as surely as they already had in the other Ellirt's timeline.

The cold lessened slightly. *It understands more than I thought possible.* Frostvine's all-encompassing voice was more muted than before. *You chose better than I believed. Perhaps there is still a chance to avert the coming destruction.*

De—struction? Haemas was so cold that it was agony even to try to think.

Of either your kind or ours. In the working out of this pattern, we cannot both continue. One kind or the other must end.

What—can I—do? Haemas forced herself to form the thought.

Return the two Youngests to their pool. Stop the male-thing from stealing more.

I will—do—my best. Her teeth chattered uncontrollably.

A hint of warmth wrapped around Haemas and she sensed the familiar thought-presence of Windsign. *The First Ones can remain out of the pools for only a limited amount of time with-*

out irreversible damage. The warmth intensified into a soothing golden glow. Feeling crept back into Haemas's face, fingers, and toes. *The Youngest that was taken only a day ago was very close to the Change and will be safe for only a few more days at most. The other has even less time before it loses its potential to enter the Change.*

Haemas drew the warmer air into her lungs. The first Youngest had to be the latteh that Diren Chee had used to assault her, the one that had disappeared with Axia into the nexus. She had no idea whether it could ever be recovered, and she could only speculate that Chee had taken the other one, too.

Rubbing her hands over her arms, she stood. The bare trees loomed over her, stark and gray against the murky sky. *I believe there is only one person involved with these thefts. I will go to him, and then I will speak to the Council to prevent more Kashi coming down to take the lattehs from the pools.*

No, small sister, you must not. Summerstone's mindvoice seemed to come from just over her shoulder, and Haemas turned to find the other ilseri had finally coalesced into solid form. *If any of your kind knows how to enslave the First Ones, then we are in danger. You must not tell your males, or the Youngests will never be safe.*

Haemas shivered again, from the chill within as much as the cold without. They wanted her to search for Axia and Diren Chee, but not to enlist anyone's aid, when even the thought of Diren Chee armed with another latteh made her more afraid than she wanted to admit.

This time, I will do whatever I must to protect the future, Frostvine's immense mindvoice said. *I will not let this come again.*

The hair prickled on the back of Haemas's neck. *What do you mean?*

It has never been given to our kind to be predatory. Frostvine's words reverberated through her head. *Not even we ilserlara, who, with our last form, come into more power than your kind will ever know. Ilseri have always fled when threatened, never able to shape our minds for any form of resistance. But since my final Change, my memories have made me different. I remember before, when your kind plundered our pools, wielding our young as crude, unthinking weapons, and I see how I might employ my strength to prevent this from happening again.*

If the Youngests are not returned, I will do whatever I must. This world belonged to ilseri first, and this time we will not be driven to the edge of nothingness without fighting back.

Haemas breathed on her hands to warm them. *It may take some time to find the one responsible.*

The ilserin are holding the male-thing, Frostvine said. *I have tried to question it, but, as always with your males, it cannot hear my voice.*

Ilserin? Haemas turned back to Summerstone's lithe green-skinned form.

The children, as you would say, our—sons, the Second Ones.

Summerstone and Windsign had explained to her long ago that all ilseri children were born male, then became female after mating, but Haemas had never seen a male. *Where are they, the—ilserin? Are they far?*

Nothing is ever far for an Oldest. The overwhelming voice reverberated through her head as if she were trapped inside a huge bell. Then Frostvine's icy presence swept back over her, drowning all sight and sensation of the winter-bound glade. She had a flash of featureless gray betweenness, then found herself standing on the bank of an immense green river that roared down from a crown of rocks to dash itself against the tumbled boulders below.

The gorge had a feeling of primordial beauty, as if no human had ever walked here. It was a place of ancient trees, huge as Highlands houses, twisted by the wind into spreading shapes. Light-headed from the abrupt transfer, Haemas steadied herself against the trunk of a gray-barked giant.

This is the place of the Second Ones. Frostvine's chill presence hovered near. *Tell the male-thing to give back the First Ones or I will deal with your kind as I must.*

Movement stirred in the canopy of branches on the other side of the rushing river, and she saw the trees swarming with green-skinned creatures. Trembling, she thought of Diren Chee's overconfident face, then put away her fear. She could not afford to be afraid. Too much depended on her now.

Come down, Frostvine commanded, and the green-skinned males jumped lightly out of the trees, glancing across the river with bright black eyes. Then a last pair of young males climbed down, supporting a stumbling figure between them. Haemas edged closer to the riverbank, trying to see. The other did look to be human, but the hair wasn't right, nothing like the bright shade of gold that Diren had inherited from his Chee bloodlines. She spoke to Frostvine. *I must cross the river.*

A chill grayness swept over her—

—and she stood on the opposite bank, knee-deep in tangled weeds doubled down to the ground by a glaze of ice from the river's spray, the hesitant ilserin so close that she could have stretched out her fingers and touched their smooth emerald skin.

The ragged figure supported between two natives raised its haggard face and tried to focus. Then it struggled erect and reached a six-fingered Kashi hand out to her. She met the hand with both of her own, human warmth against warmth, surprised and relieved. "What are you doing here?" she shouted over the thundering roar of the falls, then stared in shock as Kevisson's eyes rolled back and he wilted to the frozen ground.

Chapter Seventeen

The afternoon had finally turned fine and clear, the green sky gleaming like a finely cut emerald. Diren motioned the Lenhe girl onto the portal platform. The wind gusted, whistling through the portal's eaves, and she frowned as she struggled with a frayed cloak of Axia's that swathed her from chin to heels and dragged on the steps. Over her shoulder, the stand of pines caught his eye, swaying dark green against the lighter sky. He could smell the clean tang of the needles even all the way over here. The muscles in his jaw tightened. That grove had been Chee'ayn's pride and joy, back when the Chees had still known pride as part of their lives. No matter what it took, he would see that this neglected House was returned to its former glory.

Ignoring the way Kisa followed his every move with her eyes, he painstakingly replaced the ilsera crystals in the portal housing. He didn't like to leave the portal active, but it couldn't be helped. Chierra servants could not replace the set properly; they could not distinguish one attuned crystal from another, and the crystals had to be set in the proper sequence. It took a trained Kashi to tell them apart. Axia was the only person who could have done it for him, and she—

He flashed back to her glimmering face, trapped and terrified, suspended in a brilliant blue mist above his head. His palms went sweaty and he shivered in the chill air. What in the name of Darkness had happened after she'd entered the timeways? He had to find the Tal woman and learn if there was any way to release his sister.

"Where are we going?" Kisa asked, wrestling the bulky cloak with her small fingers.

"Shael'donn." Diren stepped up beside her and twitched his own cloak more closely around his shoulders. "I have business there." His gloved hand traced the hard-angled shape of the latteh inside his pocket, already set for the next person foolish enough to touch it with his or her bare skin.

Kisa gazed up at him, worry pouring from her loosely shielded mind in waves, but she said nothing, letting the fiction stand that he was her father.

Which, fortunately, he was not. Diren turned his face away from the shivering child. The last thing he had ever been interested in was fathering a brat on some Lowlands woman, good-looking or not. *Open your shields,* he told the child. *I'll transport us both.* Activating each crystal in turn, he attuned his mind to the similar set at Shael'donn, concentrated—then opened his eyes on a sunny but chill afternoon on the other side of the Highlands, at least three days' hard ride from Chee'ayn.

At his side, the girl studied the huge brown stone edifice of Shael'donn, then turned to look over her shoulder at the smaller House of Moons. "Are we going to get Adrina now?"

"What?" For a moment, he couldn't think what she was talking about. Then he remembered there was another Lenhe child, even younger than this one. "Not now," he said brusquely.

The young green-gold eyes seemed to accuse, staring a hole straight through him, but she said nothing. She merely hiked up the cumbersome cloak and stepped down from the portal onto the crushed-gravel path. Diren followed her, casting his mind around the quiet, snow-dusted grounds for some signs of the silshas or even Haemas Tal herself. He sensed nothing, though, except a tree barret skittering around in the shadows and a few circling Iraels in the clear green sky overhead.

The two of them walked the short distance to Shael'donn in silence, their feet crunching on the snowy gravel. At the main door, Diren nodded to the boy on duty. "We've come to see Healer Saxbury."

The youngster, a healthy crop of freckles sprinkled across his face, shook his head. "I'm sorry, Lord Chee, but Master Lising left word that she's in a very bad way."

"Well, of course, she can have no *regular* visitors." Diren pushed the cloak impatiently back off his shoulders. "But the Lord of Chee'ayn can hardly be described as that."

The boy paled. "No, sir. If you'll just let me call Master Lising or—"

Blocking Kisa's view with his body, Diren used his gloved hand to pull the latteh out of his shirt, then quickly touched it to the boy's forehead. *You will call no one. You will remember no one coming to see Healer Saxbury this afternoon except Kevisson Monmart. Do you understand that? Kevisson Monmart.*

Rigid with shock, the boy stared glassily ahead. Casually Diren withdrew the latteh and replaced it in his shirt, resetting it with his mind even as he did so. Who knew but that they might meet more students or Masters on their way to Saxbury's room who would also require a certain amount of *persuasion*.

The wintery glade wavered in and out of focus and the grinding roar went on and on, never varying in its intensity. Kevisson felt his eyes blinking, so he knew they were open, and yet for some reason he could not make sense of anything. Fingers stroked his brow and he pushed at them weakly, shuddering. Why couldn't the damned ilserin leave him alone? No matter what the green-skinned idiots thought, he hadn't taken anything!

No, it's all right, a familiar mindvoice murmured.

"Haemas?" he said, but his words were lost in the immense thunder of the falls. He realized he was stretched out on the frozen ground, his head pillowed on something warm and yielding. His fingers moved, brushing the softness of the inside of an ebari-wool cloak that had been tucked over him, and he smelled the smoke of a blazing fire close by. It might be her, he thought, but he couldn't focus his eyes enough to be sure. The light here under the trees seemed to refract in odd directions, distorting the face that looked down at him as if he were seeing it underwater. Perhaps he was just dreaming again or had even lost his mind completely. He shifted restlessly, trying to raise his head.

It is me. Warm fingers turned his face to meet her gaze.

He blinked, then blinked again, hard. Braided hair slipped over the figure's shoulder, the golden strands as pale as the third moon gliding through a star-studded night. Haemas leaned over him and the warmth of her mindpresence surrounded him, a comforting silvery glow that he would have known anywhere.

"Where in the name of Light have you been?" he demanded, then, without thinking, his arms closed around her neck and he found himself kissing her fervently, as he had never dared before, as if she were air itself and he were drowning for the lack of her.

She kissed him back, her arms twined around his shoulders, trembling, mingled anxiety and relief spilling through her shields. Finally she sat back and smiled wanly. *You had me so worried!*

He tried to sit up, but the trees spun sideways and threatened to take him off the edge of the world with them. His vision fuzzed, and sometime later he realized that his head was pillowed in her lap. He gazed up through dark-gray, bare tree limbs interlaced so thickly that the leaden green of the sky could just be glimpsed between them. Something overhead rustled, and then supple green bodies skittered effortlessly through the branches. "Not again!" he muttered hoarsely, and struggled to right himself before they could drag him off into the trees.

No, you're safe, Haemas said, but Kevisson remembered limber green hands hauling him through the trees like a piece of baggage, being so cold he would never get warm again, fearing that he would never get home.

He rolled over, fighting to push himself to his feet. "You don't know what they're like. We have to—"

She pressed her hands to his temples and willed him to meet her luminous pale-gold eyes. They burned at him like distant suns, made for some other world, where love had its season and haste and fear were unknown. *The ilserin won't bother you now.* She seemed wiser for some reason, older, more assured. The tension melted out of his arms and legs and he sagged against her.

She pulled the warm cloak back across his shoulders. *They didn't mean to be cruel. They just had no idea of how to care for a human.*

They keep saying I—took something. Unutterably weary, he closed his eyes. A spinning darkness seemed to be drawing him down.

Unfortunately, they can't tell one human male from another. Her arms encircled him, comforting and human. *I'm not sure how old they are chronologically, but mentally they're very young.*

For a while, he drifted on the edge of sleep, soaking up the crackling warmth of the fire and the balm of her touch, but there was something that nagged at him, something he ought to . . .

Then he remembered. *Where—where have you been?* He rubbed his aching head fretfully. *I Searched until I found you on the other side of the Highlands, but then something or someone shattered the link.*

It was Diren Chee. She pressed a cool ovoid into his hand. *Try to eat a little of this to settle your stomach. I'm sorry I haven't anything hot, but the poor ilserin would be horrified if they saw us eat animal flesh.*

Chee? His fingers curled around a purple nasai and brought it to his lips. *The Council?*

The Council had nothing to do with it. He had some plan to use the timeways. She raised her head, and her pale-gold braid of hair tickled his neck. *Do you feel strong enough to go back?*

Back. He turned that word over in his mind, chewing it as slowly as the bite of fruit in his mouth. *Back . . . Enissa!*

Yes. Despair glimmered in her pale eyes for a moment. *She's very weak. I thought I could find—something down here to help her, but it seems . . .* Her mindvoice trailed away tightly. Then she took a deep breath. *It isn't possible.*

Swallowing the mouthful of fruit, he attempted to sit up again, this time making it almost all the way before the dizziness set in. Hunching forward, he pressed both hands to his forehead and fought it.

Haemas pressed another wedge of the sticky purple fruit into his hand. *Here, eat a little more.*

His stomach rolled sickly, but he made himself eat another bite. Juice dribbled down his chin and he dabbed at it with the back of his hand.

Do you think you can stand now? Rising to her feet in a single graceful motion, Haemas held her hands out to him.

He reached for her, then shivered as the forest seemed to grow suddenly heavier with a chill brooding presence that he could neither see nor name.

Haemas paled and backed away. *But he has to know.* She looked sharply up into the overhanging tree branches as if speaking to someone. *He's not like the others. He's a good man. He can help.*

Kevisson struggled to his feet, trying to balance against residual dizziness. *What is it?*

Her upturned face grew ashen, making her seem older, weighing her down in some way. "But I don't know if I can *do* it by myself," she said, her words all but lost in the background roar of the falls. Her eyes closed, and she seemed to strain against something.

Kevisson touched her face and found her cheek as cold as the icy river. *Is it the ilseri? What's wrong?*

Haemas gazed at him with the same lost, bleak expression he'd seen the first time they'd met, years ago. *My father is dead!* she had insisted, falsely believing she had killed him herself. What could have happened now to match the depth of that old despair?

Staring over his head at the pounding river, she seemed to pull herself together, standing taller and straighter, certainly taller than half the men in the High Houses. *We have to—go back to the Highlands, and there are some things I must do that I can't—explain.* Kevisson heard tears in her voice, yet her cheeks were dry. *I need you to help if you can, without asking why. Do you—do you think you can do that?*

Startled by the urgency of her request, he hesitated. Then she added, *Because if you can't, I'll have to do it alone.*

Suddenly he wanted to protect her as he had all those years ago, make the world better for her, smooth away the rough edges and give her peace and security again. But she wasn't a child anymore; she was a woman with an awesome amount of power at her command, and the world was a much more complicated place. He started to nod, but then the dizziness swept back over him and he groped for support against the rough bark of a towering redthorn tree.

She laid a hand on his arm. *You need hot food and a decent night's sleep.*

I'll—be all right. A fit of shivering overtook him and she picked the ebari-wool cloak up from the ground, then wrapped it around his shoulders. His teeth chattered as he shook his head. *I'll be fine. Let's—let's go back, if you can take me, then I'll do whatever I can, although I don't promise not to ask questions.*

There are no crystals here. She looked around, the tip of her high-bridged Tal nose reddened in the chill air. *Frostvine will have to take us if she can; otherwise we'll have to walk to the closest pool.*

Frostvine? He glanced around the riverbank, but even the ilserin had fled back into the trees.

Haemas's pale eyes blinked as she seemed to look for something that couldn't be seen. *I don't think that Frostvine uses her solid form anymore. She's . . .* He felt her struggle for the proper term. *She's more advanced than Windsign and Summerstone, older. They call her an ilserlara, an Oldest. I don't completely understand what that means, except that she's somehow more than the others.*

The heavy cold filtered back through the trees, settling around them and chilling Kevisson down to the marrow. Was that what Haemas was talking about? He opened his shields and strained to hear the ilserlara's mindvoice, but there was only a vague impression of frigid anger, immense weight, and mind-numbing cold.

Haemas reached out a hand to him. *Lower your shields so that she can take us back to Shael'donn. I suppose that's a good enough place to start, and we can go to Enissa.* She gripped his fingers hard within her own, as if seeking his strength. *Maybe there is something that the two of us together can do for her.*

A snarl rattled softly from the ice-coated brambles beside the river, then a huge black silsha emerged. *Shadowfoot!* Haemas reached out with her free hand. Its eyes narrowed to yellow slits, the silsha rubbed its black-furred head against her palm.

Now lower your shields, she said, and as Kevisson did, the glade shifted, seeming to twist itself inside out, leaving him the impression of a mind-numbing blueness that glittered with the brilliance of the noonday sun on newly fallen snow. For a second he couldn't breathe; then he staggered and fell to his knees on the crushed-gravel path that led from the House of Moons to Shael'donn.

The door to the old healer's sickroom at Shael'donn stood unlocked. After directing Kisa to wait for him in the hall, Diren quietly lifted the latch. No one should be expecting trouble, but that didn't mean he could be careless. Inside the room, a girl glanced up from her seat beside the bed, her face confused.

"Can I help you?" She brushed nervously at the ash-gold hair caught at the nape of her neck.

Diren didn't recognize her, and fortunately she didn't seem to know him, either. Probably one of the unTalented brats from the House of Moons who had lingered on after its closing. He assumed a look of concern. "How is she?"

The girl's mouth tightened. "No better, I'm afraid." She turned back to peer into the colorless face in the bed. "Her breathing is very shallow."

After sliding the reset latteh crystal out of his pocket, he cradled it in his gloved hand and moved closer to the bed. "What does Master Lising say?"

"He thinks she will be gone by the end of the day." The girl closed her eyes, radiating misery through thinly maintained shields. "It isn't fair! She's always worked so hard to help anyone in need!"

"You're right, of course." He stopped by her side. "Do you know who I am?"

She turned wet-lashed eyes to him, puzzlement written across her young face. She might be no more than fourteen or fifteen, he thought, not old enough to be very well trained. That should make his task all the easier.

"No, my Lord," she said.

With a smooth motion, he pressed the latteh to the side of her forehead, catching her slender body with his free arm as she swayed. *I am Kevisson Monmart,* he said into her mind, projecting Monmart's tan features and golden-brown eyes and hair. *You will remember that it was I who came to see the healer this afternoon, and no one else. Do you understand? No one else was here.*

Her lips moved as she repeated his words without sound, her bluish-gold eyes staring straight ahead. Then he lowered her into the chair beside the bed. *You will stay here until twenty minutes after I've gone.*

He turned back to the still form buried under the comforters on the narrow bed. It was really quite amazing that the old biddy still lived. The mindblast he had given her while her shields were down would have killed most people within a few minutes. Now, more than a day later, here she was, still clinging to life. Well, that could be remedied with only a few seconds' work, and no one would remember anything except that Monmart had forced his way in here to finish her off.

Stretching his fingers out, he touched her feverish right temple. Her shields were in shreds, a good sign. This would be short work indeed. Letting his mind slide deeper, he looked for the nerves that controlled her heart. Just one nudge and he—

Noise from out in the hallway intruded—voices, loud and quarreling, breaking his concentration. Then he felt Enissa

Saxbury herself rouse somehow, sensing his presence. *Kevisson,* he whispered hurriedly to her, *Kevisson has come to finish your tough old hide off.*

Withdrawing, he rubbed his eyes. Whatever happened, he must not be caught here. He opened the door and motioned to Kisa. "What is it?"

Her back pressed to the wall, she stared up at him with bewildered eyes. "Someone is arguing—down there." Her small hand pointed back the way they had come up.

He took her arm and hurried her in the opposite direction. *Be very quiet,* he told her. *No one must know we have been here.*

Just as they reached the stairs and turned the corner, plunging safely down the steps out of sight, he heard the voices more clearly. His hand jumped on the rail as he recognized Monmart's voice—and then Haemas Tal's.

The door stood open, and the small sickroom itself was crowded with people. Riklin Senn pushed to get his breath back after enduring two flights of stairs. It was not seemly for the new Lord High Master of Shael'donn to be seen puffing.

He assumed his deepest voice. "All right. Just what is the problem here?"

Healing Master Brevit Lising glanced up from the bedside. "My Lord, come quickly!"

Straightening his brocaded tunic, Riklin pushed through the onlookers, noting with distaste that not only had Kevisson Monmart reappeared, but also that upstart Haemas Tal. Her aristocratic face was tight with tension and she looked much wearier than she had just this morning. He sniffed. It was beyond him as to why her father had never married her off so that she had children of her own to keep her busy and out of the way. Standing beside the bed, he gazed down upon the Saxbury woman's pale face, noting how her eyes were only dark smudges in her weary face. "Is she dead?"

"Not—" the older woman's bloodless lips said, although her eyes remained closed. "Not—yet." The breath wheezed in and out of her lungs.

"Enissa!" Haemas Tal pushed through the massed bodies.

Riklin glanced irritatedly over his shoulder at the willowy Tal heir who towered over him by half a head. "What's the problem, Lising?"

"I'm not worried about Her Ladyship, Lord High Master." Lising's narrow eyes darted toward the shocked onlookers. "But Master Monmart is quite another matter."

"I just want to see for myself that she's all right." Monmart's voice had the temper of cold steel beneath it. "Then I'll go."

"You'll go now!" Lising's voice rose. "And you'll answer for what you tried to do here!"

"But we've only just arrived." Haemas Tal edged closer to the bedside, her shoulder brushing Riklin's. "And we have done nothing except try to see our friend."

Enissa Saxbury's gray-haired head moved restlessly on the heap of pillows. "Why, Kevisson? Just tell—me—why."

Riklin watched closely as Monmart glanced uneasily around the crowded room. "Why *what*?"

"I'm afraid I saw him, too, my Lady." A girl dressed in the gray uniform of the House of Moons turned to her, hands clutched anxiously together. "He came to finish her off, that's what he said."

"Finish her off?" Monmart echoed. "You mean Enissa?"

"Kevisson, why?" Enissa began, then broke off in a fit of coughing that sent tears streaming down her lined cheeks. "Why—did you—want to—kill me?"

Chapter Eighteen

Haemas groped under the thick layer of quilts for Enissa's hand, then curled her own fingers around it, shocked by its chill and the looseness of the skin. The healer's head sagged back against the heaped pillows, her cheeks the color of old snow.

"It couldn't have been Kevisson," Haemas told her again. "He was being held by the ilserin, and then I was with him down in the Lowlands for hours before we came back to Shael'donn."

"No," Enissa whispered, each sound a fearsome struggle. "Kev—is—son."

But whatever had aroused the old healer had also sapped her remaining strength; Haemas felt her slipping away. She clutched Enissa's hand so tightly that her fingers ached. *I won't let you die,* she said fiercely into Enissa's mind. *You have to fight! Stay with me!*

Enissa made no answer, sinking deeper into a black exhaustion from which there would be no return. Haemas pressed Enissa's clammy hand to her cheek and closed her eyes, so desperate that she would have gone back to the pool and stolen a latteh herself if she thought she had time. But the ilseri were watching now, as well they should, and, of the two lattehs that she might have used, the one Axia had taken was probably lost forever, while the other was presumably still in Diren Chee's possession.

Chee. Suddenly Haemas knew who must have attacked Enissa, then made sure that Kevisson, of all people, was blamed. Better than anyone else in the Highlands, she knew how convincing a false memory could be, how it wove in between the cracks of what had really happened, distorting words and events until the victim believed an utter falsehood. The sight of her father lying dead at her feet still surfaced in her nightmares, even though she had fresh proof that the image was false every time she visited Tal'ayn.

Sitting back in the bedside chair, she stared blindly around the sparely furnished sickroom. Chee must be aware that she had returned without Axia, and he was making good on his threat to destroy everyone she cared about. Now that Master Ellirt was dead, only Enissa and Kevisson remained. And ten minutes ago, Senn had locked Kevisson up on the charge of attacking Enissa. Haemas had argued, protested, even threatened to call her father—which would, of course, have been of no use whatsoever, but she had thought Riklin Senn might not know that. Senn, however, had only smiled and asked her to give Lord Tal his regards, then closed his office door in her face.

Enissa's breathing grew increasingly ragged and shallow, her chest barely rising and falling. Haemas flashed back to that terrible moment when Master Ellirt had died, his life-force dimming, slipping slowly and inexorably beyond her reach. She couldn't let that happen again. She clasped her hands on the edge of the bed and pressed her forehead against them, trying to think. Before anything else could be done, Enissa must be made to breathe more easily. Perhaps she could manage that much. Closing her eyes, she opened her shields and slid into her friend's unprotected mind, searching for the nerves that controlled the breathing centers.

Shadowy images surrounded her: golden-eyed men who sneered, laughed, attacked, everywhere people who didn't understand, who—

Fear seeped into Haemas's mind, electric and razor-sharp, but she fought to shut it out. It was natural for Enissa to be afraid now, but Haemas could not afford it. She had to find the breathing nerves.

Faces crowded into her mind, people she had never seen, haggard, fresh-faced, affectionate, laughing, furious ... One after the other, she shunted the memories aside, trying to hold her concentration. A child's high, thin crying tugged at her, then the dusty, dry smell as the servants cleaned out Rhydal's study after his death . . .

Just as it seemed too late, she found the proper nerves and keyed Enissa's breathing herself, holding control and feeding it with the energy of her own body until the pattern was reset and Enissa breathed normally again.

Feeling lost, Haemas rested, knowing that what little she had accomplished so far was just the first step. Lising and Nevarr had surely done this for Enissa already, and more than once—but without mending the real damage, her breathing would only deteriorate again and she would slip away. Lising and Nevarr were both excellent, highly trained healers. What made Haemas think she could do any better than either of them?

But they had given up and she had to at least try. She drifted through Enissa's mind again, looking, searching for something that could be put right, if only she had the wit to recognize it when she saw it. Then a burst of energy blasted her, sun-bright and molten hot, almost making her lose consciousness. Tumbling through the chaos of Enissa's unconscious mind, she fell through images, sights, sounds, feelings—

An older man's face grimaced at her. "For Light's sake, Enissa, can't you behave like a proper wife in public? It's more than—"

The strong scent of hot keiria tea overwhelmed her, heavily sweetened with honey—

Pain burned through her abdomen like fire sweeping down before the wind, her son would be born any—

Footsteps echoed through the long empty hall as the servants came to carry Rhydal's bier down to the funeral pyre—

Energy, too much energy. Even as she was buffeted by it, Haemas recognized that here was the focal point of the damage. All Enissa's mental energies seemed to be grounded to this one place in her brain, so that no matter what thought was begun or memory accessed, it shunted here, then combined with the cacophony of her other thoughts into a blaring chaos that overwhelmed all autonomic functions of her nervous system.

As she was swept away by the thought-storm, Haemas fought to shut the distracting images out. Here was the place where something could be done, if only she knew what to do. The energy must be halted somehow, quieted, the thought-paths redirected until everything flowed as it was meant to. But it was tricky and baffling, and for a moment, she considered going to Lising and Nevarr for help.

Then she realized that they must have seen this, too, and already given it up for lost. She would have to work by herself. Summoning her remaining energy, she edged toward the disruption, fighting to shut the deafening half-finished thoughts out. At the first shorted neural pathway, she poured her own energy into it, trying to remember how it had felt when Ellirt had healed her with the latteh.

There had been warmth, she thought, a blissful warmth that had healed her cut and bruised face. Concentrating, she poured heat into the damaged area until she was exhausted, and then continued doggedly until a ragged blackness threatened to drown her. When she finally stopped, the pathway was complete again, the thoughts flickering along it like slim golden fish in a mountain stream. Only a rough scar remained to indicate where it had been disrupted.

She had succeeded, but all the same, she was dismayed. It had taken every bit of free energy she possessed just to heal this one pathway, and thousands of pathways fed into this disruption. At this rate, it would take thousands of days to heal her friend—if she lived that long, if Diren Chee left them alone, if Frostvine didn't take action against the Kashi because of the missing lattehs, if—

Unsteadily Haemas groped her way back to her own body, barely able to feel it slumped on the edge of bed at Enissa's side. When she opened her eyes, she found them wet with her own tears. Enissa could not survive long enough in this condition to let Haemas finish what she had begun, even if she had time to meticulously heal each pathway.

And the one thing she did not have was time.

* * *

Diren took Kisa back to Chee'ayn and set one of the few remaining servants to watch her. Then, as soon as the sun set, he entered the portal again and reached for the pattern that signaled Tal'ayn. Sleet blasted his face the instant he materialized; an ice storm was in full progress on this side of the Highlands caldera. He took shelter under the covered doorway into the main house, then glanced up. He could just make out the towering twin crags with their bridging walkway. The Tals had built this house into the living mountain and had the most interesting architecture in all the Highlands. After he had consolidated his power, Diren would spend some time here enjoying the unique amenities of this place. There was supposedly an excellent rock garden with thermal springs nestled somewhere between the house and the cliffs behind—

JUST WHAT IN THE NAME OF BLOODY DARKNESS ARE YOU SNIFFING AROUND HERE FOR, YOU WET-EARED EXCUSE FOR A MAN?

Diren's hands jumped, but he held his temper. As soon as Tal felt the kiss of the latteh, the old bastard would be falling all over himself to be pleasant. The thought of Tal's imminent downfall warmed him, even out in the biting, ice-filled wind. He looped his cloak over one shoulder and leaned against the door. *So this is how you greet your visitors. I can't say that I'm surprised. I'd heard tales of Tal "hospitality."*

WHAT DO YOU WANT? Tal's mindvoice was still deafening.

I'm on Council business, of course. Diren allowed a note of peevishness to creep into his tone. *Or do I have to discuss that with you in there sitting by the fire, while I freeze my backside off out here in the damned courtyard?*

Tal made no answer, but seconds later, the door swung open and a gaunt, middle-age servant inclined his brown-haired head to him. "My Lord?"

Diren favored him with a withering glance, then swept down the narrow stairs into the main house, shedding ice pellets as he went. "Fine sort of welcome," he muttered, shrugging out of the sopping cloak at the bottom of the steps.

"You might get a better reception," a sultry female voice commented, "if you waited to be invited."

Diren turned and stared down into the green-streaked golden eyes of a petite Kashi woman.

Her fingers trailed idly down her slender white neck, brushing the green velvet of her low-cut bodice. She was dressed in long flowing skirts, the latest fashion affected by the women of the Highest Houses, and her skin had the translucent elegance of the finest imported porcelain. She tilted her small head back, studying him with an unsettling frankness, her full red lips parted in a pout. "I am Alyssa Alimn Senn."

"Lady." He met those startling eyes, then looked away, feeling disconcertingly hot.

She waved a small hand at the servant. "Haner, you're dismissed." Then she turned her level gaze back to Diren. "My husband doesn't want to see you, of course." Her fingers traced the gold-worked sunbursts on her bodice. "And I think you'll find that he's remarkably good at doing exactly as he pleases." Then she froze, seeming to hear something he could not. Her eyes darted toward a door just down the hallway and her smooth cheek paled. A blankness descended over her face. "You'd better go on in." Lifting her cumbersome skirts in both hands, she glided down the passageway before him.

Diren followed the shapely back, trying to remember what he had heard about her. Alyssa Senn, the old Tal's very young wife—hadn't there been some sort of scandal at one time? "Has the Lady Haemas visited recently?" he asked, as if making casual conversation.

"Now I know you have no true business here." She radiated amusement, pausing with her hand on the latch of an enormous oak door decorated with carvings of the hunt. "No one who knew Dervlin well would be foolish enough to ask that question." A chilling smile flitted across her face and she suddenly looked ten years older. "Ask him yourself, if you dare." Opening the door, she stood aside.

Tal's gruff voice rang out from within. "Well, are you going to come in, or are you going to stand out there and ogle the wench all night?"

Diren tightened his shields, then entered the golden glow of firelight in the wood-paneled office beyond the door. The pleasant aromas of woodsmoke and hot mead filled the room.

Tal's lip curled. "She has all the discrimination of a starving silsha and the morals of a poisonous bavval. You can have her, if you're willing to take the risk, but I wouldn't advise it."

"Lord Tal," Diren said, trying to think of anything but the cold hard shape of the latteh secreted within his gloved hand.

The old man was smaller than he remembered from seeing him in Council. He sat in a wing-backed chair before the fire, his feet propped up, his eyes like hammered circles of gold, deep-set under bushy white brows. They raked Diren. "What in damnation is it that couldn't wait until the next meeting? I don't like visitors, especially uninvited ones."

"I have important news, my Lord." Diren glanced around for a second chair, but though the room was stuffed with a massive pine desk, cabinets, and bookshelves, there was no place where a second person might sit. "News that I'm sure you'll want no one else to overhear." Sliding his hand behind his back, he approached the old man and the huge crackling fire. "News of the Lady Haemas."

The chair creaked as the old man leaned forward, then turned his eyes moodily to the flames. "You dare speak that name to me?" His voice was threaded with menace.

"I do." Diren spread his free hand before the dancing yellow flames, glad of the warmth after being half frozen out in the courtyard. If he could just get a bit closer, he thought, no one would be able to stop him, but it was well known that the old Tal possessed both a powerful Talent and the training to use it. He had to be careful. He cleared his throat. "She has recently been my—guest—at Chee'ayn, where she and I came to an—understanding."

Tal snorted, then laced gnarled hands across his chest. His face might have been made of tempered steel. "You don't expect me to believe that, do you? That disgraceful wretch has sworn never to marry any man, not even that worthless halfbreed Monmart."

"But she has agreed to accept me." Diren held his hand out

as if in goodwill, concealing the latteh in his gloved palm. "Provided you give us your approval."

"She can do as she likes." The golden eyes blinked, reflecting the firelight like two polished mirrors. "She always does." A log shifted in the red-hot heart of the fire, shooting sparks outward. Tal seized the poker, then leaned forward, angrily spearing the logs as if he had a grudge against them. "Her decisions have nothing to do with me. I've finished with her."

"Isn't the truth more that *she's* finished with you?" Still holding his hand out, Diren laced his tone with sarcasm. "Didn't she renounce Tal'ayn?"

Holding the poker so tightly that his knuckles shone white, Tal gave him a sharp glance. "So that's what this is about, is it? My 'approval,' indeed! The last time that ungrateful wench wanted my approval, she was still in nappies!" His white brows drew together over his hawk nose.

Curling his fingers around the latteh, Diren locked his hands behind his back, seeming to give the matter serious thought. "Wouldn't you like to put all this behind you now, Tal? She is, after all, your only child. No matter what happened between the two of you, Tal'ayn is bound to come to her someday."

"Not if I entail it elsewhere!" The old man clanged the poker back onto the stone hearth. "Say one more word and I'll will it to my cousin's youngest son, Lan Kentnal! I've always meant to anyway."

So he hadn't gotten around to it yet. Diren repressed a smile. All the better, then. Now that Haemas Tal had returned from the timeways, it would make claiming her as his bride all the more appealing if she brought the wealth of Tal'ayn to him. With that much gold, a dozen Chee'ayns could be put to rights.

"Isn't Lan Kentnal only two or three years old?" he asked casually as he edged around behind the old man's chair.

"Five." Tal leaned his head back against the leather and closed his eyes. "Now get out!"

"Five years old and already a wealthy man," Diren said softly. "What a lucky youngster. I do hope he appreciates his good fortune." Then he pressed the latteh crystal to the pale, almost transparent flesh of the old man's temple. Tal's body went rigid with shock, then sagged in the chair, his mouth open and eyes staring.

Diren held the latteh in place another moment, then realized Tal wasn't breathing. After quickly pocketing the crystal, he felt Tal's face; the skin was already cooling. *Breathe, damn you!* he shouted into the other's mind, but he could sense the lack of response, the seeping dimness that signaled neural shutdown.

But it didn't fit in with his plans! He needed the old man alive, not dead. It would be disastrous for Haemas Tal to come into her inheritance before he had her under control again. As mistress of Tal'ayn, the Council might actually believe her, if she went to them about the latteh. Shuddering, Diren dropped his shields and flung himself into the dying mind, trying to make the heart beat again, the lungs breathe.

But everywhere blackness loomed, dissolution, blankness. He discovered the sites of old injuries that had healed over with fearsome twisted scars. Years ago, he remembered now, Tal had been mindblasted by his nephew and had nearly died. Obviously he had been too frail for the latteh. His brain had not been able to stand up to the power surge.

Numbly Diren withdrew, then stared down at the lifeless body. He rubbed a trembling hand over his face and felt cold sweat. What should he do? Tal's snip of a wife and at least one of the servants knew he was here. He couldn't just leave and let them find the body. Bloody Darkness, he'd been so stupid! He should have come here in secret. He should have made sure that no one saw him. He should have—

With an effort, he controlled his panic. What was done was done, and he had to make the best of it. He hauled the door open and ran out into the empty corridor. "Lady Senn!" He looked around in unfeigned wildness. "Lady Senn, come quickly!"

"Coming."

He heard her voice from a long way off and waited as she

managed to hurry without ever stooping to the indignity of actually running.

"My word, Lord Chee, what is it?" Her flushed face regarded him scornfully as she tucked a fallen tendril of bright-gold hair back into place. "Has Dervlin run out of mead again, or does he just want someone to remove his boots?"

"I'm sorry." Diren hesitated, his hands dangling helplessly. "But I'm afraid—does Tal'ayn have a healer in residence?"

"A healer?" Her eyes narrowed. "No, Dervlin can't abide them. Why?"

"Lord Tal . . ." He glanced back at the crumpled figure in the chair. "I think he's—dead."

"Really?" Alyssa Senn stood on tiptoe, trying to peer over his shoulder. "Are you quite sure?"

"I'm sorry," he repeated numbly. "It was some sort of attack. It happened—so fast. There was no time to call you before he was gone."

"Oh, I've had quite enough time with my Lord husband already." Placing one small manicured hand firmly on his chest, she pushed him aside and crossed the sitting room to gaze down at Tal's staring eyes. "In fact, he and I have had so much time together, it's a wonder we haven't killed each other by now."

The sight of her perfect features gazing so dispassionately at the dead man chilled Diren even further, and he flashed back to another moment in his life, when his father had gazed so at the broken body of his mother lying at the bottom of a rocky chasm—where he'd thrown her.

Finally, his father had said, radiating a rare satisfaction. *Finally, some peace.*

With an effort, Diren wrenched himself back to the present. "Is there anything I can do, my Lady?"

Alyssa glanced up from her husband's dead body. Her fingers played idly with one of her green koral-stone earrings. "No, thank you, Lord Chee. I think you've done quite enough. Would you care for some refreshments?"

* * *

Blue was everywhere, mind-numbing, robbing her senses of all other sensations until Axia was not even sure she existed anymore. Perhaps she was dead and this was actually the realm of Darkness where the wicked were eternally punished.

But that couldn't be. There was too much light, a searing blue brilliance that danced and glimmered and sang with a nightmarish intensity until she would have screamed if she could have found her voice in this terrible place. In her hand, the latteh crystal buzzed, overriding her thoughts and making it impossible to concentrate and find her way out. The Tal woman had done this to her—maneuvered her into touching the latteh with her bare skin, then abandoned her to die in this glittering blue wasteland where nothing was real.

Splintered scenes appeared in a dazzling circle around her: places she knew, faces she remembered, events she had tried desperately to forget. Over and over again, she saw her father pitch her mother's writhing body over the cliff, then stand with his arms crossed, staring after her.

Why, when all of time was supposed to be accessible here, she should have to endure that moment again and again, she did not know. Once she had seen Diren standing outside on the frozen grounds of Chee'ayn, and for a second she had thought she might reach him. But then the scene had faded and she had been here again, alone and hopelessly lost in the awful draining blueness.

And most frightening of all, she could feel herself changing. This place was not meant for humans. The electric blueness was invading her brain, searing the small portion that wasn't already paralyzed by the latteh. Soon she would not be able to think at all.

The scenes shifted again, as they often did, and she saw Diren in an unfamiliar place, standing in a room with an old man slumped in a chair, a diminutive, proud-faced woman at his side. If only she could reach him, take his hand, perhaps he could pull her from the nexus before it was too late. Perhaps . . .

Fire laced her brain as she struggled to make her foot step on the writhing blue line that led to Diren. The line itself seemed to fight her, whipping back and forth, and the latteh disrupted her thoughts to the point that she was not sure she even knew what she was doing.

Then she felt her foot make solid contact with the pathway, the tremendous energies surging up through her as if she were some sort of lightning rod. Good so far, but it took three steps to exit the nexus. She remembered that much from before. Her brain in agony, she tried to take another step, the blueness shining so much that she could barely see at all, her eyes dazzled until everything was just one intense field of scintillating blue.

Then, just as her foot made contact with the reluctant blue line, Diren and the room faded, and she was left alone in the nexus.

Chapter
Nineteen

Frostvine surveyed the forest passing below her nebulous body. She had spent many pleasant Interims there as an ilseri, roaming the huge trees that shadowed the birth pools, riding the air currents above to seek the sun's nourishment. Hovering, she savored the remembered sense of peace and sisterhood, then sank through the leafless trees, feeling her body drift thinner and thinner. It took constant vigilance in this cycle of her life not to let go and scatter her molecules across the face of the planet one final time, to mingle forever with the weathered cliffs and the wind, and the stars, and no matter how careful she was, her time would come soon. It almost took more density than she could summon now to communicate with the more youthful Third Ones.

Still, she must persist for a little longer. She had examined the nexus for the possible outcomes of this crisis. At the ends of more than half the lines, the ilseri were only a half-forgotten memory to the invading humans. And at the conclusion of most of the rest, the wretched human-things had decimated the forests or completely destroyed this world.

Even spread so thinly, she could feel the one that her sisters called Moonspeaker far away on the other side of the daunting mountains. What a strange creature it was, always behaving as if human and ilseri were only two branches of the same tree. Having watched the quarrelsome, greedy human-things through the many Interims of her long life, she had thought Windsign's attempt to train one would be fruitless. Human-things were obviously a less-advanced lifeform, forever fixed into a solid state, perpetually immature, really no more than cruel, careless, unthinking children.

But, for the first time since she had phased into the Last Life, she had been wrong. This particular human's mind was silver-bright and powerful. It had learned more than she had believed possible, even halting the disastrous experimenting with the timeways begun by the males of its species. Whether it could now do anything about the theft of the First Ones remained to be seen. At that thought, anger surged through Frostvine, roiling, massive, and dark, like a storm cloud blocking the sun. Down through the Interims, the Last Ones had been helpless, never able to reshape their minds to a pattern that could stop the humans when they raided the birth pools and then later attempted the timeways. This time, though, she would find a shape within her mind strong enough to do what must be done, even if it hastened her end.

The shadowfoot's shoulder pressed against Haemas as she mounted the Shael'donn portal. She rested her hand on the large head, glad of its ferocious company. If it came to a physical struggle, the creature might well tip the balance in her favor against Chee. The minds of all three silshas sent to her by the ilseri had been sealed against the Kashi, although she had never understood how.

Closing her eyes, she activated each ilseri crystal in sequence, then called up the signature vibration of Chee'ayn, praying that the crystals were in the portal right now, not removed and separated as they had been when she had been imprisoned in that strange ramshackle house.

The shadowfoot snarled as it was pulled with her into the cold gray betweenness, then emerged into the chill night on the other side of the Highlands caldera. The stars glittered down, tiny bits of broken crystal in a clear night sky that arched blackly overhead, terrifyingly infinite. The pines swayed and whispered at the edge of the cliffs. Haemas's fingers clenched in the beast's thick fur.

Would Chee be sleeping at this late hour? She shivered and stepped down from the staging platform, forcing her way through the overgrown brambles crowding the weathered wood. Everything depended on catching him unaware so she could recover the latteh without a fight. If he had time to set it for mind-binding, it would be much harder, if not impossible.

Blacker than the surrounding night, the shadowfoot flowed at her side, its great head weaving back and forth as it sampled the scents. Ahead, the half-ruined house loomed without a single light to stand against the darkness, many of the windows boarded up and ominous. The broken outline faintly echoed other, more prosperous times, when the weed-choked gardens must have been lush and cultivated, the stonework bright, the steps scrubbed. Haemas thought of growing up in this decaying atmosphere and shuddered; as oppressive as the emotional climate had been at Tal'ayn, she had at least never wanted for basic comforts.

She lowered her shields and cast her awareness through the building, seeking the mind of another Kashi, first encountering a chierra mind, muffled and quiet, lost in vague dreams, then another, and another. Concentrating, she ranged farther into the maze of dusty rooms and nit-eaten furniture, trying not to ask herself what she would do if he wasn't there. Finally, in one of the crumbling towers, she found a spark of slumbering consciousness that shone Kashi bright to her psi-senses.

She withdrew, not wanting to alert Chee to her presence. No doubt he would have the latteh close by, perhaps even on his person. Circling the house, she tried a warped side door, but it was locked. Then she circled around to another wing, but that door was also bolted. From the rundown appearance of the place, many of the doors and windows had been permanently shut for years.

Finally she wrapped a rock in her cloak and broke an unboarded window, then climbed through, nicking herself in the process in half-dozen places on the jagged splinters of glass. The silsha leaped neatly in after her without even touching the broken pane, then pressed up against her, licking her cut hands and arms with its raspy tongue.

Not now. She pushed the black-furred head away. *We have to find the latteh.*

After giving her one last warm lick, it padded on ahead of her, seeing far better than she could with its nocturnally oriented eyes. Resting a hand on the back of its neck, she let it guide her through the darkened house, thinking at each creak and groan from the ancient floorboards that someone would wake up and give the alarm. But the few servants slept on as she and the silsha mounted the old staircases, seeking the tower where she had sensed the Kashi.

After she had stubbed every one of her toes and bruised most of her body on unseen objects, she felt the sleeping Kashi mind very near. Her hair filthy with dust and webs, she stopped before the door and tried to lift the latch without waking Chee or the servant she sensed sleeping in the room next door. It was locked.

Grinding the heel of her hand against her forehead, she fought down her panic and tried to think. The shadowfoot could break the door down, but that would rouse the entire house. There had to be another way. She decided to try the door of the servant's room. Under her trembling hand, the latch gave with a rusty click. She slid into the cold, stuffy silence, the stealthy shadowfoot at her heels. The air smelled of mold and unwashed clothes. In a narrow bed shoved against the far wall, an older chierra woman stirred and mumbled in her sleep.

The back of her neck bristling, Haemas hesitated, then touched the woman's temple and spoke to her chierra mind. *Sleep*, she said. *All is well. Sleep soundly and do not wake up, no matter what you hear.*

The muttering trailed away into snores. Haemas took an uneven breath, longing for a light, but afraid to risk it. She turned to the silsha. *A door*, she said to it, and pictured what she wanted. *Is there another door in this room?*

The beast padded around her, then nosed up against the wall on the right side, waiting. Sensing its pleasure, she held her hands out to keep from bumping into anything and followed it through the darkness to find that there was indeed another door. This small room adjoined one on the other side. She lifted the latch and flinched as it gave with a squeak.

Faintly illuminated by embers in the fireplace, a sleeping

figure squirmed on a cot, then rolled over. Haemas froze, her heart hammering in her chest. If Chee woke up now, it would certainly come to a fight.

Afraid to probe him, she slid through the door, watching the dark heap on the cot all the while, listening with her mind for any sign of consciousness on his part.

The figure on the cot suddenly bolted up. "Father?"

Haemas stared in shock. The voice was a child's. She hadn't known that Chee had any family except Axia.

"Father, is that you?" the child asked again in a voice blurred by sleep.

"No," Haemas heard herself say. "I'm—looking for him. Do you know where he is?"

"He left." The child fumbled on the bedside table for an unlit candle, then her bare feet thumped on the floor. "Just a minute. I'll make a light."

Haemas sensed the child concentrating on the candle, racing through the old Kashi ritual to generate the spark. Then the flame blazed up, bright and strong, illuminating the cluttered room with its wavering yellow light.

"I'm Kisa," the child said, blinking at her with sleep-clouded eyes.

Haemas took in the long hair and the worn nightdress, much too big. A little girl, she thought numbly. She hadn't known. "Kisa—Chee?" she asked.

"No." The girl rubbed her eyes with the back of one fist, then yawned. "Kisa Lenhe."

"Lenhe?" Dumbfounded, Haemas balanced on the edge of the bed. Then the shadowfoot nosed the door aside and padded into the room. "Don't be afraid," she said quickly. "He won't hurt you."

Kisa held her free hand out to the beast and smiled as the silsha licked it. "I know."

The silsha radiated a rare contentment as it allowed the small hand to stroke its face. Haemas was utterly amazed. She always introduced each new girl accepted into the House of Moons to her silshas, but the beasts had never shown any of them more than a wary willingness to allow them to look at a distance. Even Enissa, the most Talented of all who had come to work with her, had never been accepted by them like this. For Haemas's sake, they tolerated a few other humans, but nothing more.

"He's nice." Kisa laid her cheek against the black-furred face, then looked up at Haemas. "When is my father coming back?"

"I don't know." Haemas's mouth tightened as she fingered the raggedness of the single quilt provided against the night's bitter cold. "How long has he been gone?"

"We came back this afternoon." Kisa pushed at the matted hair hanging about her face and frowned. "Then he left me with Sanna and she locked me in here. She's not nice at all, not like Dorria."

Dorria ... Lenhe ... With a shock, Haemas realized that Kisa must be Myriel Lenhe's child. Why in the name of Light had Chee brought her here? Was he really her father?

Numbly she watched the youngster stroke the strangely patient shadowfoot; the beast recognized something in her, no doubt the same sort of thing that it had once seen in Haemas. Kisa must have a potentially strong Talent, stronger than any of the girls who had been sent to her for training, the sort of child the House of Moons had been founded to train and nurture.

And she was Diren Chee's daughter.

The sweat on Diren's forehead dried in the second it took to flash through the chill gray betweenness between Tal'ayn and Chee'ayn. Chilled to the marrow, he looked up at the massive outline of Chee'ayn, black against the endless green-black of the night sky. Damnation, but he was tired. He couldn't think what to do now, how to turn the old Tal's death to his advantage. He wrenched the ilsera crystals out of their housing and stuffed them into his pockets, then hunched his shoulders against the rising wind and set off for the house, still seeing Dervlin Tal's white face in his mind as the old man stiffened at the touch of the latteh crystal, then just—died.

That wasn't his fault, he told himself fiercely, each breath puffing white in the chill night air. He couldn't have known the old man's brain was scarred from that fight with his nephew. All that had happened years ago. No one could have expected him to remember that!

At least the Shael'donn healer, called in by the old man's wife, had seemed to suspect nothing. "It was bound to happen sooner or later," he had said to Alyssa after the briefest of examinations, his aristocratic face indifferent. "And he did have a long life."

"Long enough," Alyssa had agreed, her face impassive and her shields woven tightly around her mind. Her hand strayed to the heart-shaped diamond fastened at her throat. "But I will, of course, have my memories."

Diren fumbled in his pockets for the key as he trudged wearily down the overgrown path. Tal's death had put a gigantic hole in his grand plan, but—

Ghostly blueness shimmered suddenly before him and he glanced up involuntarily into the star-scattered sky. A scintillating blue glow hovered overhead just out of reach, and in it he saw her face again—Axia's face, tormented, afraid, inhuman in the way that the bright-blue motes of light seemed to form one side of her head now. She was changing.

Her eyes, glowing with the strange light, finally came to him and seemed to focus. He shivered as her lips shaped his name, although he heard nothing but the wind moaning through the pines. Behind her, he glimpsed splintered scenes of other places and people shifting like a kaleidoscope.

His mouth hung open and his heart froze in midbeat. He shook his head as the apparition reached out a glimmering blue hand clutching an equally blue latteh. Scuttling backward, he tripped and fell, bloodying his palms on the frozen gravel. "Go away!" His voice rang past the ruined house and across the yawning chasm into which Brann Chee had once thrown their mother. "Go away!" He felt that if she touched him, he would be lost with her in the nexus, with no more life than a ghost.

Her blue lips moved again, and he heard his name, faintly, as if someone were whispering it from incredibly far away. "Diren!" Her eyes crawled with the awful blueness. "Diren, please!"

He hunched on the rough gravel, pressing his bleeding hands over his ears, closing his eyes against the ghastliness that had once been his sister. He would not hear her, would not see her! She—was—not—there!

The breath sobbed in his chest as he willed her to go away, to die, to do anything but pull him into that mind-stopping hell of scintillating blueness with her. The wind gusted, sharp and bitter against his face, and, when he finally worked up the courage to open his eyes, he was alone again in the vast, snowy wasteland of the Chee'ayn grounds.

The echoing shout drew both Kisa and Haemas to the window in time to see a ghostly blue figure reaching its hand out to Chee as he cowered away from it.

"It's that light again," Kisa said. Awe permeated her words. "It was here before and it looks just like a lady, but Father said it wasn't really." She looked up at Haemas with puzzled eyes. "Do you think it's *the* Light? Should we ask Father Orcado to come?"

"No." Haemas fought to keep the trembling out of her voice. "It's—just someone who is traveling, like using the ilsera crystals, but she can't quite get here. That's all. She's a real person, not a ghost or a spirit." Then she folded the shivering child into her arms and pressed the small head to her breast.

Kisa's lips moved against her shoulder. "Shouldn't we help her, then?" Her arms stole tentatively around Haemas's waist. "I mean, if I was lost, I would want someone to come for me."

"I'm going to help her." The child's thick tangled hair gleamed red-gold under Haemas's hand in the candlelight. "As soon as I can. I won't leave her like that. I promise."

She looked around the small, ill-kept room; it was musty and dirty as well as cluttered with moldering piles of wall hangings and rags, certainly not the room of a beloved child. Smoothing the hair away from Kisa's puzzled eyes, she looked down at the small face. "Get your things," she told her. "I'm taking you back with me."

"I don't have any things." Kisa rubbed her eyes. "Sanna took my clothes away when I went to bed. All I have is the cloak Father made me wear, and it's too big."

"Then bring that. It's very cold outside." Haemas glanced

anxiously out the window, but the snowy path was deserted now. "We have to hurry." As she bundled Kisa into the patched cloak, she wondered if Chee had already removed the ilsera crystals from the portal. If so, she would be trapped here with him—and the latteh.

She snuffed the candle so Chee wouldn't see the light, then opened the door to the adjoining room, sending the shadowfoot out first to lead the way through the dark house. "Lay your hand on its neck," she told the child. "It sees in the dark much better than we do." Then she buried her own freezing hand in the warm fur and followed the silsha into the hall. The darkness seemed to press in on her, almost vibrating, and the plaster crumbled beneath her free hand every time she tripped and caught herself against the wall.

"Shield your mind," she whispered to Kisa as they inched down the dark hall. "Don't let him know we're here."

"But he's my father." Doubt colored Kisa's young voice. "He's supposed to know where I am."

"We'll tell him later," Haemas lied as they came to the steps, feeling her face go hot. "He wouldn't understand." She felt Kisa's hand slide off the shadowfoot's neck; the beast stopped, its breath whuffing in the intense silence of the stairwell.

"You want to go with the shadowfoot, don't you?" Haemas reached through the darkness and touched the child's face; it was cold and wet with tears.

"Yes, but—" Kisa hesitated. "He didn't come for me for so long. What if he gets mad? What if he doesn't want me back?"

"Please, it will be all right." Haemas tried to hide the desperation in her voice. "We have to go!"

"Oh, I wouldn't be in such a hurry as all that, Lady Haemas." The cold tones of Diren Chee's voice echoed up the stairwell from below and she saw the faint glimmer of a light at the bottom. "You and I haven't even gotten to chat yet."

Catching Haemas's alarm, the silsha stiffened and snarled. *Not yet,* she told it. *Wait.*

"Kisa, come down here!" Chee's voice cracked at them. "At once!"

Kisa, no! Haemas groped for the girl's arm, but missed,

then heard muffled footsteps as the barefoot child felt her way through the darkness down the steps. She sank back against the peeling wall; this was worse than anything she'd imagined. Chee stood down there, blocking her, and she knew of no other way out of this tower.

"Come down, Lady." Chee's tone turned jovial. "We'll have a drink to celebrate my good luck. I thought I would have to go looking for you, and now here you are, all wrapped up like a Naming Day present and delivered right to my door."

Her fingers clenched in the silsha's fur. "And shall we drink to *Axia's* good fortune, too?"

"I would not mention that name if I were you." The humor drained from his voice. "What you did to her is abominable." He hesitated, and then his voice went smooth as silk again. "But do come down. I have something for you, in honor of our coming matrimonial."

Her heart withered as she recognized the gnawing, buzzing sensation that accompanied a latteh set for control, the feeling of power thrown out of balance. Her hands trembled as she bent to peer into the shadowfoot's yellow eyes, almost invisible in the darkness. *Guard,* she told it. *Don't let him touch me, even if you have to kill him.*

Snarling in assent, the shadowfoot surged down the steps. She braced her free hand on the outer wall, trying not to slip as it bounded downward, making her descend much faster than prudence indicated. When they rounded the final corner, she saw Chee waiting at the bottom, holding up a lamp, his golden eyes glittering. His free arm was across Kisa's shoulder, holding her in front of him like a shield. Her eyes were white-rimmed and staring.

Still charging, the silsha laid back its tufted ears and roared a full-throated challenge at the man blocking their way. The muscles rippled under its black hide as it gathered itself to spring.

Chee smiled, then glanced down at the child. Kisa stiffened and threw her small hands out in denial. "No!" she cried at the angry silsha. "Don't hurt my father!"

Chapter Twenty

The attacking shadowfoot twisted in midair, its curved claws missing Diren Chee's nose by a whisper. Chee stumbled backward, his laughter echoing from the crumbling walls as Haemas watched, dumbfounded. Landing with a thump in the inky shadows beyond, the silsha scrambled around to face the man in black, its claws shredding the rotting carpet and raising a cloud of dust. Its ears were flattened to its skull and every hair on its huge body stood on end. *Guard!* She told it. *Don't let him hurt me!*

Oh, surely you don't think that I'll have to do anything as crude as actually hurt you, do you? The latteh's buzzing intensified, and Chee's mindvoice took on the same harsh quality. *That sounds like far too much work.*

Haemas fought to stop shaking. As long as she could remember, fear had been her greatest enemy. All those years ago, she had let fear take over and make her decisions for her, but she couldn't give in to it this time. She had to consider Kisa and the helpless First One clutched in Chee's hand, and beyond that, the future of the entire Highlands. She shrugged the heavy cloak off to move more freely. With a tremendous leap, the shadowfoot bounded back up the steps to shield her from the waiting man. She placed a trembling hand on its bristling neck and looked down at the girl's pale, anxious face. "Kisa, I want you to come back with me. No matter what he's told you, I doubt he is really your father, and even if he is, he should wait until the Council of Twelve recognizes his claim. He had no right to steal you away."

Kisa frowned, then twisted around to stare up at Chee. He

set the lamp aside and touched splayed fingers to the child's temple. Kisa's eyelids fluttered, then her eyes lost their focus.

"You'll have to try harder than that, Lady." He smiled lazily. "Come into my study and we'll drink to our coming matrimonial." *Perhaps we could start the festivities early.* Stroking Kisa's cheek, he winked and projected an image at Haemas: a statuesque woman surrounded by a cloud of glittering pale-gold hair, turning slowly, her long-fingered hand extended to him in invitation, candlelight gleaming on the silken curves of her naked white body—

"You're not fit to raise a child!" Strengthening her shields, she shut him out, but the image left her shaken. Beneath her hand, the shadowfoot quivered with restrained rage, but in spite of her urging, it would not attack. Chee was safe unless he raised a hand to her, and he was not fool enough to do that. His shadowed face gazed up the steps at her, his golden eyes reflecting what little light there was and burning at her through the gloom. She read his message as plainly as if he'd spoken: Once the latteh touched her bare skin, she would either succumb to his will, or die fighting it. Her mouth tightened. Death, she thought bleakly, would be so much cleaner.

"Come, Lady." Chee sounded as if he were flirting with her at a Midwinter's Festival. "Why drag this out all night?"

Haemas gauged the space at the foot of the stairwell; perhaps if she kept the shadowfoot between them, she could slip past him and escape down the hall—but that would leave Kisa and the First One behind. Cursing herself for not having the foresight to bring a dagger or some sort of weapon, she edged down the remaining steps, sliding her back along the wall and keeping the silsha's massive body between them. Its lips were wrinkled in a snarl, and she felt the frustrated anger boiling through its mind.

Chee smiled and slipped his gloved hand out of his pocket. His gaunt face was confident as he held the dull-green latteh out to her as if it were a present. "Not as large as the other." His tone was light. "Still, it seems to be effective. At least, it was with your father earlier tonight."

Fear and guilt stabbed through her—*lying dead at her feet,*

*her father's face white and empty, his outflung hand grazing
her boot.* She faltered, her heart hammering against her ribs.

"The poor fellow wasn't up to it, but it wasn't a total loss."
Chee angled up the bottom step toward her and the silsha.
"Just before he died, he admitted that he had never changed
his will. That makes you a very wealthy Lady now."

"I don't believe you," she said in a surprisingly even voice.
"You'd never get the better of him. My father's Talent would
make ten of yours." In her mind, her cousin arched a golden
eyebrow. *"You killed him, of course. I always knew it would
come to this."* Haemas bit her lip. He was—not—dead! Shaking, she forced the hateful false memory aside and descended
the rickety steps, her back pressed hard against the wall.

"That might have been true, without the latteh." He inched
closer, then flinched as the shadowfoot bared its four-inch
fangs in an ear-rattling snarl. Reaching back, Chee jerked Kisa
in front of him, then pressed forward again, using the small
body as a shield and reaching for Haemas with the crystal.

She dodged under his arm, twisting to avoid the latteh—and
slipped. The steps caught her across the diaphragm as she fell,
slamming the breath out of her lungs. She sprawled headfirst,
gasping, a red-hot band of pain constricting her ribs. The
silsha's momentum carried it on down the steps.

Chee moved in, the harsh planes of his face triumphant, the
latteh glowing dully in his outstretched palm. "Here, let me
help—"

A shimmering light erupted in the dim hallway behind his
head and spread outward. Haemas stared past his hand as the
unnerving brilliant blue of the temporal nexus spilled through
the old house.

"Diren?" The faint voice crackled with overstressed energies. Chee spun around, his face ashen. His fingers tightened
around the latteh and he thumped back into the opposite wall.
On the steps, Haemas struggled for breath as an outline
formed in the blueness, flickering from haze to solidity, then
haze again, all within the space of a second.

"Help—me!" Axia stood several feet above the floor, her

blue hair swirling around her face, blown by some wind unfelt in this dimension. "Diren, for the love of Light, help me!"

Beyond her, Haemas glimpsed other places, faces, events, then, with a chill, the churning dark blue of the maelstrom, the end result of disrupted time. She stretched her arm out to the apparition. "Axia!" Her voice was wispy for lack of breath. "Follow the sound of my voice!"

The air began to stir, cold and dank, electric. Axia's eyes wandered the hall, focused on her cowering brother. "Diren, it's so cold here. I—can't think."

"Reach out to her!" Still half stunned, Haemas braced her throbbing ribs and levered herself up against the wall. "Look behind her—at the whirling dark-blue mass—that's not normal! It's a sign of time disruption!"

Chee suddenly came back to himself and yanked Kisa before him, scuttling away from his sister's reaching fingers.

Haemas transferred her weight to the shadowfoot, fighting the pain in her ribs to breathe. "She doesn't see anyone but you. Call to her before it's too late. The latteh must be causing a temporal disruption. Everyone in this When could die!"

"No!" Chee's white-rimmed eyes were staring at the apparition. "Keep it away from me!"

Haemas edged toward the blue woman whose hair glowed around her head like a constellation of blue stars. *Axia, open your mind to me.*

Axia's haunted blue eyes looked straight through her.

Axia, there must be a blue line under your feet. Look down and walk along it.

"Diren." Axia's face contorted. "Father is here. I keep finding him, just when he's—he's—" Her reaching fingers strained toward him. "Diren, please!" The eerie blue face drifted closer; another second and her fingers would graze his cheek.

"No! Leave me alone!" Chee shoved Kisa at his sister, then ran down the hall, his footsteps echoing behind him.

Horrified, Haemas watched Axia's fingers touch Kisa's hair and transform the tumbled red-gold to blue. "No!" she called. "Axia, no!" But the other woman drew the unresisting child up to her breast and hung there above the floor, the two of them suspended in fountaining blue. Any second, Haemas knew Axia would lose this line—she did not seem capable of completing the final step that would lead her back into this When—and then Kisa would be lost, as well.

She bared her mind to the opening Axia had created. For a second the nexus of glowing lines was superimposed over the shadowy hallway; then Chee'ayn faded from her awareness.

Kevisson awoke with a start. He had been dreaming of moonlight-pale hair and mysterious white-gold eyes that hinted at something just beyond his reach. She had kissed him, held him as a woman holds a man, and then, just before he'd awoken, she'd spoken to him, but now the thread of her words unraveled and he could not remember what she had said.

His heart thumping, he glanced in puzzlement around the narrow room with its single barred window, then remembered—he was locked up in the depths of the old North Wing of Shael'donn by order of Riklin Senn, where he could do nothing and no one any good, not even himself.

His hair was damp and plastered to his head, as if he had been feverish, but the decent meal and a night's sleep had helped. He felt much more himself. Squinting up at the wan sunlight filtering in from the window, he tried to remember what day this was. How long had it been since Haemas had found him among the ilserin and brought him somehow back to Shael'donn? Had that really been only yesterday?

The door swung inward with a creak and a tow-headed youngster peeked around the edge. "Master Monmart? I've come with your breakfast."

"Thank you . . . ?" Kevisson squinted at the young face.

"It's Emayle, sir, Emayle Ferah." The boy carried a tray over to a rough table beside the bed and set it down. The rich smell of hot buttered porridge and steaming tea filled the room. "You tutored me last year."

"Yes, Emayle." Kevisson sat up and massaged his temples. "I appreciate—"

The solid spine-wood door banged back against the stone wall. Kevisson blinked at the velvet-clad expanse of Riklin

Senn crowding the doorway, resplendent this morning in a tunic of burnt umber.

"Who in the name of Darkness authorized this?" The words came out in a bellow suitable to a bull-ummit in full rut.

"No—no one, my Lord," the boy stammered, his fingers clutching at the linen napkin he'd been about to hand to Kevisson. "I—I just th-thought Master Monmart would be— hungry."

"It was not your place to think!" Senn planted a fist on his hip and glared from underneath bristling eyebrows. "Now take that sop and get out of here!"

Kevisson swung his legs over the edge of the cot while the boy struggled with the tray.

"I suppose you coerced him." Senn slammed the door behind the boy's departing back. "You don't care how you abuse your Talent or flout Shael'donn's traditions, do you? First Myriel Lenhe, then the Saxbury woman, and now even your own students! You're a disgrace!"

Kevisson couldn't grasp what Senn was talking about. He rubbed the itchy, unshaved bristles on his chin and blearily studied the other's florid face; how strange to think that only a ten-day or so ago, it had seemed he would be Lord High Master of Shael'donn in accordance with Ellirt's last wishes and stand here in Senn's place.

Ellirt . . . what would Kniel Ellirt have done at a moment like this? The wily Andiine Master had never let anything throw him off his stride, not blindness, misfortune, or, especially, fools. Kevisson pictured the cheerful old man with the ready smile that had always twinkled, no matter what the occasion. Kniel Ellirt would have laughed in this posturing idiot's face, even if he were about to die.

Kevisson looked up into the fierce little eyes that reminded him of an enraged tree barret—and smiled.

A twinge of doubt leaked from Senn's mind before he could damp it. "I see." He strained the velvet down over his chest. "Several Council members have already been hinting about your disposition; after your Talent has been burned out, they'll remand you to a Lowlands farm where you'll serve as the meanest chierra for the rest of your days." He flicked an invisible mote of dust on his sleeve. "However, I would prefer not to have Shael'donn's honor stained with this matter. I will leave this door unlocked when I go, and I expect you to be gone when I come back—forever." He paused with his hand on the latch. "Have I made myself clear?"

Kevisson rose. "You can't be serious. As soon as Enissa recovers some of her strength, she'll clear me. I did not hurt her."

"As you didn't half-kill me that day before the Council?" Senn's lip curled disdainfully. "Unfortunately, the Saxbury woman will not be 'recovering,' as you put it. You did a far better job on her than you did on me. She died last night."

Kevisson's head reeled; Enissa couldn't be dead! Surely he would have felt her passing? He reached for the feisty healer's presence in the West Wing, but felt no trace of her. He shivered and his eyes darted helplessly around the bare walls.

"I blame myself, of course." Senn opened the door, then hesitated on the threshold. "I should have set a guard to protect her. I, better than anyone else, should have known exactly how much violence you were capable of. Do all of Shael'donn a favor, as well as yourself. Leave before the Council gets around to passing sentence on you. Don't force your former students to watch what's coming to you." Then the door clicked shut behind him.

Enissa—dead. The enormity of it stunned him—and where in the blazes was Haemas? He paced almost blindly around the dim room. Had she left Shael'donn, believing he'd killed Enissa? He could make no sense of any of this. He had to get out, breathe fresh air, find some room to think things through. Stopping at the door, he leaned against the wood and listened, both with his ears and his mind. It was time for the boys to be in class and the hall seemed to be deserted. He fumbled at the unlocked latch.

The nexus was filled with coruscating blue motes of light that danced and sparkled, obscuring the ends of the shifting timelines, and nowhere was there any sign of the woman or the girl. One hand pressed to her aching ribs, Haemas shaded her eyes with the other, squinting as she scanned the lines that led to everywhere and everyWhen. The light had a violent, overbright quality she had never seen in this place before, continually phasing from bright blue into a hellish purple-white more akin to lightning.

After long minutes of anxious searching, she caught a glimmer of Axia's mindpresence along one writhing temporal pathway, partially hidden by the wildly gyrating energies. Concentrating, she matched her foot to the erratic line. It thrummed with an angry energy she'd never experienced in the nexus before—an odd, heavy, throbbing rhythm that threw her off balance.

Fighting to keep her feet, she glimpsed golden hair amid the actinic flashes of light ahead. It disappeared, and abruptly the pathway calmed. The energies wound down, leaving only the usual background crystalline vibration, almost silent in comparison. She could make out the scene at the end of this particular line now—a night of dark, low-hanging clouds with occasional lightning and the faraway figure of a man carrying a lantern.

She stepped on the line a second time, and the scene sharpened. A golden-haired man and woman were talking, perhaps arguing. His heavy-browed face was furious, hers, thin, fragile-boned, afraid. The pair of them seemed somehow familiar, yet the woman wasn't Axia, and Kisa was nowhere in sight. Haemas took the third and final step—

—into sharp-bladed, rain-soaked grass. The clouds were scudding overhead and the wind smelled of rain. She took a shallow breath of the oppressively hot, humid air.

"You're not going anywhere!" Downslope from her, the man held a leaded-glass lamp high in one hand while he twisted the woman's arm with the other. He was tall and broad-shouldered, but soft around the middle and jowls. The yellow light threw the overpadded folds of his face and neck into harsh relief.

"For the love of Light, Brann, *let me go!*" The woman's

piercing cry reverberated through the night. "I will not be treated this way!"

Although she didn't see Axia, Haemas felt her presence there. She turned slowly, trying to locate her before the arguing man and woman took notice of her. High above, incandescent lightning split the dark roiling clouds. A heartbeat later, thunder cracked like a huge tree being broken. She glanced reflexively over her shoulder—and saw the unique stand of immense, arrow-shaped pines, and beyond, the crumbling portico of a once-proud house.

The woman shrieked, and Haemas's nails dug into her palms. She now knew where—and When—Axia had brought her. Against all odds, the Chee woman had somehow found her way to this crucial and terrifying moment from her past.

"Leave me, will you?" the man snarled.

Sweat trickled down Haemas's face as Brann Chee dragged the struggling woman through the mud, past the tumbled rocks, all the way to the cliff's edge, every detail the same as it had been when Axia had branded them into Haemas's mind through a blood-chilling nightmare.

But this time, it was real.

Knowing what was to come, she blanched at having to witness the playing out of this old tragedy. Nothing could prevent Brann Chee from doing exactly what he had done all those years ago. In accordance with the rules of the temporal nexus, even if she prevented him from murdering his wife, this When would merely split, creating an Otherwhen, while the Truewhen leading to her own time would remain the same.

In her When, and Axia's, Nells Cassidae would always die at the hand of Brann Chee.

Nells had fallen to her knees now, flailing weakly at his hands clenched in her hair, her face tear-streaked and dirty, too winded to cry out again. A jagged gash was bleeding from her right temple. Haemas's heart thumped painfully against her ribs, and she suddenly knew that she could not stand by and watch this, no matter how meaningless her interference ultimately was.

"Stop!" She slogged down the muddy path toward Chee.

He hesitated at the edge of the cliff, his feral face surprised. Then his lips twisted in a fierce grimace and he looked down at his feebly struggling wife. "Sent for reinforcements, have you? Well, it's too damn late!" His words echoed downward against the sides of the yawning chasm as his shoulders heaved to cast his wife over the edge and onto the jagged rocks below.

Haemas seized his arm, lowering her shields in the same second, and struck him with the full power of her Talent. His shields deflected the worst of the blow, but he stumbled backward, dazed, and sat down hard in the wet grass. His foot dislodged a fist-size rock that careened crazily down the cliff, ricocheting from side to side. Haemas knelt in the mud and drew the exhausted woman back from the edge, holding the thin shoulders tightly.

"Mother!" A voice rang out from the pines, then Axia drifted toward them like a blue-tinged ghost, followed by a smaller shadow, the Lenhe child.

The woman stiffened in Haemas's hands. "Lord of Light!" she said hoarsely. "What's wrong with her face?"

"It's—an effect of the ilsera crystals," Haemas said. "It will fade."

Nells rubbed her abraded throat, then touched her bleeding temple. Her hand came away dark with blood, and she stared down at it in the dim light without surprise. She sighed finally. "Thank you, whoever you are." She looked up into Haemas's face with Diren's and Axia's dark-flecked eyes. "He would have done anything to keep me from taking the children. I'm afraid he's quite mad."

Axia halted a few feet away, her hands clenched at her sides. The side of her face glowed eerily blue in the darkness. "Mother," she said again, "it *is* you."

Thunder cracked in the distance. "I don't know what you're talking about." Nells put a trembling hand to the mass of hair that had come loose and fallen around her face in sweat-soaked strings. "My daughter's just a bit of a thing yet, barely able to sit at table with us." She wavered to her feet and wiped her muddy, bloodstained hands on her skirt. "Now, I must find my children and leave before Brann recovers his wits. He's—unstable. When he get these temper fits, I never know where it will end." She glanced down at the torn sleeve of her tunic, soaked with blood from her scrapes and scratches. "My father will be furious when I show up, of course, but I can't think about that. I have to do what's best for my children."

"You—were going to take them?" Still glimmering with the blue of the nexus, Axia's eyes followed her, drinking in her every move. "That's why he was so angry?"

Nells nodded, then retreated out of reach as her dazed husband tried to stand. "Chee stock is notoriously unstable. There are rumors, of course, and none of the High Houses will marry into this Line anymore, but my father made me come to Brann. He wanted a High House for his grandchildren." She bent to the rock-littered ground to pick up the discarded lamp. "Well, at least I have two fine children from this marriage. I will come away with something."

Wearily, she lowered her head and trudged back up the slope toward the house and the children who must be hiding within earshot, since Axia had seen this as a child in her own When.

"No!" Axia's agonized voice rang out in the darkness. "Don't leave me here with him again!"

A warm raindrop spattered Haemas's cheek. "She's not." She tried to make Axia meet her eyes. "Not in this When, at least. She's taking you and Diren back to the Lowlands to live a better life."

"But I'm *here*, not up there!" Axia took two stiff steps after the retreating figure of Nells Cassidae.

"You can't go with her." Two more fat raindrops splashed the back of Haemas's neck. She felt the energies gathering in the clouds above, the interplay of humidity and temperature differential, wind and static electricity. Any minute, the storm would sweep back down across this corner of the Highlands.

Axia grimaced. "Leave me alone." Her eyes still radiated a faint, luminescent blue.

"Where's the latteh?" Haemas asked.

"I made the brat take it," Axia said in a flat voice. She

gazed stonily at the speck of yellow light that was Nells and the children returning to the house. "I had to get rid of the damn thing before it tore my mind apart, and now I can't get near it."

Haemas's heart raced as she turned to the silent child and held out her hand. "Kisa?" But the girl didn't speak, didn't move. Since the crystal had been triggered by Axia, who had been the first to touch it after it had been set, it couldn't be affecting Kisa. Axia must be controlling the girl's untrained mind. Worried, she moved wearily toward her, the soaked grass clinging to her legs. "Kisa, we have to go back now."

"Oh, you can forget that." Distaste radiated from Axia's mind. She laughed and the cold empty sound of it reverberated in the gaping black chasm. "We're never going back."

Chapter
Twenty-one

The air at the edge of the cliff had gone still and heavy, and the night was mind-numbingly silent. The impending storm hovered overhead like a great weight about to break loose. Haemas turned back to Axia and forced her voice to reasonableness. "There's no reason for you to stay here." She glanced over Axia's shoulder at the child standing far too quietly under the emerald-black pines. "You have no place in this timeline, no friends, no one who will ever recognize you as family. I'm not even sure you *can* stay indefinitely without disrupting time."

Lightning flickered overhead, crooked as a bavval's tongue, illuminating the low roiling mass of clouds. Thunder answered almost immediately in a low rumble that shook the ground.

Axia's head turned restlessly, as if seeking something. "I'll go to Cassidae'ayn and stay with my mother." The unnatural blue glow in her eyes guttered, flared, then finally faded away.

"You saw how she was when you approached her a few minutes ago. If you follow her to the Lowlands, she'll think you're insane." A wave of weariness rushed over Haemas and her knees sagged. She straightened again only with great effort. Her reserves were spent; it had taken the last ounce of her strength to stop Brann Chee from killing Nells. She passed a shaky hand over her sweat-dampened face. "And what about your brother?"

"Diren wants his precious latteh back, but he doesn't care a damn thing about me." Axia crossed to where Brann Chee still sat in the wet grass, his round face dazed and staring out into the chasm's black emptiness. "Isn't that so, *Father*? Diren only cares about himself. Isn't that what you always taught us—take care of yourself first and let Darkness have the rest?"

He glanced at her with baffled eyes, then his hand shot up and anchored itself in the hem of her gown. "Leave me, will you?" His voice was slurred, his features contorted into a snarl. "You think you're too damn good for Chee'ayn?" He lurched onto his feet and began to manhandle her through the grass and rocks toward the edge of the cliff.

No! Haemas shouted into his clouded mind. *That's not Nells!* She stumbled after the struggling pair.

"You will not shame Chee'ayn by running back to that Lowlands hovel!" He slipped in the mud, then struggled upright, never loosening his hold. "And I will not have my children brought up by some ragtag, chierra-tainted Line!"

"Father, no, it's *me*, Axia!" Axia fought like a wild creature, kicking and scratching, but he was a massive man, at least double her weight. Inch by inch, he forced her toward the edge.

Haemas wrenched at his hands, but he backhanded her to the muddy ground, then renewed his efforts to cast his daughter into the chasm. Axia screamed as he forced first her head over the sheer edge of the cliff, then her right shoulder. The straining muscles stood out in his clenched jaw.

Her cheek throbbing, Haemas scrambled back up and seized his arm. *Look at her!* she commanded. *It's not Nells! It's not!* The white-heat of his unreasoning, unshielded fury burned across the link created by the contact of her flesh on his—he didn't understand, didn't *want* to understand. He wanted only to hurt the world back, make it pay for all the pain and disappointments he had suffered. *You can't do this!* She hauled back on his arm with all her might. *Let—her—go!* From somewhere deep inside, she summoned enough energy to buckle his still-shaky shields, then slumped to her knees. His locked hands fell away, and he stared down at them numbly, as if they belonged to a stranger.

Axia rolled over, then staggered upright. Her tangled hair covered her face and her gown was soaked through with mud.

"Everything—*every*thing always had to be done your way,

didn't it?" She stiff-armed the unresisting man backward. He stumbled, dangerously close to the cliff's edge. "You never listened to anyone! Well, it's not going to be that way, not anymore!" Her voice spiraled into a thin shriek.

"Axia, don't!" Haemas tried to get up, but her legs gave way. She found herself on her hands and knees, struggling to see through the haze behind her eyes. "It won't change anything!"

"I'll see you in Darkness!" Axia shoved him again, her face triumphant. "You'll never—"

Losing his footing, Brann flailed, his hands clutching as if the air could hold him up above the soulless black emptiness below. He caught at the hem of Axia's gown, then toppled over the edge. Haemas heard the green velvet give with a sickening rip, watched him tumble backward into the waiting abyss. His hoarse scream echoed against the sheer rock cliffs.

Thrown off balance, Axia teetered, her face terrified. Haemas made a desperate lunge for her legs, but her hands came up empty as the other woman slipped over the edge. Axia's cry, more the wail of a scavenging Irael than a human, reverberated from the sides of the chasm. Frozen on her bruised knees, her empty hands clenched, Haemas stared down into the blackness. She felt Brann strike the jagged rocks first, then, a full second later, Axia, their minds flaring lightning-bright, then shattering in crimson star-bursts of pain.

A few drops of rain spattered her hair. Her chest heaved as if she had run for miles and she felt as empty as the two lifeless bodies below. She couldn't move—indeed, she might never find the energy to move again.

Something touched her shoulder and she jumped. A small, forlorn face blinked at her through the darkness. "Lady?" Kisa rubbed at her eyes with the back of one hand. "Can we go now? I'm hungry."

Tears threatened Haemas's eyes, but she wiped them away along with the warm rain. After levering herself up from the ground, she took Kisa's small hand in hers, and felt the cool, hard shape of the latteh crystal inside the child's fist.

* * *

Staring out his study window at the pine grove, Diren narrowed his eyes, outraged. After turning his sister into some sort of ghost, Haemas Tal had actually dared invade Chee'ayn, coming and going at will apparently, and even attempting to steal Kisa from him. A muscle twitched in his jaw as he remembered how she had threatened him with a silsha on the stairwell. And now, even though she had disappeared with Axia, the damn beast was still prowling the grounds. He had watched through the window earlier as it nosed around the portal.

He snatched up his cloak and settled the worn wool around his shoulders. Well, she wasn't going to spoil his plans! The latteh was the key to everything, and even she could not stand against it. He had seen the naked fear in her pale-gold eyes last night when he had come within a hairsbreadth of touching it to her cheek. It was only a matter of time before she was his again, and they both knew it. Tomorrow a funeral pyre would burn at Tal'ayn to see the old Tal into the Light. She would have to come then. And Diren would be there—waiting.

He ordered a chierra servant armed with a crossbow to follow him and watch for the silsha, then exited the main doors, heading into a winter wind out of the east so intense that his face was numb before he'd gone two steps. Snow had fallen sometime in the early-morning hours and was ankle-deep now as he and the servant crunched through the icy top layer.

He replaced the ilsera crystals, then activated each in the proper sequence. The cold flash of betweenness enveloped him—and he opened his eyes on the ancient grillwork of Senn'ayn. A thin smile twisted his lips.

Since Dervlin Tal, the Head of the Council of Twelve, had passed from this life into Darkness, the next in line for leadership was Seffram Senn, current Lord of Senn'ayn and a fitting candidate to meet the latteh nestled inside Diren's shirt.

Kevisson blinked up at the clearest green sky he'd seen in days as he retraced the snow-covered path down to the portal. The breeze was feather-light against his face, but so cold that it snatched his breath away. He lowered his head and blew on his reddening hands as he walked. Ahead of him, the House of Moons loomed, silent and empty. Without hope, he reached within it for Haemas, but she wasn't there. As far as he could tell, she wasn't anywhere in the Highlands now, and the implications of that concerned him more than Riklin Senn and the Council put together.

He abandoned his shields and called to her, baring his mind until the slightest answer would have been deafening. *Haemas? Are you all right? Where are you?*

Somewhere behind the thickly interwoven trees, a hungry barret chittered, and on the other side of Shael'donn he heard the faint cries of boys at play—nothing else. Had that supercilious Council bastard Chee gone after her again? Worry and anger boiled through him. He stopped in the middle of the path and closed his eyes, his head thrown back, and sent his awareness surging across the Highlands to Chee'ayn, straining to find her, reaching ... *reaching* ...

Nothing, not the faintest trace of her mindpresence. He shivered and cracked his eyes open, squinting at the play of sunlight on the reflective snow. Although Haemas had told him very little down by the falls, she had mentioned that Chee wanted access to the timeways. Perhaps she had gone through the nexus where no man could follow and was far beyond anyone's reach at the moment. He would have given anything to know she was all right.

So, he told himself as he flapped his arms in an effort to keep warm, what should he do now? Nobody had paid him any heed as he left Shael'donn, so he was apparently free until the Council noticed his absence. Senn had released him only so he would flee the Highlands and disappear, leaving Senn and his Lord uncle to mold Shael'donn in any way they chose, but Kevisson had no intention of going anywhere that Haemas couldn't follow, even if staying here cost him his freedom, his mindsenses, his very life. Whether he was worthy of her or not, he understood now that he needed her in his life on whatever basis she would allow—friend, lover, wife.

He stared across the diamond-topped snow. To have any

sort of future among the Kashi, he had to prove his innocence, and the elderly servant, Dorria, was the key. If someone had come to Myriel on the night that she died, Dorria must have seen him, and, since Enissa had been attacked in the very same room, Dorria might have witnessed that, too. He had to—

A low rattling snarl made him look at the surrounding trees; a pair of massive black silshas bounded through the snow toward him, tufted ears flattened to their skulls and fangs gleaming bone-white in the sun. He blanched. There wasn't even a decent-size rock readily to hand, and the Shael'donn portal lay a good fifty feet away.

He bolted anyway, his boots slipping in the wet snow. The silshas flanked him easily, black fur bristling, their hot yellow eyes pinning him between them. Throwing open his shields, he reached for the mind of the closest, knowing even as he tried that it wouldn't work. These beasts had been protected in some way by the ilseri before they had been sent to the Highlands. Everyone knew their minds were inviolable, and they answered only to Haemas Tal.

The black-furred beast regarded him with whiskered disdain while he probed, but he found no sense of what it wanted from him, no emotions or simple animal thoughts, just the frustrating blankness that protected it far better than the shields of any Kashi protected a human mind from meddling.

It padded closer and nosed his leg. When Kevisson stiffened, its ears flattened and it nipped his thigh. Startled, he jumped forward. The beast snarled and nudged him again. Relief flooded through him as he realized they weren't going to tear him into bloody bits; for some reason they wanted him to go with them.

He traipsed across the snow, herded by the two beasts, then stopped before the portal housing, puzzled. The silsha on the left batted him with a huge velvet paw and he darted up the steps. They flowed onto the platform with him, closing off his escape. Kevisson stood in the center and took a deep breath. Well, it would be relatively easy to leave them behind if he traveled by crystal. He had only to pick a suitable destination.

Lowering his shields, he tried to remember the vibrational signature for Lenhe'ayn, a difficult proposition with two snarling silshas breathing hotly in his face. Before he could summon the proper pattern to mind, he felt the crystals' energies surge. Someone was using another portal to reach this one. The silshas turned and darted out of the portal housing into the night and he tried to follow, but it was too late. An unfamiliar mental touch, rife with odd harmonics, aligned the crystals' vibrations with that other portal, and Kevisson fell into gray betweenness, the place that was no place at all, colder than a thousand Highland winters. Then, just as suddenly, he was blinking under a canopy of long, bare tree limbs interwoven high above his head.

An upside-down, green-complected face dropped abruptly in front of him, staring with Leafcurl's unblinking bright-black eyes. *Male-brother, the mothers want to know where Moonspeaker has gone.*

"Of all the bloody nerve!" Seffram Senn stirred restlessly in his favorite overstuffed chair before the roaring hearth. How dare that Chee upstart show up without so much as the slightest hint of a summons! He scowled, hoping Chee wasn't there to discuss that little deal they had made to promote his nephew's installation as Lord High Master of Shael'donn. He had no idea how Rald had been persuaded to withdraw his candidate, but it was probably more prudent not to know. He had paid off the debt in full the next day, and such things were better off never being mentioned again. It was an old adage that the less one had to do with Chee'ayn, the better. Everyone knew it was just a matter of time until those crazy damn Chees bred themselves out of existence. That Line had been notoriously wild and unstable for over five generations.

"Tell the little bastard that I'm occupied." Senn waved one hand lazily at the waiting chierra servant. "Have him make an appointment."

The servant nodded, his tan face tense, then turned back to the ornate carved wooden doors just as they swung open.

"I'm afraid my business can't wait." Clad in black trimmed

with silver, Chee smiled at the servant, who paled and dropped his dark eyes.

"My Lord?" The servant caught Seffram's eye, with the unspoken question ringing in his mind: *Should he call Security?*

"No, Franel." Seffram fingered his jaw, trying to judge how best to handle this. Chee did have a vote on the Council. It would be foolish to turn him away at this point. "Wait outside. Lord Chee will not be staying."

Chee braced his arms behind his back and strolled across the dark maroon carpet to the huge windows that stretched from ceiling to floor, looking out on the snow-covered expanse of Senn'ayn's fabled grounds. "You must lend me your head gardener this summer, Senn. I have a number of renovations planned at Chee'ayn."

"Renovations?" Seffram felt a laugh bubbling up. "The only way to renovate that nit-eaten wreck would be to level it and start over. There's nothing left there worth saving, even if you had the gold, which you do not."

"You haven't heard, then." Chee turned away from the windows and slid a hand inside his tunic. "I'm getting married."

"Oh, really?" The laugh moved upward, tickling his ribs. "Did some Lowlands House come calling?"

Chee drew his hand out, then thrust it casually behind his back. "Haemas Sennay Tal, actually. Really, I'm surprised you haven't heard."

"Haemas Tal?" The suppressed mirth escaped and ricocheted through him until he was helpless with laughter. "You can't be serious! Not only has her father just died, but that snip has sworn never to marry. By the Light, she once turned down the *Killians*! She would never settle for a Chee." Warm tears of laughter rolled down his cheeks.

"Obviously, my charms escape you." Chee's voice was strained. "Still, who knows what lies within the heart of a woman?"

"Not that one, anyway." Seffram wiped his eyes. "Even if it's true, why are you here? You certainly don't expect me to mix the anizt at your matrimonial?"

"Well, I hadn't considered that." Chee smiled thinly. "Perhaps we can discuss it later."

Something hard jammed against Seffram's temple. He stiffened in shock as a hideous grinding buzz tore through his brain. The air whooshed out of his lungs and a black fog shivered behind his eyes.

Oh, no, you don't, Chee said into his mind. *You don't get off as easily as old Tal.*

Seffram's diaphragm contracted. He took a long, shuddering breath, then another.

"That's better." Chee secreted the object inside his tunic again. "Now we're going to set up a response pattern in that moribund old brain of yours." His eyes seemed to grow larger until the dark flecks riding within them were all that Seffram could see. "From now on, anything I suggest is going to be more dear to you than your own skin. You will support me in all things, without asking any questions. Do you understand?"

The two eyes merged and formed one huge orb slivered with Darkness itself. "I—understand," Seffram heard his voice say.

"Now, you will forget this conversation and remember only that your young friend Diren spent the afternoon, exchanging pleasantries." A hand touched his temple, then suddenly he was blinking at Diren's concerned face. "You look tired, Seffram." Diren clapped him on the shoulder. "Are you all right?"

Seffram stared at the hand on his shoulder. What had they been talking about? He tugged at his ear, feeling foolish. For the life of him, he couldn't remember. Even the bright sunlight streaming in through his favorite windows looked oddly colored and strange. "I—I—"

"It's all right." Diren opened the sideboard and extracted a bottle of Nivan wine with easy familiarity. He poured a generous measure and handed it to Seffram. "Here. You've been working too hard, what with Tal's sudden death and all."

Seffram watched his shaking fingers curl around the fluted glass as if they belonged to someone else. "Tal, yes, that was a—shock."

Diren poured another portion of the amber-colored liquid for himself and settled into the chair on the opposite side of the hearth. "Well, I have a plan." He smiled, and his eyes shone across the space between them like two newly risen bright-gold moons. "I should share some of the burden you're carrying. After all . . ." He tossed off the expensive wine as lightly as if it were water. "What are friends for?"

As always, the nexus was cold, glimmering with blue light too bright to focus on, yet as Haemas stepped into it with Kisa, she could feel the same brooding rhythm that had prevailed earlier. She glanced down at the latteh in her hand and realized it was still set in the controlling mode.

She wasted a moment trying to rearrange the flickering energy pulses within the dull-green crystal, but they eluded her, maintaining the mind-binding pattern Axia had set. She glanced around at the glittering array of lines and splintered scenes; it was difficult to concentrate amid all this. Perhaps it would be better to wait until she returned to her own When to free the latteh.

She pictured her study in the House of Moons, but none of the scenes that appeared at the end of the lines were familiar. No doubt, the rattling, teeth-on-edge vibrations of the latteh were interfering, but she didn't want to waste energy exiting the nexus, then reentering, and she couldn't go back without it. Frostvine had demanded the return of this First One above all other priorities. She held the equivalent of an ilseri child in her hand, and the ilseri had every right to issue ultimatums.

Kisa's fingers tightened on hers. *I can't breathe very good here.*

Haemas concentrated harder, trying to focus the timeways as the ilseri did. She glimpsed something vaguely familiar at the end of a line to her right, just an impression of a shadowed room, but she felt that she had been there before. Clasping Kisa's hand tightly, she drew her over to the writhing blue line. *Watch,* she told her. *When the line crosses in front of you, step down on it.* Then she took the first step herself and felt the power of the nexus humming up through the sole of her foot.

Behind her, Kisa watched soberly, then did the same.

Good, she told the child. *Now we must take two more on the same line and then we will be there.* After waiting for her chance, she took a second step and then a third, feeling Kisa correctly follow her each time.

The glimmering blue faded away, leaving them in a darkened room with a vaulted ceiling, far too big to be in the House of Moons. Spicy-sweet incense filled the air and she saw fluted vases of mind-conjured chispa-fire placed around the outside of the walls. Long rows of highly polished dark wood benches had been pulled back to make room for a single shrouded bier containing the richly dressed figure of an older white-haired man.

"Oh, my Lady, I knowed you would come!" The quavering voice spoke behind her, and her heart sank as she recognized the speaker. She turned to see her old chierra nurse, Jayna, huddled by the doors in a woolen shawl. "He were took that fast." Her brown eyes were reddened and tears streamed down her lined face. "There were nothing that anyone could do, not even the healers."

Kisa tugged at Haemas's hand and whispered, "Where are we?"

"This is the chapel at Tal'ayn." Haemas's hands were cold and clammy, her heart racing like a runaway horse. Had she blundered into an Otherwhen, or was this what her When had become? She released Kisa's hand to approach the bier carved of oak.

There had been a period in her life when she had seen this scene every time she'd closed her eyes, when it had formed the substance of her every nightmare, but that had been a fabrication of her cousin Jarid, crafted to make her run away and abandon her inheritance. Her father's death had been only a sick fantasy spun by Jarid's twisted mind.

But this time ... She stopped at the edge of the bier and gazed down at the still face, white as marble beneath the silken shroud.

This time, apparently, it was real.

Chapter
Twenty-two

Leafcurl slithered out along the branch over Kevisson's head, then peered anxiously down at the small campfire burning beneath the tree. *If Moonspeaker does not return soon, the mothers say it will be too late.*

Kevisson reached for another stick of wood from his dwindling pile and tossed it into the hungry flames. He rested his chin on his knotted hands and stared moodily into the weaving flames. When he squinted, he could see Haemas's face in them, somber and yearning, anxious. Where in the name of Darkness was she? "Too late for what?" he asked dourly.

Leafcurl leaped down from the tree, a drop of at least fifteen feet, and landed lightly on his feet with dancerlike grace. He hunched his head between his shoulders and held his four-fingered hands protectively before his face as he warily circled the fire. *We may not say.*

Kevisson glanced into the trees, sensing how the other ilserin lingered out of sight amid the dark massive trunks, unnerved by the flames. Apparently, the adult ilseri had made them understand that he had to have warmth and sleep and appropriate food in order to survive. Still—he grimaced—he was stranded there, just as he was finally figuring out what was going on, with no way to return to the Highlands unless he hiked to the nearest Kashi portal, and because of the confusing manner in which he'd arrived, he had no idea as to where that might be, just so the ilseri could repeatedly ask him a question to which he had no answer—where was Haemas?

Braving the fire, Leafcurl settled an arm's length away, curling his four green limbs as neatly as a silsha. Kevisson leaned his head back against the tree's rough gray bark, thinking. Evidently, from the way the ilserin had hounded him before, a human had taken something from the pool, but that in itself was baffling. Why would a human want anything from an ilseri pool?

Because it was valuable, the back of his mind whispered, because it would bring him money or power or prestige. *Him* . . . he stared up at the tree-slivered green sky. Why had he assumed that a man had taken the object?

Because the ilserin had mistaken *him* for the thief, and although the youthful, inexperienced ilserin obviously understood very little else about humans, they did seem to know the difference between males and females.

A strong feeling grew in Kevisson's mind that a single hand lay behind everything that had happened, no matter how disconnected the events seemed—the attack on Lenhe'ayn, Riklin Senn's appointment over him to the Lord High Mastership of Shael'donn, Myriel's death, the attack on Enissa, the theft of something apparently crucial from the ilseri pool, Haemas's subsequent erratic comings and goings, the closing of the House of Moons . . .

Haemas had said Diren Chee was responsible for her disappearance, that he wanted access to the timeways. The altering of Dorria's memory and the mindblow that had led to Enissa's death all spoke of someone with a strong Talent—and Chee did hold a seat on the Council. Kevisson got to his feet and scavenged more deadfall wood from the brush, still thinking. It must have been Chee who had broken his Search link and almost killed him. He piled an armful of sticks beside the fire, then closed his eyes and settled back against a hollow log, slowing his breathing, letting his mind drift, Searching his memory much as he had Searched the Highlands for Haemas.

When he had found her the night after she'd disappeared, he'd had an impression, just for an instant, of a tall rambling house built of crumbling gray stone and weather-blasted wood. That must have been Chee'ayn. He remembered something Myriel Lenhe had said before she'd died, about the leader of the chierra attack—something that had made no sense at the time. "There was something wrong with his eyes," she had insisted. "They were the wrong color."

At the time, he'd thought perhaps they had been blue or gray, like those of Outlanders. Had she meant instead that his eyes were Kashi-gold, not chierra-brown? Had *Chee* led the attack on Lenhe'ayn, then killed Myriel to guard his secret? Opening his eyes again, he watched his exhaled breath misting white in the frigid air. He had to return to the Highlands and find Chee—before there were more deaths.

He glanced into the thickly set trees, feeling the childlike ilserin's eyes studying his every move. He couldn't afford the days that hiking back would cost, even if the ilserin would let him go this time, and they very likely would not. He had to persuade the older ones, the ilseri, to send him back, but how? He couldn't even see them, let alone communicate with them.

"Leafcurl?" He motioned to the slim green creature that was closest, although to his eyes all ilserin looked enough alike to be seeds in the same callyt pit. "I have to go back."

Why? Leafcurl advanced over the frozen ground, his naked four-toed feet making no noise at all in the crackly dead brush.

"To find Moonspeaker." Kevisson concentrated, producing in his mind Haemas's oval face surrounded by a cloud of shining pale-gold hair.

But she is on the business of the mothers. Leafcurl looked anxiously over his shoulder as the other ilserin crept through the trees like dim green shadows to stand behind him. *Such things are forbidden to male-brothers.*

"Among ilseri and ilserin, I'm sure that is true, but not among the Kashi." Kevisson unclenched his fists, trying to curb his mounting impatience. "I must find her. She may be in terrible danger."

The ilserin's head whipped around. The others froze in place, like a herd of startled ebari, then leaped almost as a single creature into the trees and clambered high over Kevisson's head. *Windsign says Moonspeaker has returned!*

"To the Highlands?" A surge of excitement ran through him. If so, he could Search for her, as he had done before.

Then doubt surfaced; what if Chee sensed him and broke his link again? The last time had nearly killed him, and there were no healers waiting to save his life down here in the forest.

To the high places,' yes. Leafcurl's eyes, bottomless as two holes, gazed down at him through the leafless branches. *But ilseri cannot travel there. Windsign and Summerstone ask: Do you wish to go to her?*

"Yes!" Kevisson rotated, peering through the densely packed trees, but he could see no sign of the elusive ilseri who had to be there—somewhere. "Tell them I will help in any way I can. I will give my life for her!"

Leafcurl reached down and bracketed Kevisson's face with cool green fingers. *Open your mind, male-brother, and the mothers will send you. They say there is little time left.*

For a second, Kevisson hesitated, reluctant to drop his shields before creatures he could neither sense nor communicate with. He squinted up into the layer upon layer of tree limbs surrounding him, pinning him in this cheerless place so far from everything he knew. He didn't want to stay shut up here with the children while Haemas was in danger back somewhere in the Highlands.

Haemas ... She trusted the ilseri implicitly, and he had no choice but to do the same. He could either believe them and join the fight, or wait things out down here with the rest of the males in this blasted nursery.

He flung open his mind, laying himself bare before the unseen and unseeable natives, concentrating on his desire to find Haemas and fight at her side in any way possible. A moment of fierce blueness overwhelmed him; an alien presence swept through his mind, blinding him to everything else, stealing the breath from his lungs. He swayed, unable to command his limbs or receive any input from his senses. Then a great roaring surfaced in his head, and he crumpled to his knees, instinctively throwing his hands out to break his fall. His outspread fingers slid through new, wet snow, which soaked coldly through the legs of his pants. He took a spasmodic lungful of achingly chill fresh air as he waited for his vision to clear.

Whatever had brought him here was like nothing he had ever encountered before.

Blinking furiously, he wiped away tears and glanced up at the twin crags with their bridging tower—the famous, never-to-be-forgotten sight of Tal'ayn.

"The mourners will be arriving that quick, coming through those very doors." Jayna wrung her work-roughened hands in her apron. "The family, what little there is of it, should be down here in the chapel to greet them, but Lady Alyssa—" Her mouth compressed and she dabbed angrily at the tears leaking from her reddened eyes. "*She* won't come!"

Haemas stared down at the empty face of her father, feeling as if she made the slightest movement she would break into slivers and scatter across the floor. This wasn't real; it couldn't be. Down through the years, she had seen him dead in her mind a thousand times, and yet known all the while that he lived. Guilt bubbled up through tiny cracks in her reason, unexpected and fever-hot.

A distant part of her understood that the damage Jarid had done her all those years ago was resonating now with this scene; she'd never been able to completely eradicate the false memory he'd spliced into her drugged mind. She and Master Ellirt had only been able to subordinate it to the truth of what had actually happened on that terrible night—that it had been Jarid who had attacked her father and the chierra servant Pascar who had died, not her father.

But the image still lurked below the surface, painfully sharp. *He sprawled across the rug, one limp hand grazing the toe of her boot. She wanted to run, to scream, to do anything but just stand there, frozen, gazing down at her father's white and empty face.*

Sweat beaded her forehead, chilling her in the cool air of the chapel. She felt Jayna's warm fingers on her clammy arm. "How—" She couldn't make her head turn, couldn't look at the beloved chierra servant who had raised her. "—how—did this happen?"

"It were, as they say, natural causes." Jayna's voice was

only a whisper in the still, incense-permeated air. "One minute, he were visiting with Lord Chee in his study, and the next he were lying there in his chair, eyes staring, cold and dead. It were that fast."

An icicle formed around Haemas's heart. She forced herself to look at Jayna's tear-swollen face, touched her wet, wrinkled cheek. "Lord—Chee?"

"Yes." Jayna reached past her to pick up a basket, then folded back the silk veil over the bier and began spreading the traditional tiny white anith flowers around her father's body. "He came to speak with his Lordship last night. Lady Alyssa took him into the study herself. His Lordship were that angry at first. Ivva and I could hear him yelling all the way down the hall, even through the door."

Sick flutters exploded in Haemas's stomach, as if she were full of lightwings trying to batter their way out. Diren Chee had come here, to her father's house, and now her father lay dead. What was it that Chee had said to her? *"The poor fellow wasn't up to it, but it wasn't a total loss. Just before he died, he admitted that he had never changed his will."*

He had told her, had all but pushed her nose in what he had done, and she had dismissed his words as a weak bluff. Her throat closed; she might as well have killed him herself. She should have stopped Chee somehow, should have told the Council about the latteh when she'd first returned from the Otherwhen, should have made them believe her and demanded their help!

The blood pounded in her temples, and she knew that no matter what she had said, the Council would not have taken her word against Chee's. The Lords disdained her because she made no pretense of being a traditional Kashi wife and daughter. And then there was the promise she had made to the ilseri to keep the secret of the latteh crystals. If she had enlisted the help of any other Kashi, she could not have made that promise, and a whole new era of cruel power plays among the Kashi, not to mention extinction for the ilseri, would have begun. Unwittingly, Chee had pitted Kashi against ilseri once again, and Haemas was caught squarely in the middle. It had to be her fight and no one else's.

She watched Jayna's hand tremble as she scattered the fragile white flowers along the length of the bier. Tears coursed down the old woman's faded cheeks in an unending stream, but Haemas's own eyes were hot and dry. She wondered where her tears had fled.

The doors to the chapel creaked inward, admitting a frigid draft. Haemas caught a glimpse of gold-encrusted robes as Father Orcado's staid presence swept into the room.

"Peace be with you, my child," he said, his voice loud in the chapel's stony silence.

Kisa darted out of the shadows to press against Haemas's side. She glanced down at the child's drawn face, catching the memory of this man presiding at another funeral only days before, *Kisa's mother and brother consigned to a huge pyre while the orange-yellow flames leaped up and up . . .*

She put her arm around the trembling girl and turned to Jayna. "Please take Kisa down to the kitchen and get her some warm food. Then have Ivva bathe her and put her to bed in my old room. Perhaps some of my old clothes will fit her."

Jayna nodded and looked down, seeming to notice the exhausted child for the first time. "Of course." She reached for the small hand. "Poor little barret, she looks half starved, as well as all done in."

Kisa shrank back from Jayna's chierra hand. Haemas bent down and stroked her tangled red-gold hair. *It's all right. Jayna will take good care of you. She looked after me when I was growing up here at Tal'ayn.*

Jayna smiled an encouraging gap-toothed smile, crinkling her face into a maze of wrinkles. "Now, lass, you just come with old Jayna and she'll see you're looked after proper like."

Kisa stared at Jayna's hand for another few seconds, then took it reluctantly. "But what about my father?"

"We'll talk about him later." Haemas caught a flicker of interest from Father Orcado. "Go with Jayna."

Hesitantly Kisa allowed the old chierra servant to lead her past Orcado's narrowed eyes.

"What was that all about?" The priest drew Haemas away from the bier as Jayna shepherded the child through the rows of polished hardwood benches. His brows knotted. "No one has come forward to declare himself father to either Lenhe girl, and the Council has been deliberating on their disposition."

"I—can't talk about that right now." Haemas flinched as the doors settled back into place with a solid thunk. She rubbed her cold arms and gazed up into the shadowed eaves, feeling shut-in, buried in this dimly lit place.

"No, I suppose not." Orcado turned to the bier, his heavily brocaded robes rustling. His face looked an unhealthy gray-white in flickering blue chispa-fire. "Has the pyre been completed yet?"

"The pyre?" she echoed hollowly.

Orcado glanced sharply over his shoulder at her. "The funeral pyre—for your father. To send him on to the Light."

Her father . . . involuntarily, her eyes went back to the stern face, blurred by the silken veil, so still that he might have been carved from the same wood as the bier. She had wanted so badly for him to love her all these years, something he had never been able to do. Now . . . her empty hands clenched. Now they would never make peace with one another.

With a wrench, she pulled herself back to the present. If the funeral was to be soon, she didn't have time to stay. She had to return the latteh to the pool and she had lingered here too long already. Frostvine had insisted the nascent ilseri had very little time left before it lost its ability to enter the Change. If she stayed for the ceremony, it might be too late and everything she had labored to build between the Kashi and the ilseri would be lost.

She touched the hard shape of the crystal inside her mud-caked tunic. "I can't stay," she heard herself say absently to Orcado. "I have something—important—to do."

"Something important?" Orcado's voice rang out and the mind-conjured chispa-fire in the urns lining the walls flared at his intensity. "More important than seeing your father on into the Light?" He seized her wrist. "More important than doing your duty?"

She felt his pompous mind pushing at her shields, demanding to know what led her to deny this last of all family duties, and suddenly she was filled with outrage. What right did he. have to judge her? He had no idea of what was at stake here or what she had suffered to come this far. She jerked her wrist, but he only tightened his grip, his fingers digging painfully into her flesh, his flat golden eyes glowering at her. Furious, she shoved him back against a long wooden bench. He stumbled, releasing her to catch himself, then lost his balance and sprawled facedown across the flagstones.

She backed away and reached inside her pocket to cup the latteh in her palm, assessing the energy patterns that flickered within it. Was it her imagination, or were they waning?

Without warning, the chapel doors flew inward, hitting the inside walls with a dull, reverberating clang. A narrow-faced man stepped into the open threshold, his dark-clothed body framed in thin wintery sunlight. "Well, my dear, this *is* fortunate. I had very much hoped to be able to pay my respects to you as well as your departed father."

Haemas's fingers tightened around the dying crystal.

It was Diren Chee.

As Frostvine's diffuse mass rode the morning's warming air currents up over the rugged mountains, she watched the striated gray rocks and stunted trees below for some sign of human habitation, but there was none on this side of the great mountain. Halfway up, she passed a barrier of crystal-generated energies that she could easily surmount. Still, she perceived that the humans of the lower regions who were without mindstrength would not have been able to do so, and saw that this must be how they were kept out of the mountains.

It made her realize there were many mysteries left in this world that she would like to know and understand. She felt reluctance to leave this plane of existence, and yet it was clearly her time. She had spent portions of the long Interims of her life studying the puzzling pale-skinned invaders, and instinct insisted that now was the moment when the future would be made. Long ago, when the humans had nearly eradicated her kind, she had been very young and her older sisters had lacked the understanding of how to take action, but this time was different. She had come into her final strength and the ilseri would prevail.

Topping the last ice-crowned peak, Frostvine rode the cold air currents, sinking down to a great sweeping plateau that would have been lush with trees and vegetation in the warm season. High overhead, the orange sun gleamed in the cloudless green sky, seeding its energy over the human domains. Spinning herself thinner and thinner, she soaked the free heat energy up, drawing it all into herself to starve the land and its denizens below.

The temperature beneath her plummeted, creating an area of cold so absolute that no living thing, large or small, could continue to exist. Then she seeped toward a human habitation that lay ahead. As she passed, the tree limbs below froze, then shattered into crystalline shards at the slightest gust of breeze.

She knew the absorption of so much energy would incinerate her like a leaf that had blundered into flame, but before the end she would have traversed the entire area of this high plateau and made this world safe again for her kind.

Several horned beasts looked up from the snow below where they were foraging for dried vegetation, their shaggy blue-gray fur almost hiding their bright-black eyes. Sensing the approaching cold-death, they spun on their haunches to flee, then staggered as she passed over them and stole the life-sustaining warmth from their flesh. Their bodies broke with a brittle crash as they hit the hard-frozen ground, scattering across the snow in icy splinters.

Chapter
Twenty-three

Wedged between a storage shed and the courtyard wall, Kevisson shivered and tugged his collar up. Even though he could see little of what was going on, he could hear the ring of the ax down at ground level as the chierra staff cut wood. Between the activities below and the number of incoming guests, there was no mistaking that preparations were being made for a funeral pyre—but whose?

Hugging his arms around his body for warmth in the frost-laden air, he tried to convince himself that these preparations weren't for Haemas. Surely the ilserin would have told him if she was dead. Tilting his head back, he squinted at the winter sun's pale-orange disk riding above him in the green sky. It was probably somewhere around the Twelfth Hour, although it was hard to be sure. The enticing smell of fresh-baked bread drifted from the Tal'ayn kitchens over on the far side of the house, no doubt being prepared for the huge influx of mourners.

Blue flashed in the ornate Tal'ayn portal in the middle of the courtyard, and he hastily reinforced his shields as another incoming party of richly garbed Kashi arrived. He leaned against the freezing stone wall, fighting his impatience. Where was Haemas, and why had she come *here*, of all places? He wanted to reach out to her and tell her that he was there, but with so many trained Kashi roaming about, he was afraid of being detected. If he hadn't been a wanted man, he would have eavesdropped on some of the lesser-Talented Kashi minds arriving for the ceremony, but if he was going to be of any help to Haemas, he had to stay free to move about.

He heard shouts from the ground below, and then the squeals

of harnessed ebari pulling chopped wood up in large sleds from
the groves that surrounded the main house. His hands felt like
blocks of ice as he beat them against his sides to restore circu-
lation, and he suddenly knew that if he stayed out there in the
courtyard one more minute, he would go insane. He didn't care
if someone from Shael'donn or the Council apprehended him
right away. He had to find out whose pyre was being laid.

Because if Haemas wasn't safe, nothing else mattered.

Stepping into the dim, quiet recesses of the Tal'ayn chapel,
Diren savored the startled feel of Haemas Tal's mind before him,
worn and weary like a rock barret run to ground after a long and
grueling chase. He glanced at the priest sprawled against one of
the benches. "Why, Father Orcado, I believe they were just looking for you at the pyre." He reached down and helped the older
man to his feet, then shoved the bench back into place. "Go on
ahead and I'll bring Lady Haemas in a few minutes."

Orcado tugged his brocaded cassock back into place, his
eyes furious. "I'm afraid Lady Haemas says she has more *important* things to do than attend to her father's pyre."

Diren cocked his head. "She's distraught," he said smoothly,
"as she has every right to be, under the circumstances." He
glanced at the flower-strewn bier and folded his hands. "I'll
speak to her after you leave. I'm sure she'll see reason."

Orcado sniffed, then lowered his head and bulled through
the chapel doors. A gust of chill air stirred the stuffy room as
they clanged shut behind him.

Diren pulled a black leather glove from his belt, then thrust
his hand into it, taking care to snug each finger down. Haemas
backed away from him, her face thinned by weariness and
grief, her eyes haunted. Diren smiled. "Why do you fear me,
Lady? You must know by now that I bear you no malice."

After drawing the other glove, he donned it, too, then flexed
his fingers several times, studying her out of the corner of his
eye. Her face was smudged, her hair loosened across her
shoulders, her tunic torn, yet the exotic pale eyes stared at him
so fiercely that they seemed to be illuminated by an inner
light. He could feel the air crackle around her. She was more

than magnificent—along with the latteh, she was the key to his future, a prize beyond price.

He drew the incense-laden air deep into his lungs. "If I didn't care for you, I would not have selected you as Lady of Chee'ayn." He let his gaze drift past her to the bier. "And you would be dead."

Her white-gold eyes glittered in the suddenly flaring chispa-fire. She shifted, trembling and poised for flight.

Her fear and indecision intoxicated him like a heady perfume; soon, yes, *soon* she, and everything she represented, would be his. He drew the new latteh from his pocket and held it up. The irregular facets glimmered dull green in the blue glow of the chispa-fire. "Really, I should be quite vexed with you." He turned the crystal over in his gloved hand and watched the light play across it. "You have no idea how much trouble it was to obtain this."

She stiffened. "Is that how you—killed my father?" Her voice was low.

He caught at the edges of something unexpected in her mind, an emotion so strong that, for a second, it shimmered white-hot through her shields. He held his breath, standing absolutely still so that he could read the faint, already-receding traces of . . . guilt.

A thin smile twisted his lips. *Yes,* he whispered forcefully into her mind, *I would not have come to him if you had accepted me. Why didn't you just give me what I asked for? I wasn't unreasonable; it is a Kashi daughter's first obligation to marry and produce children. It's your fault that Tal lies there cold and dead, food for the flames.*

Her high-cheekboned face had gone as pale as that of her dead father. Diren strolled toward her, his boots loud on the flagstones, the latteh extended in his gloved hand, already set for control. *Aren't you tired of fighting?* He schooled his tone to reasonableness, then, letting his desire for her wash outward like a warm tide, he stretched out his other hand. *Accept me and I'll take care of you. We will rule the Highlands together.*

Unexpectedly, the despair in her mind lashed out, raw and aching, battering his shields, but it was not nearly as powerful as he would have expected. With a laugh to hide his exertion, he sloughed it off. "Is *that* how you got rid of Axia? You'll have to do better than that with me."

More guilt surged up in her mind. Then, with an effort, she shielded it, but not before he caught the echo of a shrill scream in her mind. He slipped around the flower-strewn bier, narrowing the distance between them.

She held her ground, hands clenched at her sides, jaw set. "Don't you want to know where she is?"

"No," he said glibly, and with a shock, realized he really didn't. "She obviously bungled things, as usual, but I don't have to put up with fools anymore." He edged closer.

"She died at the hands of your father!" She backed away from him until she tripped and caught herself against the far wall.

"Don't be ridiculous. Our father died years ago." Diren dodged around the bier and angled to cut her off from the door.

"She went back without me—after she took Kisa." Her eyes flickered to the right as she realized he now stood between her and the only way out. "She found that last night with your mother—"

"You're just playing for time." A muscle jumped under his eye. "That's the last place she would have gone."

"It was an Otherwhen." She passed a grimy hand over her face and straightened her shoulders. Pain glimmered in her eyes. "I stopped him, but it made no difference here."

"What do you mean—'you stopped him'?" His fingers tightened until the latteh's facets bit through the glove's soft leather.

"I couldn't let him kill her." Slowly she reached into the pocket of her torn tunic and pulled out an oblong shape. "So now, in that timeline, Nells survives to take her children back to the Lowlands and raise them at her father's house."

She was holding the other latteh, he realized suddenly—the one that Axia had carried into the temporal nexus on that ill-fated expedition. He took an involuntary step back. Then he saw her eyes drop to the latteh crystal cradled in her hands; even as the two of them watched, its color was fading visibly from dull green to gray.

"What have you done to it?" He leaped forward and wrenched her wrist in his free hand.

Alarmed, she jerked back, but couldn't break free. "It's dying!" Her words came out in a rush as she struggled against his grip. "I have to take it back to the pool!"

"How in the name of Darkness do you know about the pool?" He tightened his fingers and dragged her toward him, bringing up the primed latteh in his other hand.

Her eyes widened until they seemed to make up half her face as he brought the latteh closer. "No, it has to go back to the pool before it's too late!"

Lightning blazed through his hand where he touched her; then the tiled floor rose up to smack him from behind. He sprawled there, his ears roaring and his vision obscured by a white haze. Dimly he made out the figure of Haemas Tal as she staggered into a glittering whorl of blue that disappeared as suddenly as it had come.

Obliged to slow as she came to the first widespread human habitation, Frostvine continued to bleed the warmth out of each field and orchard and herd beast as she passed. It grieved her to be responsible for the ending of so much blameless life, yet it was the nature of these human-things to exploit the land and the creatures that thrived upon it. Nothing must be left, not the tiniest beast, nor the least blade of vegetation—nothing that they could live upon if she died before killing the last of their prolific kind.

The structure rising up before her had been constructed of the heavy gray stone native to this region and was very dense on the outside. Flowing around it, she lingered, letting her tenuous body seep through the most minute of cracks until she filled the building and drew out the last bit of life-sustaining energy. Inside, the humans lay scattered on the floor, their frozen bodies broken into icy shards by the impact of their falls.

Heat energy seethed within her like a lightning-laden storm. Never had she been so full, yet she had barely begun. The path of destruction she was weaving would take all of a day and perhaps part of the night, if she could hold together that long.

Withdrawing from the stone building, she surged onward, continuing to snuff out each spark of life below with her death-dealing shadow.

Haemas felt the latteh failing as she fled into the sheltering blueness of the nexus. Dropping her shields, she stripped her mind bare to its need, funneling her own life energy into its waning core. Her knees melted and she had to fight to keep her feet, to go on thinking and breathing.

The dim green pulses flickered on the edge of extinction, then steadied and held at a critically low level. She cradled the latteh in her hand and searched for the temporal line that would take her back to an ilseri pool in her own When. Blood pounded in her ears as she tried to calm herself. If she focused correctly, the exit had to be here; she had only to find it, but her eyes kept blurring and she was so tired, so achingly cold.

Moonspeaker . . .

Her head jerked around. *Summerstone?*

There is not much time.

Haemas studied the glittering array of lines, each leading to a scene that sometimes varied from the one beside it in only the slightest of details—a scaly tree branch that grew to the right instead of the left, a cloud marginally bigger or whiter or wispier than the one in the adjacent scene. It was the same old problem: so many Otherwhens mixed in with the Truewhen she had to find.

She spread her fingers protectively over the failing crystal, feeling its need increase. *Which is the Truewhen?*

Empty your mind, then choose, the ilseri bade her. *Truewhen is a thing beyond mere knowing; it must be felt.*

Empty her mind. They always said that to her, and though she tried, understanding never came. She suspected it was a basic difference in the way ilseri and human minds were put together. Human minds simply could not reliably distinguish between Truewhen and Otherwhen.

And yet she must.

Closing her eyes, she pressed the latteh crystal to her heart, trying to let everything go: pain . . . anguish . . . guilt . . . try-

ing to float in a bright-blue sea of light where nothing intruded, not even hope. In the recesses of her mind, something
stirred. Without thinking, she took a step and felt the temporal
line humming beneath her foot.

She opened her eyes and studied the scene at the end of the
line: a forest glade in winter—and a half-frozen pool. With
two more steps, she emerged from awesome blue brilliance of
the nexus into the chill gray bite of a Lowlands winter day.

A green shape appeared behind a sheltering tree trunk.
Hurry, small sister!

She passed the fading latteh into Summerstone's four-
fingered hands, then watched the ilseri plunge into the freezing
water to place it beneath the surface.

"Is it too late?" Haemas hovered anxiously at the edge of
the ice-rimmed pool, seeing herself reflected like a rippled
ghost on the water's surface.

It is very weak. Summerstone's head surged out of the water. Her impassive alien eyes riveted Haemas as she climbed
up the smooth white stone steps, shedding icy droplets.

A gust of wind scritched the bare tree limbs against each
other and Haemas thought of the second latteh left behind at
Tal'ayn, as well as the girl, Kisa. "I have to go back."

To the high places?

Haemas rubbed her eyes. Every muscle in her body ached.
She longed to burrow into a heap of dead leaves at the foot of
one of these trees and sleep for days. "I have to reclaim the
other First One."

Frostvine has already gone before you. Summerstone's outline
softened as the ilseri altered her density until she was only a
vague green haze. *She did not believe you would be successful.*

Haemas watched her drift up through the twisting branches.
"Tell her that I have brought the one in the most danger and
am going back for the other."

*We cannot. In her present state, she cannot hear us, and
there is little time left.* The dissolving black eyes bored into
her. *We cannot survive in the high elevations long enough to
find her. You must recover the other First One, then make
Frostvine understand before it is too late.*

"What is she going to do?" Haemas asked, but received only an increasing sense of confused despair from the ilseri's mind, as if the answer was something terrible for which Haemas had no concept.

You must find her! Summerstone insisted, and then would say no more.

Wearily Haemas opened her mind to the ilsera crystals set into the rim of the pool and sorted out the spatial vibrations that would transport her from one place to another instead of one When to another. The gray betweenness flashed by; then she found herself standing in the Tal'ayn portal, blinking at the backs of three Kashi who had arrived just seconds before her.

A stocky Lord jerked around. "What the—" Then he stared. "Lady Haemas?"

She knew she should recognize this man, but her exhausted mind would not supply his identity. "Please excuse me," she murmured, and tried to slip past him.

"Have we missed the pyre?" His thick fingers closed around her arm. He smelled of woodsmoke and freshly oiled leather, and his eyes were kind. "We're sorry to be so late, but I see something has kept you, too."

"I—I really don't have time to talk." She gazed pointedly at his hand on her arm until his fingers loosened. "Please excuse me." Then, as she descended the portal steps two at a time, she remembered his name: Ellric Bramm, the father of one of her students at the House of Moons, who was no doubt wondering how he could ever have entrusted his daughter to such a rude, untidy, wild-eyed creature as she must now appear.

So my bride has returned.

Her head whipped around, but Chee was nowhere to be seen in the snow-dusted courtyard.

How touching that you couldn't bear to be separated from me for more than a few minutes. She could feel the amusement in his mind. *Shall I give you your matrimonial gift now?*

Ellric Bramm pulled his wife closer to his side, staring at her from under shaggy gold eyebrows. "Is there some— problem, Lady Haemas?"

Down here, Chee said. *On the ground.*

Turning away from the Bramms, Haemas crossed to the parapet, then shaded her eyes and looked down to the Tal'ayn grounds below, where the chierra servants were putting the last touches on the huge funeral pyre. A tiny figure waved up at her, the winter sunlight glinting on his bright-gold hair. Beside him stood another, smaller figure, its hair a redder shade of gold. With a pang, Haemas realized it was Kisa.

What do you want? She shivered as the wind whipped through the elevated courtyard.

I want you to come down here and behave like a proper woman—for once. The amusement died out of his tone. *You must see your father into the Light, of course, but then, after the ceremony, we'll announce our coming matrimonial.*

Don't be ridiculous! she flung back.

Well, then, I suppose I'll just have to marry Kisa here. I doubt she'll mind.

Haemas's nails dug into the frigid stone and she cursed herself for stupidity. She must appear to agree with him, play along, say anything to get close enough to steal the latteh and return it to the pool. *It would be pointless to marry her. She's far too young,* she answered, letting a faint hint of jealousy infiltrate her thoughts.

They say the young meat is the most tender. Still, the matter is open for discussion. Come down.

Fighting a shiver that had little to do with the chill of the afternoon air, she turned away from the wall. She had to get the latteh; she tried to concentrate only on that and not think ahead to what would happen if she failed.

The servants glanced worriedly at her as she hurried down the familiar passageways, taking the shortest route to the main entrance below. Several sober-faced guests tried to speak to her, but she pretended not to hear, brushing past before they got out more than two words.

Her old nurse, Jayna, waited by the front door, bundled up in a patched cloak, her eyes red. "There you be." Relief welled up in her simple mind. "I was so feared none of the family would be here, but I should have knowed, no matter what, that *you* would not let the old Lord down."

But she *had* let her father down, Haemas thought bleakly as she pushed past Jayna's comfortably round body without replying. She should have stopped Chee before he had ever thought to come here. Now her father was dead and Chee still had the latteh.

She rushed outside into a staggering wall of pain as Chee's mind battered her in an all-out assault to break down her shields. She huddled on the steps, pouring all her strength into resisting, swaying as the energy drain made her light-headed. She'd had no sleep and nothing to eat, and had used far more energy than she could afford in the last few hours. She put her hands to her spinning head, then caught herself against the iron rail.

Abruptly he backed off. *We were meant to be together.* She could see him more clearly now, dressed in his usual black trimmed with silver, standing before the unlit pyre, his shoulders square and his hand resting lightly on Kisa's shoulder. *Stop fighting me.*

I might marry you, she said, her heart hammering, *if you discard that wretched thing. I have no intention of being your slave!*

Ah, but I can't get rid of this, he answered. *Not when it's brought me so many wonderful new friends.* He smiled as a group of men dressed in fine dark velvets and wools emerged from behind the towering pyre to flank him.

Haemas backed away as she recognized portly Seffram Senn, who would now head the Council of Twelve in her father's place, and stern-faced Himret Rald, current Lord of Senn'ayn, standing next to the elegant frame of Aaren Killian, who had once contracted for her to marry his son. With them were all the others, the remaining High Lords who made up the Council.

"What—?" Haemas could not find her voice.

I want only the best for you—that you take your place among us as a Kashi wife and mother. Chee swept his arm at the others. *And they're all quite willing to help.*

A wave of compulsion swept over her like a block of granite descending relentlessly upon her head as eleven of the strongest, best-trained Kashi in the Highlands combined their will against hers, trying to break her shields and lay her mind bare to Chee's desires.

Chapter
Twenty-four

Below Frostvine, the land folded into sharp rock-covered hills, forcing her to flow down into the angled nooks and crannies, through snow-covered thickets, and into every outbuilding and cave. She would leave no human alive up here in these snowy lands, even though the ilseri had traditionally avoided this country as too cold for their life cycle. The wretched human-things of power had menaced the ilseri lives for the last time. Though it was her final act, Frostvine would cleanse them from the surface of this planet and leave it safe for her kind.

Coming upon another large cluster of human habitations, she slowed again, spreading her heat-stealing substance everywhere, leaving nothing behind but the momentary absolute cold of deepest space. Beneath her, she saw the creatures stumble and fall to the ground, hard-frozen lumps that would never again know life.

But several human-things raced ahead of her and then, to her annoyance, disappeared. She realized they had used ilsera crystals to travel to another location here in the high country.

It did not matter. Wherever they had gone, she would find them before the end.

Even as Haemas fought against Chee's amplified compulsion, she felt her leaden right foot slip, unbidden, forward through the slushy, ankle-deep snow. The world around her, the cold, the snow-covered Tal'ayn grounds, the huge pyre of wood rising to meet the green sky, the eleven Kashi men arrayed before it, everything disappeared in a buzzing white-hot haze.

YOU SEE? Augmented by ten trained minds all equal to or greater than his own, Chee's words thundered in her head. *IT'S NO USE FIGHTING.*

Her left foot lurched another step forward against her will, and panic ate through her. It wasn't even necessary to compel her to go to him. He only had to pin her there until he touched her with the latteh. Then she would be finished.

As would the rest of the Highlands, the back of her mind whispered. If she lost this fight, Frostvine would make good her threat and then everything would be lost. Taking a shuddering breath, she forced the raw, achingly cold air into her lungs and fought to clear her head.

YOU'LL MAKE A VALUABLE BRIDE, Chee said. *AND THINK OF THE CHILDREN YOU'LL BEAR ME. WITH THE LATTEH BEHIND THEM, THEY'LL RULE THE HIGHLANDS LIKE THE GREAT LORDS OF OLD.*

Sweat trickled down her neck and froze as she poured everything she had into her shields, trying to shut Chee out. The crushing onslaught gave a little and she thought she caught the faint swish of hurried footsteps approaching in the snow. Her stomach tightened—was that him?

But she could hear again; she seized upon that fact. And if she could hear, perhaps with just a little more effort she could regain her sight, too. Then, from out of nowhere, a familiar, sun-gold presence enveloped her, offering a quiet, steady strength. She turned her head blindly, seeking its source. *Kevisson?*

In the house behind you. Take as much as you need. I give you control. His mindpresence melded with her shields. The pain eased and then her vision cleared. She saw Chee striding quickly toward her, the latteh thrust out in his gloved hand.

She backed away. If Chee hadn't been hammering at her, she would have tried to disarm the latteh as Master Ellirt had taught her, but as it was, she could only protect herself. She jerked off her cloak and hastily swathed her hands in it.

A few feet away, Chee paused, his black-clad body dark

against the artificial mountain of the funeral pyre. "So your chierra lover has returned." A bitter smile ghosted across his face. "It won't matter. Monmart is nothing compared to us. What little he can give you won't last more than a few minutes. You're only postponing the inevitable."

White points of light shimmered behind her eyes for a second as Chee channeled the power of the ten men behind him, and she realized he was right. Whatever advantage she had gained from Kevisson was only temporary. Even this melding of his strength and hers would soon fail.

She glanced around the familiar grounds, the home from which she had been estranged for so many years, and suddenly anger flashed through her—a staggering, white-hot fury that she had lost her father and the House of Moons, that all Kashi might now lose their homes and lives, all because of the greed of this one crazed man who would not put away the forbidden lore that this When had sensibly abandoned generations ago.

Concentrating that anger, she focused it into one stunning burst and let it fly at Chee. *It's your fault, all your fault!* Deathly cold from shock and exhaustion, yet molten-hot with anger, she watched him stumble backward, then sink to the ground like a puppet whose strings had been severed. *You have stolen my father, and Enissa, and the House of Moons, and the Mastership at Shael'donn, and now the rest of us will probably lose everything, all because you must have what never was due you!*

For an instant Chee's stunned mind lay bare before her. She saw her father's shocked expression as Chee pressed the latteh to his temple . . . saw Chee whispering into Kevisson's unconscious mind as he set up the attack on Riklin Senn . . . saw him leading a group of mind-controlled chierra men against Lenhe'ayn and striking down a fair-haired boy who penetrated his overstressed shields . . . saw him returning to Lenhe'ayn to snuff out the life of Myriel Lenhe as she lay deeply asleep . . . glimpsed her own face, pallid and barely breathing after being bludgeoned with the grinding force of the latteh . . . saw the calculated attacks on Enissa both at Lenhe'ayn and later at Shael'donn—and something more that she had never suspected: She saw Master Ellirt's ashen face as he lay dying from a little-known poison, a poison that Diren Chee had slipped into his drink.

Haemas slumped to her hands and knees, wrist-deep in the cold, wet snow, utterly drained.

You! Kevisson's mindvoice was thready and weak; she realized guiltily that he had already expended more energy than he could afford in order to back her up. *It was you . . . all the . . . time!*

Sprawled in the snow, Chee struggled to right himself. "I couldn't let the old ummit live—he knew more than the rest of the Highlands put together. Every time I carried the latteh, he sensed something and was after me about it. He would have always stood in my way."

You—you'll . . . Haemas could barely hear Kevisson now. She shivered as his comforting presence abruptly faded from her mind.

She turned back to Chee. "Give me the latteh!" She wavered onto her feet. "Much more is at stake here than your foolish, senseless greed."

Chee brushed the wet snow from the dull-green facets and staggered back onto his feet. Beside the funeral pyre, the waiting Lords blinked, then crunched through the snow as one to stand behind him. She felt his mind gather in their strength again, braiding it like a strong rope, binding each element firmly into the rest until he reached the same level of power as before. The fiery white mist resurged behind her eyes, and her stomach contracted with fear as she tried to fight him off, knowing this time she was alone.

Then a tendril of thought pierced the roaring haze that surrounded her. *Moonspeaker?*

Windsign? She reached through the pain for the ilseri thought-patterns. It was Windsign, she realized, but also Summerstone, and more—a host of ilseri minds linked together in a smooth amalgam of energies. Alien strength flowed into her mind like a river in full flood, ice-green, full of odd whorls and complex nuances that stretched her mind sideways. The haze retreated, but for an instant the sky arching above her was no longer green, but gray, and the snow beneath her feet a bloody crimson. *Take our strength,* Summerstone said to her. *Bring the First One back to us.*

She felt detached now, as if there were no Kashi Lords bent on hammering her shields to shreds, as if she and Diren Chee could merely stand there and trade words in the snow as any two people might have talked about the next festival or the weather. When she spoke, her voice was rich with odd harmonics. *"Chee, give me the latteh before everyone loses."*

His face grayed as the tremendous energy drain told on him. She saw his forehead crease as he drew upon the other Lords for more and more power, but the ilseri strength bolstered her shields until she was invulnerable to his efforts. One of the Lords standing behind him crumpled to the snow and lay there unmoving, then another. The latteh glowed a muddy green in Chee's black glove, dangerous and yet innocent, the cause of so much death and pain, but no more a part of it than a dagger in the hand of a murderer.

Poor thing, she thought distractedly, to have been snatched out of its birth pool and used in this way without ever understanding. She stretched out her hand, still wrapped in the cloak, but Chee scrambled back toward the Kashi Lords who stood anchored like posts behind him.

Another vacant-eyed Lord succumbed to the power drain and tumbled unconscious into the snow. Then, as Chee's power wavered, Haemas felt him wrench Kisa Lenhe into the bond and draw upon her powerful but untrained mind to break the ilseri protection. In the first second, Kisa cried out and slumped at his feet, a forlorn heap of clothing that none of the others heeded.

Chee's augmented power flared at the edges of Haemas's mind, but her shields held, and Haemas realized he could come at her all day without hurting her now, until he and the rest were mindburned husks. But Kisa did not have the training to last that long. Another few minutes bound into Chee's network at this intensity would finish the child forever.

Casting aside the ilseri strength, she dropped her shields and laid her mind bare to the latteh in his hand, trying to link with it before Chee's stolen power could overwhelm her. She sensed the flickers of energy deep within the crystal, still aligned in the pattern that spelled mind-binding. *You are meant for more than this!* she cried into the latteh's unaware mind. *You are meant for the freedom of the trees and forest pools and waterfalls and the wind.* As she spoke to it, she tried to nudge the painful energy pulses into a randomized pattern.

Before she had barely begun, though, Chee's rock-hard will swept over her shieldless mind and smashed her concentration.

THOUGHT YOU WERE SO BLOODY CLEVER, DIDN'T YOU? Suddenly she could not feel her body standing in the snow, could hear nothing but the deafening echoes of his amplified voice in her mind. *SURRENDER AND I MAY STILL SPARE YOU. SAY YOU WILL SERVE ME!*

Pain sizzled through her every nerve. She clenched her jaw, fighting for a few more seconds of consciousness. She sensed the latteh, half aware, waiting, pulsating, alive, and powerful, yet helpless. *Resist!* she cried to it as the agony closed in. *You are meant to be an ilseri, proud and independent, not some human's toy! You don't have to be used like this!*

Dimly the latteh stirred, and its energy pulses strained out of the mind-binding pattern into a more natural randomness. Haemas called to it again, becoming aware of shouting somewhere in the background ... screaming ... panicked voices ... She realized the air had grown bitterly cold, much worse than before—the sharpest cold she could ever remember there at Tal'ayn, and the winters were notoriously fierce in this corner of the Highlands.

She reached out into the haze in front of her eyes, seeking Chee by touch, but the cold intensified, an aching, numbing, bone-chilling cold that was turning her body to stone and cutting off what little of her senses remained.

The temperature continued to plummet, the frigid air searing her lungs. Ice crystals formed on her lashes as her vision cleared. A few feet away, she could see Chee's black tunic hunched in the snow as he clasped the latteh to his chest.

Another incoming wave of glacial air rushed against her numbed face and she suddenly felt a presence, as if an immense, unseen living creature hovered very close to her. Behind Chee, the remaining Lords had collapsed to the ground, their unseeing faces turned like stones to the sky.

Inching forward on hands and knees that she could no longer feel, Haemas fumbled for the latteh in Chee's shaking hands. He blinked at her, but he was shivering too hard to resist. Clumsy with the cold, she pulled the green-faceted alien child from his stiff hands and cradled it to her breast, feeling even as she did how the energy pulses within it were slowing, though it hadn't been absent from the pool nearly as long as the other had.

The temperature dropped another notch so that now it was agony to breathe, and then Haemas *knew* what was wrong. The savage cold was killing the latteh, just as it was killing every other living thing at Tal'ayn—including her.

She tried to think, but her thoughts were dull, frozen things lying at the bottom of her mind, refusing to come together and make sense. What was it, she wondered, that Summerstone had said?

Frostvine has already gone to the high places.

It must be Frostvine's powerful presence that she felt all around her now. *Frostvine!* she cried out to the ilserlara, but there was no slowing of the cold's advance, no sign that she knew Haemas and the latteh were there.

The dull-green crystal was rapidly fading to gray; she thrust it inside her tunic next to her naked skin, then huddled over it, trying to share what little warmth remained in her body. If ilseri and human were going to continue living together on Desalaya, this First One had to be saved. Beyond that, everything else paled in importance.

Reaching for the ilsera crystals in the Tal'ayn portal, Haemas tried to find the vibrational signature that would let her enter the temporal nexus and save both herself and the dying latteh. But as she concentrated, she heard only silence. The ilsera crystals must have already shattered in the terrible, bone-breaking cold.

Speak to her! she said to the failing latteh. *She is of your kind. Tell her you are here.*

Dimly the latteh responded to her again, its energy pulses quickening for an instant as it phased toward a more conscious state, but it was too weak. The slim green energy pulses slowed and nearly flickered out. Blindly Haemas poured the remaining energy of her mind into the crystal, all that she had, far beyond the safety point, in an effort to preserve this one small life that meant everything.

On and on she went, until it seemed that she was the latteh and it was she, while her body lost all feeling and there was nothing left but searing cold that at last stole even the thought from her head.

Below Frostvine, the human-things fled for short distances and then fell to the ground, stiff and lifeless under the blight of her path. The habitation before her was vast this time, the largest she had come upon yet, built into the dense gray rock behind it and spanning two tall crags.

Flowing over it, she fed on the heat energy, feeling her fabric expand and grow even more all-encompassing and deadly. A group of humans ran toward a set of ilsera crystals, but this time she anticipated that ploy and directed the devastating cold of her body so that the crystals shattered into useless shards.

Then a tiny voice cried out to her, familiar and yet strange. Pausing, she tried to fix upon it, but in her tenuous condition, she could communicate with no one, not even another of her Last One sisters.

The voice sounded again, so piercing and clear that she paused to gather her being into enough density to hear. Surely it wasn't one of those disgusting human-things. They had no mindvoices capable of such power and clarity.

The mindvoice came again from the grounds outside the construction of rocks and wood where most of the humans had congregated. *Here!* it cried to her in the simplest of ilserin modes. *Here . . . here!*

Ilserin? Surprise rippled through her. How had a Second One come to be stranded in this high place? As far as she knew, no ilserin had ever left the great forest below before phasing into an ilseri and riding the wind, and no ilseri could survive long in the chill and thinner atmosphere of these high reaches. Quickly she released some of the heat energy trapped within her far-flung body, knowing that nothing—ilseri, ilserin, or human—could live long in the cold she was generating.

Where? she sent back to it, even though she was far too dispersed to rescue it herself. *Where are you?*

Here! The mindvoice was weak. *Here!*

Following it, she found a place in the snow littered with the twisted shapes of human bodies, all sprawled around a huge pile of cut wood. The ilserin was in the arms of one who had curled itself about it as if to protect it.

Here! the ilserin said again.

The creature who cradled it was almost dead itself, the last sparks of its primitive mind ebbing even as she watched. With a pang, Frostvine realized that the ilserin voice was an unphased First One, the lost child stolen from the pool and never returned. But First Ones did not achieve consciousness until after they Changed and emerged from the pool as slim-bodied, playful ilserin. How, then, had this one spoken to her?

Gently probing the newborn mind, she saw how this human-thing had called to it, prodded it into consciousness and urged it to speak so that it might save itself—how the human had poured the last energy of its own body into the small one so that it might live.

Wavering there, she perceived a last flicker in that dying human mind. *Here!* insisted the ilserin in its limited vocabulary. *Here! Here!*

Then she knew what it asked. Hovering over the human, she wondered at the fact that a race so selfish and aggressive and wasteful could still spawn individuals who were capable of such sacrifice.

Here! the ilserin cried into her mind, full of urgent sorrow.

Concentrating the stolen energy, Frostvine directed a measure into the human creature's mind, and was rewarded with the faintest of glimmers. Perhaps it was not too late. She fed it another small dose, then another out of the almost immeasurable amount stored within her vast body, trying not to overload the fragile creature.

Slowly the human began to revive, stirring in the snow, its odd, six-fingered hands clasping the latteh close to its nearly frozen breast.

Live, Frostvine told it. *Live and instruct the others of your kind. Because of the First One, I have spared you, but we shall never do so again. If another latteh is taken, we shall finish what was begun.*

The human tried to stand up, but its legs gave way and it collapsed back into the snow, still holding the First One close. A wave of sorrow emanated from it and Frostvine was perplexed. She watched it crawl across the snow-covered ground to touch another of the fallen humans, much smaller than itself, then gather the stiff body into its arms.

Here! the ilserin cried again, as urgent as before. *Here! Here!*

The feeling was composed of mingled sorrow and guilt, but Frostvine was too widely dispersed for closer communication, and her body was too full of heat-energy to even attempt a more cohesive form.

Reaching inside its outer clothing, the human touched the First One. The nascent ilserin changed its wording. *Child!* it shouted into Frostvine's mind. *Child! Child! Child!*

For a moment, Frostvine was puzzled. Of course the ilserin was a child. That was obvious. Then she observed how the human held the smaller one in its arms, how it smoothed the tumbled hair away from the small face—

Child! the ilserin insisted.

Then she understood. The smaller human was also a child, a new human, no more guilty of the theft than the First One itself. Peering into the smaller one's mind, she saw the dimmest of mindflickers. It, too, was almost past any help, but she released a minute quantity of energy into its being, fearing that too much would be as bad as none. Then she watched to see if the human child responded.

Child! Child! the ilserin cried.

Yes, small one, Frostvine soothed. She administered another infusion of energy even though there had been no response yet and she thought that it would do no good. The larger human

touched the child's forehead, and Frostvine felt it attempt to
pour its own strength into the dying child, even though it had
none to spare at this point.

Shamed, Frostvine made a link between herself and the human child, pouring energy into the other's mind as if it were
water. At first the older human resisted her, then seemed to understand and only watched silently as Frostvine gave and gave.
She would make it live, she decided. As the First One had
been saved, this human child would also survive.

And after she would have sworn that no human could have
taken so much raw unfiltered power, the child stirred and
opened eyes that glimmered a deep, pure emerald green.

Chapter
Twenty-five

The huge Tal'ayn ballroom was crowded with those fortunate enough to have been inside when the killing wave of cold
hit. The injured, chierra servants and Lords alike, huddled together on the floor, shrouded in blankets and cloaks, their eyes
dazed, still shivering though every fire in the huge house had
been stoked to roaring. Those most badly hurt lay on pallets
on the highly polished hardwood floor. A resourceful servant
had retrieved an old set of portal crystals packed away in one
of the basement storerooms, and now a dozen healers, summoned from the untouched Highlands Houses as well as
Shael'donn, moved among the wounded, treating the wide va-
riety of injuries where possible, and easing pain where nothing
else could be done.

And none of them, Haemas thought as she surveyed the
devastation, would ever truly understand what had just happened, because she would never be allowed to explain. She
curled her arm around Kisa's trembling shoulders as she
watched Healer Nevarr kneel on the floor to examine
Kevisson's broken arm. The healer ran his hands over the purpling flesh, then glanced up at her, his freckles standing out
sharply in his weary face. "It's not too bad. The bones didn't
come through the skin, but I can't spare the energy to start it
healing right now. Too many others are in need. I'll splint it,
then finish the real work later."

She nodded. "I'm going to Shael'donn to check on Enissa."

"Enissa?" Kevisson, his face white with fatigue and pain,
looked up at her in shock. "But—they said she was *dead*!" Ig-

noring Nevarr's protests, he tried to get up, then sagged, his face pinched, biting his lip to keep from crying out.

The healer eased him back to the pallet. "She's not dead yet, but very near it, I'm afraid." He placed a hand across Kevisson's forehead and concentrated to block his pain.

Kevisson's eyes fluttered. "But Senn came down yesterday morning to that room where they had me locked up," he murmured. "He said Enissa had died during the night."

Nevarr shook his head, then began to splint Kevisson's arm. "She's still over at Shael'donn in a shielded room, but in a very bad way. Senn moved her there, saying as long as you thought she was dead, she would be safe."

Kevisson covered his eyes with his good arm. "I have to see her."

"No." Haemas touched his clammy face and felt his spinning exhaustion. He was running mostly on raw nerve. "You rest for a few minutes. I'll be back as soon as I can, but I have to go, even if it's only to say good journey."

Kevisson turned his head to the wall. "She wouldn't want me there anyway." His tone was bitter. "She'll die thinking I tried to kill her."

Haemas laid her hand along his cheek and turned his face to meet her eyes. *I'll make her understand,* she said into his mind. Then she looked down at Kisa and stroked the child's copper-gold hair. "I'll only be gone a little while. Why don't you stay here with Kevisson?"

Kisa huddled closer, clinging to Haemas's tunic with both hands and blinking up at her with those alien green eyes that no longer held the slightest trace of Kashi gold. How much had Frostvine changed this child in the process of saving her life? Kisa had yet to speak or make any sign that she understood what was going on around her.

Do you understand? Haemas said into her mind. *Stay with Kevisson. Everything will be all right.*

In answer, Kisa only buried her face in Haemas's tunic, holding on as if she would never let go.

Nevarr sighed and touched Kisa's cheek, narrowing his eyes

appraisingly. *Why don't you take her with you? She's in shock and it might do her good to get away from the sight of all this.*

Haemas looked into the child's ilseri-green eyes. *All right.*

Gripping Kisa's small hand, Haemas stepped into the Tal'ayn portal. Before she could go to Enissa, she had one more secret task: The First One had to be returned to the pool. The outside air was still far too cold, even for the depths of a Highlands winter. Her teeth chattered as she sorted out the portal vibrations, then reached for the signature of the ilsera crystals set into the ilseri pool. Grayness flashed, bitter, but not half so debilitating as Frostvine's deadly presence.

The forest glittered with frost and, although she couldn't see them, she sensed the murmuring presence of many ilseri, more than she had ever encountered before. Kisa blinked at the seemingly empty trees, but said nothing, her small hand clenching Haemas's. Ice crystals pinged as tree branches swayed in the breeze.

Moonspeaker, you have done well, Windsign said.

A fresh pang of loss stabbed through Haemas as she drew the latteh from her bodice. Her eyes stung as she held it out. She had not done well. A string of senseless deaths lay behind her, Master Ellirt's and her father's and half the members of the High Houses—and she still had one more painful leave-taking to endure.

Summerstone's green outline appeared, rapidly solidifying. The flowing white fabric settled around her overtall, regal body as she accepted the latteh and bowed her tendriled head over it. *This one has been awakened early and promises to grow strong. It will make interesting times, watching him grow.*

Perhaps, Haemas told herself. It would be a blessing if something good came of so much tragedy. She glanced down at Kisa's disturbing emerald eyes, then wrapped her arms around the unresisting child.

We have examined the nexus. Summerstone waded into the frigid pool and sank beneath the silvery surface to replace the First One. *The possibilities abound, and many timelines show great potential for our two kinds at this juncture. Go in the knowledge that you have made this possible.*

Haemas nodded tightly, then reached for the vibrational signature of Shael'donn's portal, both longing and dreading to see Enissa again, knowing she had failed her as she had failed so many others.

She and Kisa emerged in the small portal set halfway between the two schools. Snow was falling in fitful bursts from low-hanging gray clouds as she urged the child down the gravel path toward the huge brown-stone building. It was cold there, but not nearly as bad as Tal'ayn. She held Kisa's hand tightly as they reached the broad steps, thinking back to the first time she had come here, little more than a girl herself, walking at Master Ellirt's side.

The door swung back before she could touch it, but she ignored the startled snub-nosed boy's request for her to wait. She had done with waiting and trying to live by other people's rules. From now on, she would do what *she* thought best.

Having gotten the room's location earlier from Nevarr, she headed for the East Wing, passing chattering clumps of students. She wondered how much any of them had heard of the tragedy that had struck the Highlands. Her father's funeral had been heavily attended and many of these boys must have lost relatives in Frostvine's devastating attack. None of the High Houses had escaped loss.

A chunky adolescent boy sat in a chair outside of Enissa's room with his feet braced against the wall. "Can I help you, Lady?"

Haemas lifted the door's latch, but it was locked. She met his young eyes. "You can give me the key."

He sniffled, then wiped his nose on the back of his sleeve. "I'm sorry, but—"

But she had no time for this. Even now, Enissa might have slipped beyond her. *Unlock the door,* she said, backing her mental voice with all the power of her Plus-Eleven Talent.

His mouth sagged open. Then he pulled the key out of his pocket, unlocked the door, and stood aside. Holding Kisa's hand, Haemas pushed past him into the stuffy, dim room beyond. A half-seen figure rose beside the bed. "Lady Haemas!"

It was Meryet Alimn, one of Enissa's best trainees. "Meryet, how—" Her throat closed. "How is she?"

Meryet's chin trembled. "Very poorly, Lady. The healers say there's nothing left to be done." A tear trickled down her face, gleaming in the candlelight.

Haemas squeezed her shoulder. The figure under the quilts seemed too small to be her old friend, as if her body were fading along with her spirit. Haemas slid into the chair and reached for the pale cheek. "Enissa?"

"She's—she's gone beyond hearing, Lady." Meryet's voice was strained.

Even though she'd thought she would be prepared, Haemas was shocked at the coldness of Enissa's skin. *Enissa?* she said into her mind. *Don't leave me.*

But there was only a soft, slow fading, as if her friend were dying one cell at a time. *No, you can't go!* Haemas groped under the quilts for her hand. *Not like this! You can't let Chee win!* With reckless abandon, she cast her shields aside and plunged into the blankness, seeking some semblance of the Enissa she knew, some hint of the crotchety friend who would risk anything for anyone but couldn't abide being laughed at. *Enissa!*

After a moment she caught a trace, something, but it was receding from her faster than she could follow. Pausing, Haemas tried to think. The damage—she needed to go back to the mindburned area again. Perhaps she could heal a pathway as she had done before and buy Enissa a little more time.

Guided by memory, she groped through the frustrating blankness, finally finding it again: the thousands of disrupted neural pathways that dumped every half-formed thought in the same place, creating a blaring chaos that no mind could survive. But there was little chaos or anything else left, almost no thought processes at all. Enissa was nearly gone.

Haemas hesitated, no longer sure she even had the right to try to pull her back. There was a sense of peace in the vast silences of Enissa's mind, a coming to rest that she was almost loath to disturb. After all, what could she bring her back to, except a few more minutes of dying?

Letting go, she drifted back until she could feel her own body, then opened her eyes and laid her head on Enissa's barely moving breast, feeling the life ebb from her friend even as she clung to her. A latteh could have supplied the power that she lacked. If only she could have brought one back just long enough to heal Enissa as Ellirt had shown her ... but lattehs were not unknowing things, to be used as mere tools. Even to ask such a favor of the ilseri would bring Frostvine back to the Highlands—and that would be the end of the Kashi.

A small hand touched Haemas's shoulder and she blinked through her tears to see Kisa's solemn face watching her. A strange, tingling energy surged from her shoulder through her entire body, powerful, energizing, potent. She looked down and saw her hands gripped together on the bed, outlined in shimmering emerald.

For a moment, Haemas forgot to breathe. Then, behind her, she heard Meryet gasp. "Lady, what is it?"

She raised one hand and touched her own cheek where Brann Chee had struck her in the struggle at the edge of the cliff, feeling the contradictory warmth of that cool greenness, its soothing power, and then knew it for what it was. "It's all right, Meryet," she heard herself say.

Closing her eyes, she loosed herself from her body again, riding the current of green ilseri energy flowing from Kisa, seeking the terrible wound in Enissa's brain. Coming back to the vast damage, she almost despaired all over again, but then put away her fear. She was not a healer, but she didn't have to be. Through Kisa, she had the awesome power of the ilseri behind her, and, by the Light, she could at least *try!* She began with the nearest damaged neural pathway, pouring the potent ilseri energy through it until it was smooth and conductive again. Then she went to the next and did the same, and the next, and the next ...

From time to time, it seemed that people came and tried to talk to her, but she shut the insistent voices out of her mind and held her concentration. The damage was so great that if she stopped even for a second it might be too long. If Enissa was to have any chance at all, she had to finish what she had begun without delay. And through it all, she felt Kisa's steady, uncomplaining presence beside her, channeling the apparently limitless cool green fire that made it all possible.

Eventually, although she had no idea how long it had been, she could find nothing else to work on. But she drifted in Enissa's mind, searching. She had to be sure; she could not stop until she was sure. It could not all have been for nothing.

Haemas, a voice said insistently, *it's finished. Come back.*

Finished? Was Enissa dead? Weariness dragged at her until she could hardly think. She wanted to go back, to rest, but what if she'd missed a pathway somewhere? She'd failed her father and all those people at Tal'ayn, she'd even failed Axia, and now Enissa had only this one last chance. She had to be sure. She lingered on in Enissa's mind, alone, looking for something she might have missed.

Then she felt a steadying hand on her face, breaking her concentration, startling her after she had left her body behind for so long. She tried to shut the sensation out and stay with Enissa.

No, he said, *there's nothing more to be done.*

A cool cloth bathed her forehead, her cheek, her throat . . . She felt herself losing focus, leaving Enissa's mind, going back, but it was so far, like trying to wake up after a long and overdeep sleep. She couldn't seem to make her body answer her.

That's right. A warm hand smoothed her hair back from her face. *Open your eyes now.*

But she was floating somewhere beyond bodies or voices . . . so tired . . . she couldn't . . .

Yes, you can. Open your eyes.

And there was just enough of a command in that mindvoice that some part of her responded. Her eyelids flickered, and then she could feel her eyes again, could make them work. She blinked up into Kevisson's worry-lined face.

Clutching her to his chest with his good arm, he buried his

face in her tumbled hair, his relief fierce and overflowing. Slowly she reached up and touched his cheek.

"Are—are you—all right?" she asked.

"Me?" He tried to smile, but didn't quite make it.

Haemas saw Kisa's cool green eyes peering over his shoulder. "And Enissa?" she asked.

"Sleeping," he said. "There may be some residual damage, but Lising and Nevarr think she has a good chance to recover. And Kisa is doing fine. It's you that we've been worried about."

"Me?" She tried to sit up in the chair, but her muscles were made of lead.

"It's been two days." He reached for a mug and held it to her lips. "You have to get some of this down. The healers say you're half starved."

She swallowed the rich meat broth, letting it roll down her parched throat like the finest of wines. Then she looked across the bed at Enissa's sleeping, pink-cheeked face and finally believed.

The five-cornered funeral pyre reared high over Haemas's head, a deep, impenetrable blackness against the lighter, cloud-covered night sky. Hugging Kisa's slender body closer, she thought again of those green eyes and knew she was no longer the same child, perhaps not even strictly human anymore.

Kisa and Adrina's father had finally been named. The Karoli family, who held a sweep of rich farmland on the far western edge of the Lowlands, had finally come forward and said that one of their younger sons had registered paternity of the girls in the family records before dying in a hunting accident four years earlier. Karoli'ayn had since presented a claim for Adrina that would have to be ruled upon by the Council; but taking Kisa, so altered by the ilseri, was out of the question. Even the Castillans, Myriel's maternal line, had come to examine the child, then dissolved their claim.

The forest of torches hammered into the frozen ground cast crazy, shifting shadows over the silent, stricken host of Kashi who had come to pay their respects to the dead of the many

Houses that shared this pyre. Their colorless faces stared from the fringes of the torchlight, stunned, weary, each one struggling with pain, both physical and emotional. Father Orcado paused before the wooden mountain, gazing at the multitude of silken shrouds that billowed with each twist in the wind, then began his slow, halting steps through the trampled snow, winding his way around the pyre the first of the traditional five times. The tang of freshly cut wood filled the air.

She had urged Kisa to stay inside with Jayna, but although she didn't speak or cry or do any of the things a normal child should, the girl still refused to be separated from her, even for a second. Actually, Haemas would have forgone this somber spectacle herself, but the body of her father lay on the pyre, as well as that of his bitter young wife, Alyssa. Stacked up there, too, like so much wood, were the bodies of everyone who had been outside when Frostvine came, except for herself and Kisa. More than two-thirds of those who had been in the House had survived, but a great many of the unfortunate guests had perished—as well as the ten High Lords who had been used to augment Chee's power.

Diren Chee shared this pyre, too, laid out in his silver-trimmed black tunic, the last of his House, his face appearing in death curiously young and peaceful. Had he ever understood the nature of the doom that he had called to himself? Haemas thought not. No one here but she, and perhaps Kisa in some measure, understood Chee's part in all this, and she could not tell yet how much Kisa actually remembered. To protect both the Kashi and ilseri, the rest of Highlands must never know what he had done.

Father Orcado passed before her a second time, the torchlight glinting off his gold-and-yellow brocade, his frostbitten lips moving in a silent invocation.

So many dead, so many she would never see again ... Master Ellirt, her father ... Haemas stared at the wood heaped before her, feeling the eyes of the survivors as they waited for her to step forward and enact the ancient ritual of Leave-taking and make them all feel as if there was some sort of structure to life—that, despite all their losses, there would be a meaningful tomorrow after all.

But would there be? Her fingers tightened on Kisa's shoulders. Tal'ayn was badly damaged, while at Brint'ayn and Dynd'ayn, the first two estates to suffer Frostvine's wrath, there had been no survivors at all.

Only a few minutes before, one of her father's friends had come to her and confirmed that Tal'ayn had indeed passed into her hands; Chee had been right about that. For some reason, her father had never changed his will. Her eyes sought the top of the pyre where an hour or so earlier the chierra servants had struggled to place the old Tal's bier at the very top. She felt the hot salt sting of tears. Perhaps Dervlin Tal had finally forgiven her for shaping her life to her own pattern after all, at least as much as he was able.

But she didn't want Tal'ayn. She had renounced it long ago. What use was a huge estate that would require a firm and vigilant hand in the coming years if it was to be properly rebuilt? It would take her total concentration, and if the next Council allowed her to reopen the House of Moons, she would not have time to run both it and Tal'ayn.

Her mind turned again to her old dream of a school where Kashi daughters could come to be trained in the mindarts, where they could realize the full potential of their Talents as so few of them were ever allowed. Even though it had cost him his life, Chee had still managed to destroy that. Her throat knotted as she thought of the endless hours of negotiation and capitulation and undignified downright haggling that had gone into building and funding her school, now all scattered to the winter winds. If Master Ellirt had not been there to back her before, the High Lords would never have listened to her.

And Ellirt was dead.

Orcado passed her a third time, glancing aside at her and Kisa with eyes that were only two dark-shadowed holes in the twisting torchlight. Even though he was trying to shield it, she was Talented enough to read his disapproval of her, disapproval and disdain of anyone who defied tradition, who wanted to think for herself and did what she thought was right instead of the proper, accepted thing.

But she knew as well as she knew her own name that she would never be a proper Kashi daughter or a proper anything else. And there must be others like Enissa and Meryet Alimn who wanted something more out of life, something that their fathers and brothers and husbands did not understand. She might be able to provide that, if only she had an adequate setting and the funds.

The chill wind gusted, bending the yellow torch flames double. She shivered as she looked over her shoulder at Tal'ayn rising up behind them. It was a vast estate, the biggest in the Highlands, as well as the richest. It was too bad that her father had not sired seven children to share it, as his counterpart had in Ellirt's Otherwhen. It ought to have had whole families living in its vast wings, children to play in the nasai groves and the thermal gardens, laughter ringing down from the great bridging towers.

Perhaps she should ask her father's cousins, the Kentnals, to oversee the reconstruction while she went back and tried to reopen the House of Moons. Perhaps it would even be best to cede Tal'ayn over to them and put the past behind her forever.

Jayna opened the main doors and hurried down the steps toward them, carrying several thick cloaks over her arm. Haemas had to smile. No doubt Jayna, who had taken care of her as a child, would like to have more children to look after, youngsters to fill this bitter, staid old house and make it live again with love.

Children like Kisa, the back of her mind whispered, and she looked down at the silent girl's red-gold head. What if, she thought suddenly, the House of Moons were located *here*, instead of in that small dreary building constructed in the shadow of Shael'donn? It was so obvious. If she brought her students here, not only would she have all the funds she needed, but the Council of Twelve would never be able to dictate to her again.

And perhaps there were other children like Kisa and her sister, Adrina, who had no one and needed a home. She could begin by opening Tal'ayn to other orphans of this disaster whom no one wanted.

Even boys?

Haemas turned back to see Kevisson's tall, broad-shouldered frame pushing through the crowd of spectators from the other side of the pyre, his right arm in a sling.

His lean, tan face smiled slightly as he caught her eye. *Or doesn't your generosity extend to the opposite sex?*

Father Orcado plodded around the corner again, now swinging a tiny pierced-metal censer to spread the smoldering scent of spicy incense in wide arcs through the frigid air.

But boys can always go to Shael'donn, she answered after the priest had passed.

I didn't expect you—of all people—to hold that against them. Kevisson's mindvoice was heavy with mock surprise. *And besides, do you really think Shael'donn will be the same now with Riklin Senn running it?*

But—boys? she replied lamely.

Actually, they're remarkably like girls. His tone was thoughtful. *And almost as Talented.*

For a second, she just stared at him, seeing how his golden-brown hair caught the flickering torchlight. Then she smiled back. *And just exactly who would teach these Talented boys?*

I might be willing to give it a try. He slipped into place at her side and pulled her close.

Male and female, she thought, working together instead of separately. It was a different vision from any she had ever had, and yet it sounded promising.

Father Orcado came around for the fifth and last time and stopped before her. "Haemas Sennay Tal, you are the last surviving kin of Dervlin Kentnal Tal?"

The lightness and hope she had felt bantering with Kevisson melted, and her eyes returned to the top of the pyre, to her father and all the rest who had suffered because she had not found the strength and wisdom to stop Chee until it was too late. She nodded, fighting the sudden tears that threatened.

"Then it falls to you to Light his way, as well as that of his guests, into the next world." Orcado pushed an unlit torch into her hands.

She felt the crowd's eyes as they waited for her to generate the first spark. Her fingers tightened on the coarse wood. Even after this huge pyre had burned down to the snow-covered ground and guttered out in the ashes, it would all still be with her, the pain, the loss, the failures.

And the successes, Kevisson whispered into her mind, *and the love.*

She felt his left hand slip under her cloak to rest against the bare skin of her neck, ready to lend her his strength.

Light the spark, he said. *Send the past on its way and make a new tomorrow.*

Hesitantly she clasped the dark torch in one hand and stretched the other toward it as she began the ancient ritual in her mind. *Fire is the first aspect of the Light..*

Attuned to Kevisson as she was, she heard him echoing the litany, participating with her. The flames blazed up in her mind, bright and golden, shot through with orange highlights like the center of the sun, warming her inside as well as out. She caught a whiff of pungent woodsmoke in the chill air. The spark leaped from her outstretched hand to the waiting wood and blazed up there for the crowd to see, bright and strong.

Orcado took the torch, turned back to the pyre, and put the flames to the heaped wood. "So do we all return to the Light."

Kisa shuddered, pressing back against Haemas, and Kevisson added his hand to the child's shoulder, radiating comfort. "It's not just an ending this time," he told her softly. "It's a beginning."

Haemas leaned against the steady warmth of Kevisson's side and watched the flames creep up the pyre while heavy gray smoke curled into the cloud-ridden night sky. Perhaps all endings carried within them the seeds for something better, she thought, if you could find the strength to see it.

Above the pyre the clouds parted, and she caught a fleeting glimpse of all three Desalayan moons riding high in the sky—silvery, serene Sedja, pale-gold Lydriat, and tiny blue Mishva, the most rarely seen of all.

ABOUT THE AUTHOR

K.D. WENTWORTH is the author of five novels, including *Moonspeaker* and *House of Moons*, the first two books in the House of Moons Chronicles, as well as more than fifty published short stories. She won the Writers of the Future Contest in 1988 and, since that time, her work has twice been nominated for the prestigious Nebula Award. She is a teacher and, in 1991, won the Field Publications Teachers as Writers Award. She lives in Tulsa, Oklahoma, with her husband, Richard.

ALSO AVAILABLE

MOONSPEAKER
THE HOUSE OF MOONS CHRONICLES, BOOK 1
by K.D. Wentworth
ISBN: 0-7434-7983-1

In this first book in the "House of Moons" series, we are introduced to Haemas Sennay Tal—the Moonspeaker. Daughter of one of the most powerful families of the mindtalented Kashi, Haemas lived a life of privilege until the brutal attack on her father—and the accusation that she committed the heinous crime.

Forced to flee across the Forsaken Barrier, she learns that her father's death was only a small part of a much larger plot to tear apart the fabric of reality itself!

Haemas must master her extraordinary mindtalents before she is killed—and her world is destroyed.